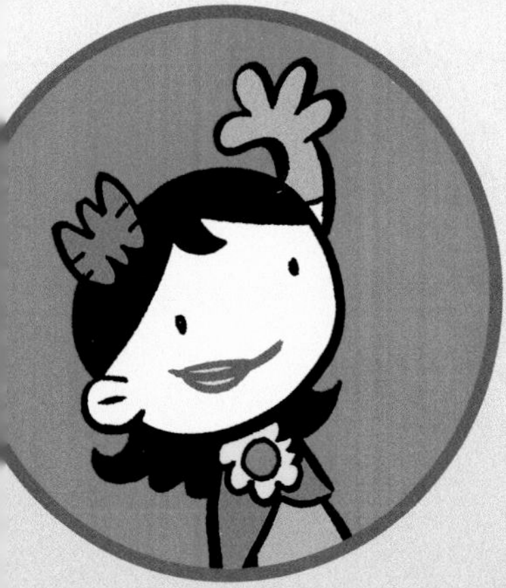

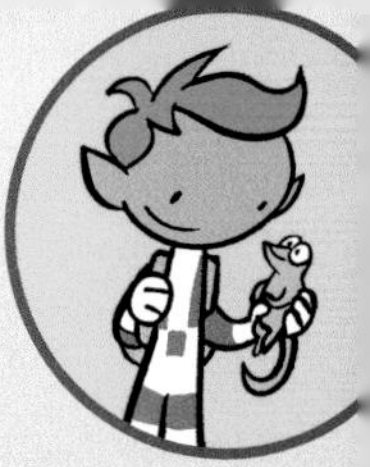

by

ART BALTAZAR

writer & artist

and

FRANCO

writer

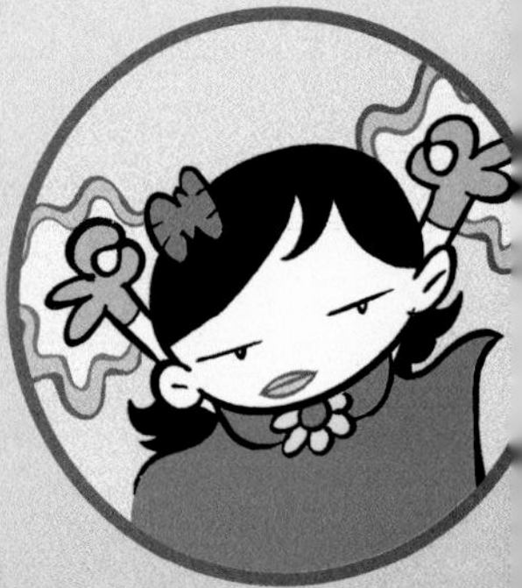

NICK J. NAPOLITANO

letterer

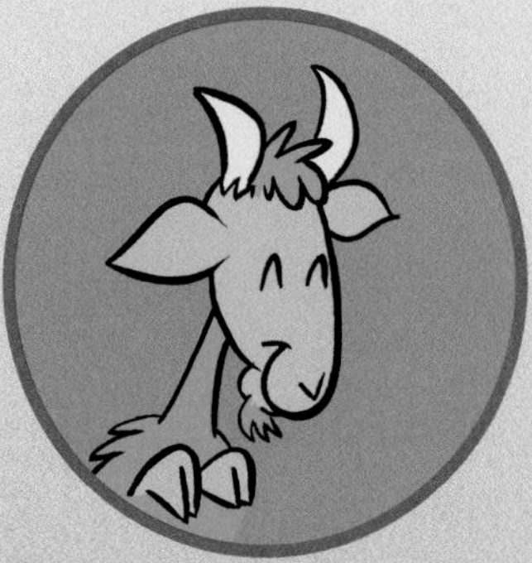

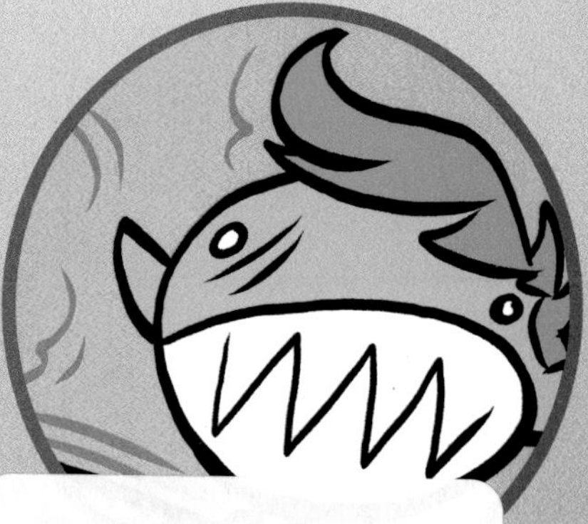

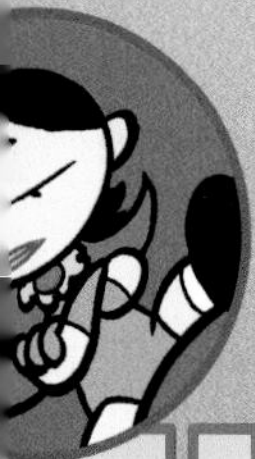

original series and
collection cover art by
ART BALTAZAR

TINY TITANS
BEAST BOY & RAVEN

JANN JONES
ELISABETH V. GEHRLEIN
KRISTY QUINN
Editors - Original Series

STEPHANIE BUSCEMA
ADAM SCHLAGMAN
SIMONA MARTORE
Assistant Editors - Original Series

JEB WOODARD
Group Editor - Collected Editions

REZA LOKMAN
Editor - Collected Edition

STEVE COOK
Design Director - Books

AMIE BROCKWAY-METCALF
Publication Design

KATE DURRÉ
Publication Production

BOB HARRAS
Senior VP - Editor-in-Chief, DC Comics

JIM LEE
Publisher & Chief Creative Officer

BOBBIE CHASE
VP - Global Publishing Initiatives & Digital Strategy

DON FALLETTI
VP - Manufacturing Operations & Workflow Management

LAWRENCE GANEM
VP - Talent Services

ALISON GILL
Senior VP - Manufacturing & Operations

HANK KANALZ
Senior VP - Publishing Strategy & Support Services

DAN MIRON
VP - Publishing Operations

NICK J. NAPOLITANO
VP - Manufacturing Administration & Design

NANCY SPEARS
VP - Sales

JONAH WEILAND
VP - Marketing & Creative Services

MICHELE R. WELLS
VP & Executive Editor, Young Reader

TINY TITANS: BEAST BOY & RAVEN

Published by DC Comics. Compilation and all new material Copyright © 2020 DC Comics. All Rights Reserved. Originally published in single magazine form in *Tiny Titans* #1-4, 6, 8, 12-14, 17, 20, 26-27, and 44. Copyright © 2008, 2009, 2010, 2011 DC Comics. All Rights Reserved. All characters, their distinctive likenesses, and related elements featured in this publication are trademarks of DC Comics. The stories, characters, and incidents featured in this publication are entirely fictional. DC Comics does not read or accept unsolicited submissions of ideas, stories, or artwork. DC - a WarnerMedia Company.

DC Comics, 2900 West Alameda Ave., Burbank, CA 91505
Printed by LSC Communications, Crawfordsville, IN, USA. 10/23/20. First Printing.
ISBN: 978-1-77950-717-4

Library of Congress Cataloging-in-Publication Data is available.

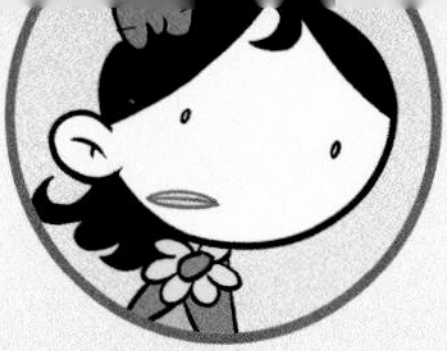

CONTENTS

BEAST BOY

RAVEN

BEAST BOY & RAVEN

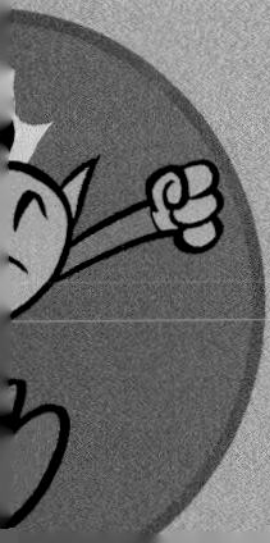

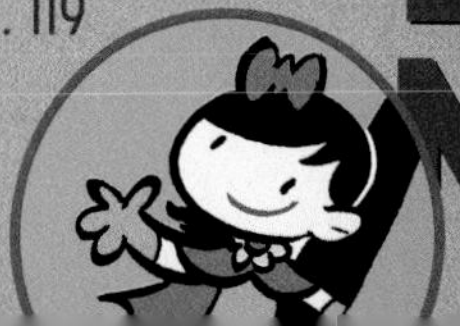

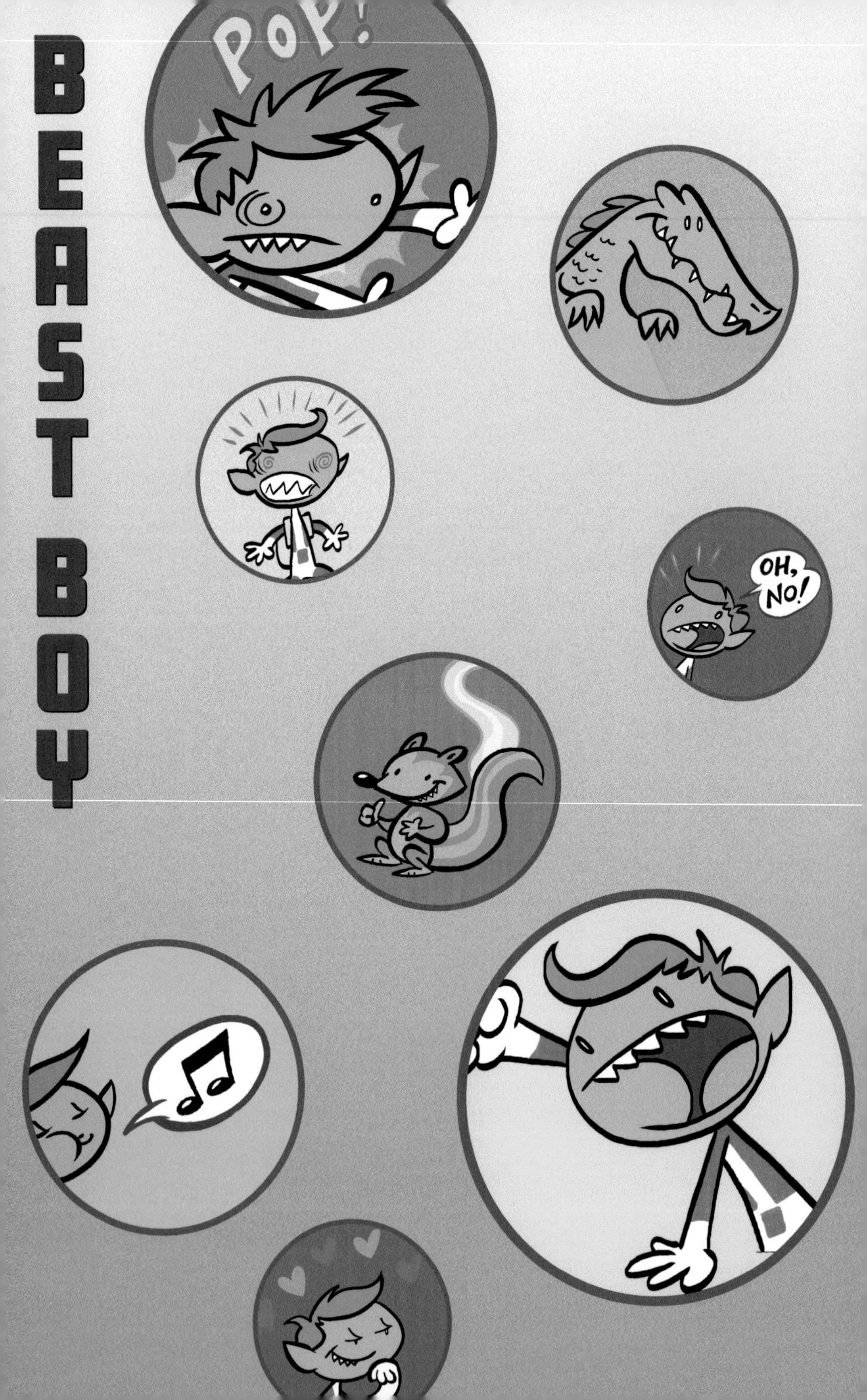
BEAST BOY
POP!
OH, NO!

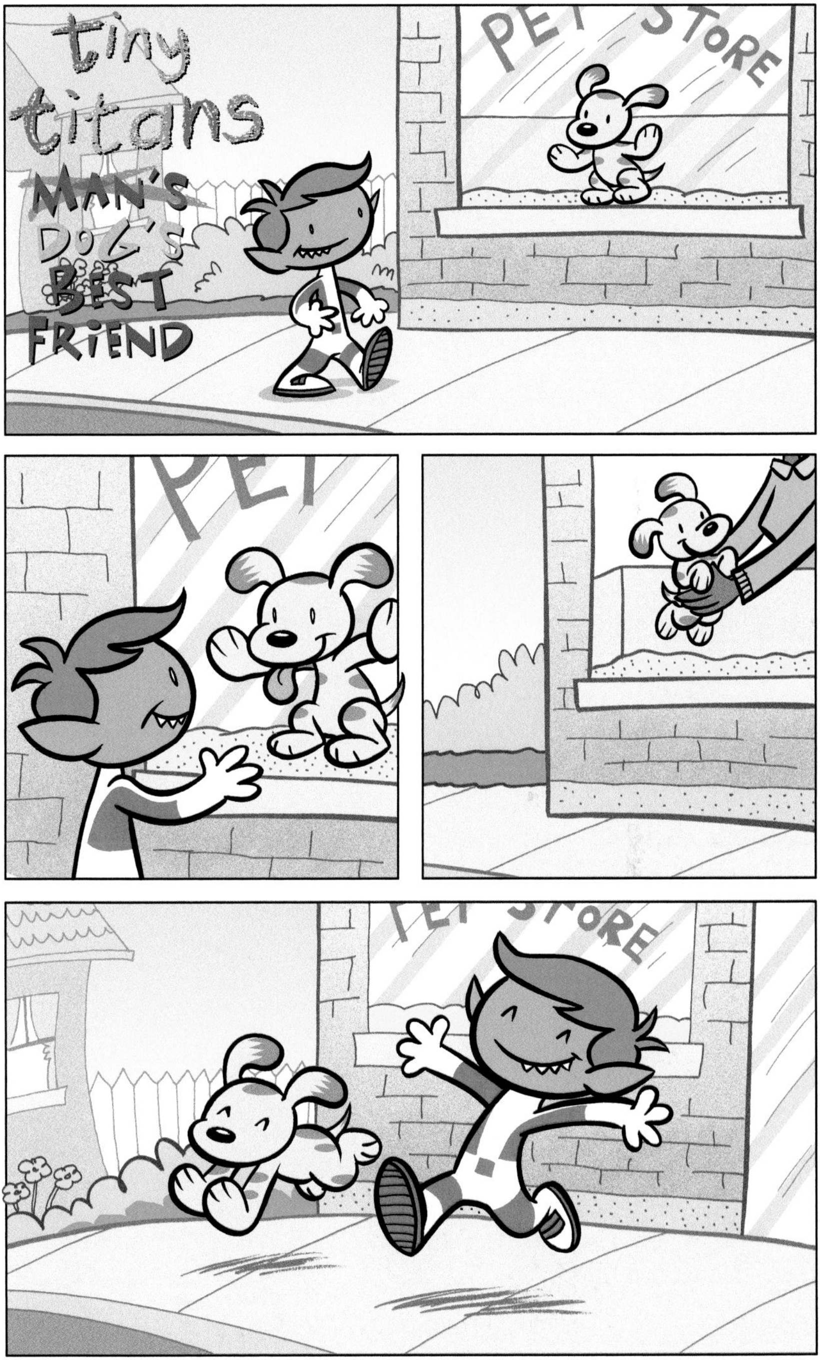
tiny titans
~~MAN'S~~
DOG'S
BEST
FRIEND
PET STORE

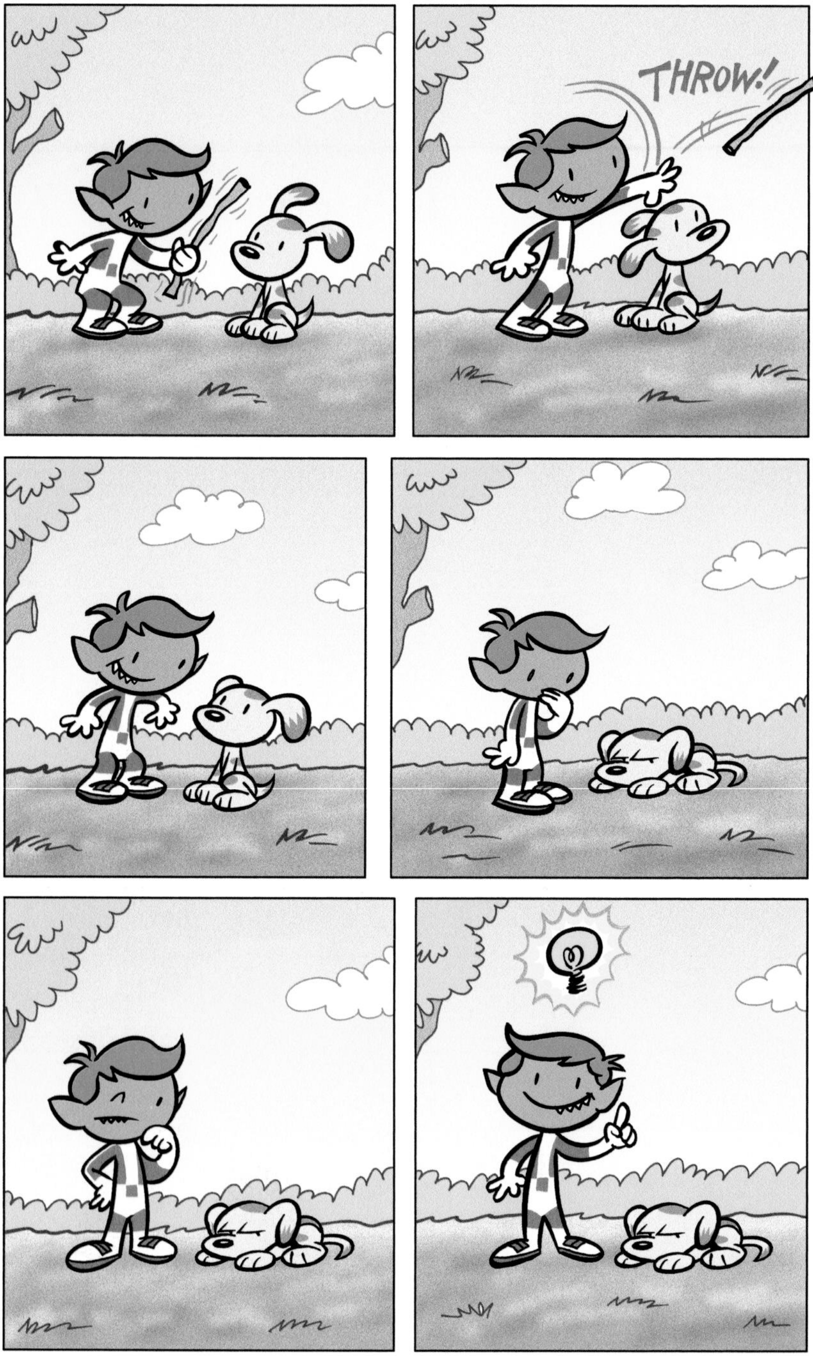
THROW!

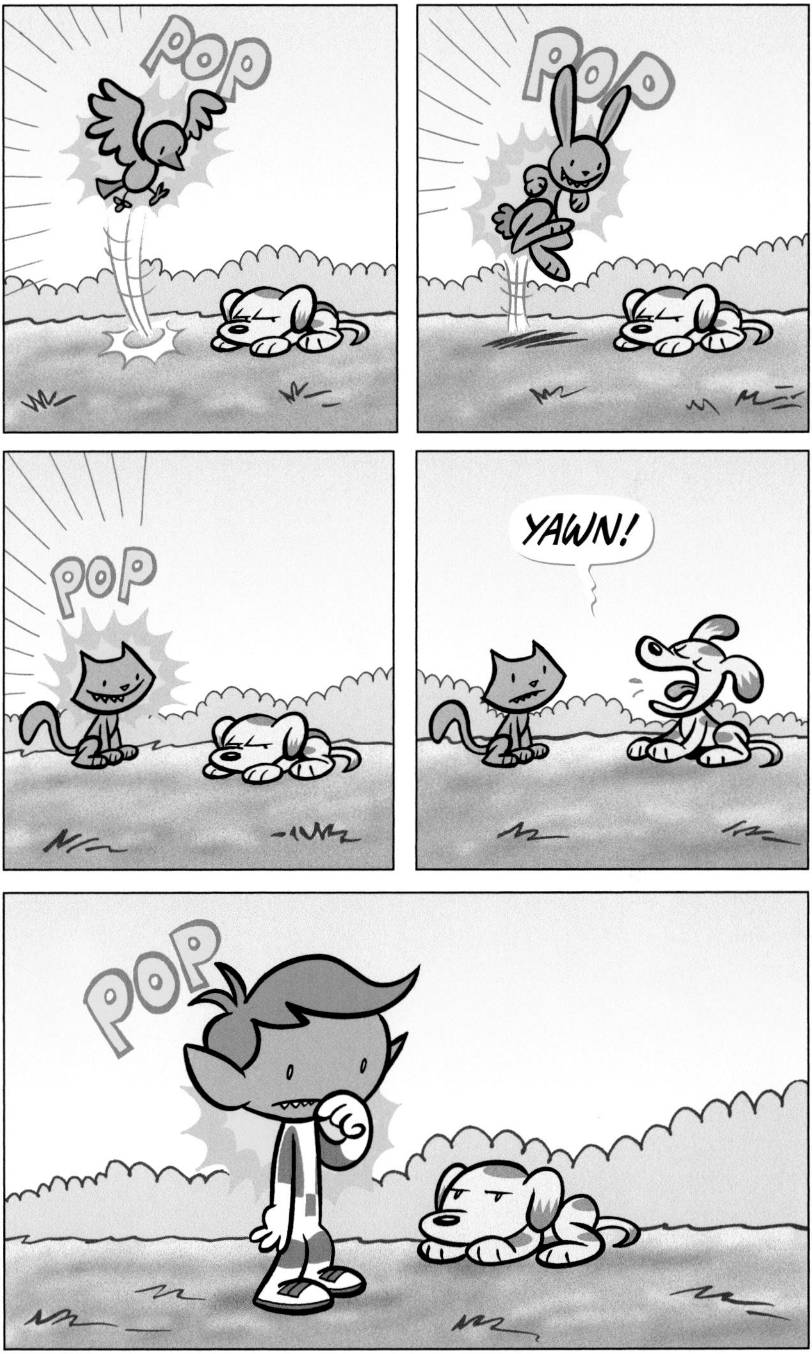
POP
POP
POP
YAWN!
POP

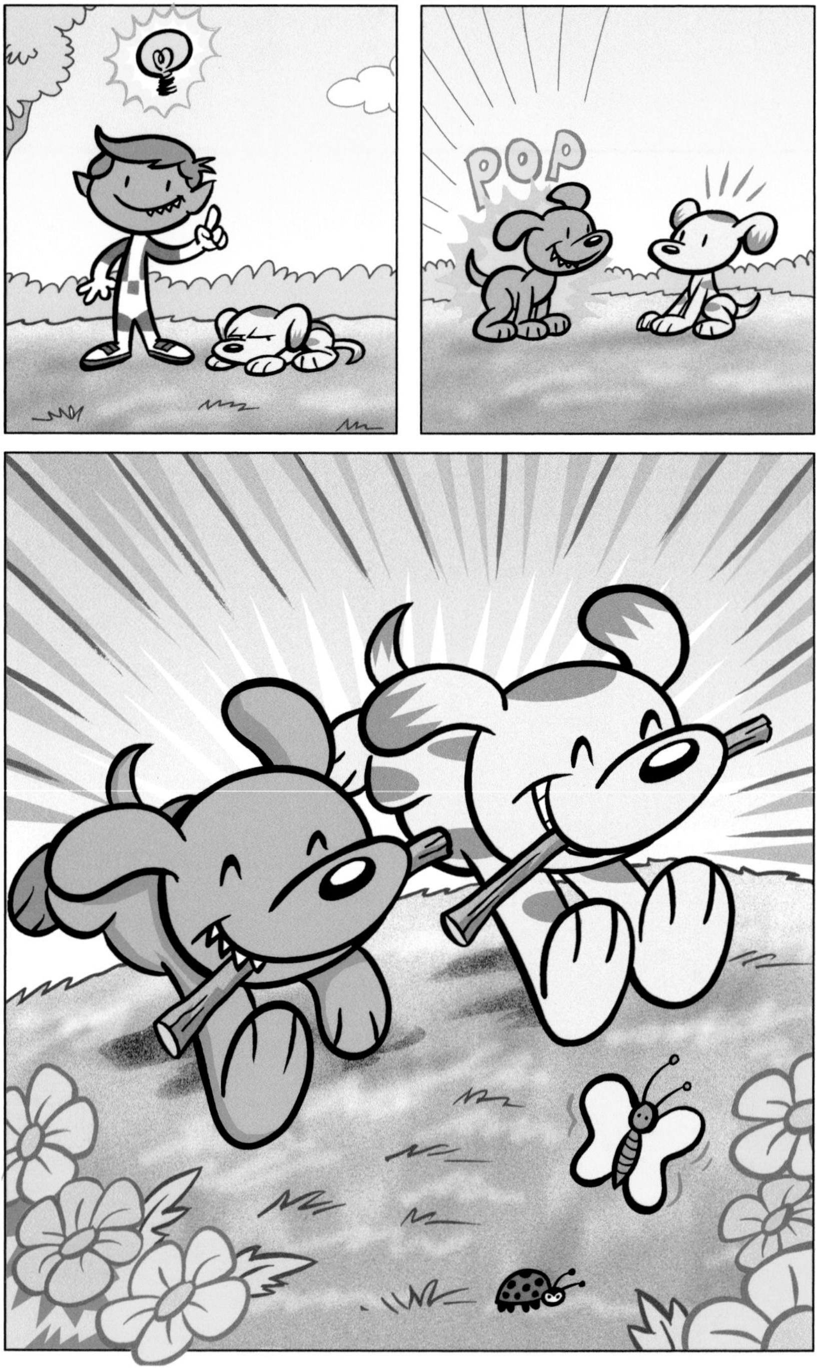
POP

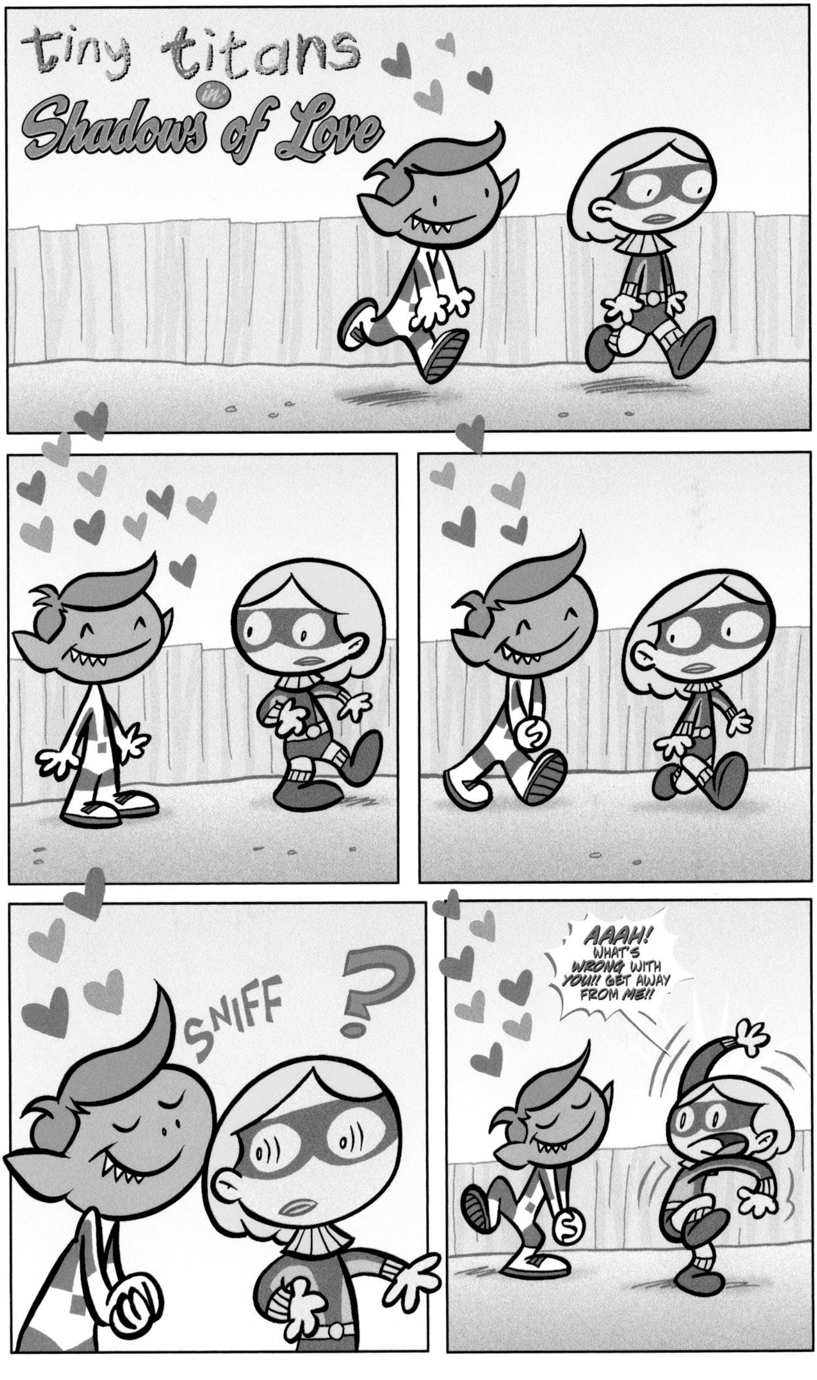
tiny titans
in
Shadows of Love
SNIFF
?
AAAH! WHAT'S WRONG WITH YOU!! GET AWAY FROM ME!!

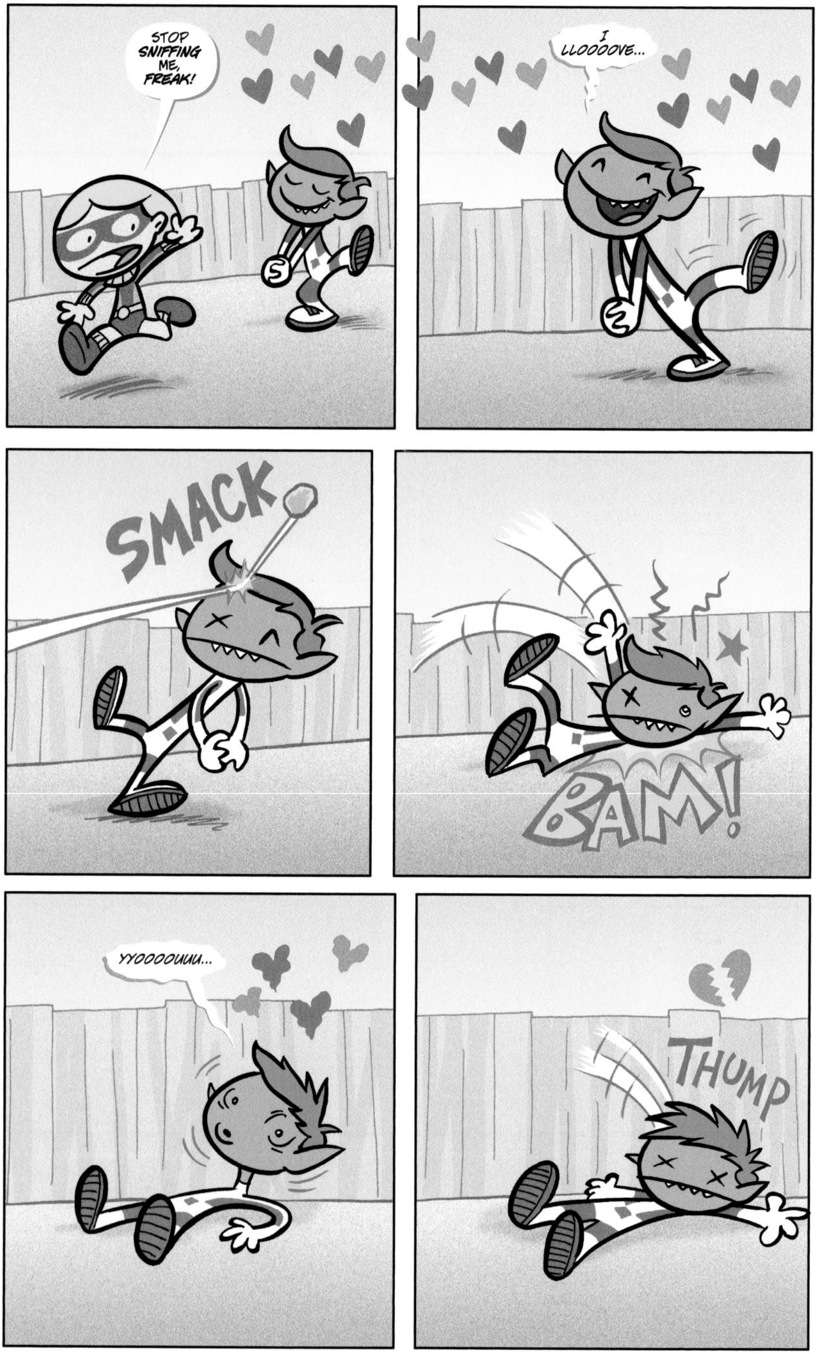
STOP SNIFFING ME, FREAK!
I LLOOOOVE...
SMACK
BAM!
YYOOOOUUU...
THUMP

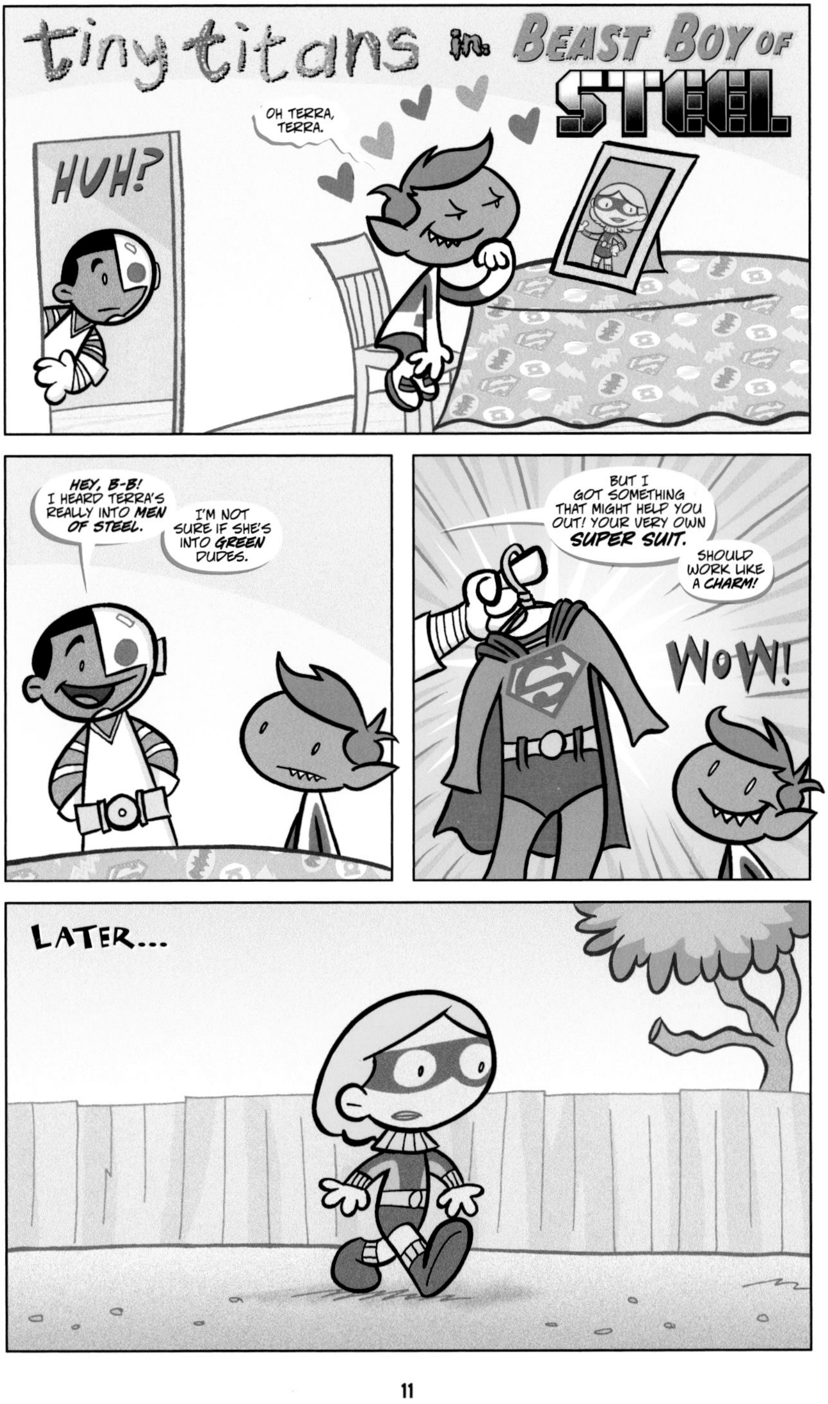
tiny titans in: BEAST BOY OF STEEL
HUH?
OH TERRA, TERRA.
HEY, B-B! I HEARD TERRA'S REALLY INTO MEN OF STEEL.
I'M NOT SURE IF SHE'S INTO GREEN DUDES.
BUT I GOT SOMETHING THAT MIGHT HELP YOU OUT! YOUR VERY OWN SUPER SUIT.
SHOULD WORK LIKE A CHARM!
WOW!
LATER...

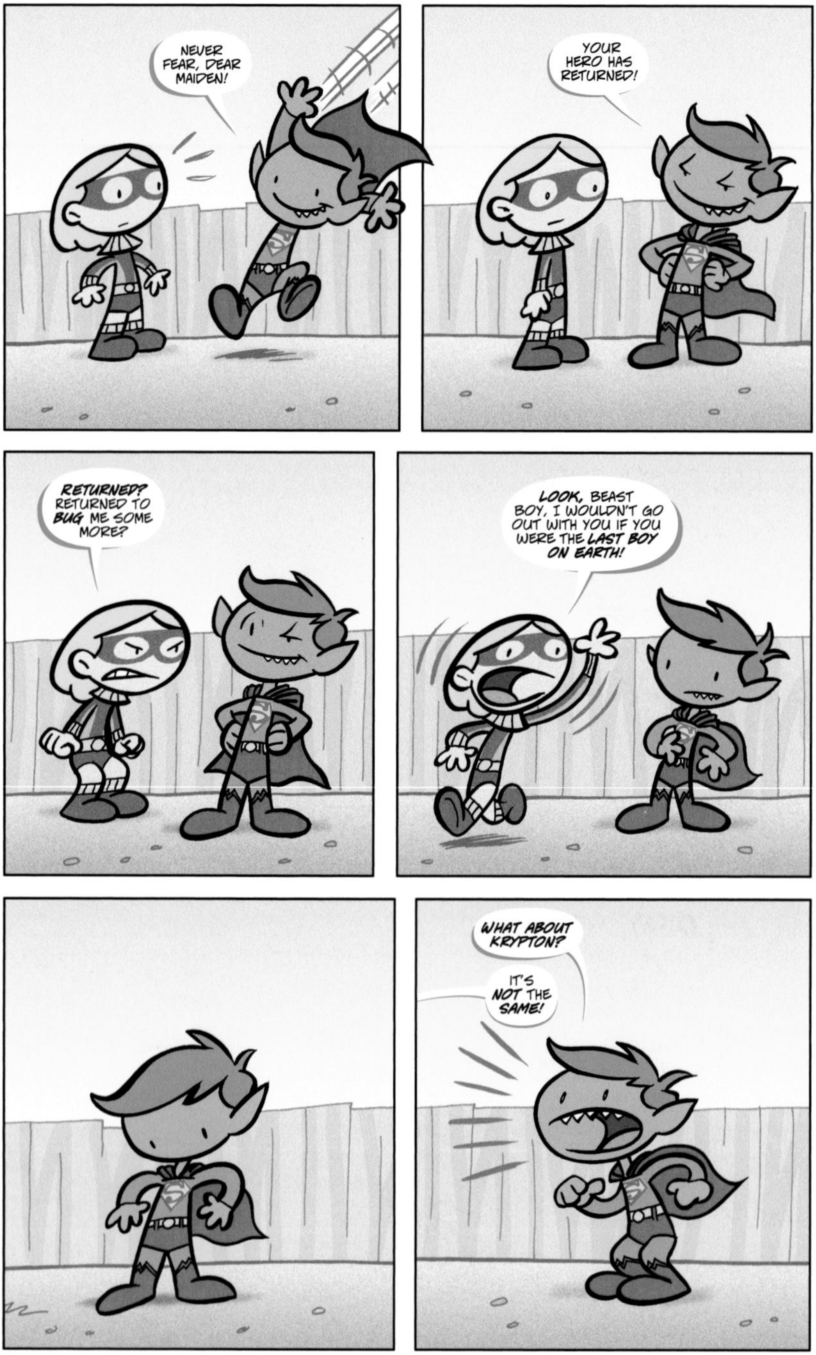
NEVER FEAR, DEAR MAIDEN!
YOUR HERO HAS RETURNED!
RETURNED? RETURNED TO **BUG** ME SOME MORE?
LOOK, BEAST BOY, I WOULDN'T GO OUT WITH YOU IF YOU WERE THE **LAST BOY ON EARTH!**
WHAT ABOUT KRYPTON?
IT'S **NOT** THE **SAME!**

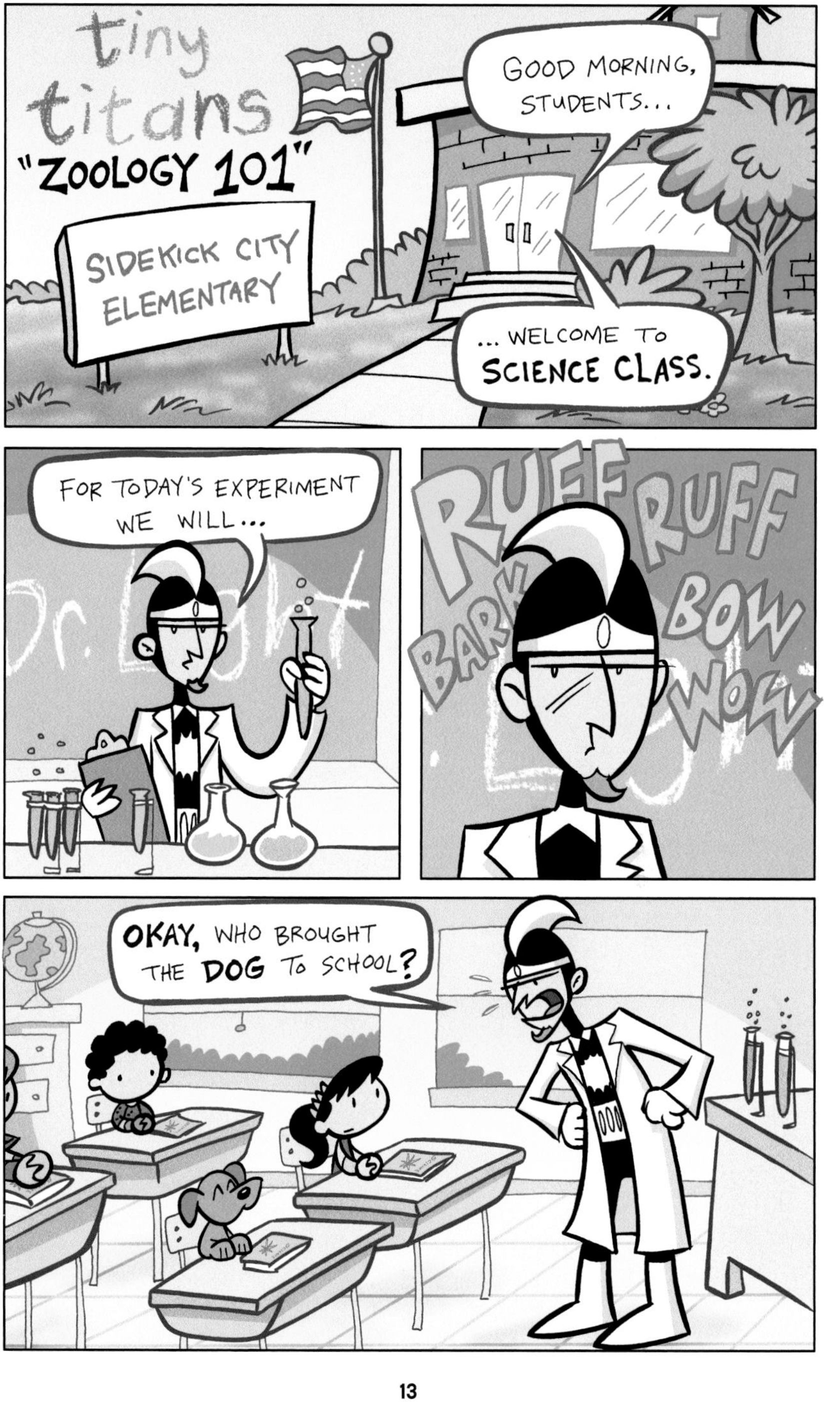
tiny titans
"ZOOLOGY 101"
SIDEKICK CITY ELEMENTARY
GOOD MORNING, STUDENTS...
... WELCOME TO SCIENCE CLASS.
FOR TODAY'S EXPERIMENT WE WILL...
Dr. Light
RUFF RUFF
BARK BOW WOW
OKAY, WHO BROUGHT THE DOG TO SCHOOL?

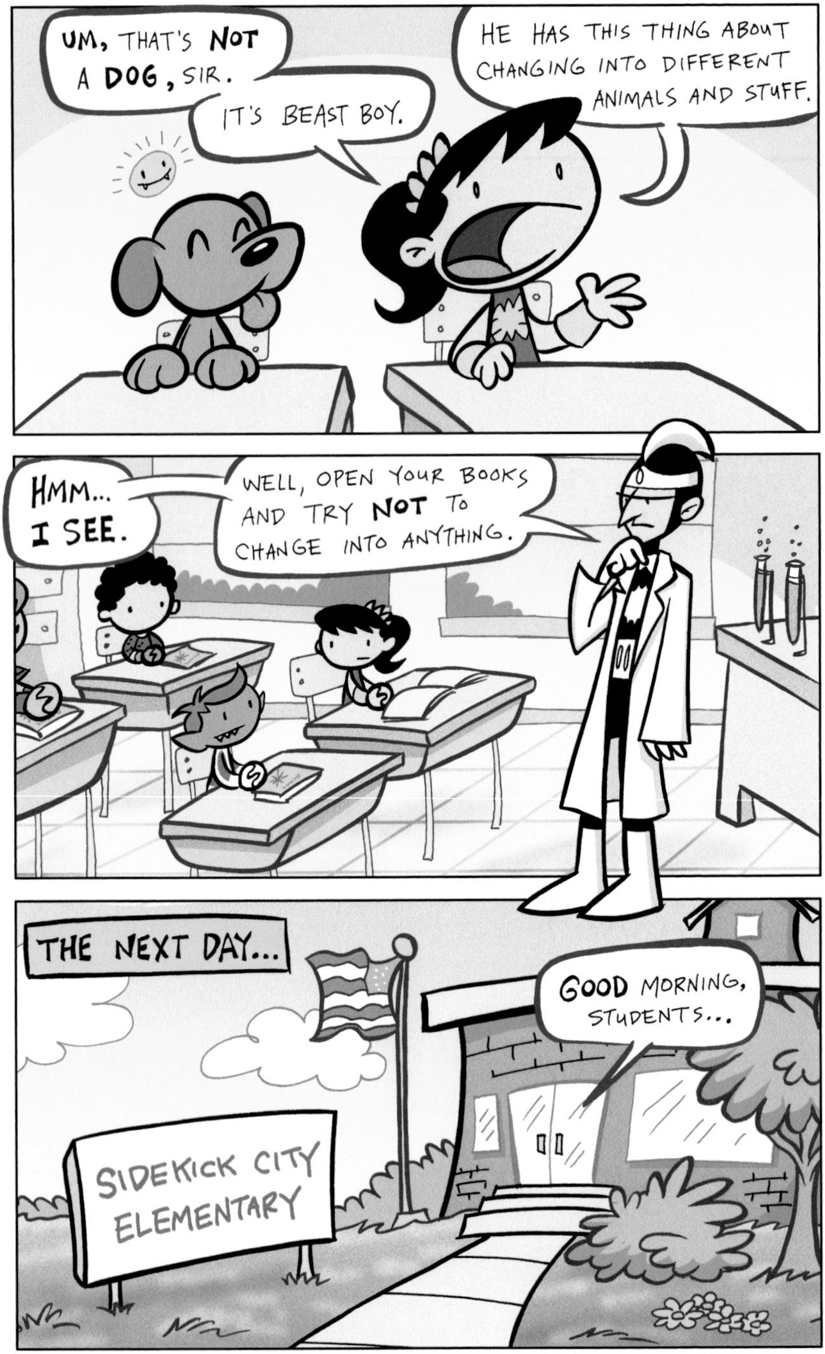
UM, THAT'S **NOT** A **DOG**, SIR.
IT'S BEAST BOY.
HE HAS THIS THING ABOUT CHANGING INTO DIFFERENT ANIMALS AND STUFF.
HMM... I SEE.
WELL, OPEN YOUR BOOKS AND TRY **NOT** TO CHANGE INTO ANYTHING.
THE NEXT DAY...
GOOD MORNING, STUDENTS...
SIDEKICK CITY ELEMENTARY

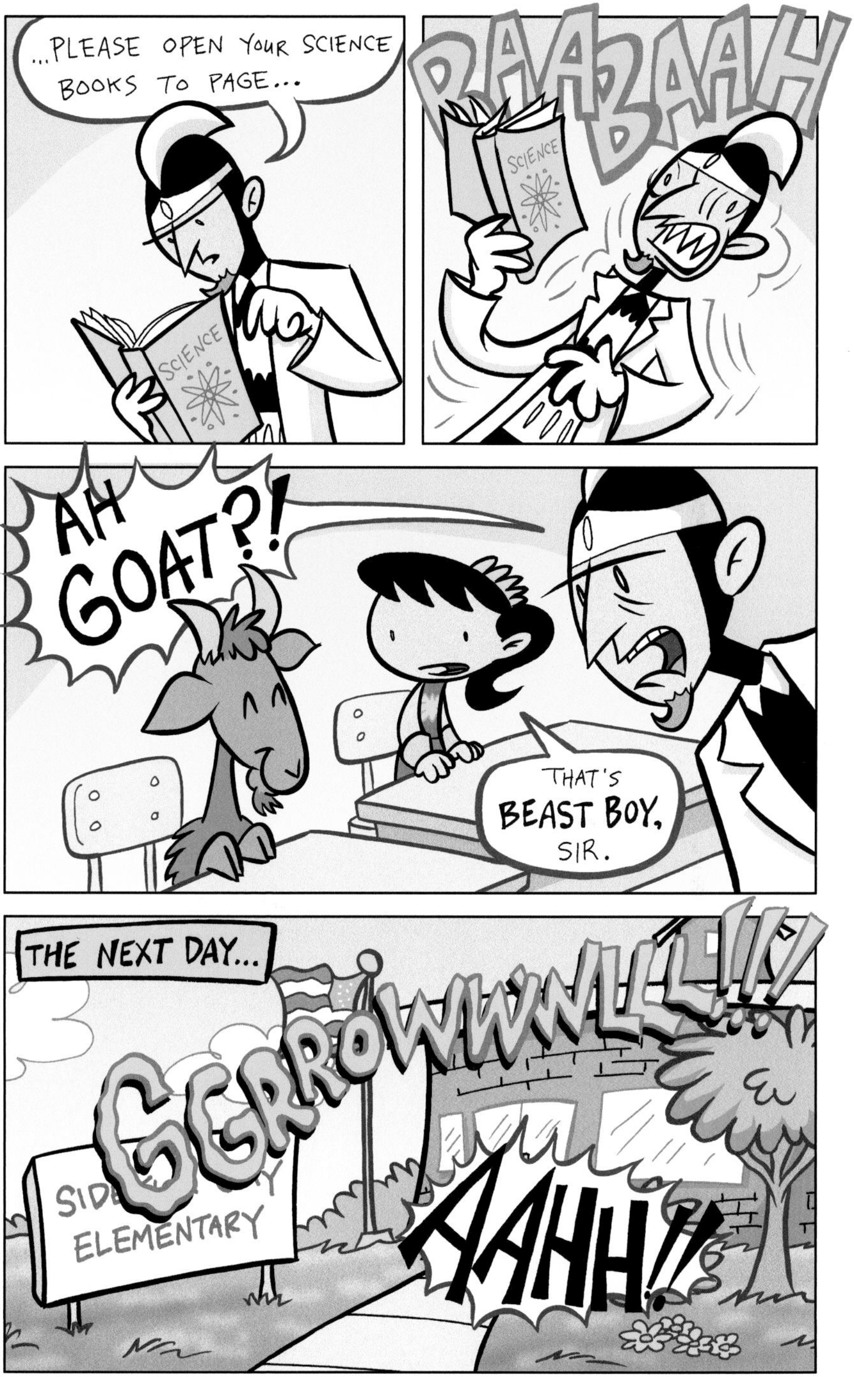
...PLEASE OPEN YOUR SCIENCE BOOKS TO PAGE...
SCIENCE
RAABAAH
SCIENCE
AH GOAT?!
THAT'S BEAST BOY, SIR.
THE NEXT DAY...
GGRROWWWLLL!!!
ELEMENTARY
AAHH!!

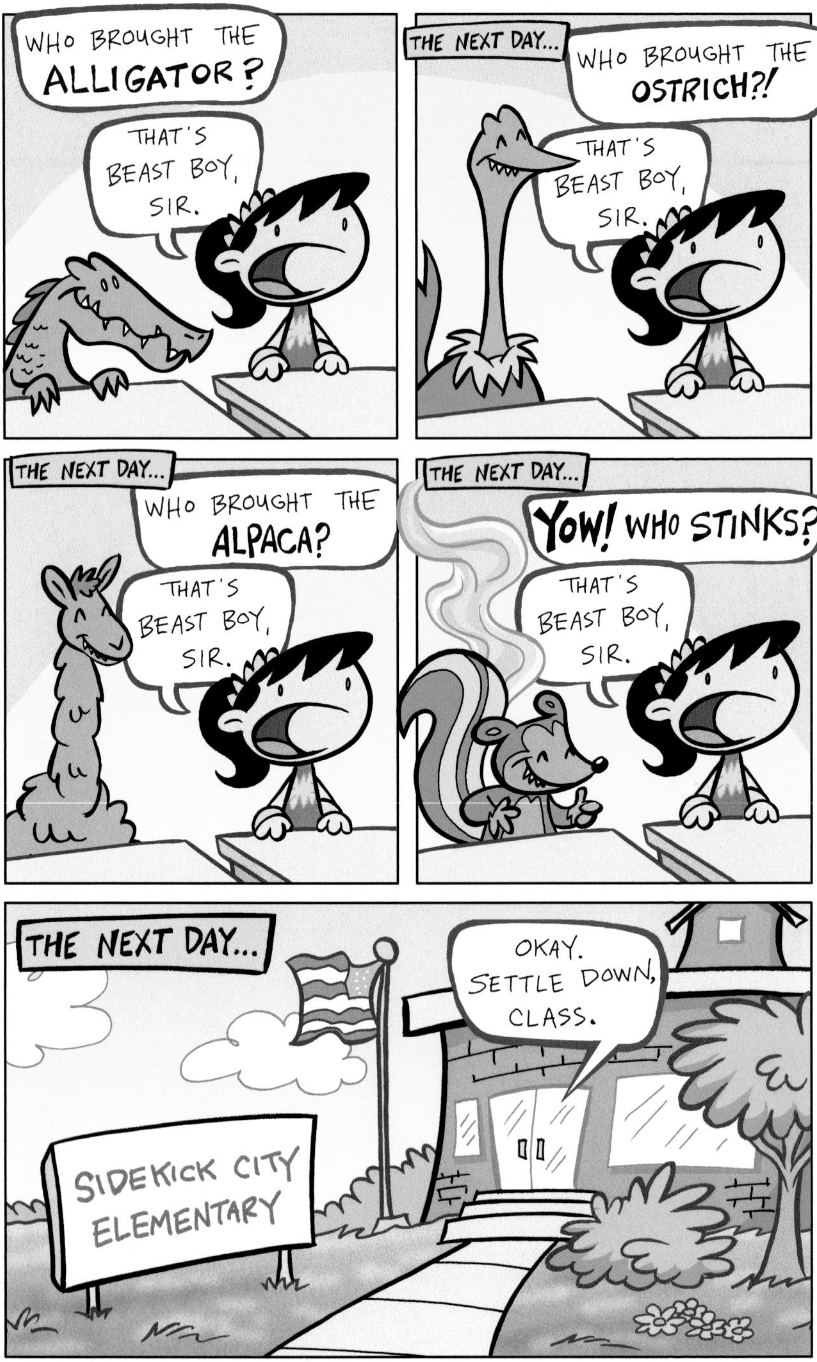
WHO BROUGHT THE ALLIGATOR?
THAT'S BEAST BOY, SIR.
THE NEXT DAY...
WHO BROUGHT THE OSTRICH?!
THAT'S BEAST BOY, SIR.
THE NEXT DAY...
WHO BROUGHT THE ALPACA?
THAT'S BEAST BOY, SIR.
THE NEXT DAY...
YOW! WHO STINKS?
THAT'S BEAST BOY, SIR.
THE NEXT DAY...
OKAY. SETTLE DOWN, CLASS.
SIDEKICK CITY ELEMENTARY

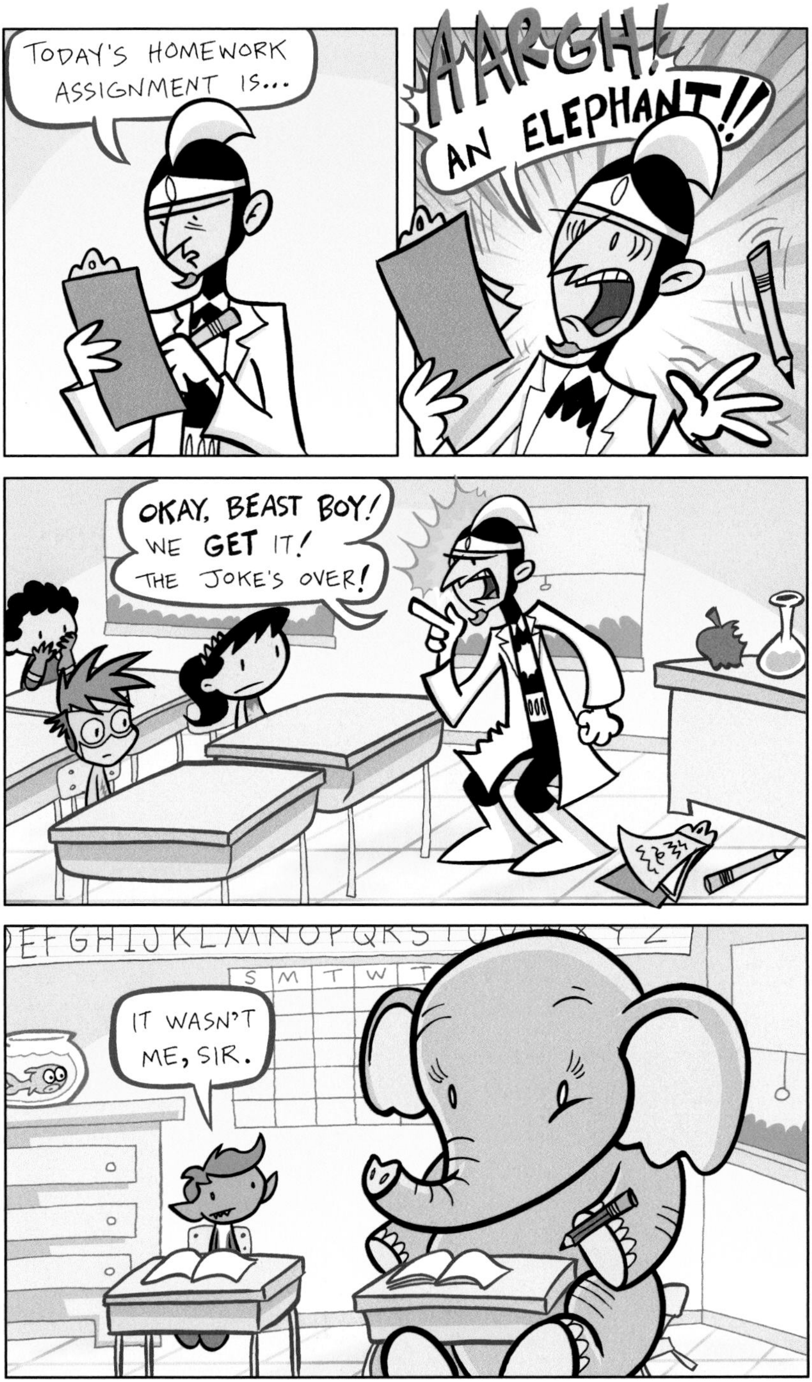
TODAY'S HOMEWORK ASSIGNMENT IS...
AARGH!
AN ELEPHANT!!
OKAY, BEAST BOY! WE GET IT! THE JOKE'S OVER!
IT WASN'T ME, SIR.

HELP BEAST BOY FIND HIS PUPPY FRIEND!

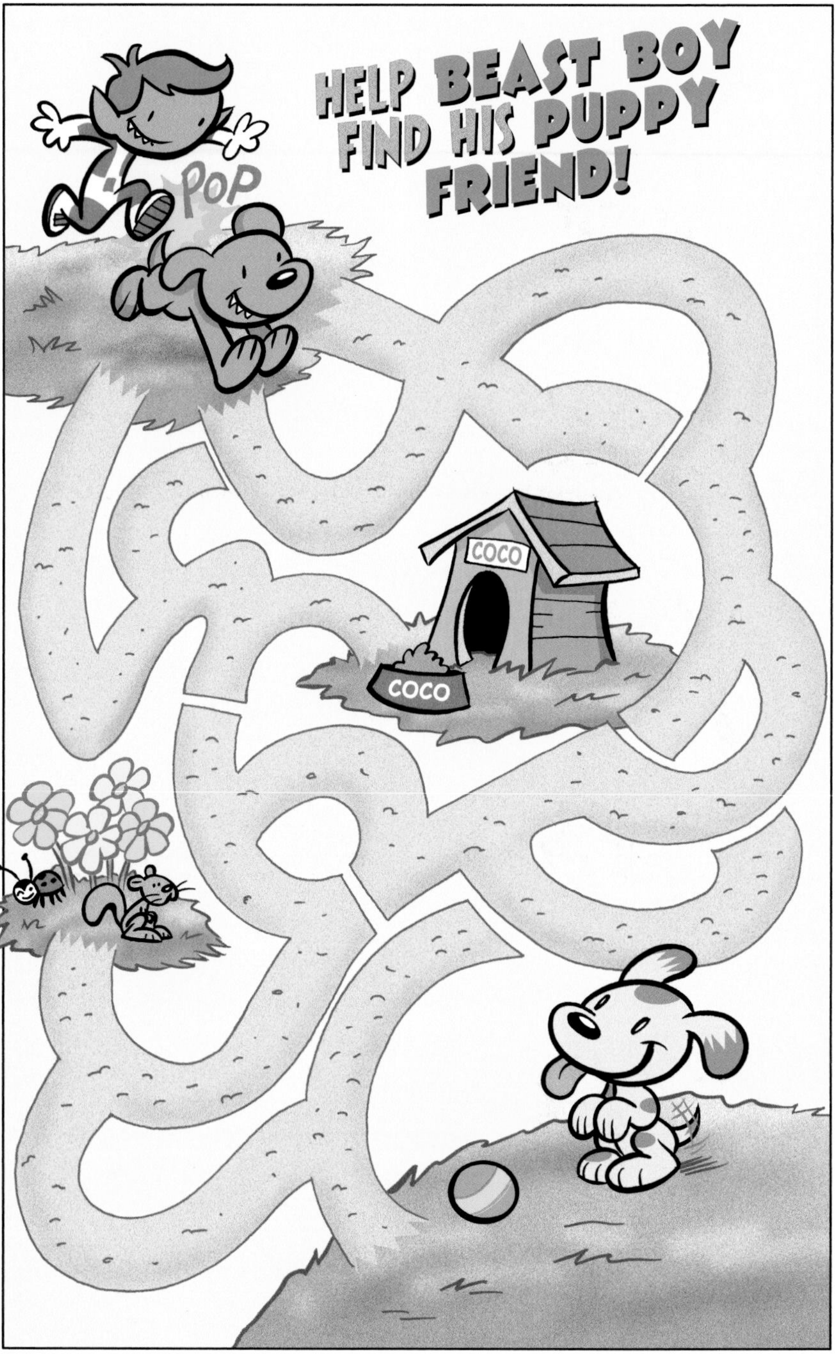
POP
COCO
COCO

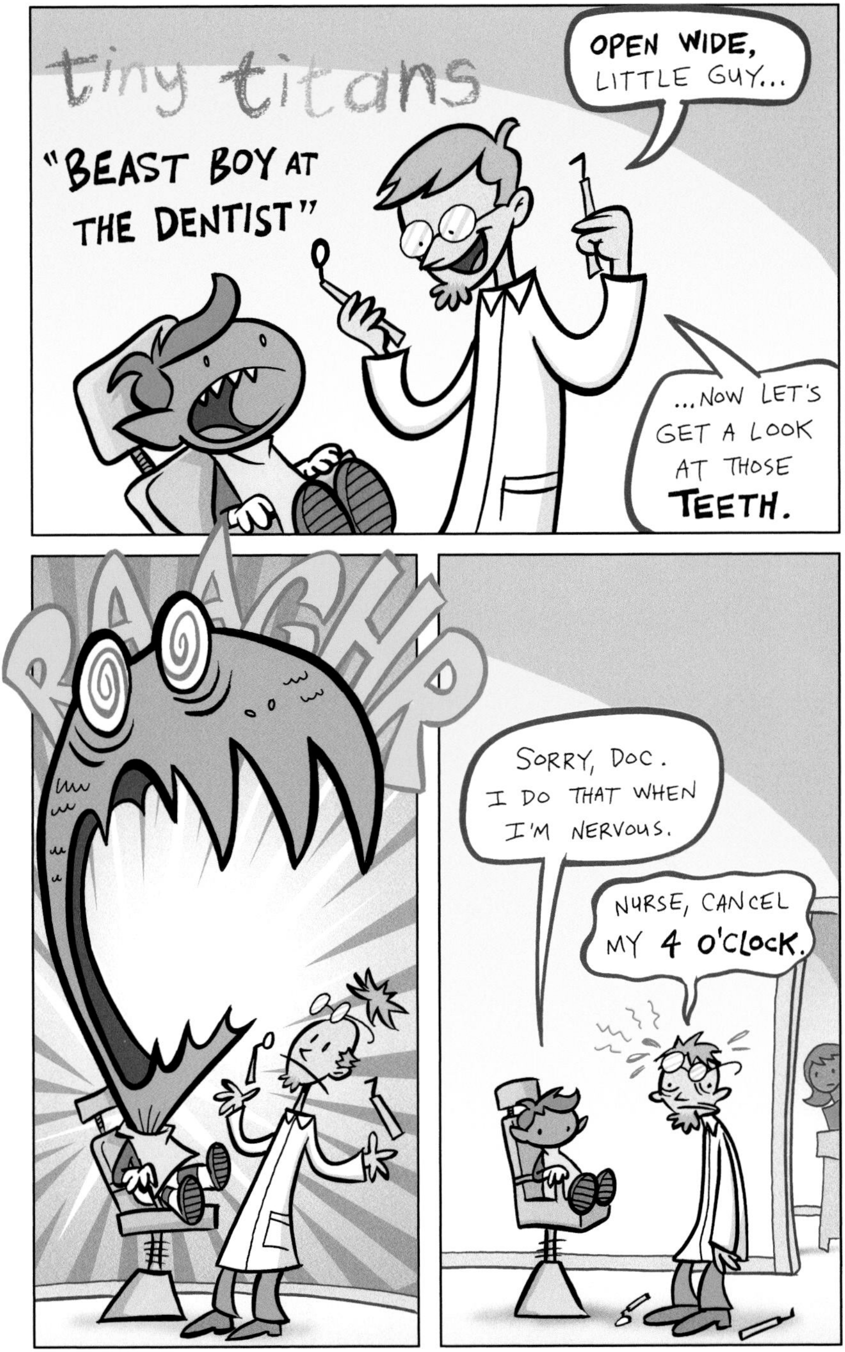
tiny titans
"BEAST BOY AT THE DENTIST"
OPEN WIDE, LITTLE GUY...
...NOW LET'S GET A LOOK AT THOSE TEETH.
RAAGHR
SORRY, DOC. I DO THAT WHEN I'M NERVOUS.
NURSE, CANCEL MY 4 O'CLOCK.

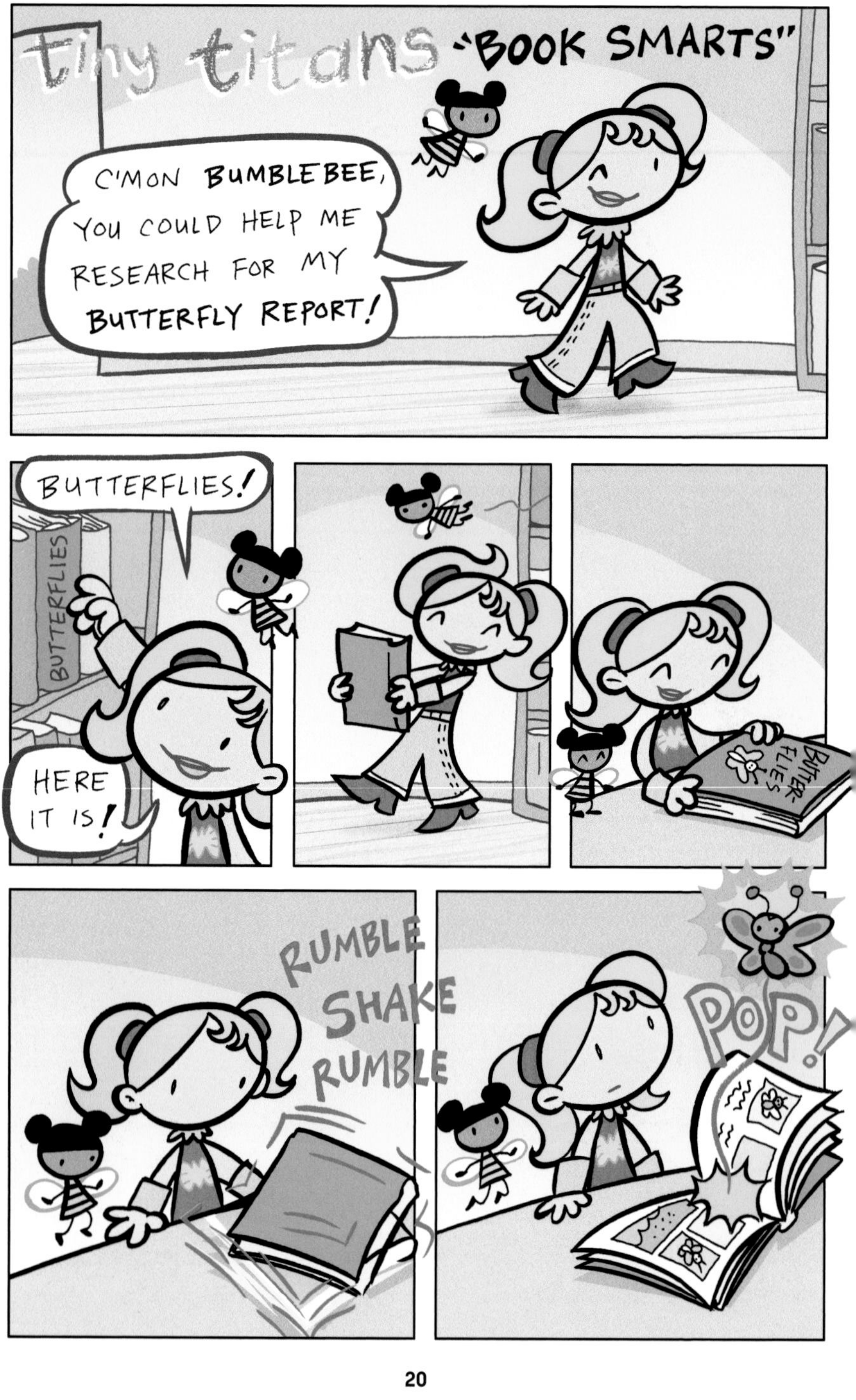
tiny titans
"BOOK SMARTS"
C'MON BUMBLEBEE, YOU COULD HELP ME RESEARCH FOR MY BUTTERFLY REPORT!
BUTTERFLIES!
BUTTERFLIES
HERE IT IS!
BUTTER-FLIES
RUMBLE
SHAKE
RUMBLE
POP!

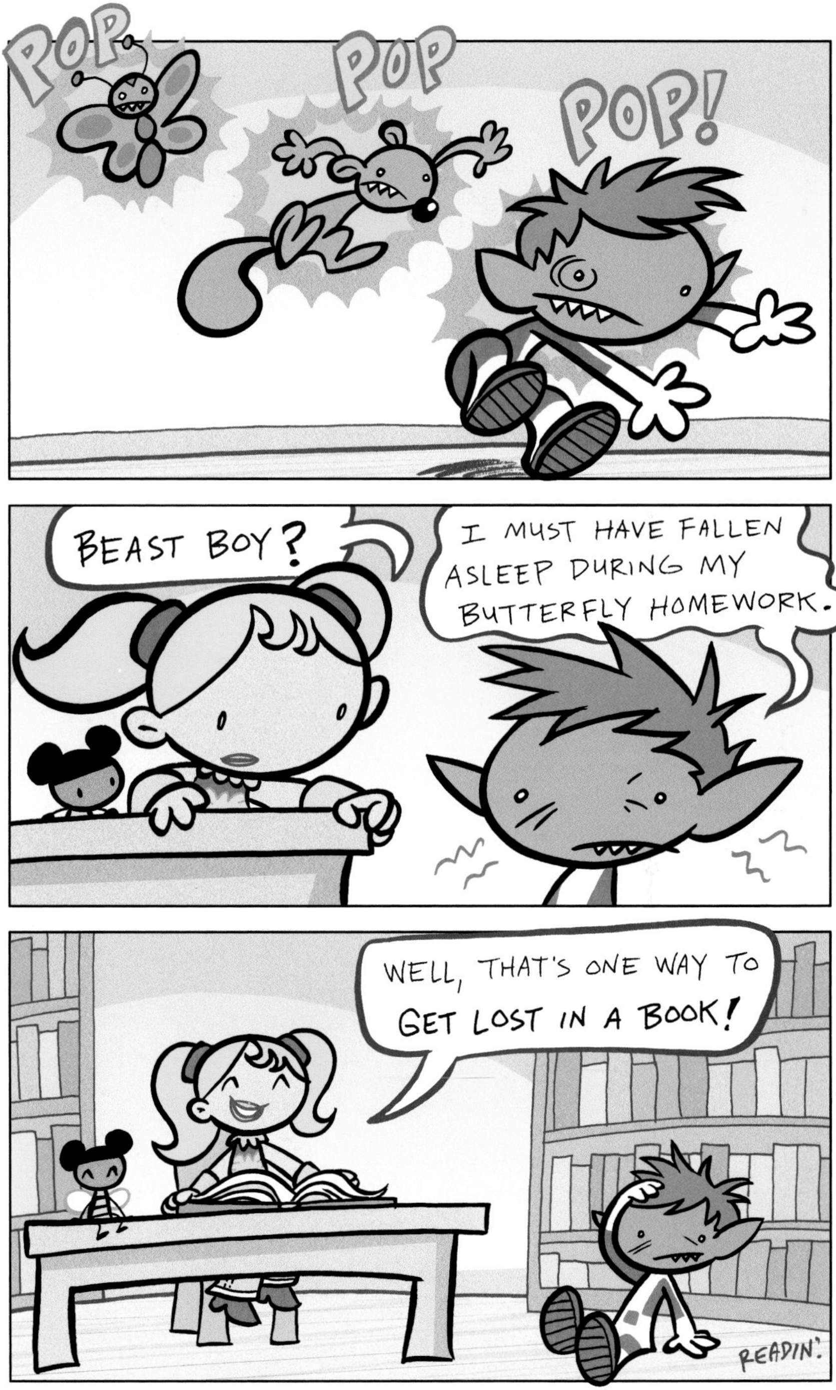
POP
POP
POP!
BEAST BOY?
I MUST HAVE FALLEN ASLEEP DURING MY BUTTERFLY HOMEWORK.
WELL, THAT'S ONE WAY TO GET LOST IN A BOOK!
READIN'.

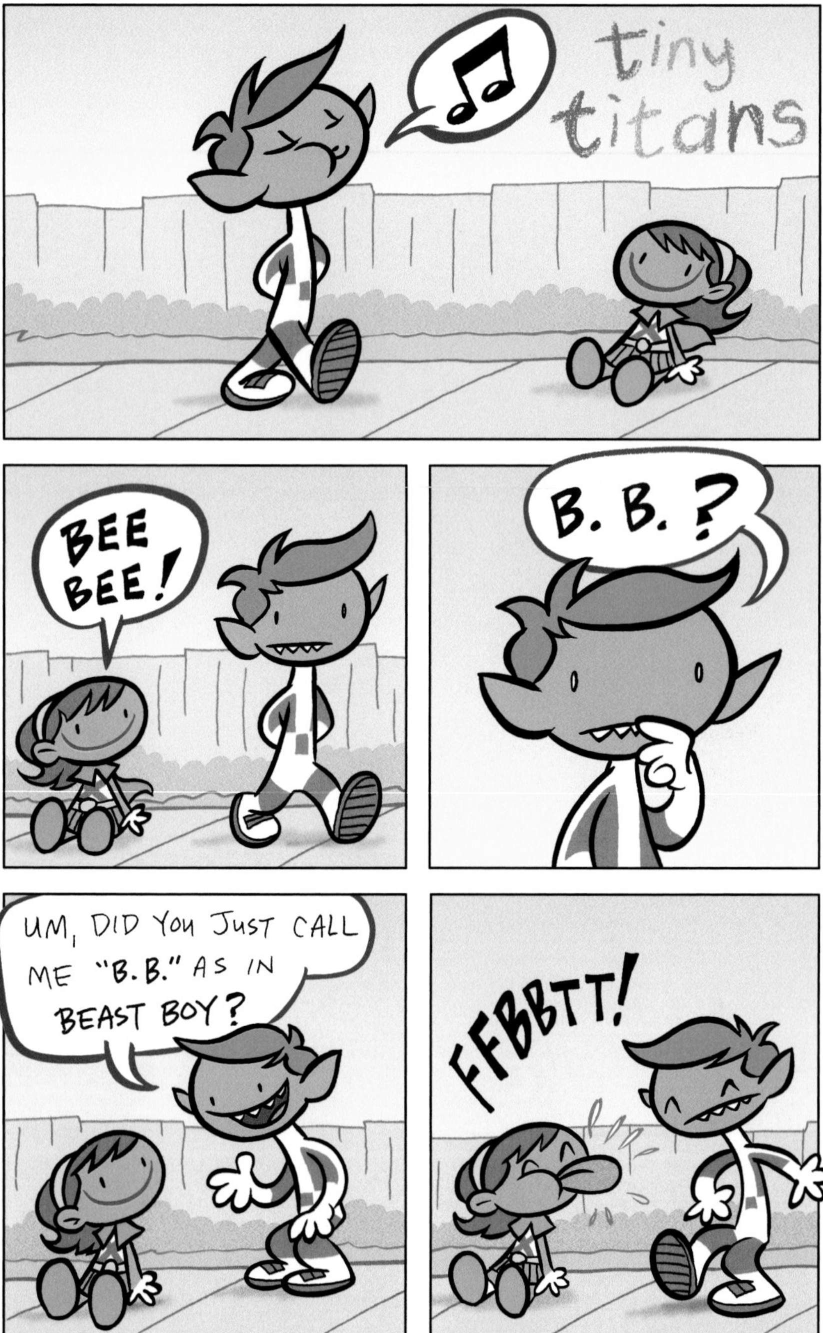
tiny titans
BEE BEE!
B. B.?
UM, DID YOU JUST CALL ME "B.B." AS IN BEAST BOY?
FFBBTT!

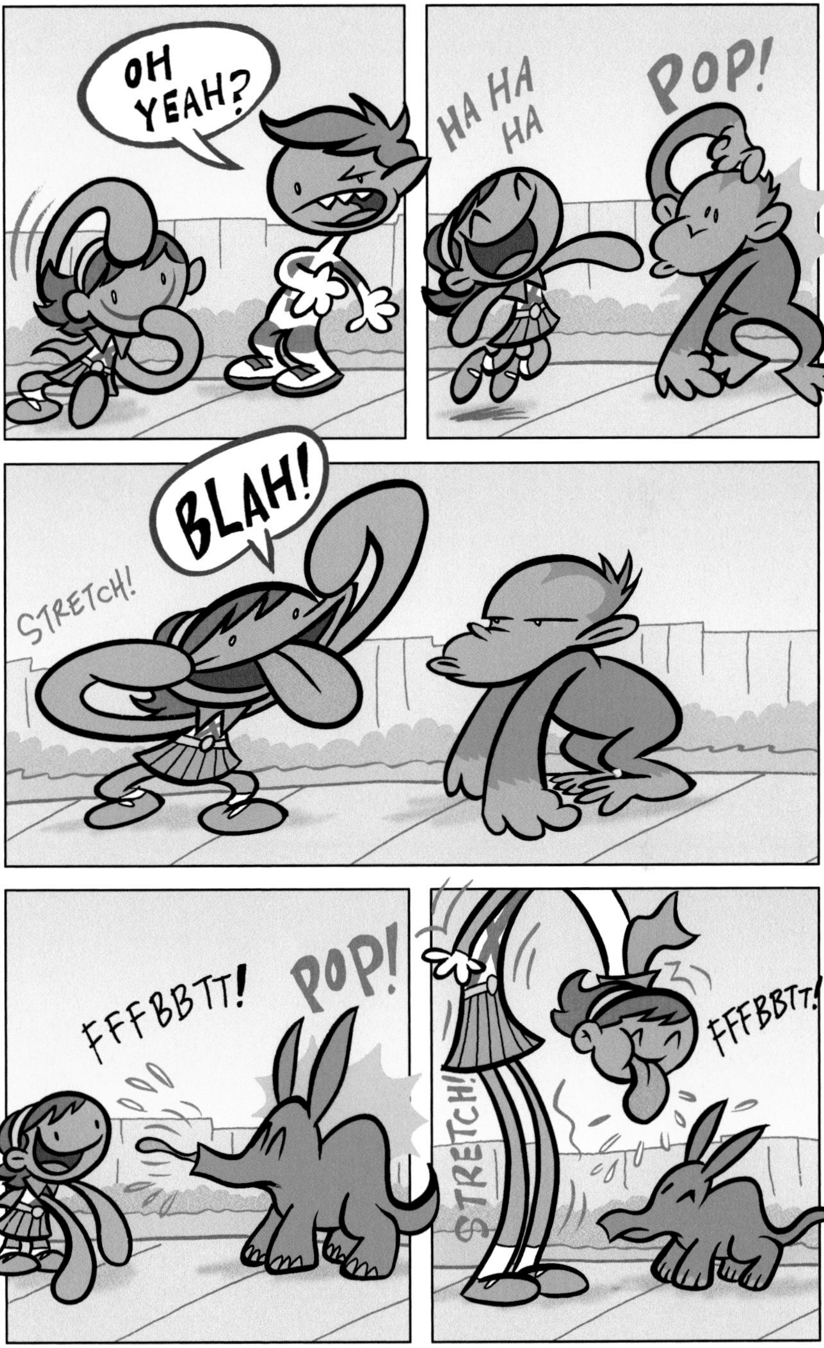
OH YEAH?
HA HA HA
POP!
BLAH!
STRETCH!
FFFBBTT!
POP!
STRETCH!
FFFBBTT!

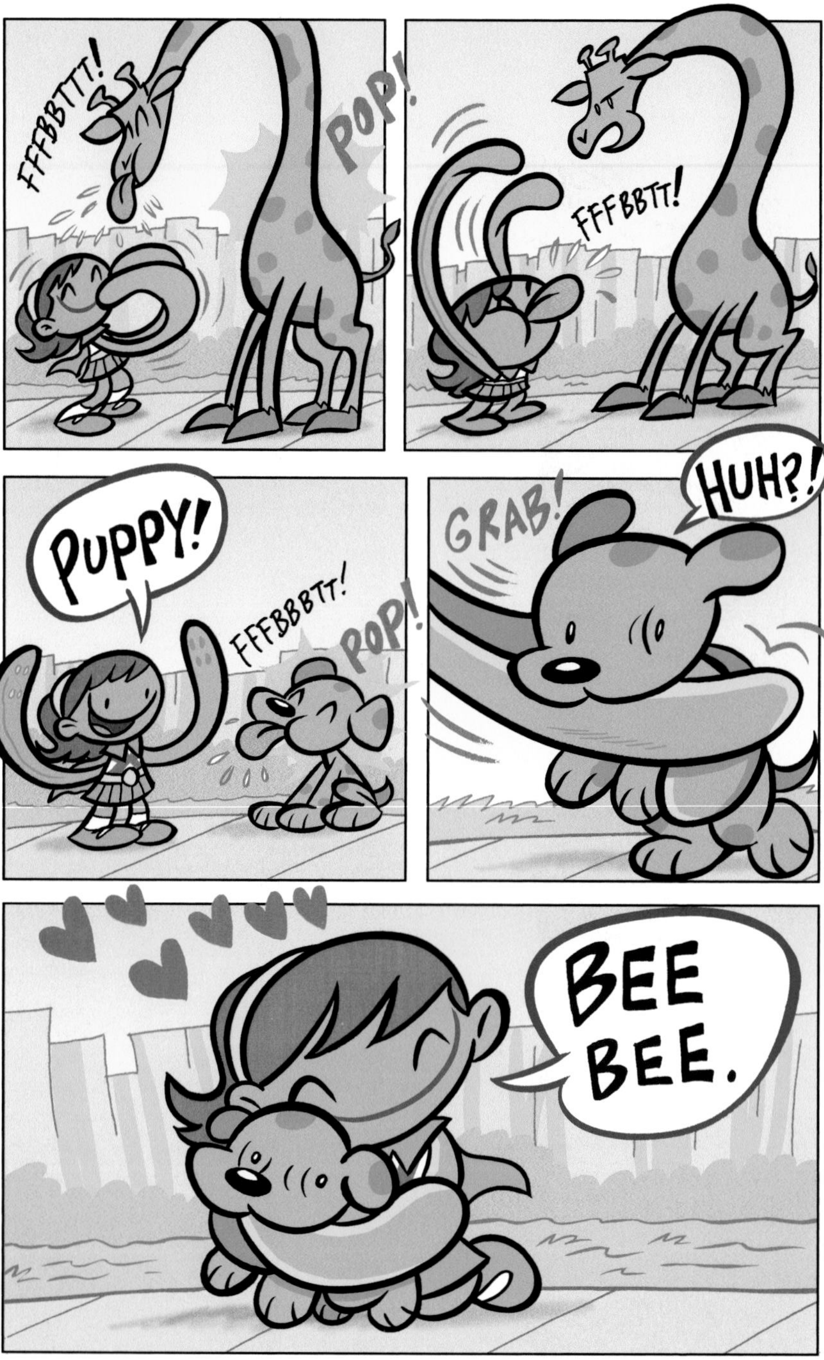
FFFBBTTT!
POP!
FFFBBTT!
PUPPY!
FFFBBBTT!
POP!
GRAB!
HUH?!
BEE BEE.

-Awww! ♥

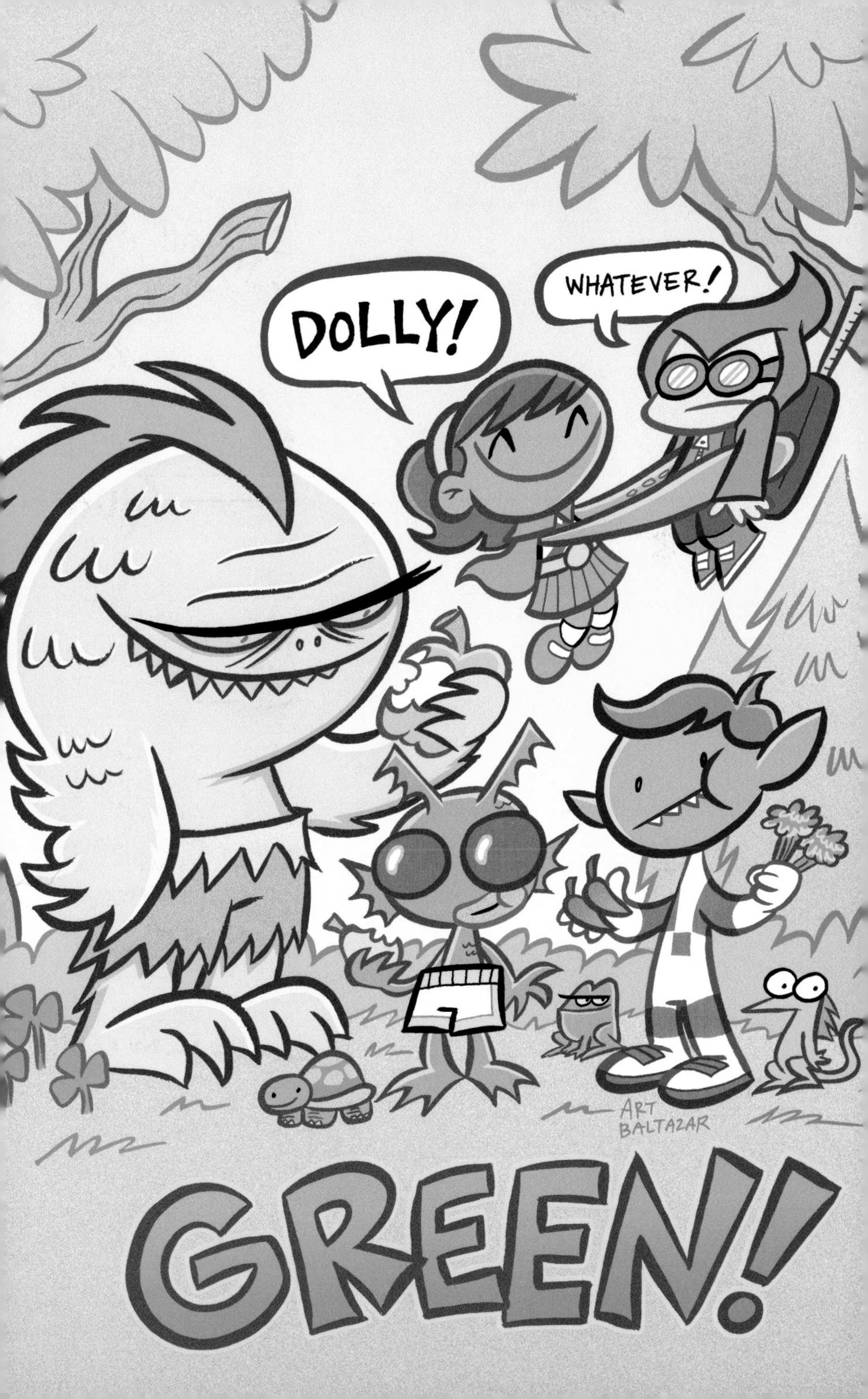
DOLLY!
WHATEVER!
ART BALTAZAR
GREEN!

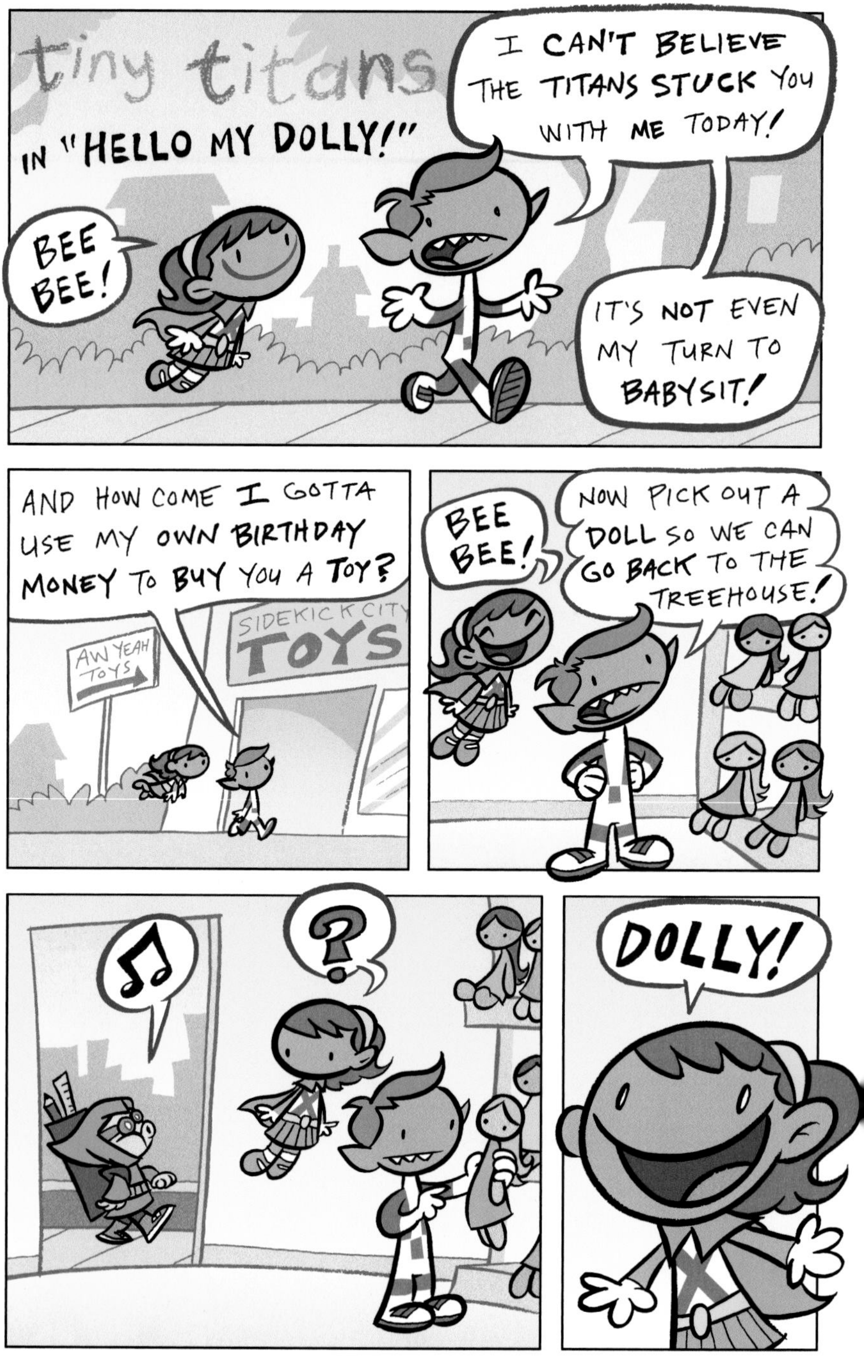
tiny titans
IN "HELLO MY DOLLY!"
I CAN'T BELIEVE THE TITANS STUCK YOU WITH ME TODAY!
BEE BEE!
IT'S NOT EVEN MY TURN TO BABYSIT!
AND HOW COME I GOTTA USE MY OWN BIRTHDAY MONEY TO BUY YOU A TOY?
SIDEKICK CITY TOYS
AW YEAH TOYS
BEE BEE!
NOW PICK OUT A DOLL SO WE CAN GO BACK TO THE TREEHOUSE!
?
DOLLY!

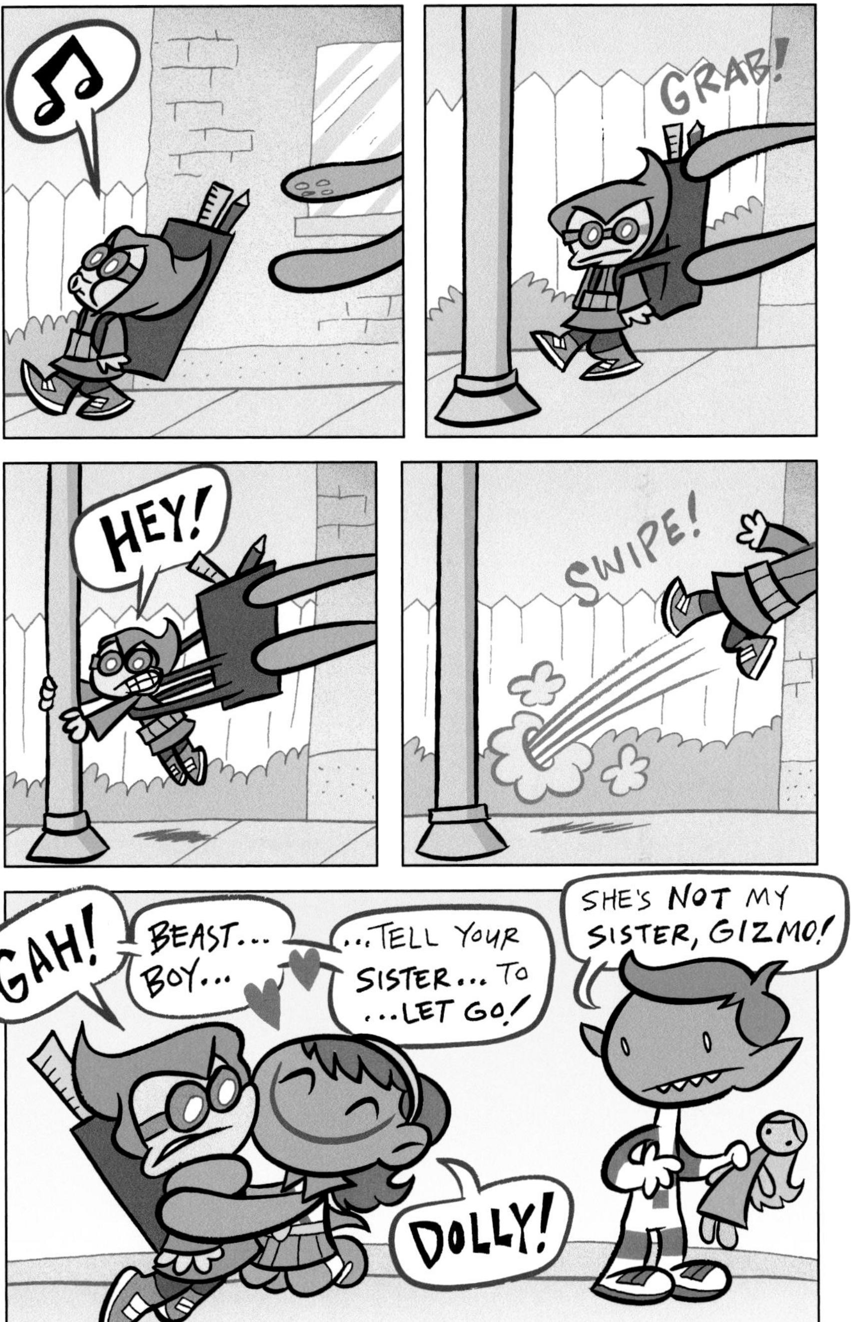
♫
GRAB!
HEY!
SWIPE!
GAH!
BEAST... BOY...
...TELL YOUR SISTER... TO ...LET GO!
DOLLY!
SHE'S NOT MY SISTER, GIZMO!

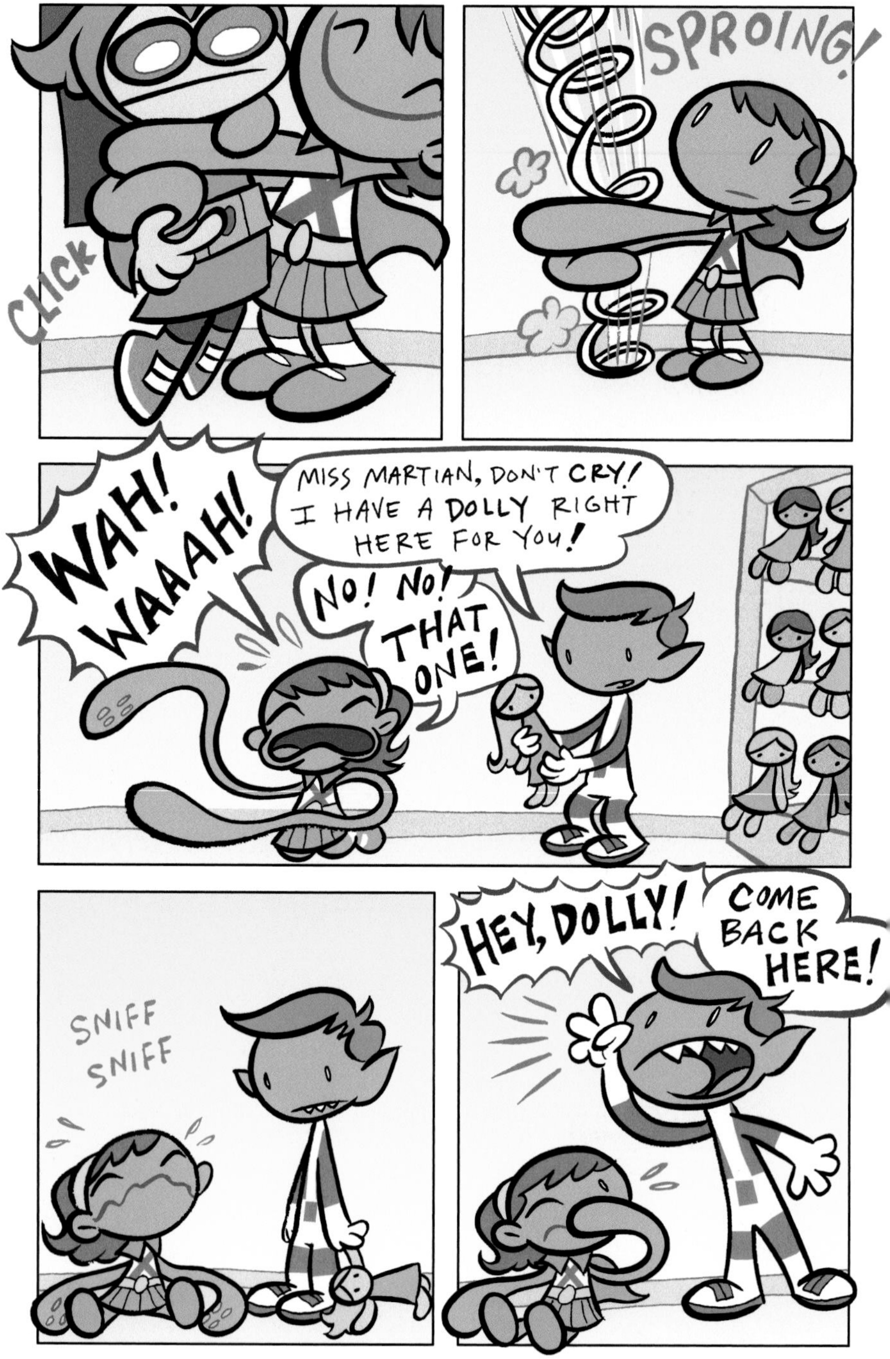
CLICK
SPROING!
WAH! WAAAH!
MISS MARTIAN, DON'T CRY! I HAVE A DOLLY RIGHT HERE FOR YOU!
NO! NO! THAT ONE!
SNIFF SNIFF
HEY, DOLLY!
COME BACK HERE!

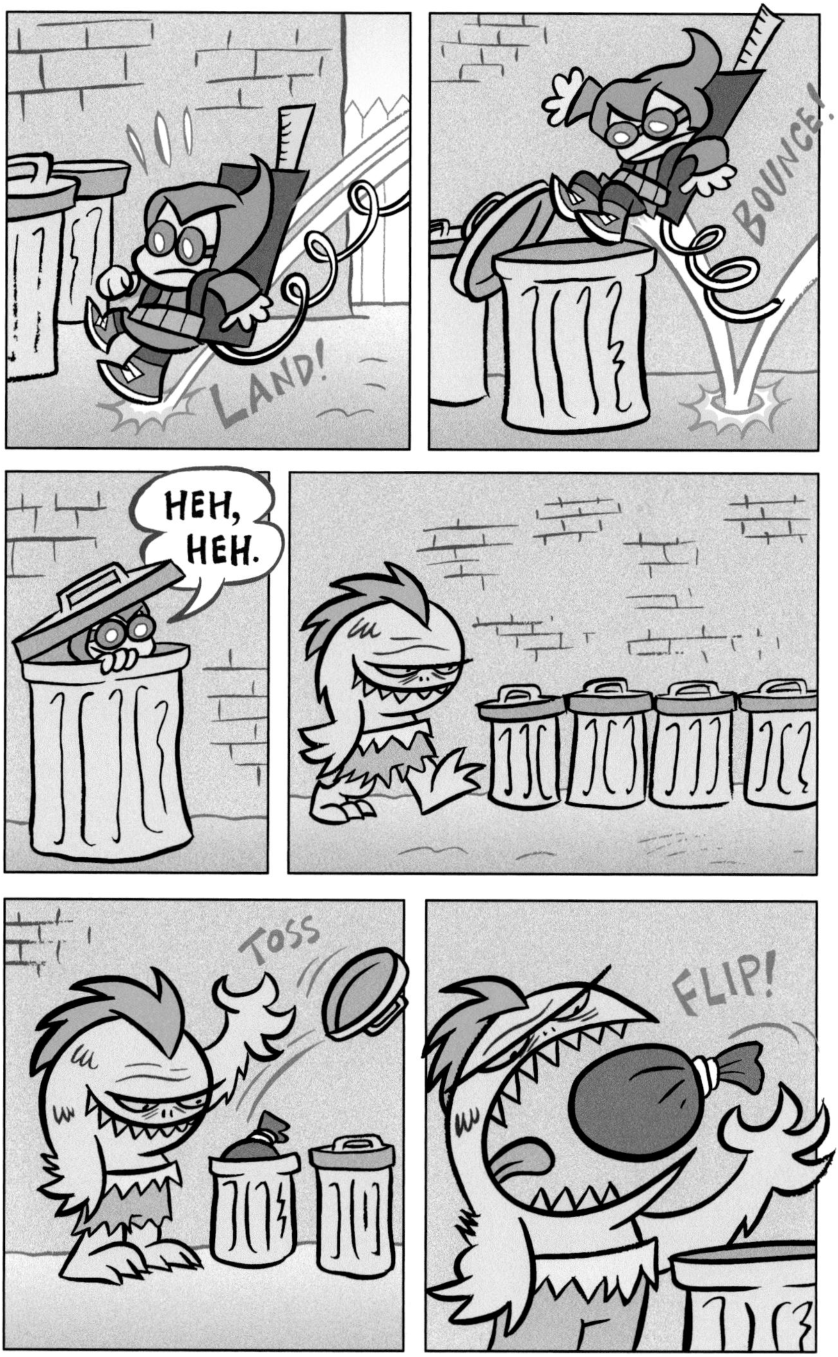

LAND!
BOUNCE!
HEH, HEH.
TOSS
FLIP!

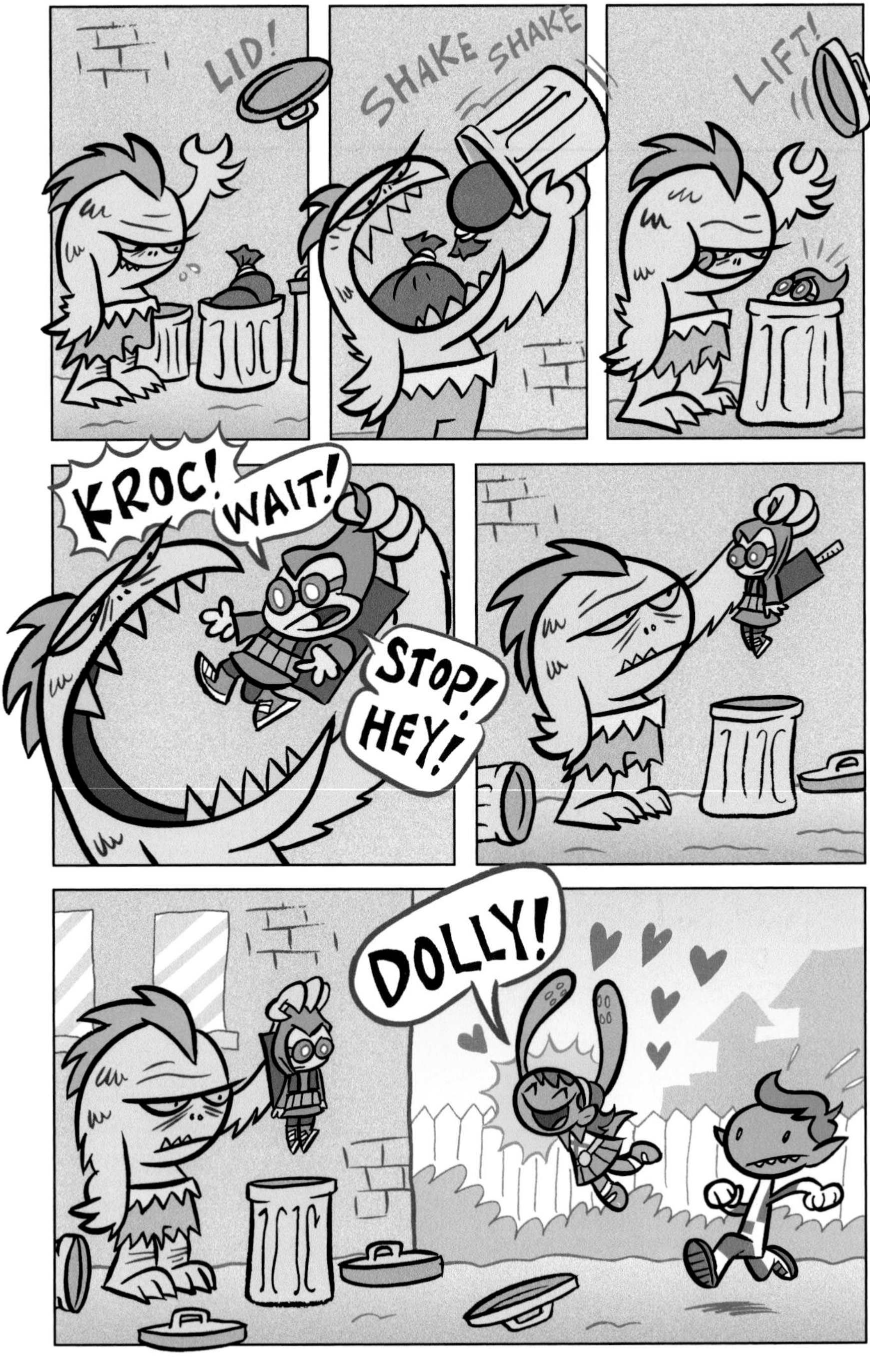

LID!
SHAKE SHAKE
LIFT!
KROC!
WAIT!
STOP!
HEY!
DOLLY!

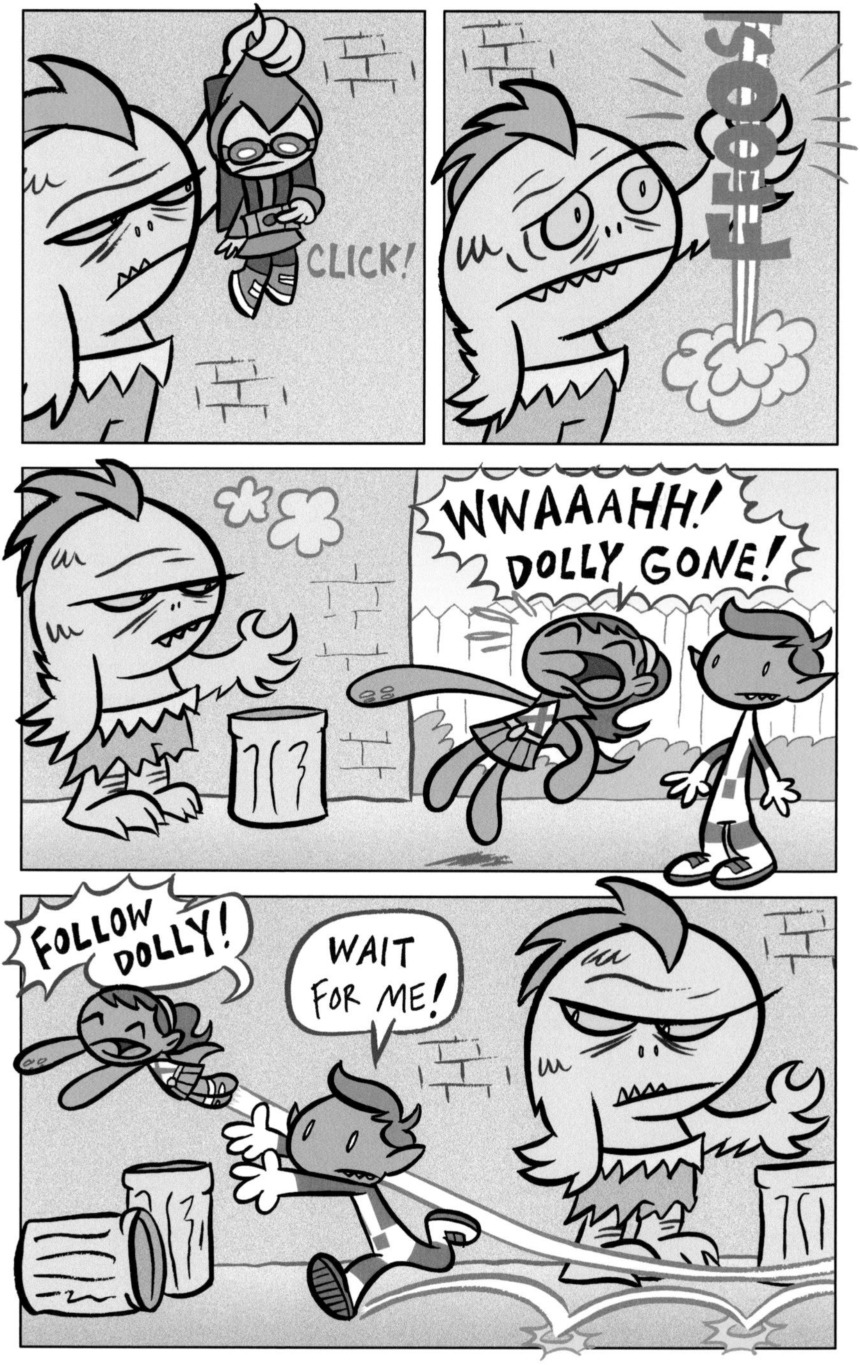
CLICK!
FOOSH
WWAAAHH! DOLLY GONE!
FOLLOW DOLLY!
WAIT FOR ME!

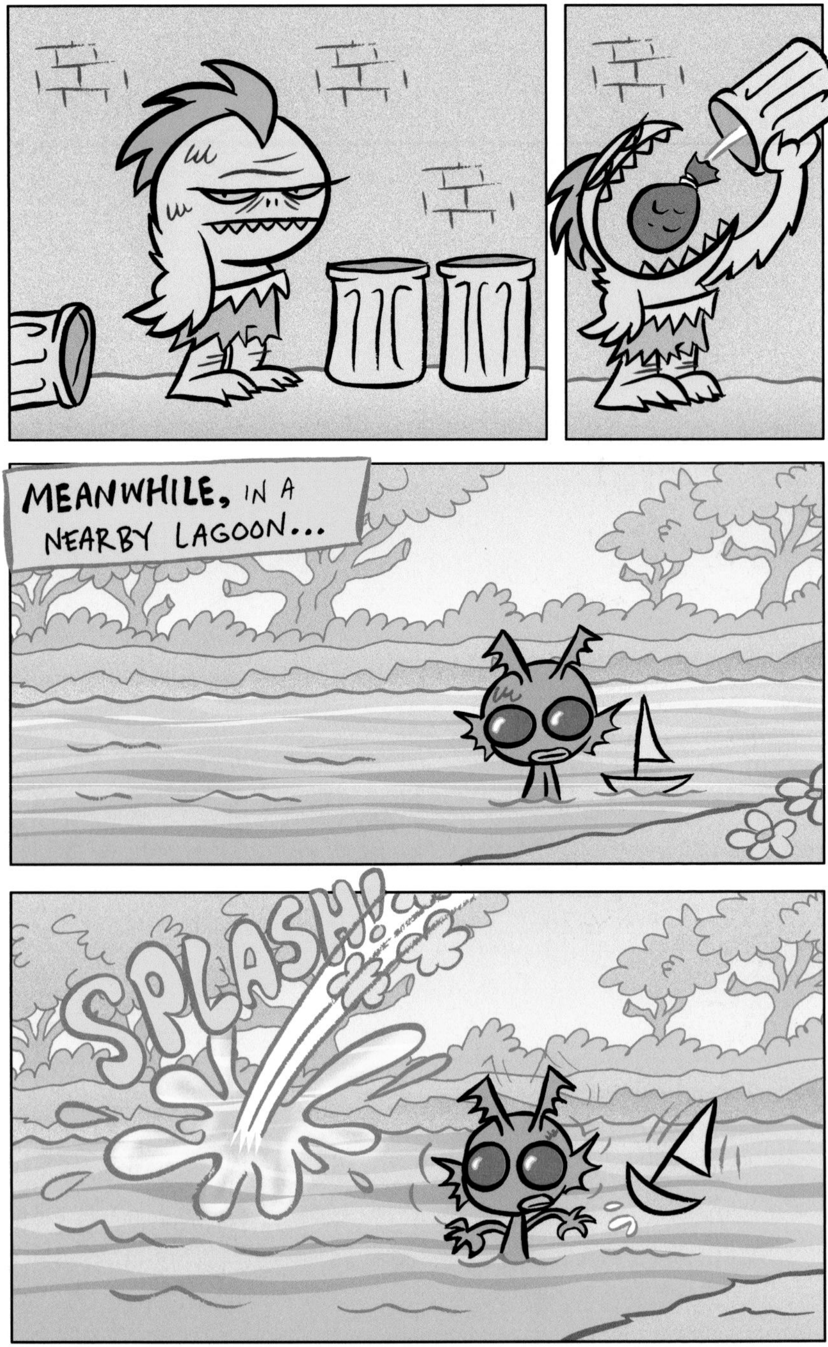
MEANWHILE, IN A NEARBY LAGOON...
SPLASH!

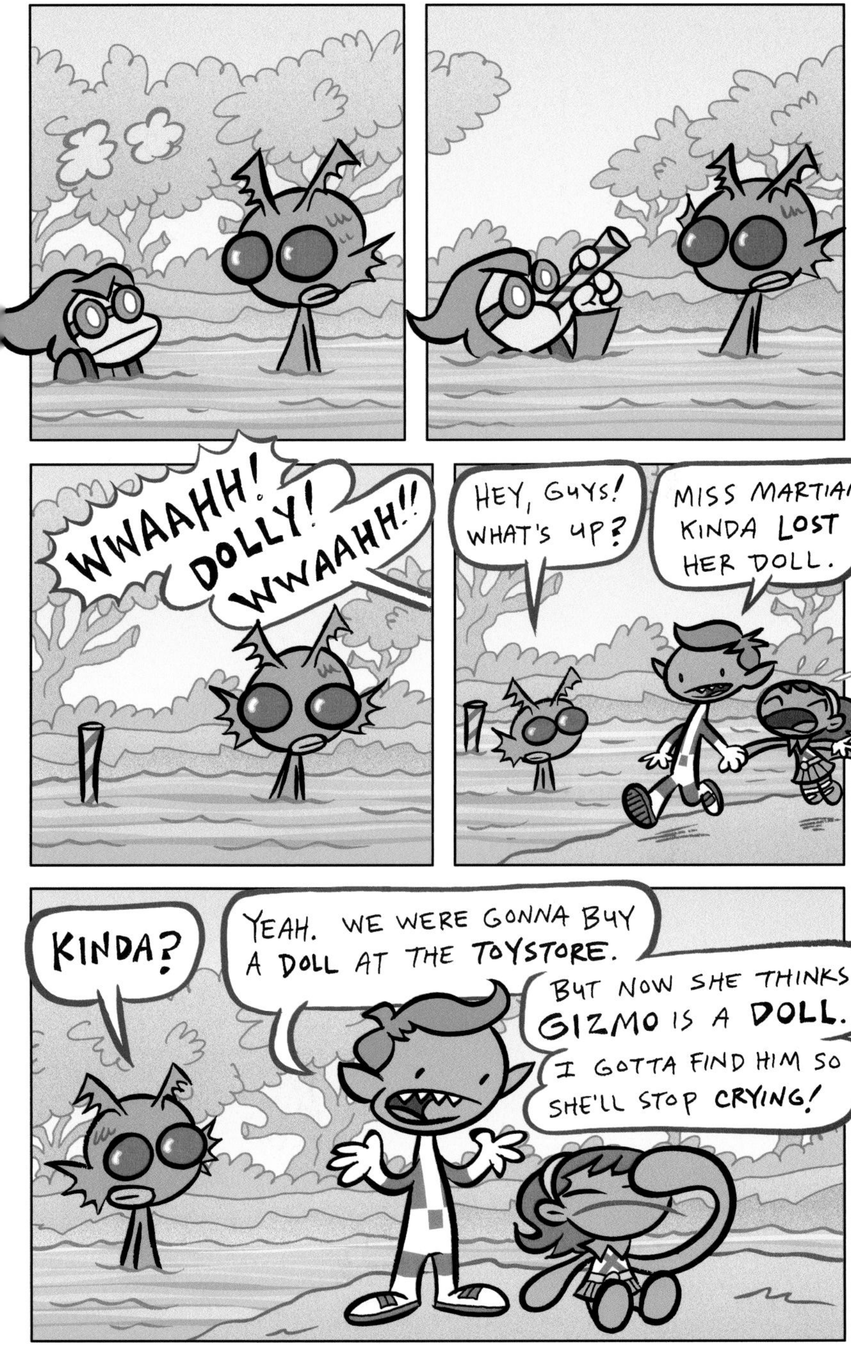
WWAAHH! DOLLY! WWAAHH!!
HEY, GUYS! WHAT'S UP?
MISS MARTIAN KINDA LOST HER DOLL.
KINDA?
YEAH. WE WERE GONNA BUY A DOLL AT THE TOYSTORE.
BUT NOW SHE THINKS GIZMO IS A DOLL.
I GOTTA FIND HIM SO SHE'LL STOP CRYING!

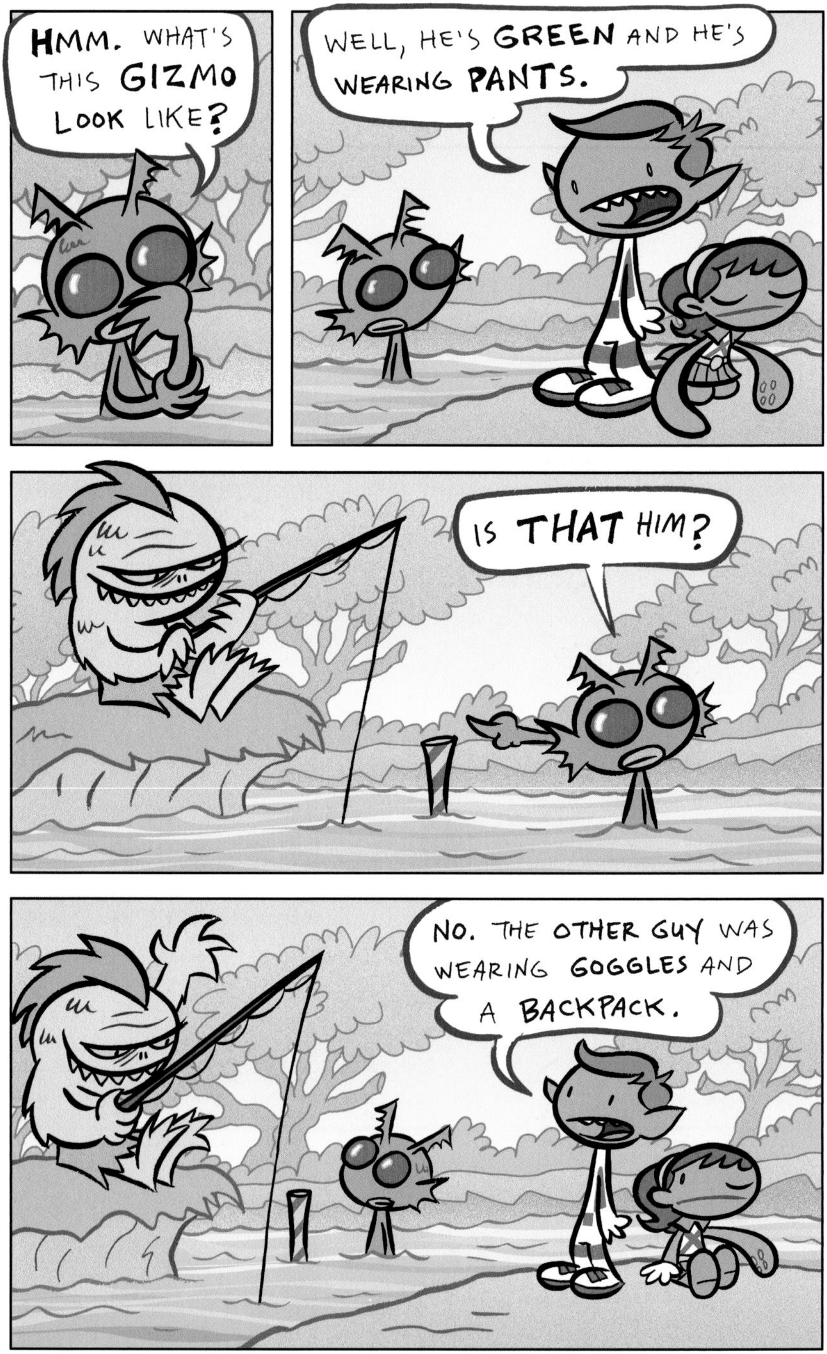
HMM. WHAT'S THIS GIZMO LOOK LIKE?
WELL, HE'S GREEN AND HE'S WEARING PANTS.
IS THAT HIM?
NO. THE OTHER GUY WAS WEARING GOGGLES AND A BACKPACK.

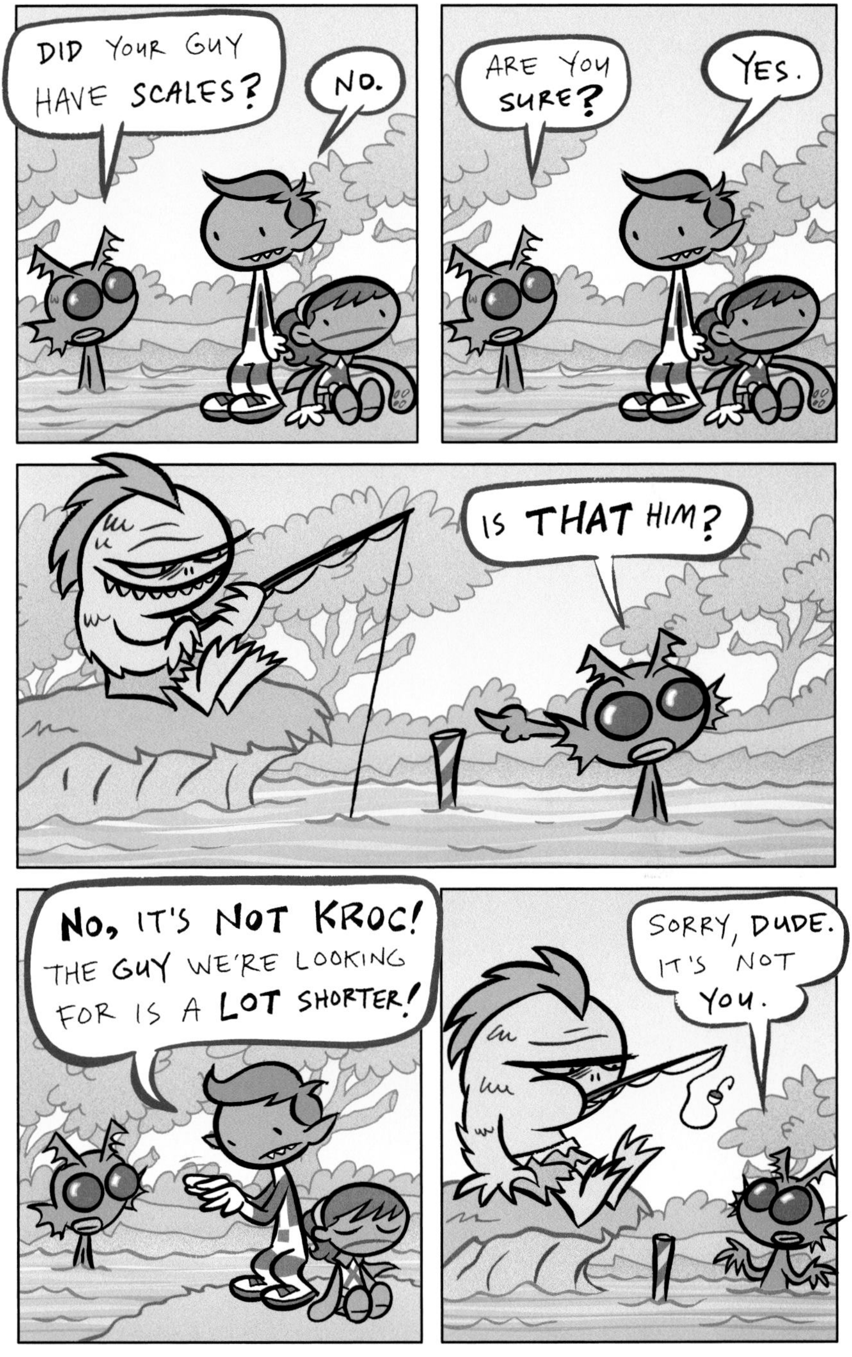
DID YOUR GUY HAVE SCALES?
NO.
ARE YOU SURE?
YES.
IS THAT HIM?
NO, IT'S NOT KROC! THE GUY WE'RE LOOKING FOR IS A LOT SHORTER!
SORRY, DUDE. IT'S NOT YOU.

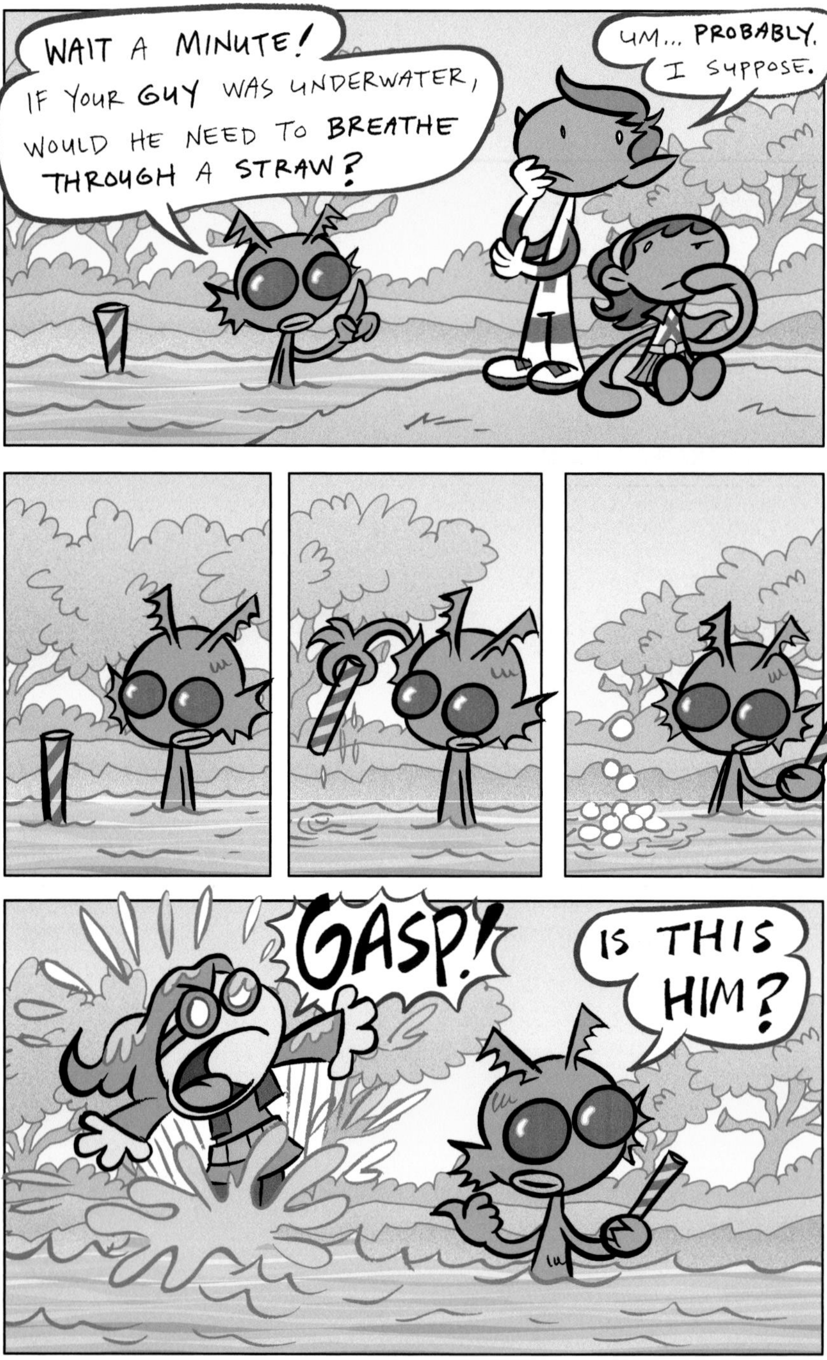
WAIT A MINUTE!
IF YOUR GUY WAS UNDERWATER, WOULD HE NEED TO BREATHE THROUGH A STRAW?
UM... PROBABLY. I SUPPOSE.
GASP!
IS THIS HIM?

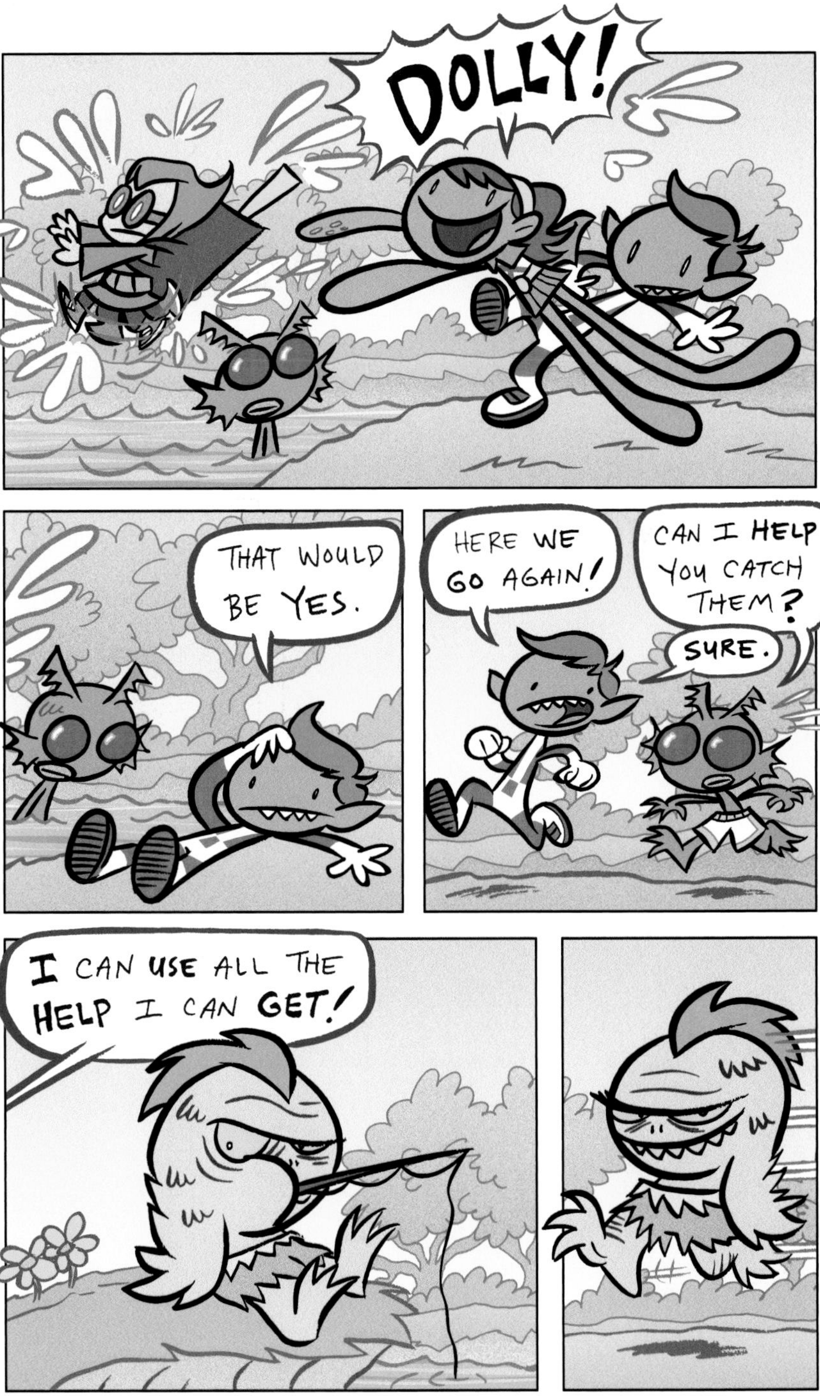
DOLLY!
THAT WOULD BE YES.
HERE WE GO AGAIN!
CAN I HELP YOU CATCH THEM?
SURE.
I CAN USE ALL THE HELP I CAN GET!

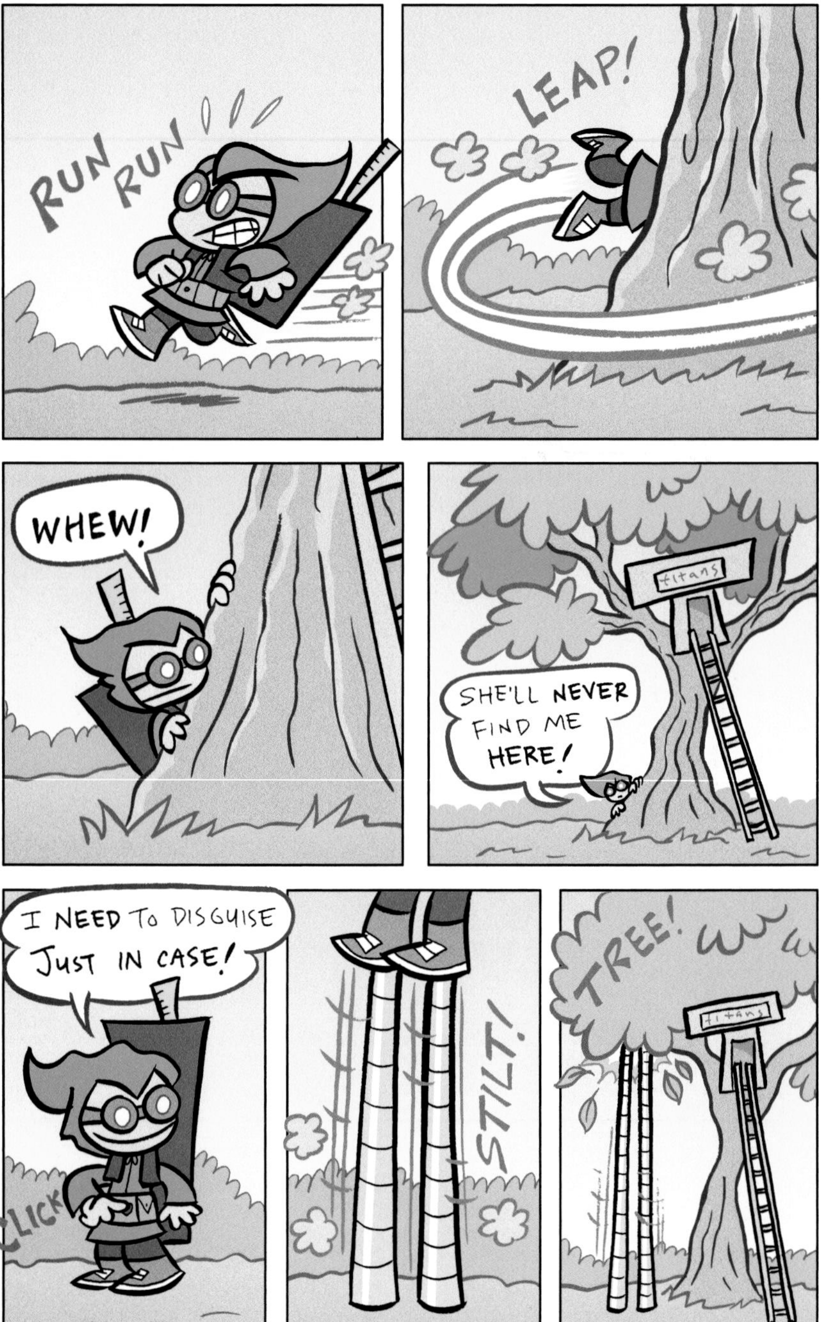
RUN
RUN
LEAP!
WHEW!
SHE'LL NEVER FIND ME HERE!
titans
I NEED TO DISGUISE JUST IN CASE!
CLICK
STILT!
TREE!
titans

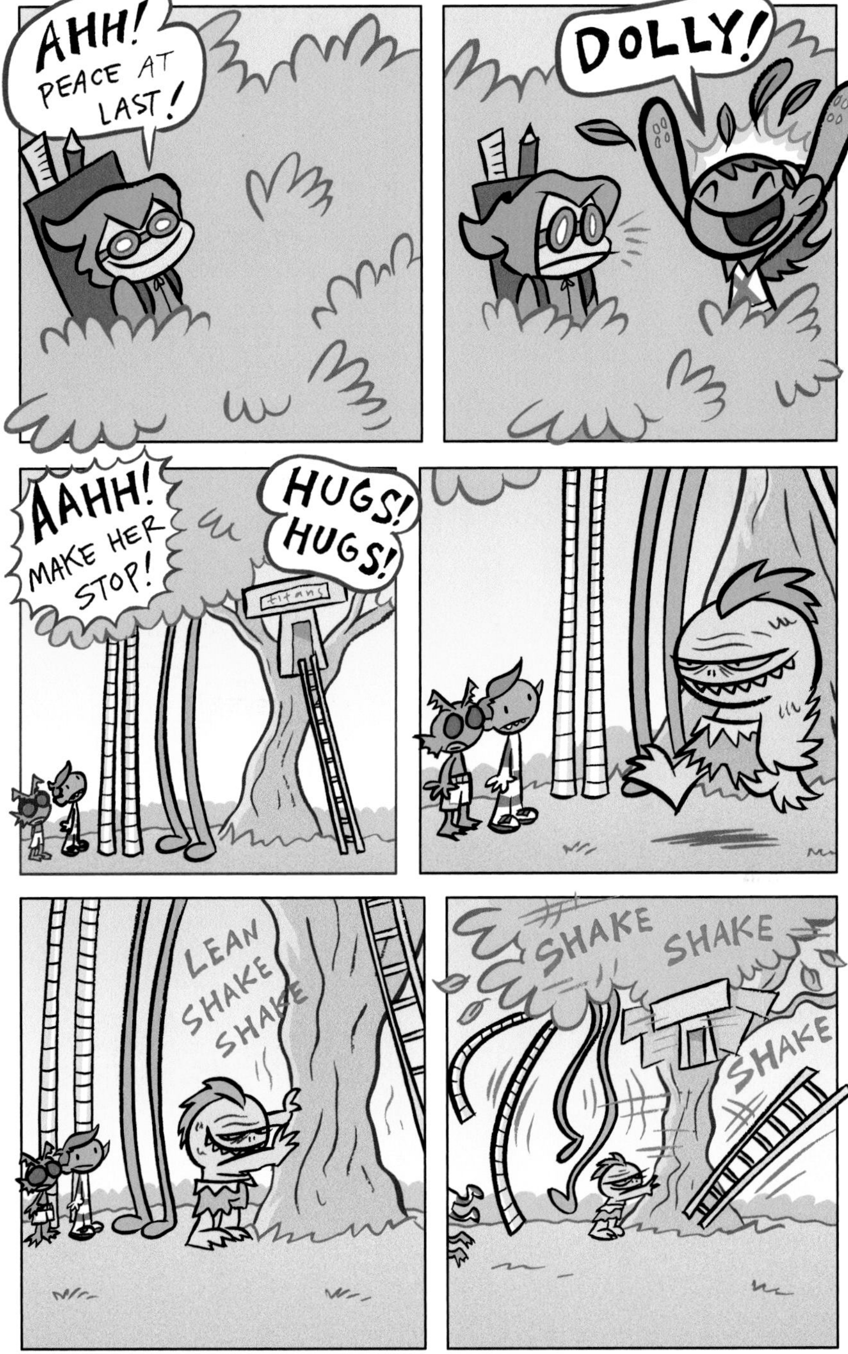
AHH! PEACE AT LAST!
DOLLY!
AAHH! MAKE HER STOP!
HUGS! HUGS!
titans
LEAN
SHAKE
SHAKE
SHAKE
SHAKE
SHAKE

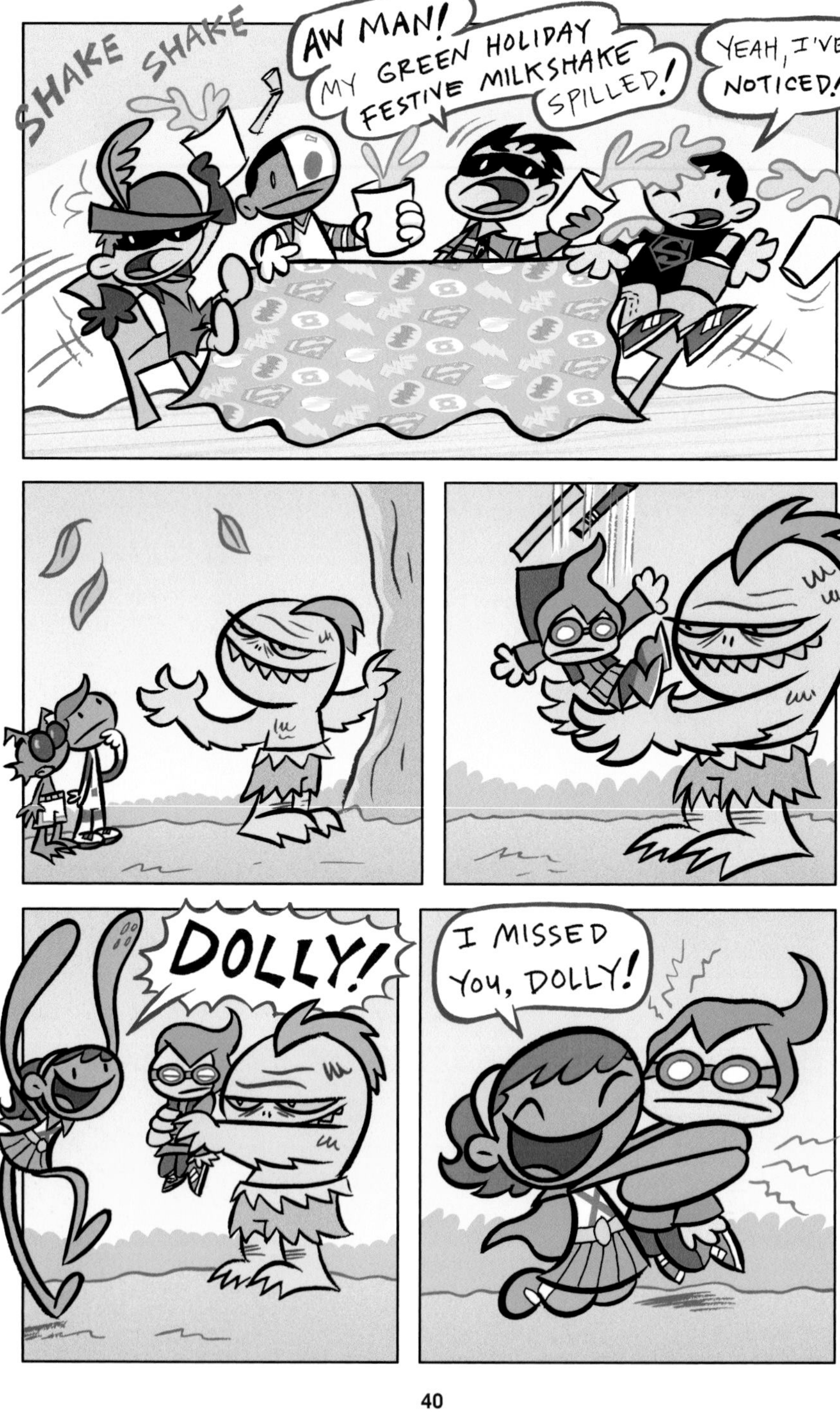
SHAKE SHAKE
AW MAN! MY GREEN HOLIDAY FESTIVE MILKSHAKE SPILLED!
YEAH, I'VE NOTICED!
DOLLY!
I MISSED YOU, DOLLY!

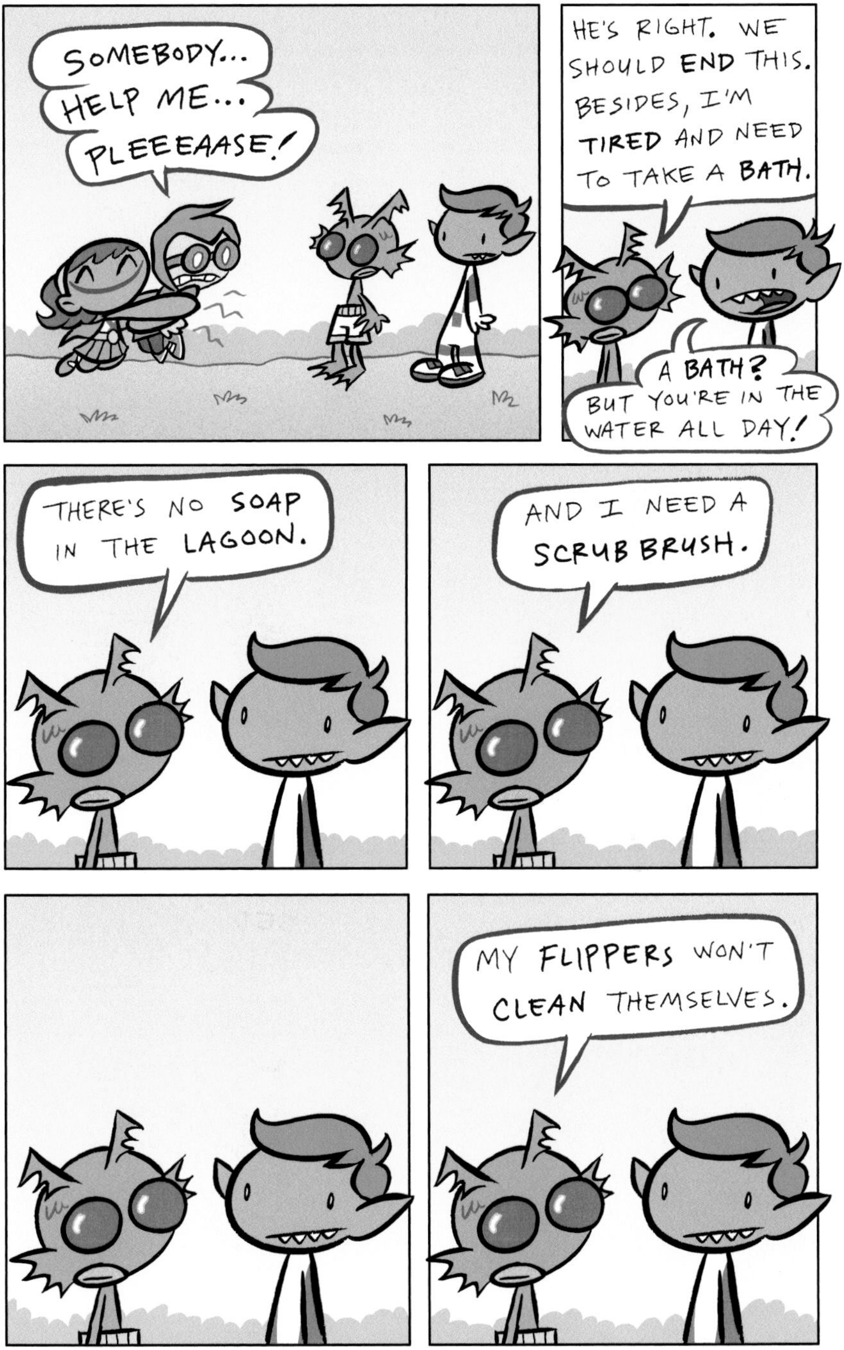
SOMEBODY... HELP ME... PLEEEAASE!
HE'S RIGHT. WE SHOULD END THIS. BESIDES, I'M TIRED AND NEED TO TAKE A BATH.
A BATH? BUT YOU'RE IN THE WATER ALL DAY!
THERE'S NO SOAP IN THE LAGOON.
AND I NEED A SCRUB BRUSH.
MY FLIPPERS WON'T CLEAN THEMSELVES.

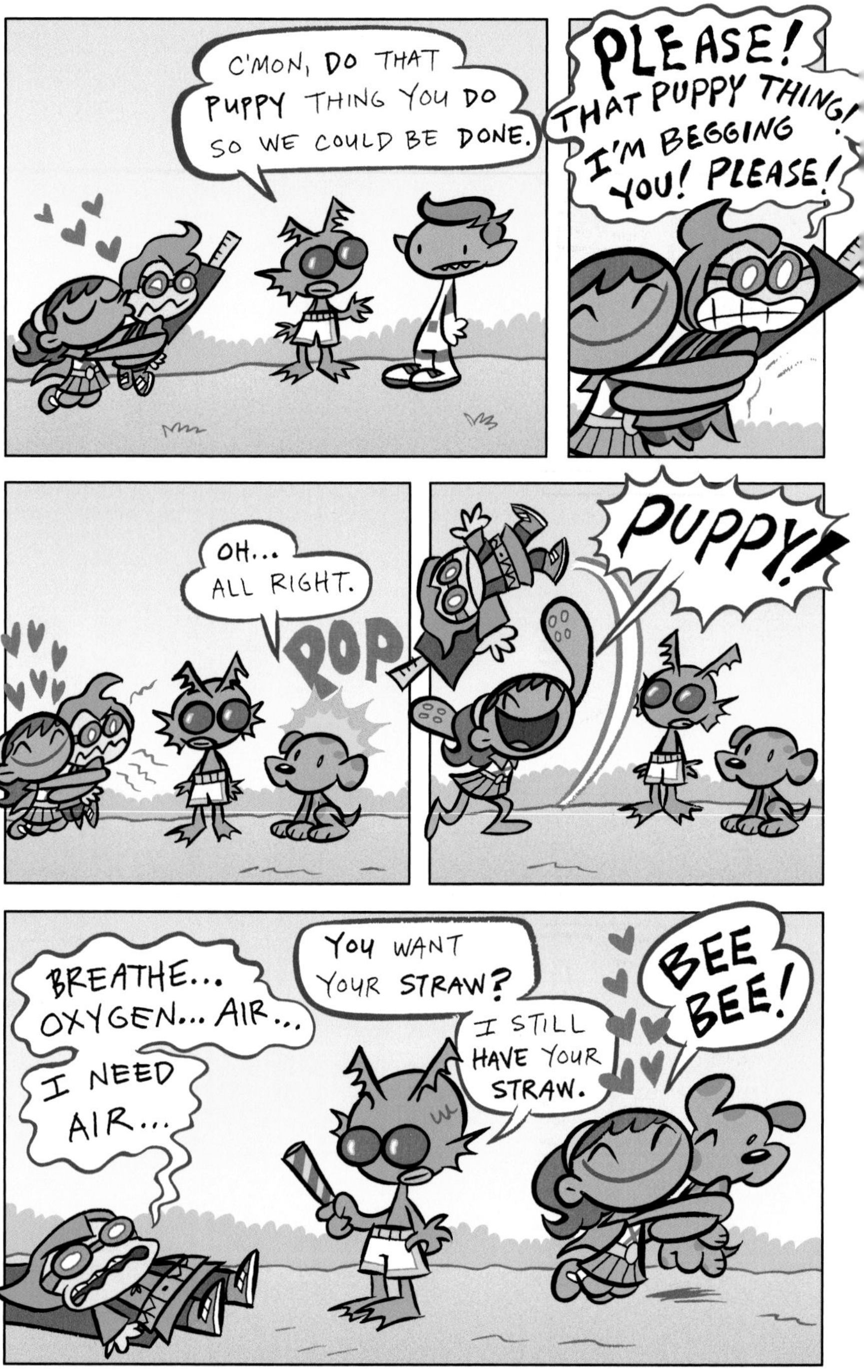
C'MON, DO THAT PUPPY THING YOU DO SO WE COULD BE DONE.
PLEASE! THAT PUPPY THING! I'M BEGGING YOU! PLEASE!
OH... ALL RIGHT.
POP
PUPPY!
BREATHE... OXYGEN... AIR...
I NEED AIR...
YOU WANT YOUR STRAW?
I STILL HAVE YOUR STRAW.
BEE BEE!

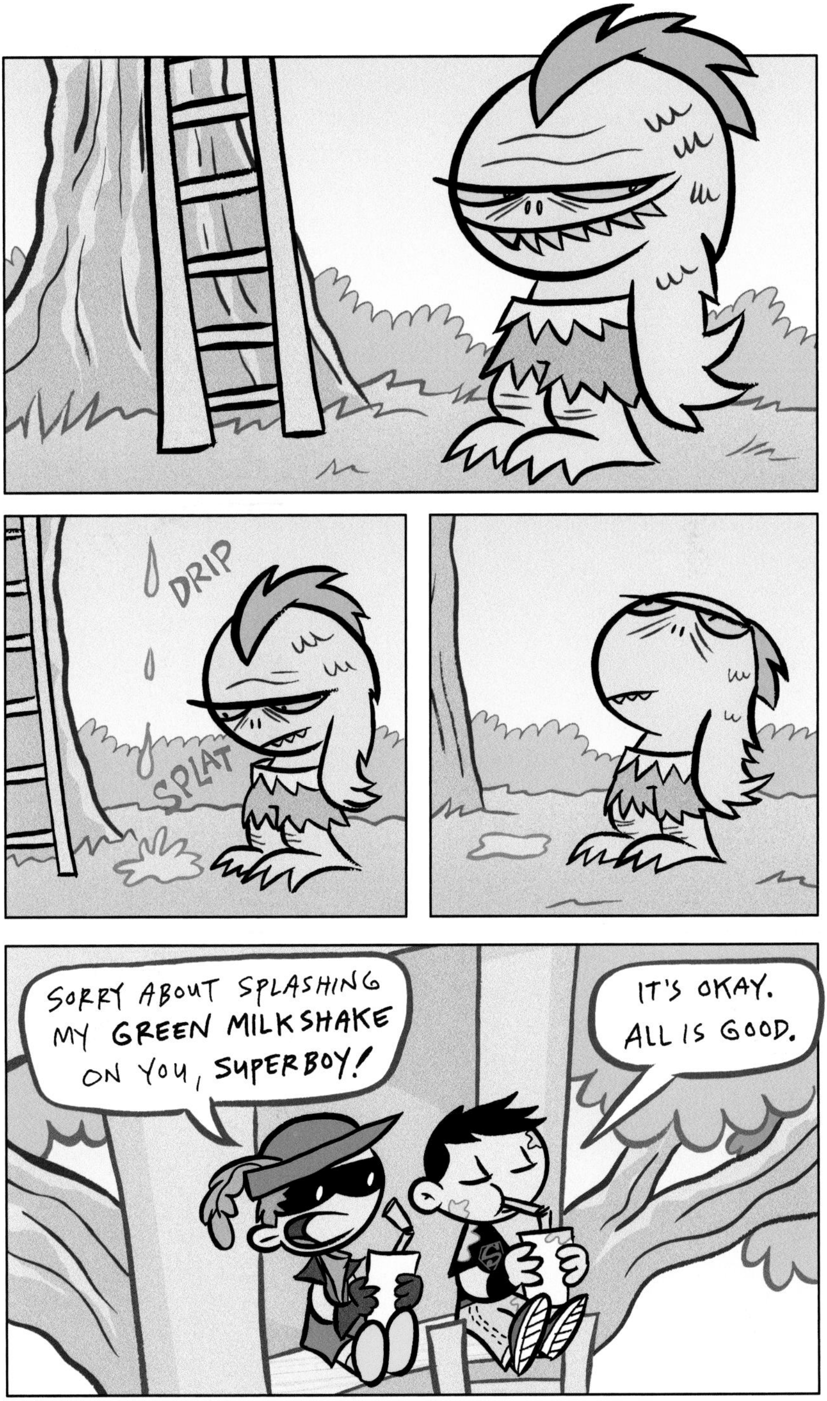
DRIP
SPLAT
SORRY ABOUT SPLASHING MY GREEN MILKSHAKE ON YOU, SUPERBOY!
IT'S OKAY. ALL IS GOOD.

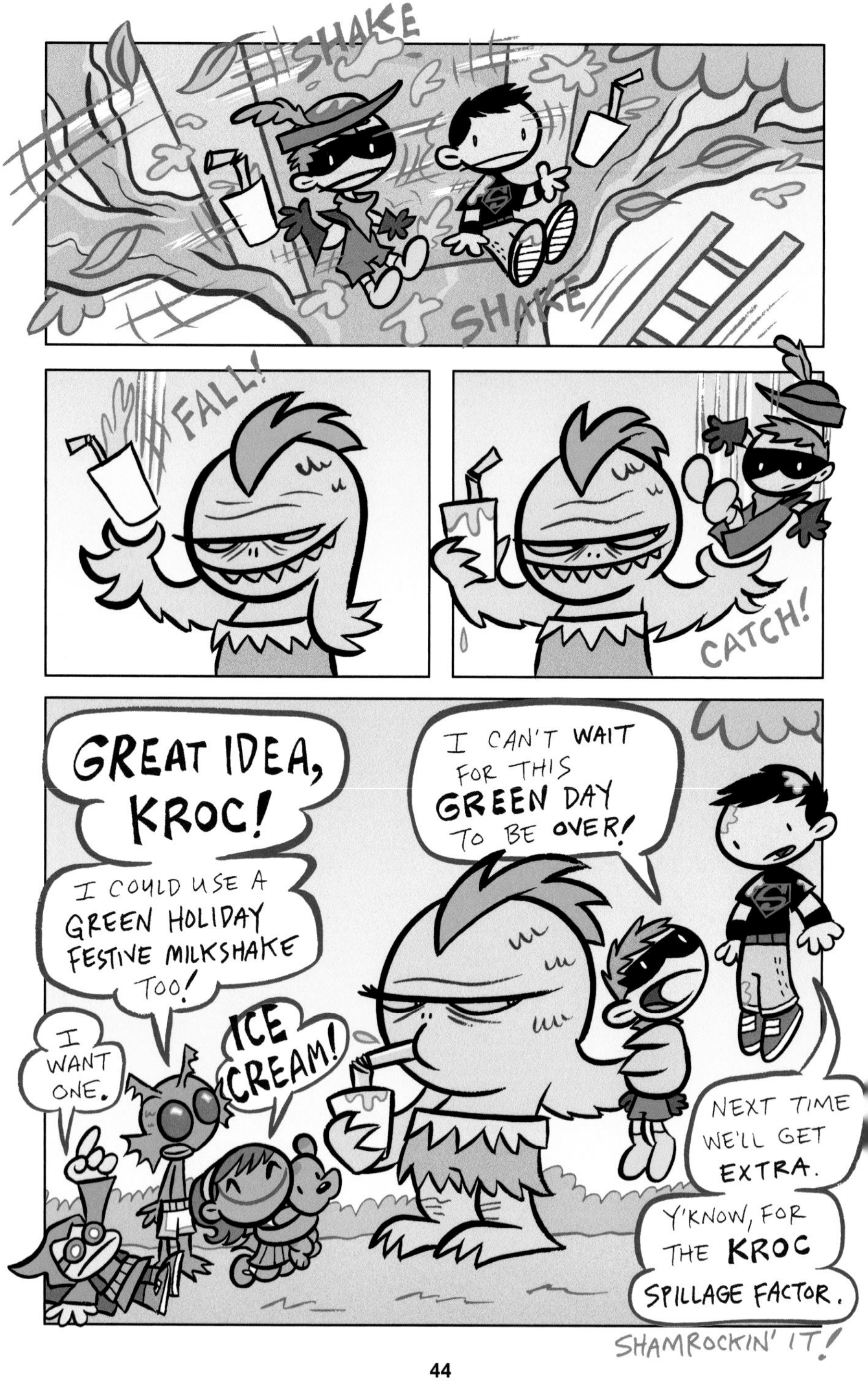
SHAKE
SHAKE
FALL!
CATCH!
GREAT IDEA, KROC!
I COULD USE A GREEN HOLIDAY FESTIVE MILKSHAKE TOO!
I CAN'T WAIT FOR THIS GREEN DAY TO BE OVER!
I WANT ONE.
ICE CREAM!
NEXT TIME WE'LL GET EXTRA.
Y'KNOW, FOR THE KROC SPILLAGE FACTOR.
SHAMROCKIN' IT!

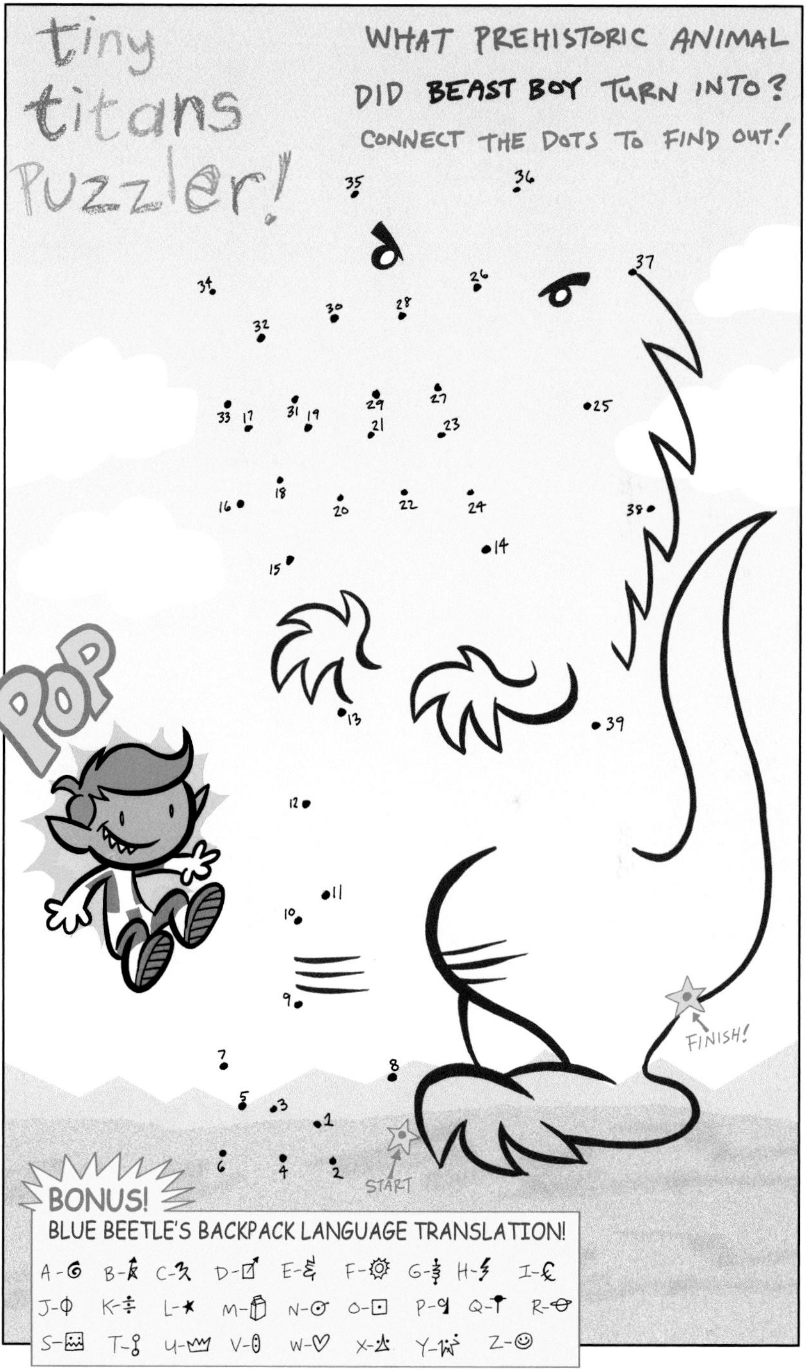
tiny titans Puzzler!
WHAT PREHISTORIC ANIMAL DID BEAST BOY TURN INTO?
CONNECT THE DOTS TO FIND OUT!
POP
START
FINISH!
BONUS!
BLUE BEETLE'S BACKPACK LANGUAGE TRANSLATION!

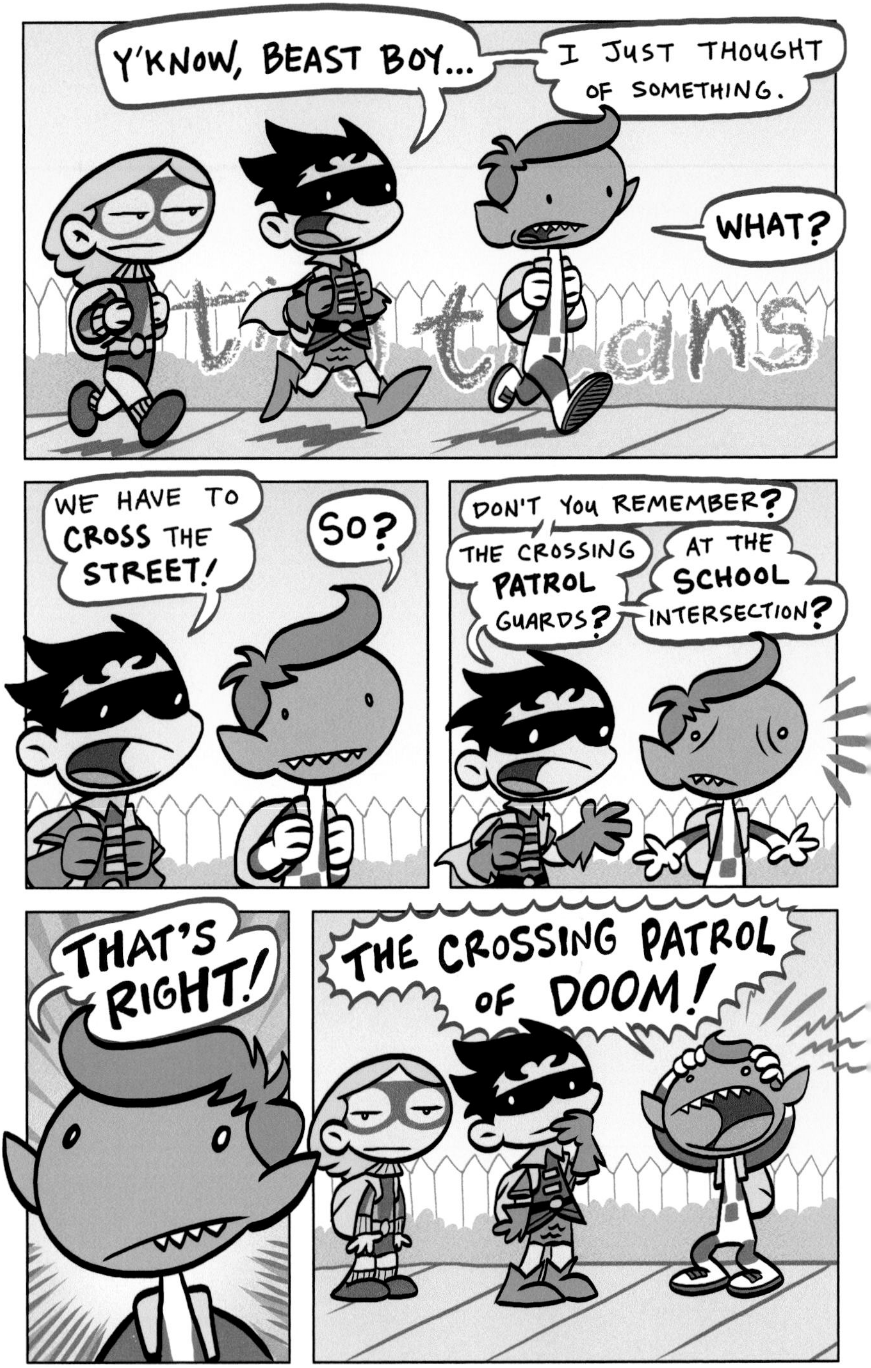
Y'KNOW, BEAST BOY...
I JUST THOUGHT OF SOMETHING.
WHAT?
WE HAVE TO CROSS THE STREET!
SO?
DON'T YOU REMEMBER?
THE CROSSING PATROL GUARDS?
AT THE SCHOOL INTERSECTION?
THAT'S RIGHT!
THE CROSSING PATROL OF DOOM!

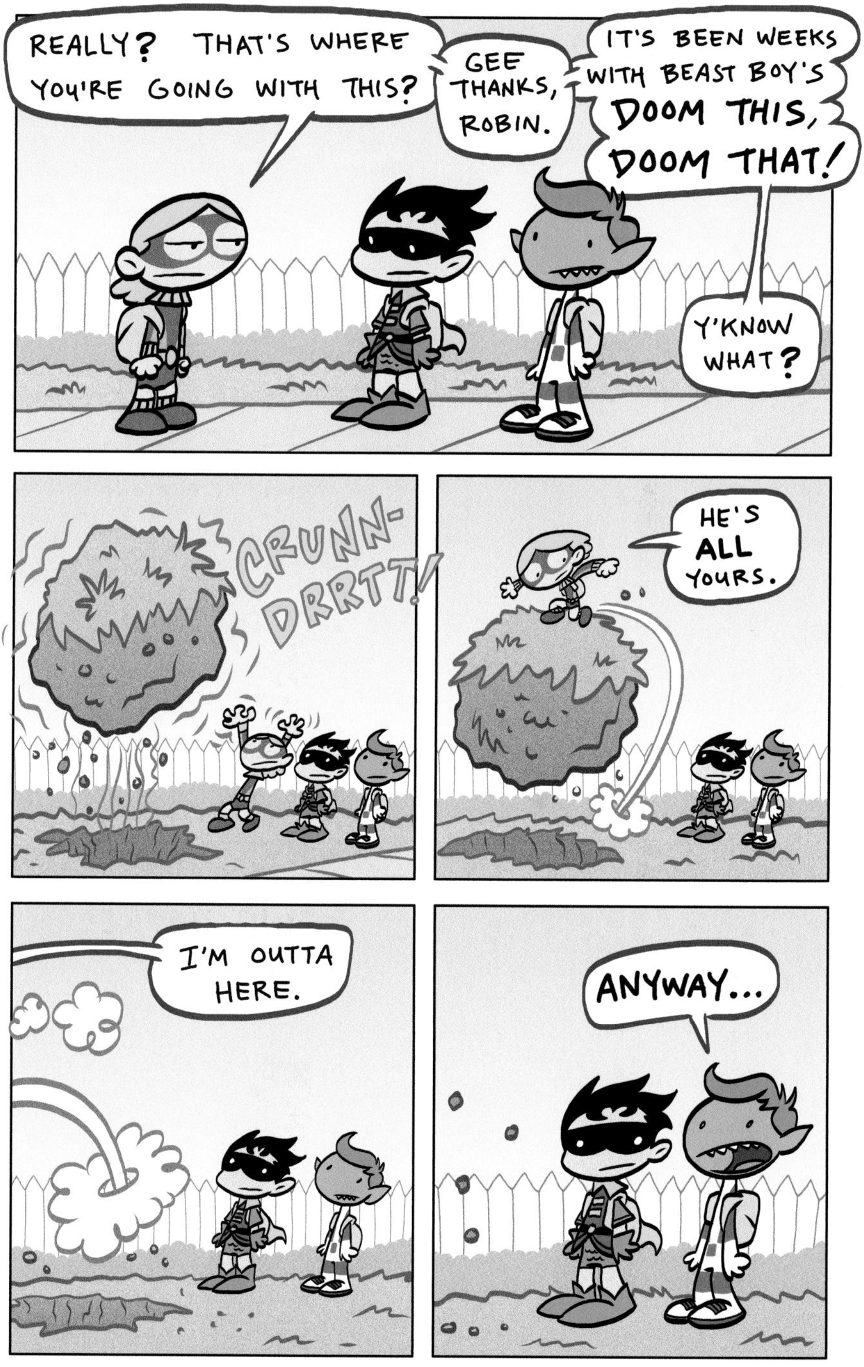
REALLY? THAT'S WHERE YOU'RE GOING WITH THIS?
GEE THANKS, ROBIN.
IT'S BEEN WEEKS WITH BEAST BOY'S DOOM THIS, DOOM THAT!
Y'KNOW WHAT?
CRUNN-DRRTT!
HE'S ALL YOURS.
I'M OUTTA HERE.
ANYWAY...

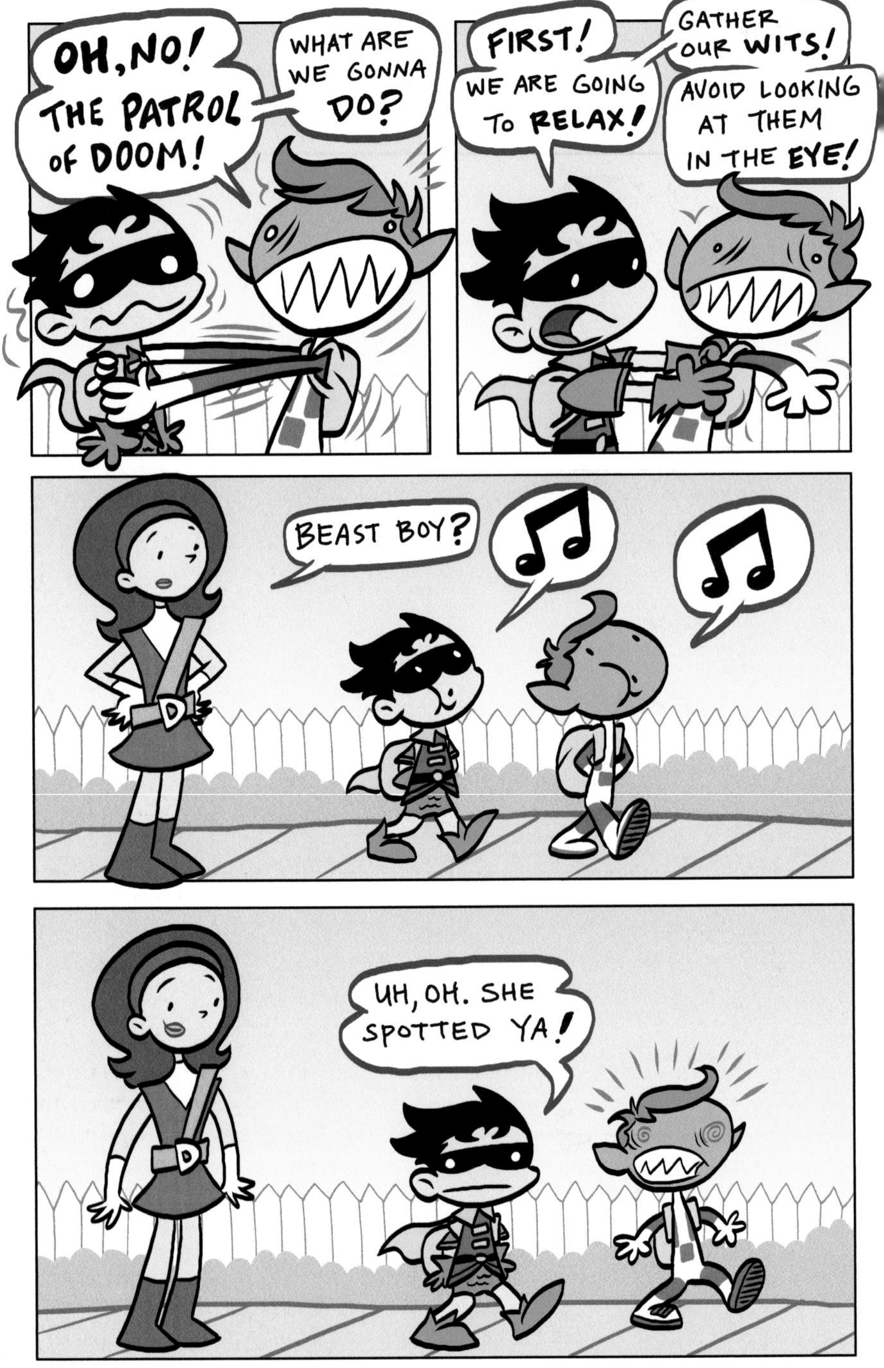
OH, NO! THE PATROL OF DOOM!
WHAT ARE WE GONNA DO?
FIRST!
WE ARE GOING TO RELAX!
GATHER OUR WITS!
AVOID LOOKING AT THEM IN THE EYE!
BEAST BOY?
♫
♫
UH, OH. SHE SPOTTED YA!

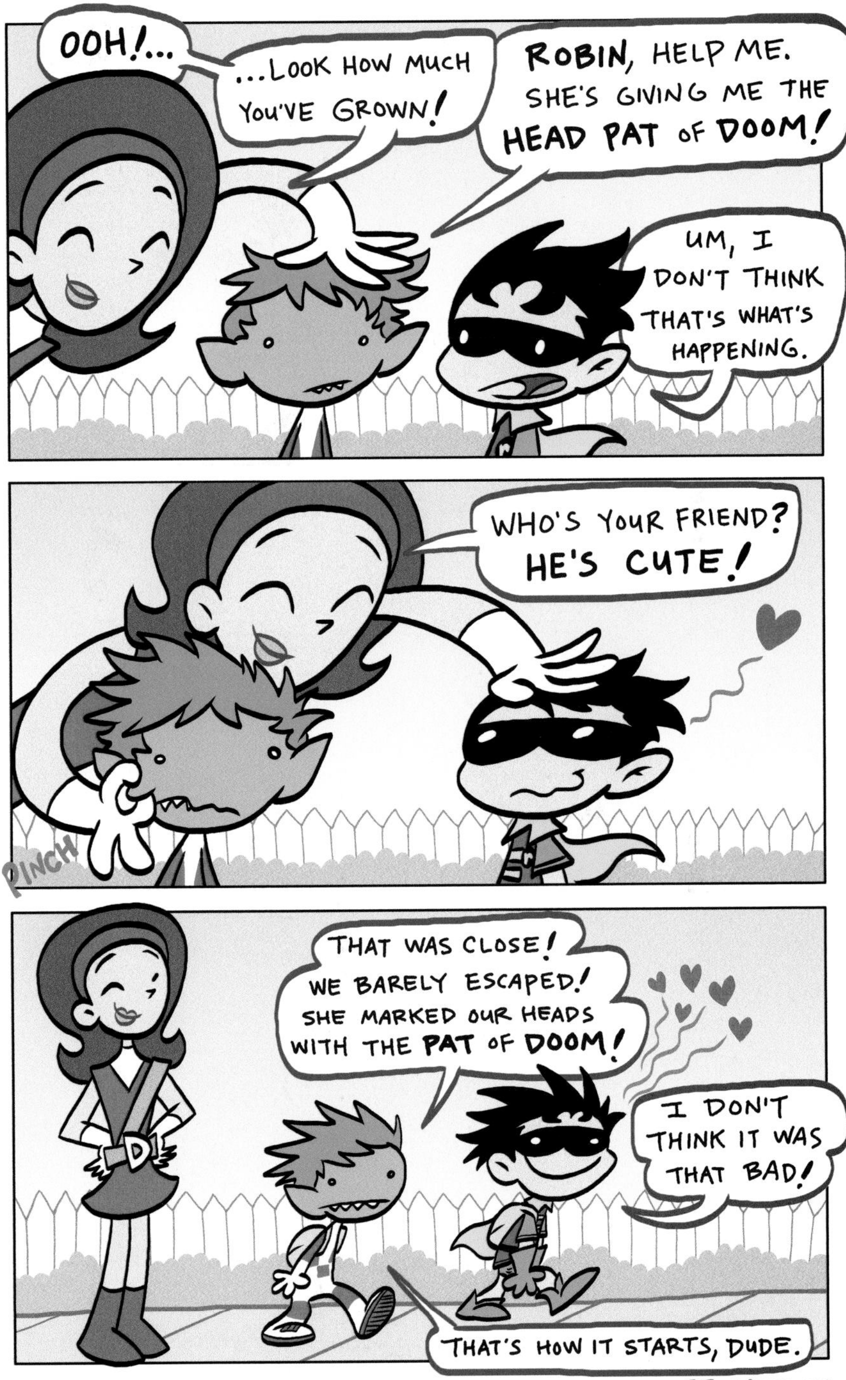
OOH!...
...LOOK HOW MUCH YOU'VE GROWN!
ROBIN, HELP ME. SHE'S GIVING ME THE HEAD PAT OF DOOM!
UM, I DON'T THINK THAT'S WHAT'S HAPPENING.
WHO'S YOUR FRIEND? HE'S CUTE!
PINCH
THAT WAS CLOSE! WE BARELY ESCAPED! SHE MARKED OUR HEADS WITH THE PAT OF DOOM!
I DON'T THINK IT WAS THAT BAD!
THAT'S HOW IT STARTS, DUDE.

–BE CAUTIOUS.

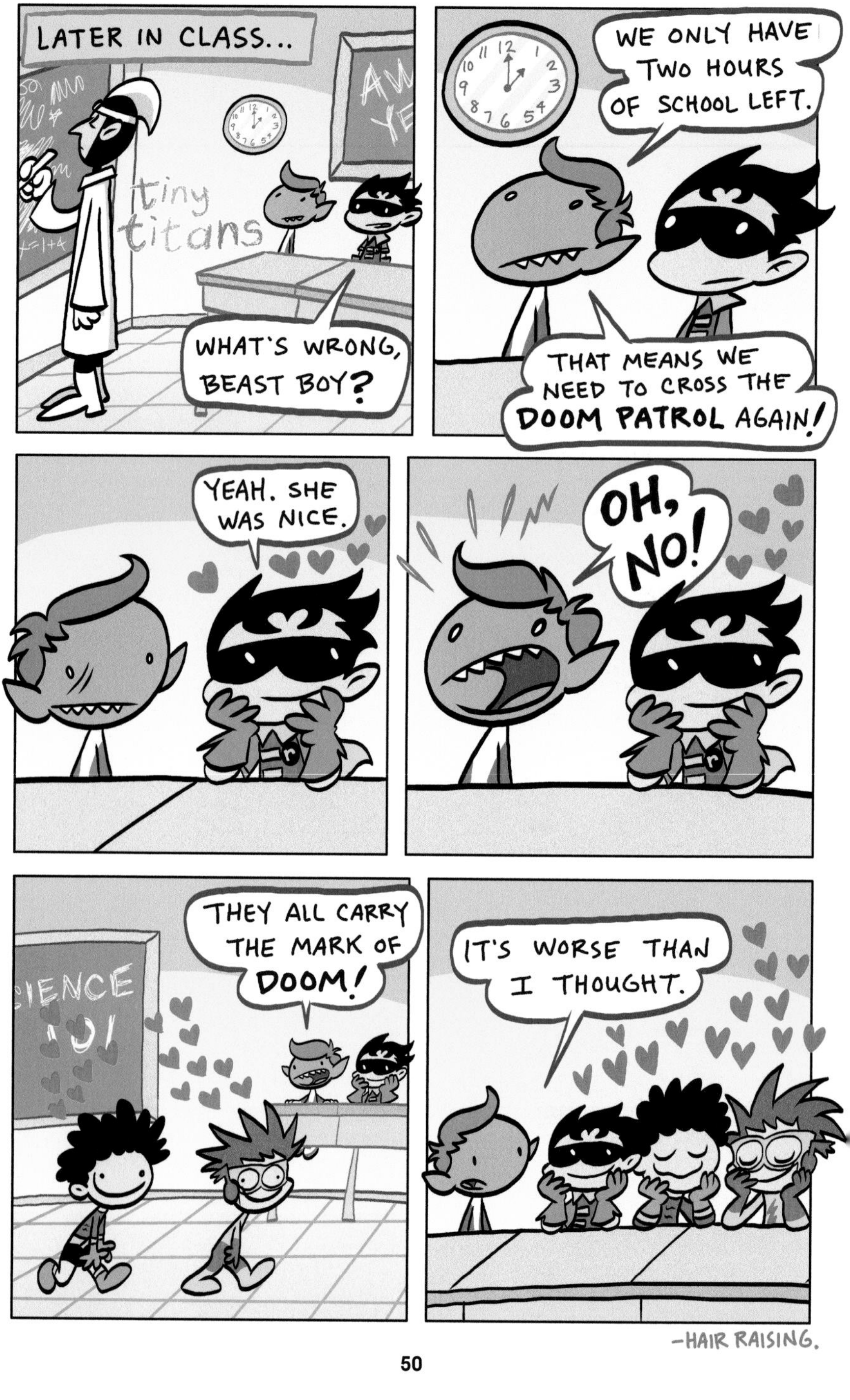
LATER IN CLASS...
tiny titans
WHAT'S WRONG, BEAST BOY?
WE ONLY HAVE TWO HOURS OF SCHOOL LEFT.
THAT MEANS WE NEED TO CROSS THE DOOM PATROL AGAIN!
YEAH. SHE WAS NICE.
OH, NO!
SCIENCE 101
THEY ALL CARRY THE MARK OF DOOM!
IT'S WORSE THAN I THOUGHT.
-HAIR RAISING.

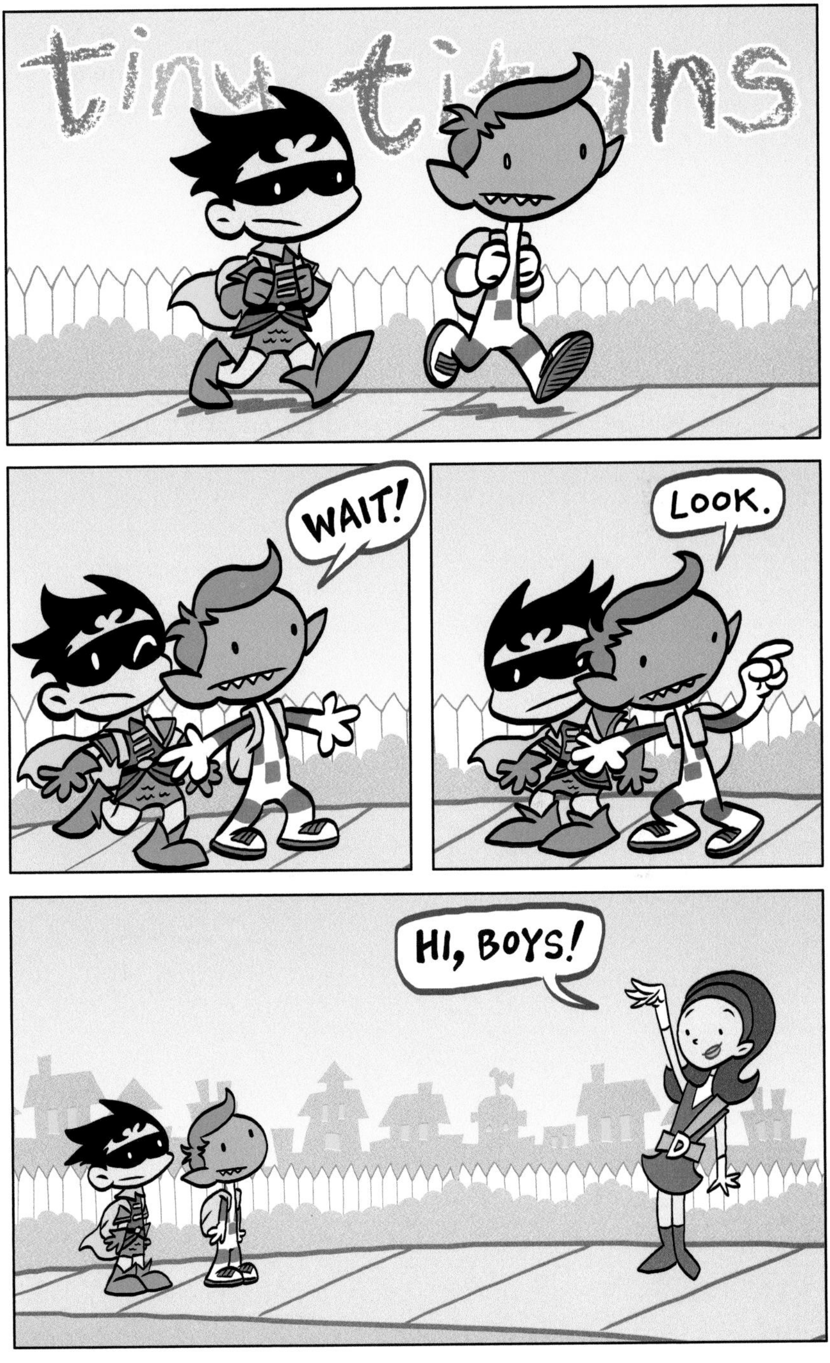
tiny titans
WAIT!
LOOK.
HI, BOYS!

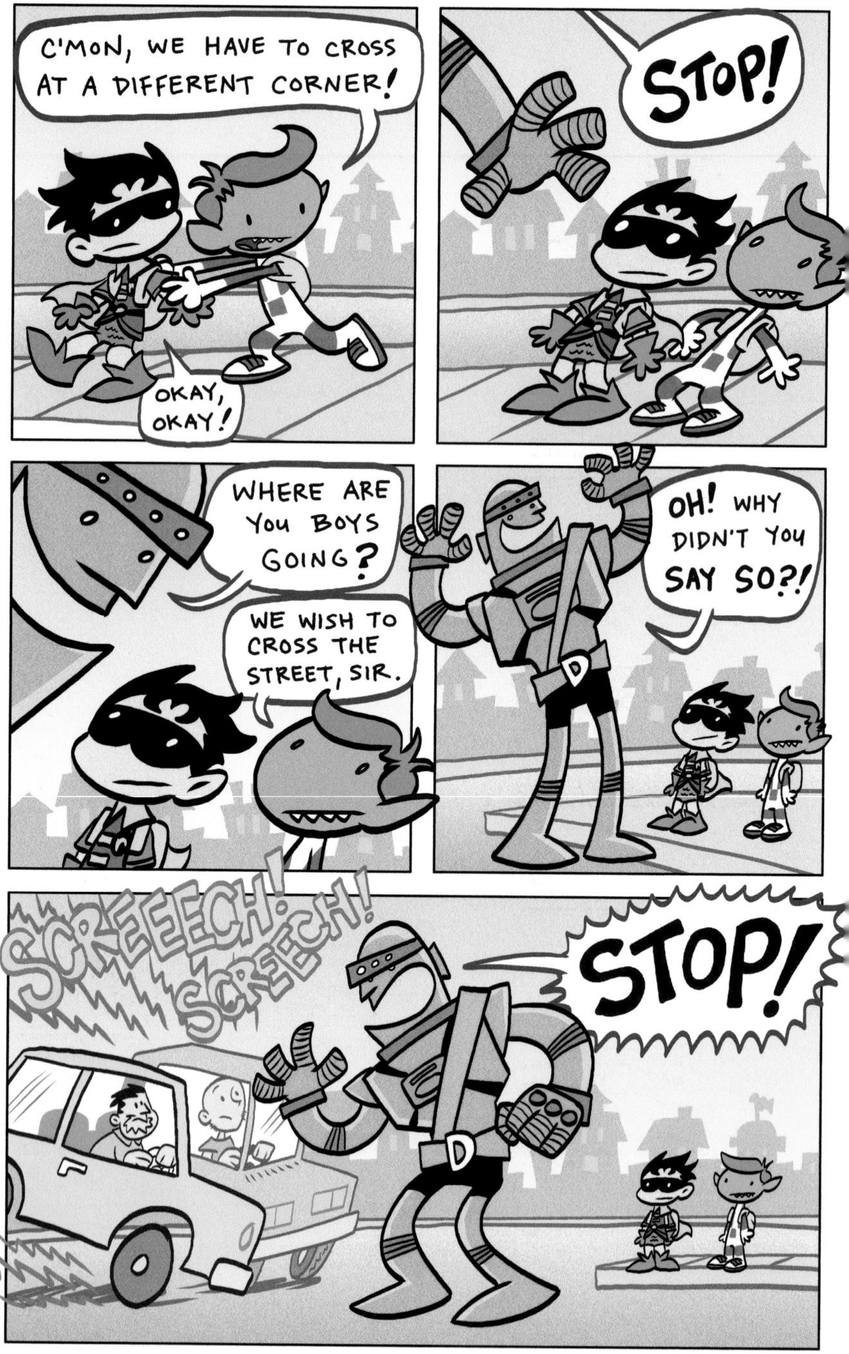
C'MON, WE HAVE TO CROSS AT A DIFFERENT CORNER!
OKAY, OKAY!
STOP!
WHERE ARE YOU BOYS GOING?
WE WISH TO CROSS THE STREET, SIR.
OH! WHY DIDN'T YOU SAY SO?!
SCREEECH! SCREECH!
STOP!

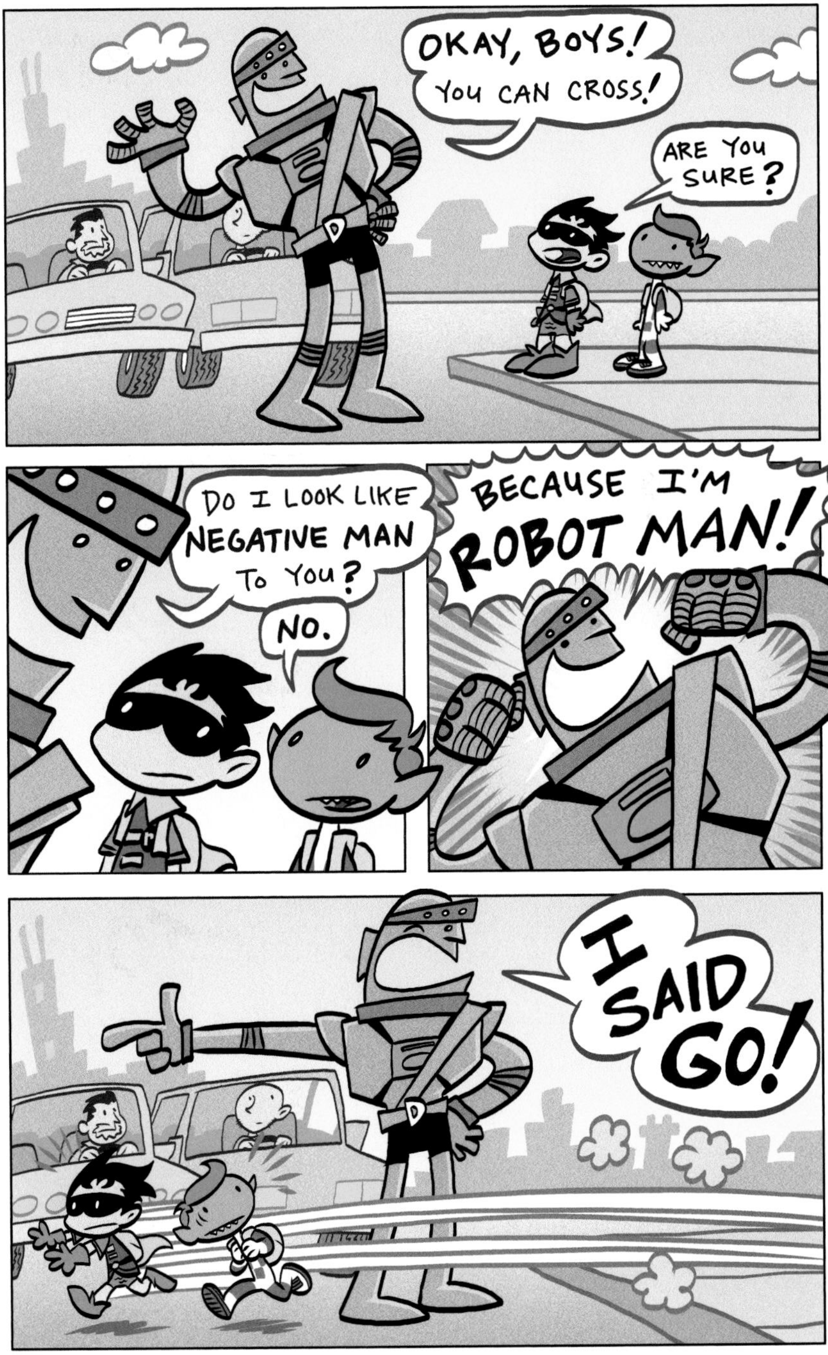
OKAY, BOYS! YOU CAN CROSS!
ARE YOU SURE?
DO I LOOK LIKE NEGATIVE MAN TO YOU?
NO.
BECAUSE I'M ROBOT MAN!
I SAID GO!

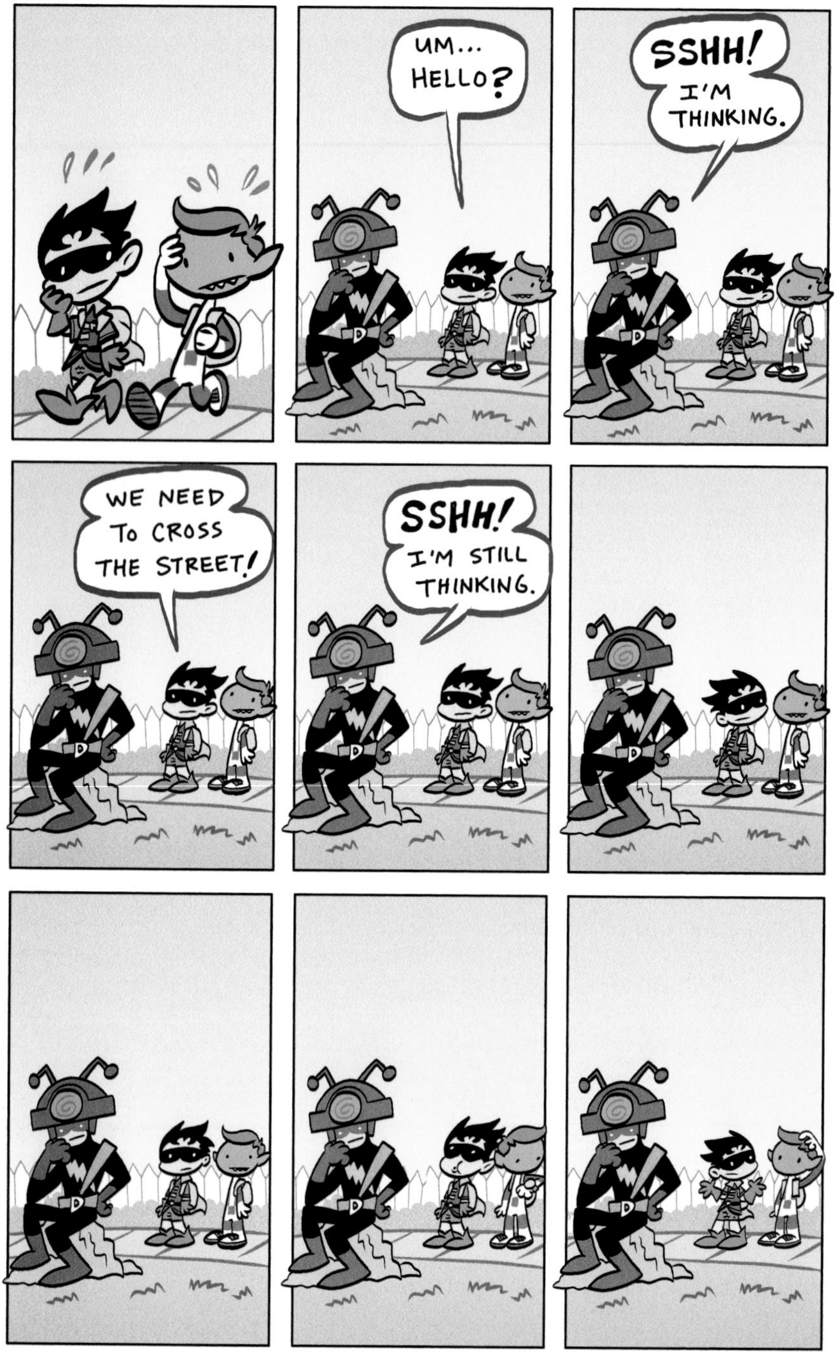
UM... HELLO?
SSHH! I'M THINKING.
WE NEED TO CROSS THE STREET!
SSHH! I'M STILL THINKING.

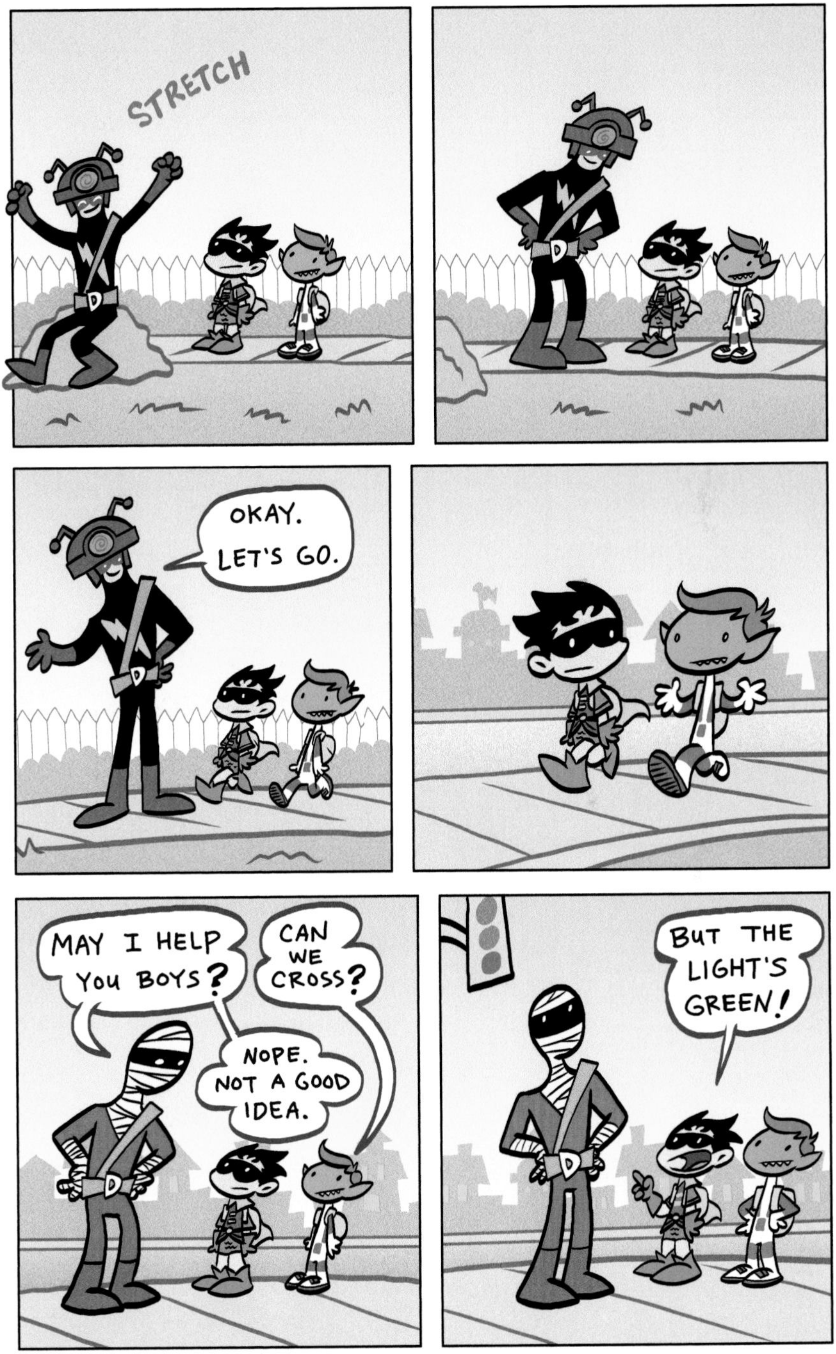
STRETCH
OKAY. LET'S GO.
MAY I HELP YOU BOYS?
CAN WE CROSS?
NOPE. NOT A GOOD IDEA.
BUT THE LIGHT'S GREEN!

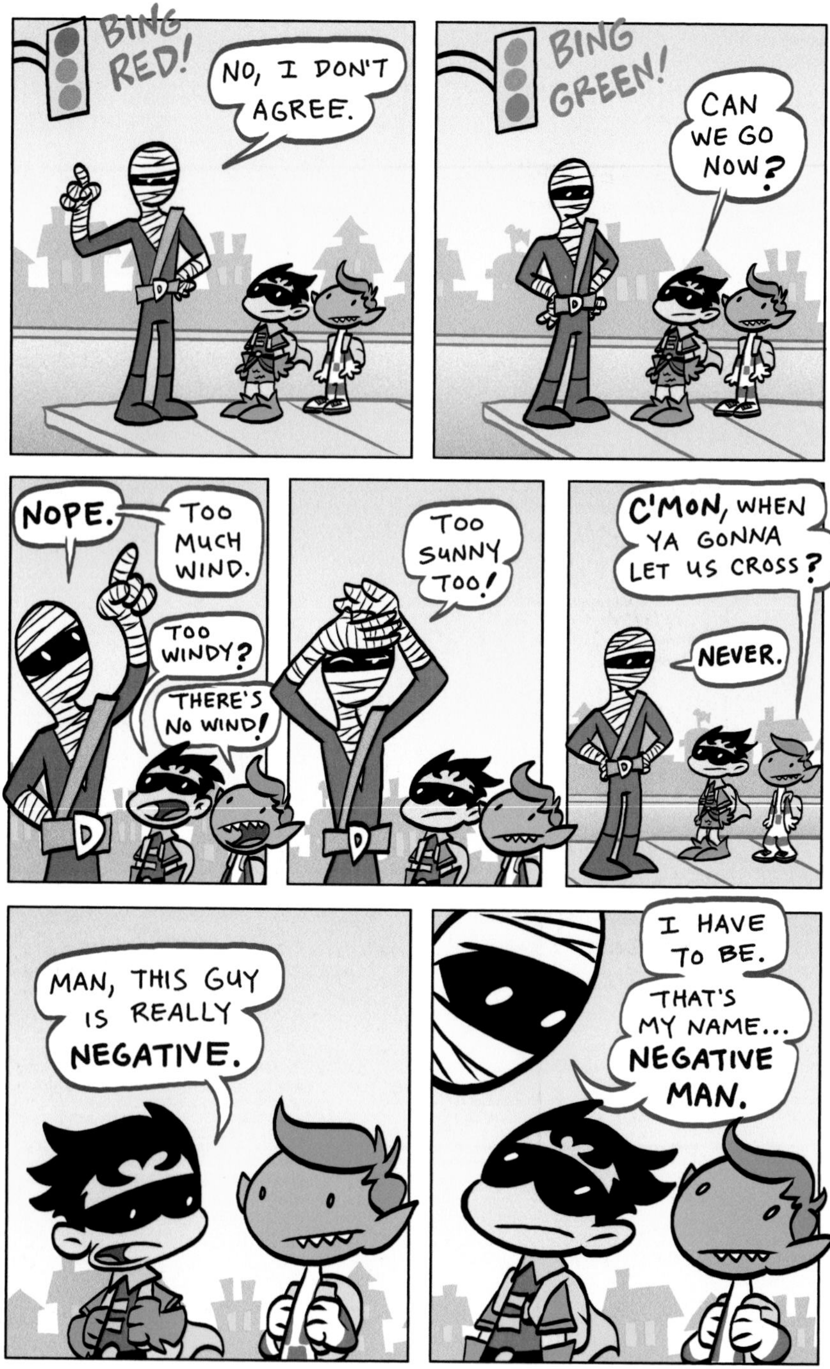
BING RED!
NO, I DON'T AGREE.
BING GREEN!
CAN WE GO NOW?
NOPE.
TOO MUCH WIND.
TOO WINDY?
THERE'S NO WIND!
TOO SUNNY TOO!
C'MON, WHEN YA GONNA LET US CROSS?
NEVER.
MAN, THIS GUY IS REALLY NEGATIVE.
I HAVE TO BE.
THAT'S MY NAME... NEGATIVE MAN.

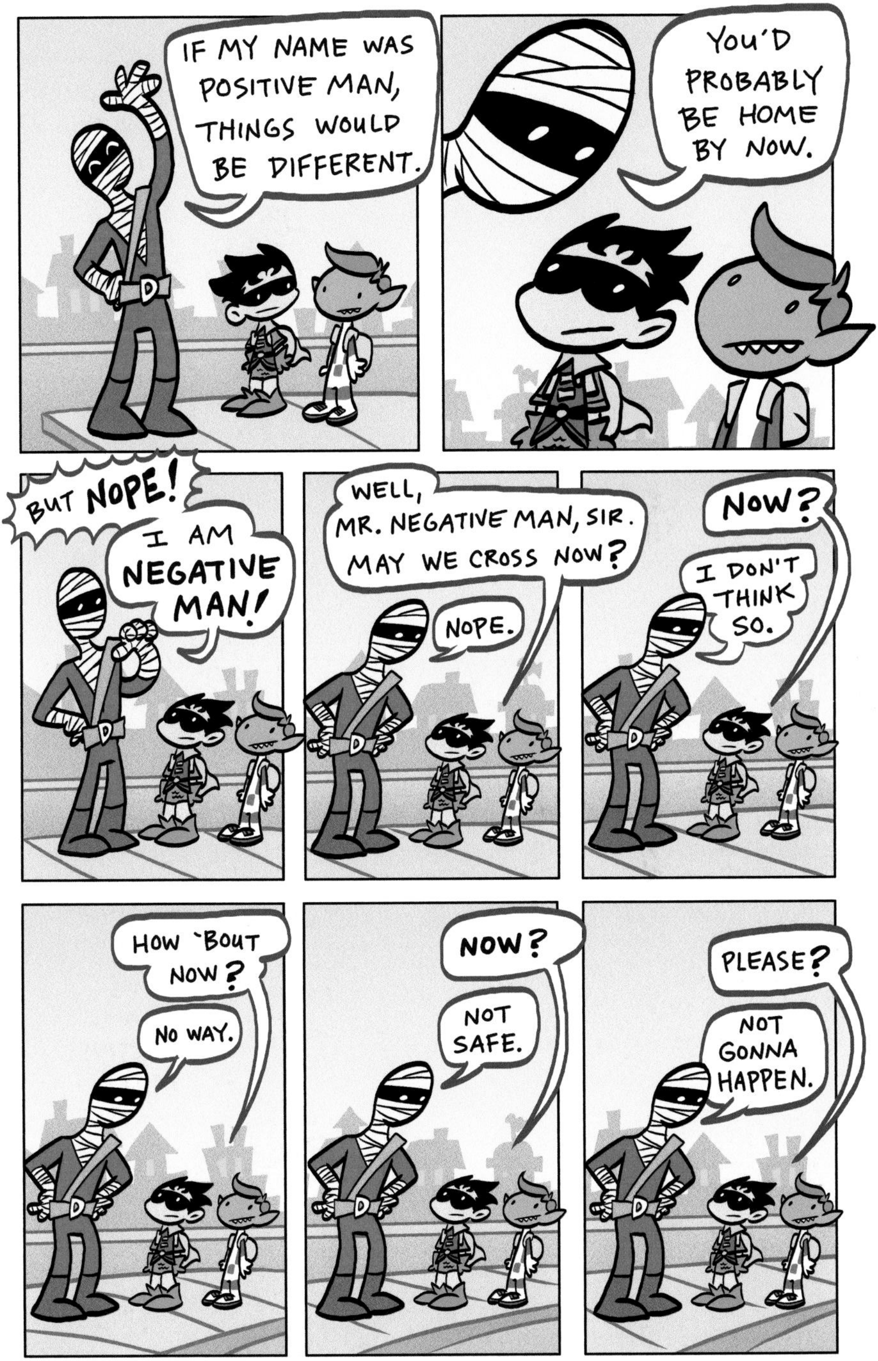
IF MY NAME WAS POSITIVE MAN, THINGS WOULD BE DIFFERENT.
YOU'D PROBABLY BE HOME BY NOW.
BUT NOPE!
I AM NEGATIVE MAN!
WELL, MR. NEGATIVE MAN, SIR. MAY WE CROSS NOW?
NOPE.
NOW?
I DON'T THINK SO.
HOW 'BOUT NOW?
NO WAY.
NOW?
NOT SAFE.
PLEASE?
NOT GONNA HAPPEN.

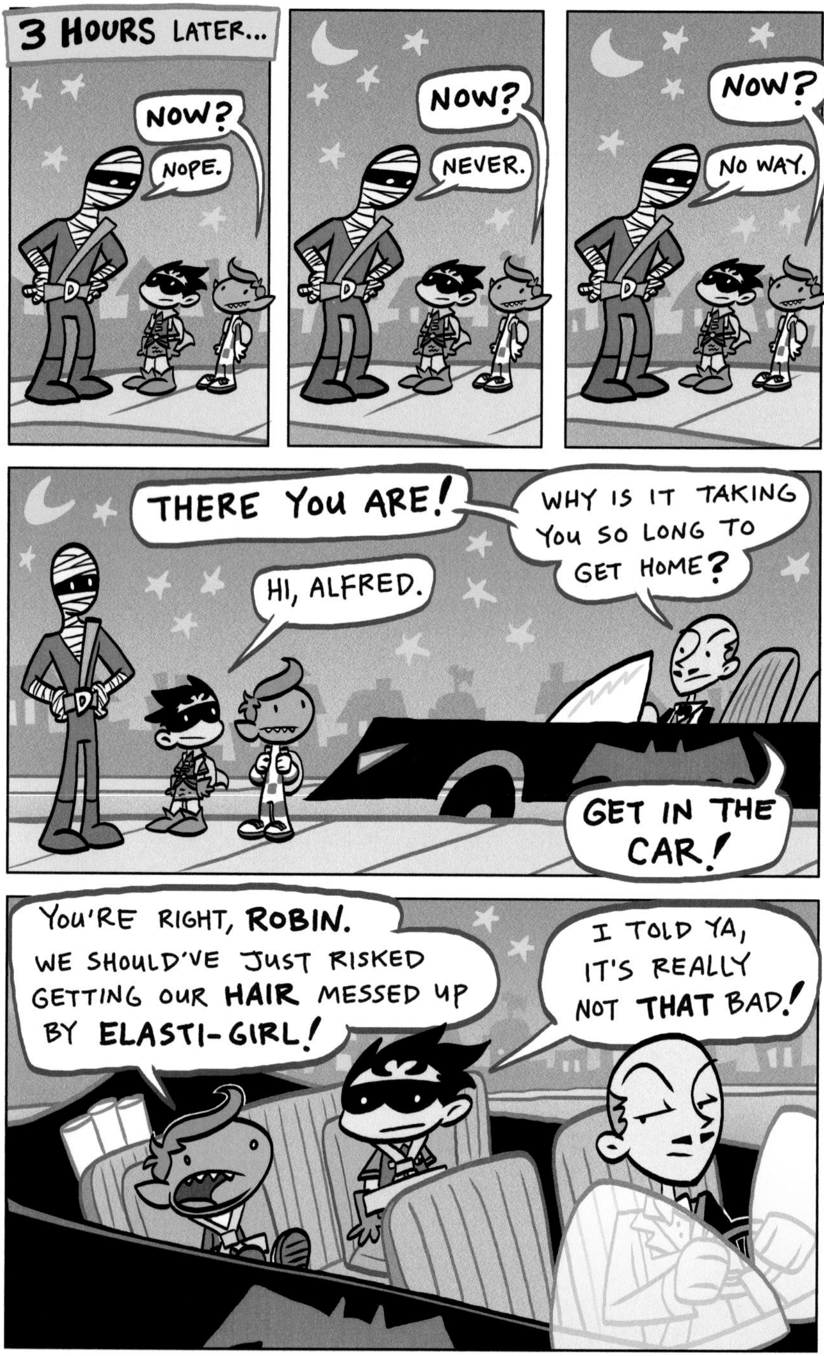
3 HOURS LATER...
NOW?
NOPE.
NOW?
NEVER.
NOW?
NO WAY.
THERE YOU ARE!
WHY IS IT TAKING YOU SO LONG TO GET HOME?
HI, ALFRED.
GET IN THE CAR!
YOU'RE RIGHT, ROBIN. WE SHOULD'VE JUST RISKED GETTING OUR HAIR MESSED UP BY ELASTI-GIRL!
I TOLD YA, IT'S REALLY NOT THAT BAD!

—NOPE.

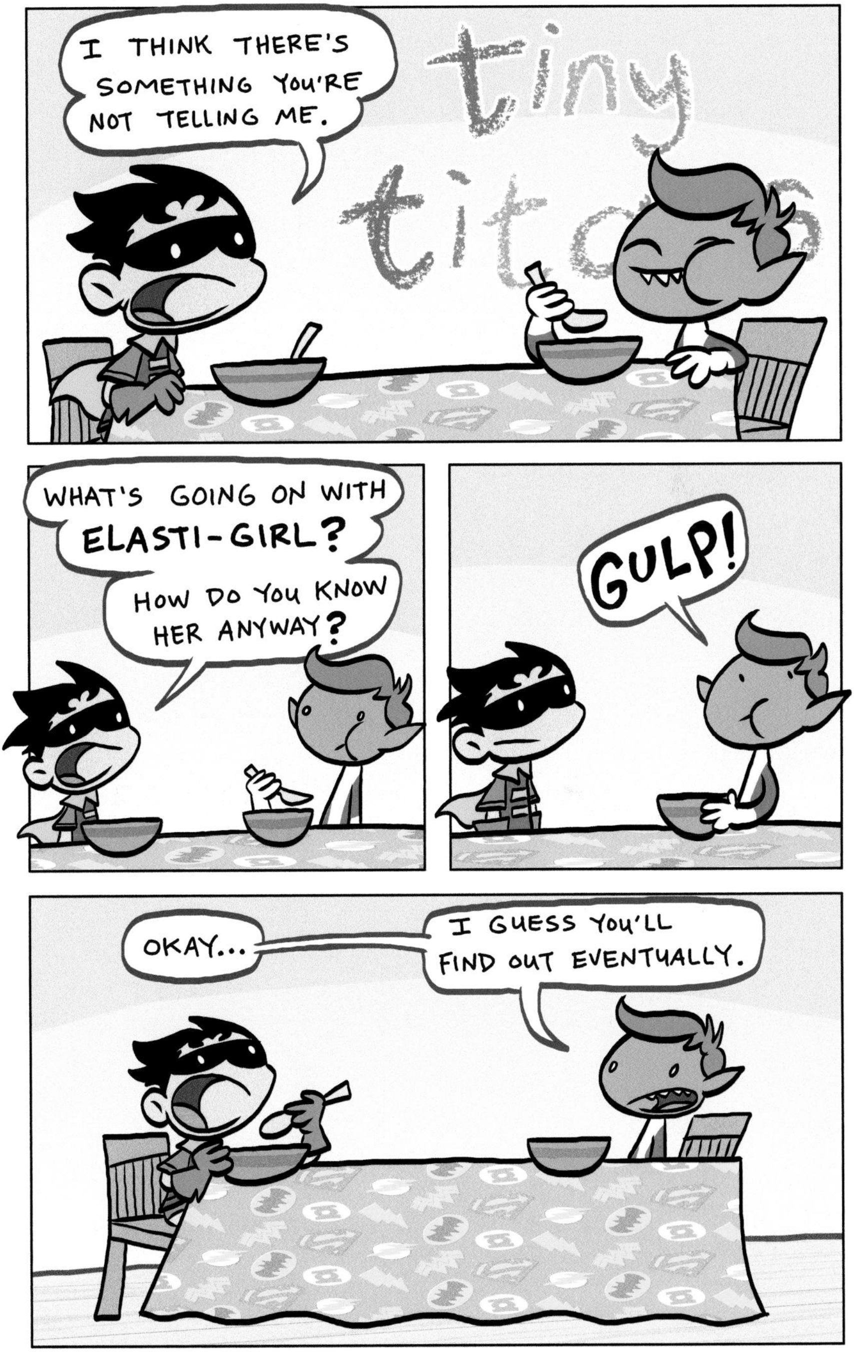
I THINK THERE'S SOMETHING YOU'RE NOT TELLING ME.
tiny titans
WHAT'S GOING ON WITH ELASTI-GIRL?
HOW DO YOU KNOW HER ANYWAY?
GULP!
OKAY...
I GUESS YOU'LL FIND OUT EVENTUALLY.

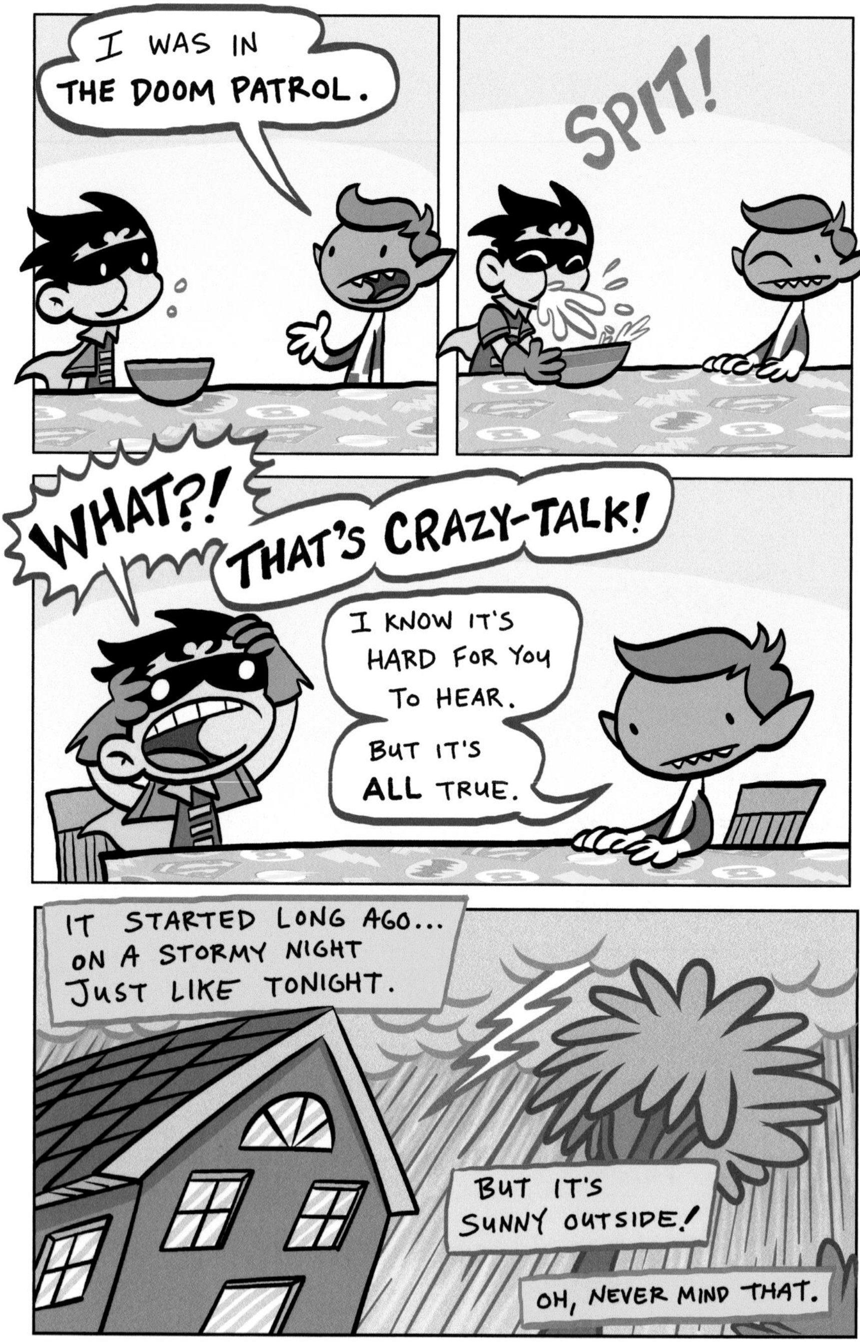
I WAS IN THE DOOM PATROL.
SPIT!
WHAT?!
THAT'S CRAZY-TALK!
I KNOW IT'S HARD FOR YOU TO HEAR.
BUT IT'S ALL TRUE.
IT STARTED LONG AGO... ON A STORMY NIGHT JUST LIKE TONIGHT.
BUT IT'S SUNNY OUTSIDE!
OH, NEVER MIND THAT.

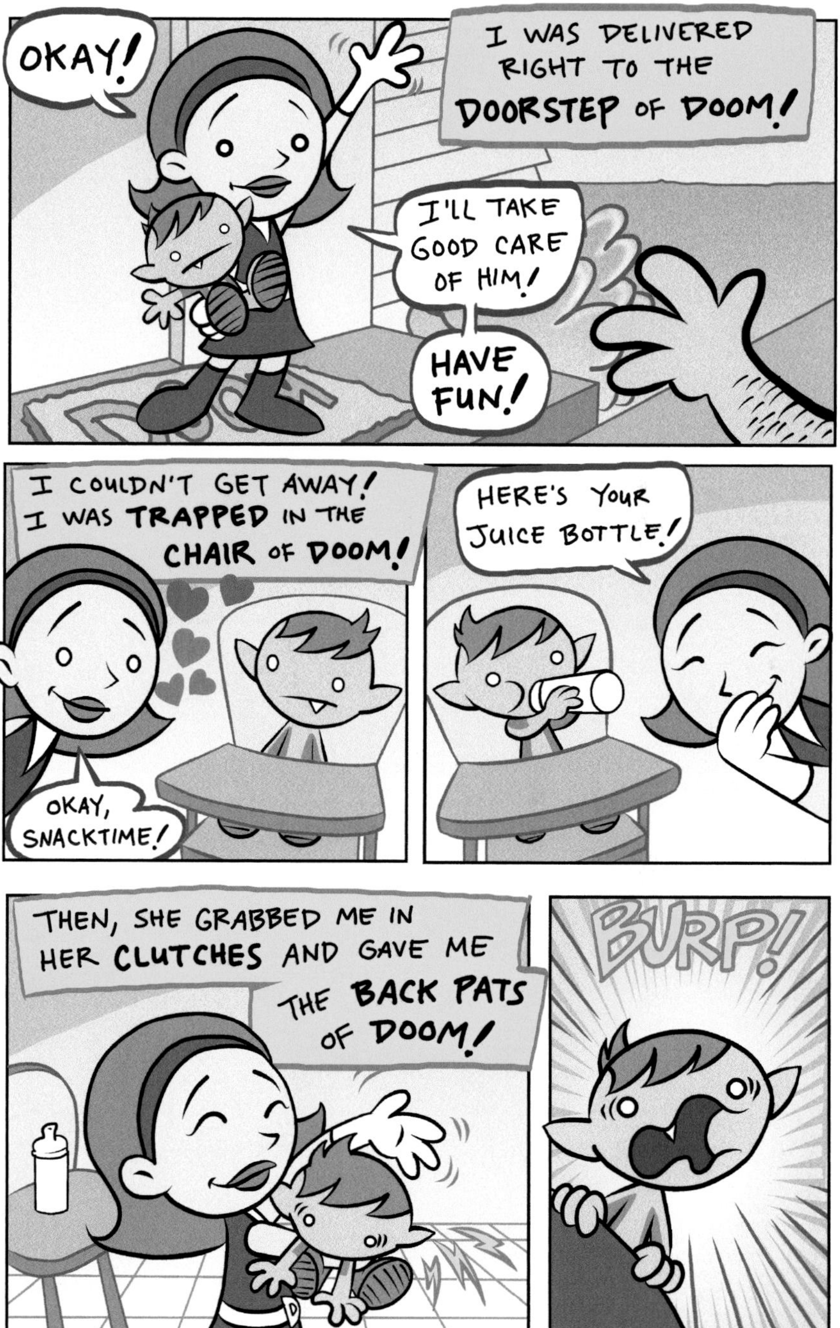
OKAY!
I WAS DELIVERED RIGHT TO THE DOORSTEP OF DOOM!
I'LL TAKE GOOD CARE OF HIM!
HAVE FUN!
I COULDN'T GET AWAY! I WAS TRAPPED IN THE CHAIR OF DOOM!
OKAY, SNACKTIME!
HERE'S YOUR JUICE BOTTLE!
THEN, SHE GRABBED ME IN HER CLUTCHES AND GAVE ME THE BACK PATS OF DOOM!
BURP!

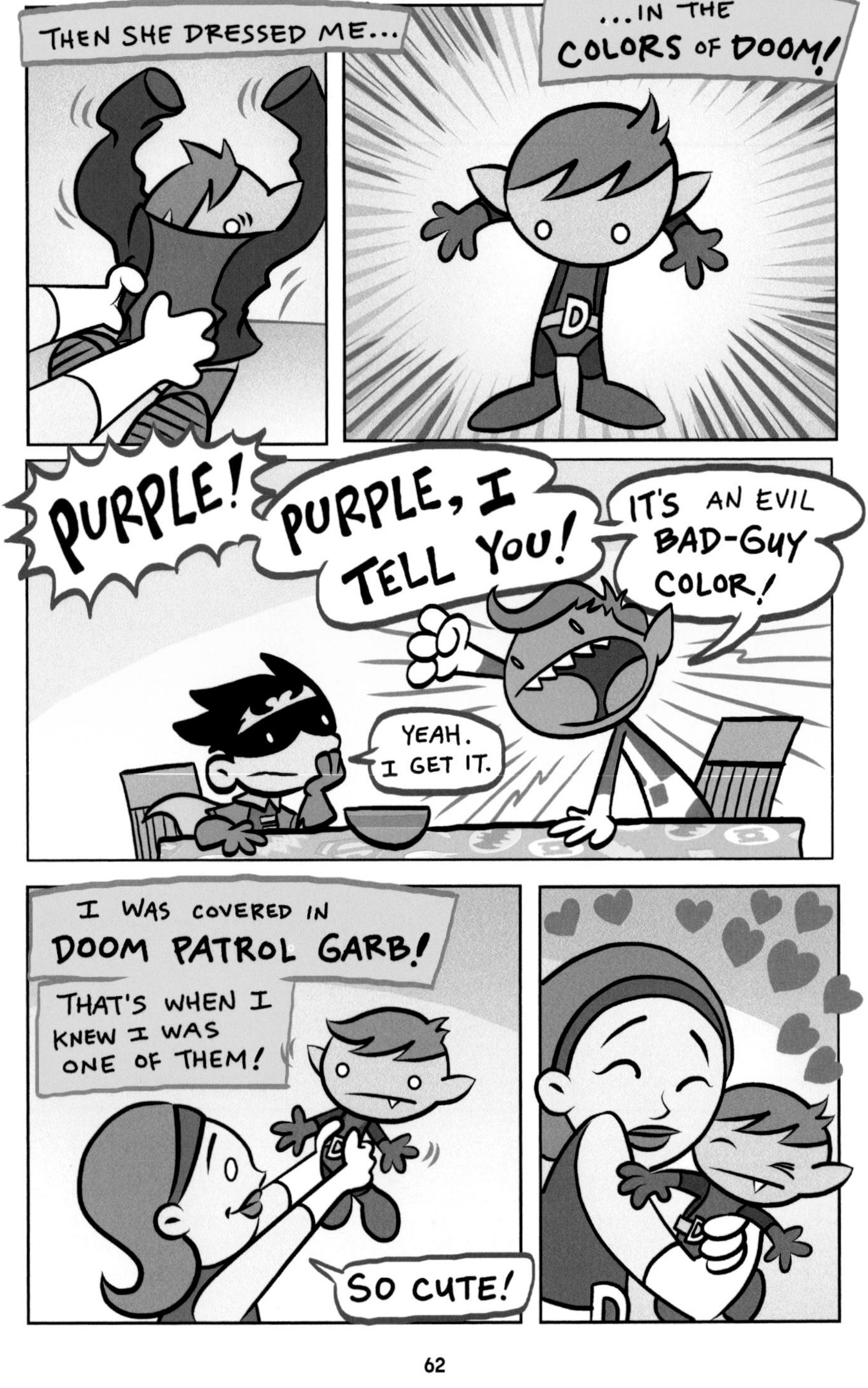
THEN SHE DRESSED ME...
...IN THE COLORS OF DOOM!
PURPLE!
PURPLE, I TELL YOU!
IT'S AN EVIL BAD-GUY COLOR!
YEAH. I GET IT.
I WAS COVERED IN DOOM PATROL GARB!
THAT'S WHEN I KNEW I WAS ONE OF THEM!
SO CUTE!

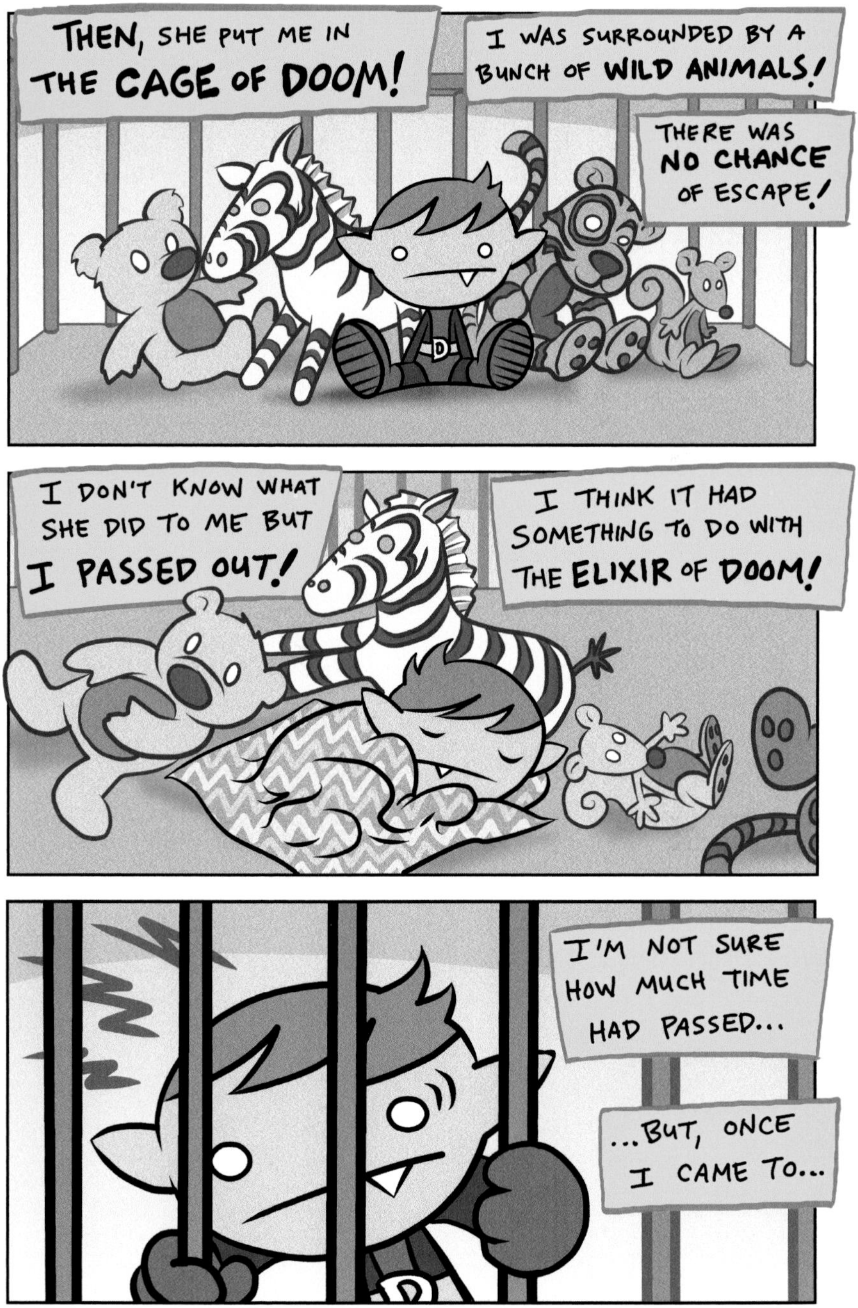
THEN, SHE PUT ME IN THE CAGE OF DOOM!
I WAS SURROUNDED BY A BUNCH OF WILD ANIMALS!
THERE WAS NO CHANCE OF ESCAPE!
I DON'T KNOW WHAT SHE DID TO ME BUT I PASSED OUT!
I THINK IT HAD SOMETHING TO DO WITH THE ELIXIR OF DOOM!
I'M NOT SURE HOW MUCH TIME HAD PASSED...
...BUT, ONCE I CAME TO...

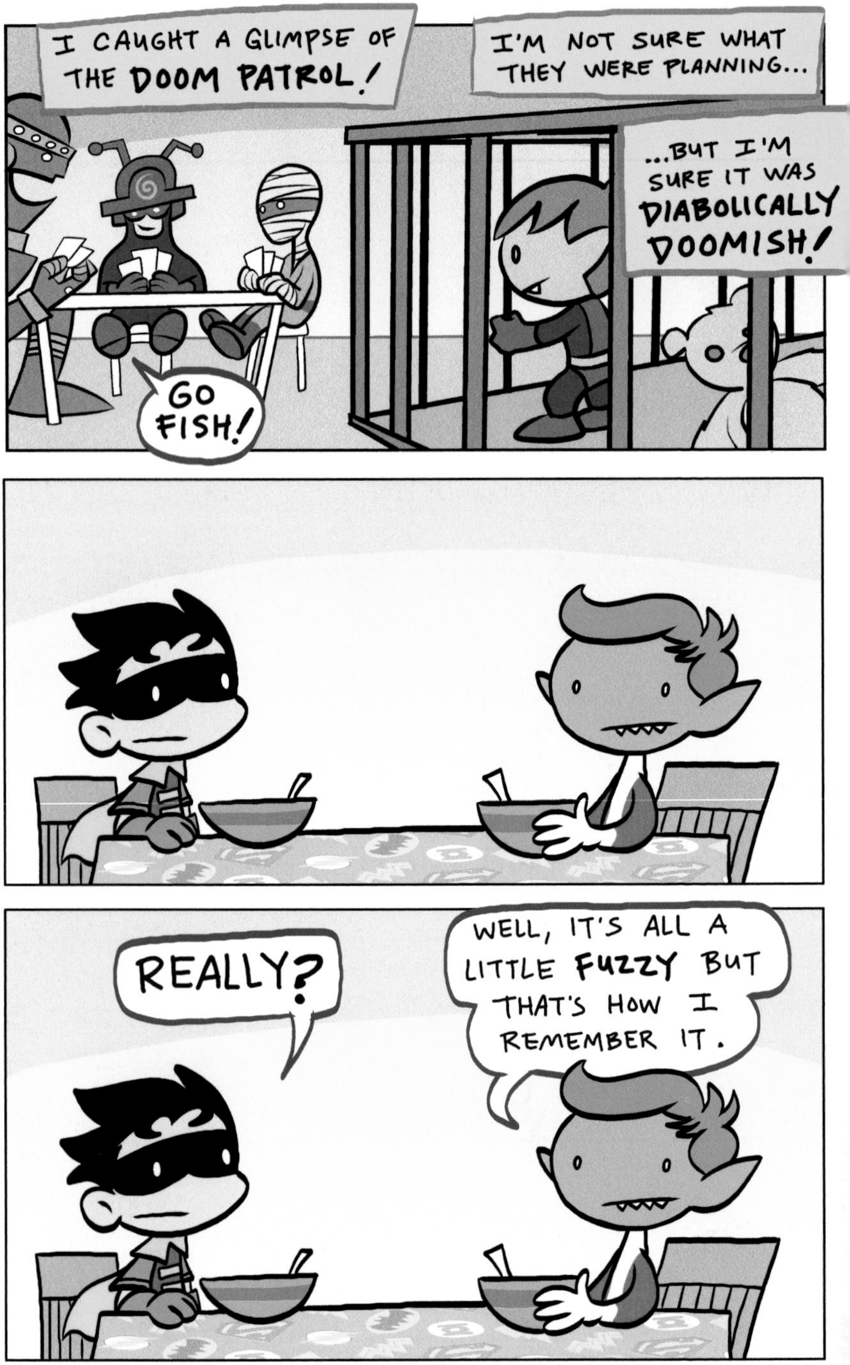
I CAUGHT A GLIMPSE OF THE DOOM PATROL!
I'M NOT SURE WHAT THEY WERE PLANNING...
...BUT I'M SURE IT WAS DIABOLICALLY DOOMISH!
GO FISH!
REALLY?
WELL, IT'S ALL A LITTLE FUZZY BUT THAT'S HOW I REMEMBER IT.

–JUST DOOM IT!

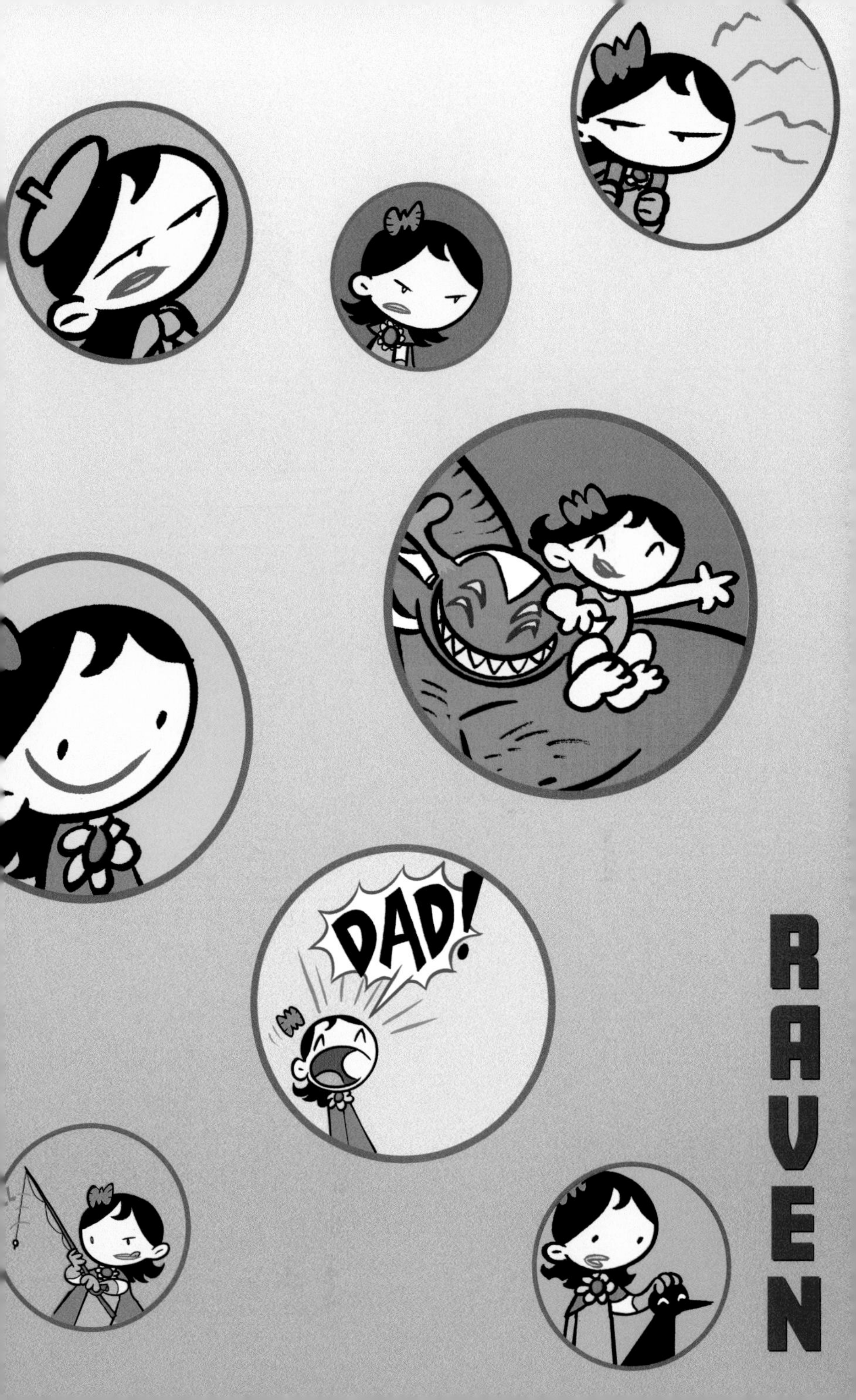
DAD!
RAVEN

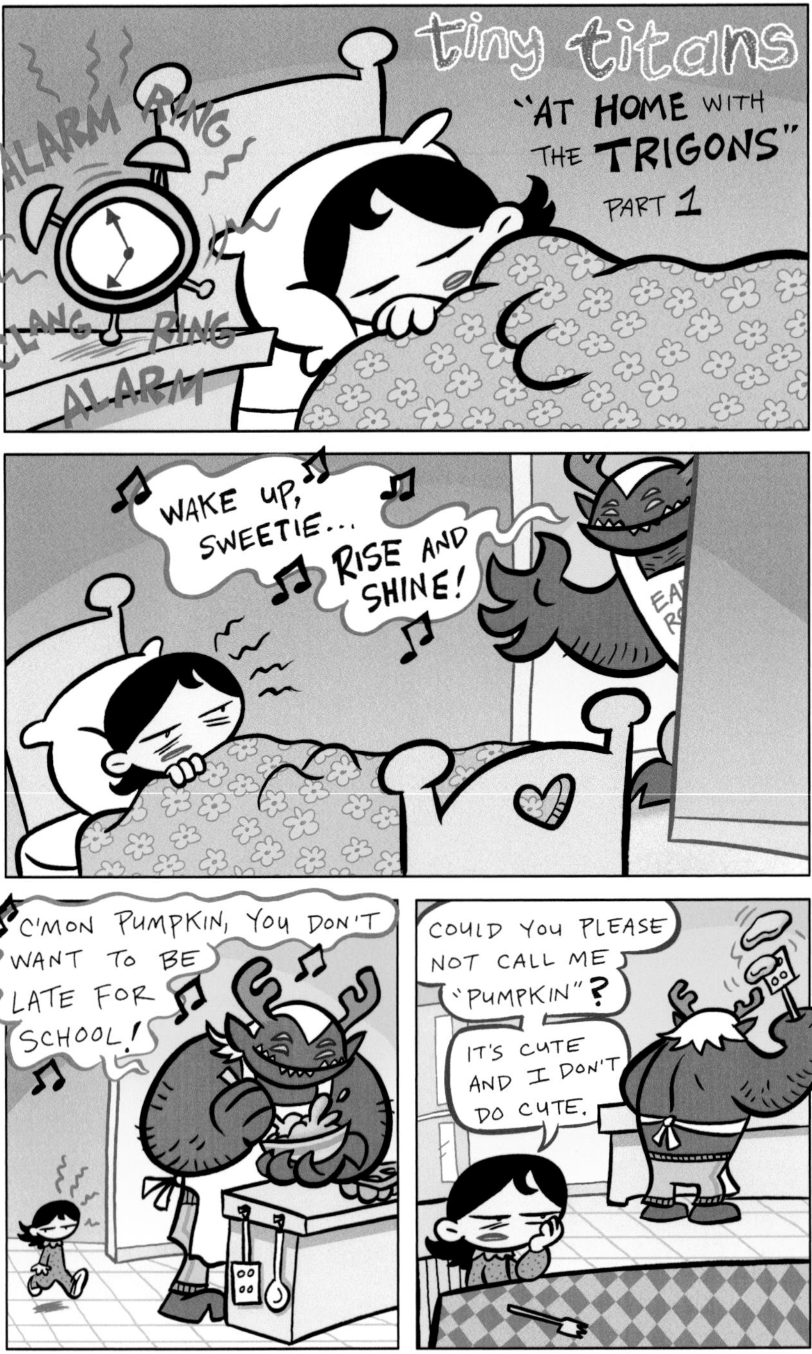
tiny titans
"AT HOME WITH THE TRIGONS"
PART 1
ALARM RING
CLANG RING
ALARM
WAKE UP, SWEETIE... RISE AND SHINE!
C'MON PUMPKIN, YOU DON'T WANT TO BE LATE FOR SCHOOL!
COULD YOU PLEASE NOT CALL ME "PUMPKIN"?
IT'S CUTE AND I DON'T DO CUTE.

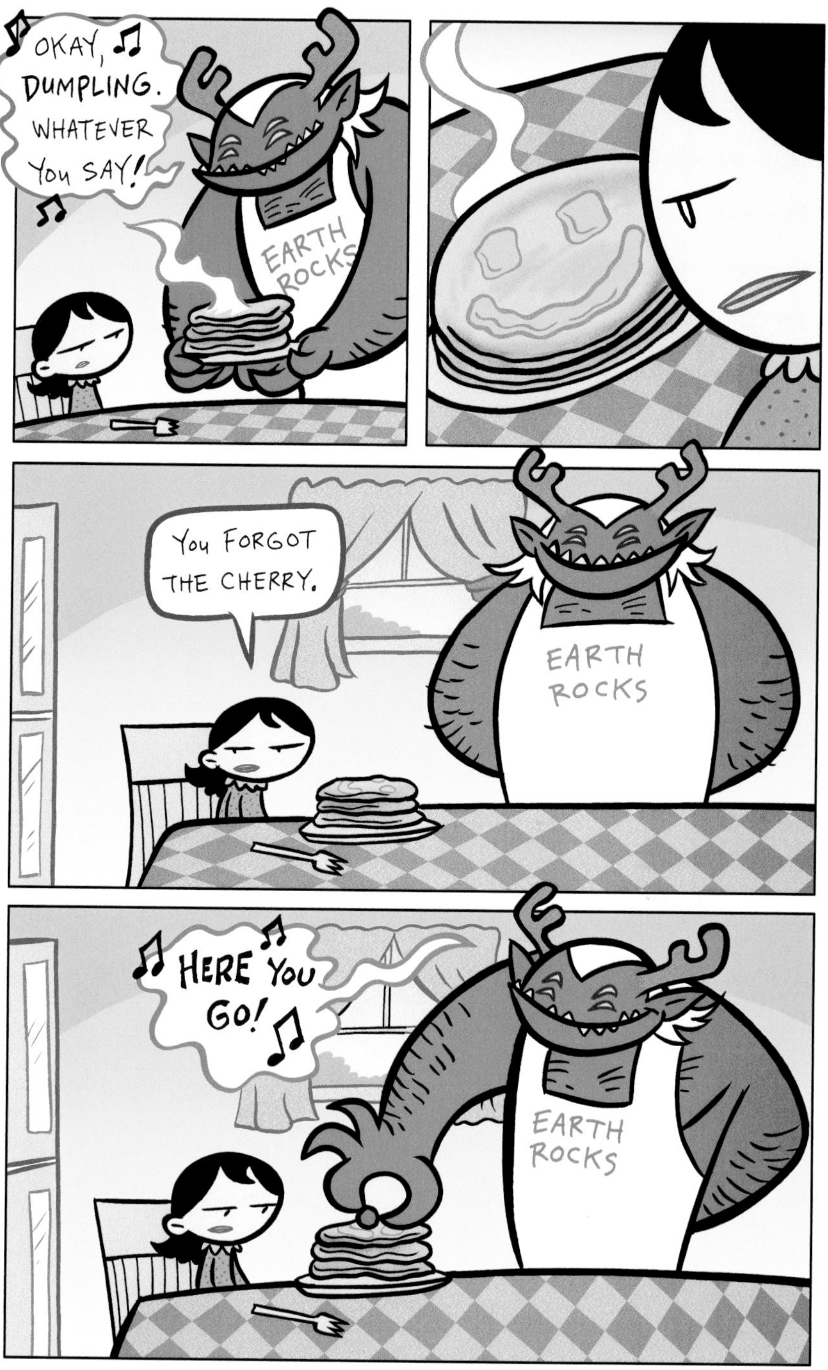
OKAY, DUMPLING. WHATEVER YOU SAY!
EARTH ROCKS
YOU FORGOT THE CHERRY.
EARTH ROCKS
HERE YOU GO!
EARTH ROCKS

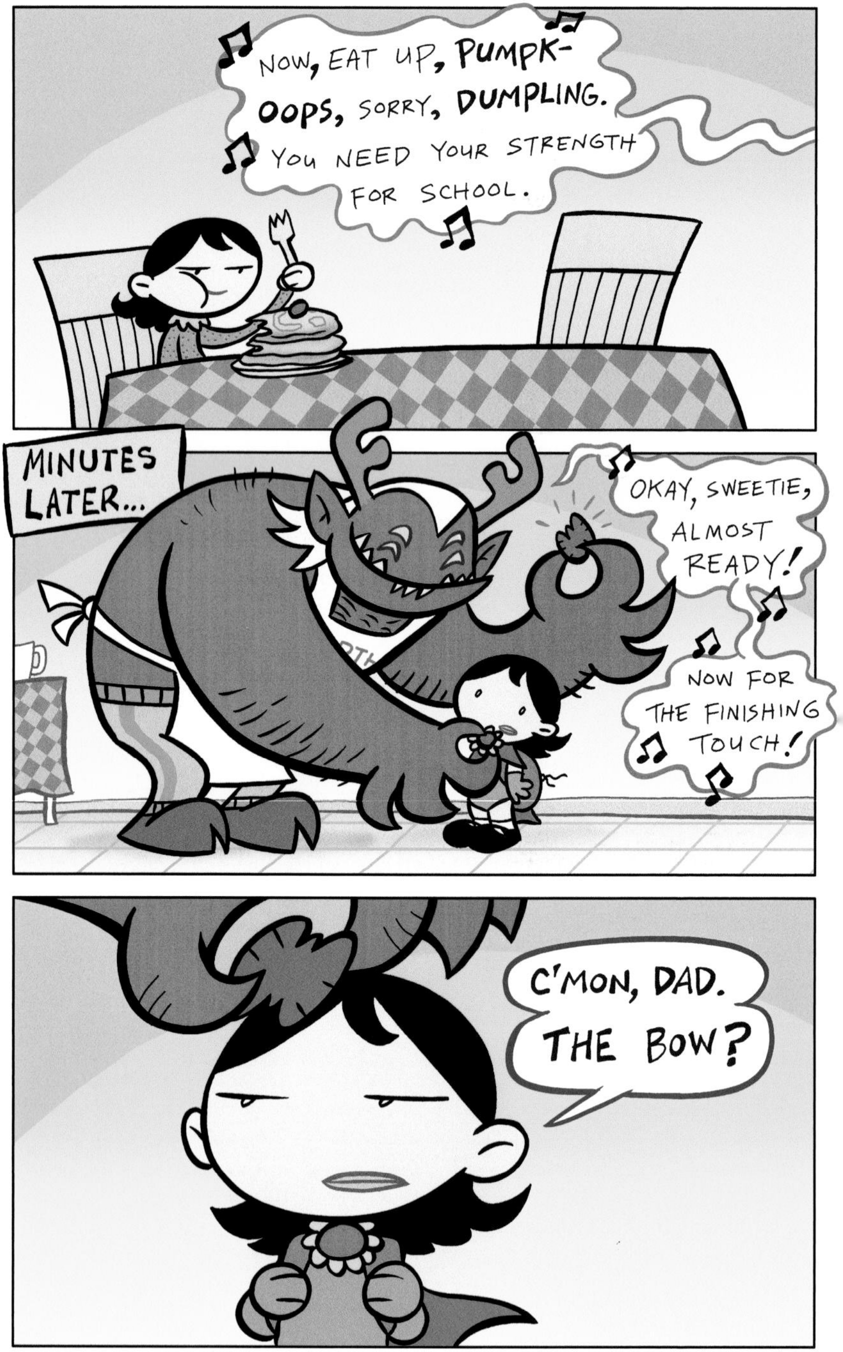
NOW, EAT UP, PUMPK- OOPS, SORRY, DUMPLING. YOU NEED YOUR STRENGTH FOR SCHOOL.
MINUTES LATER...
OKAY, SWEETIE, ALMOST READY!
NOW FOR THE FINISHING TOUCH!
C'MON, DAD. THE BOW?

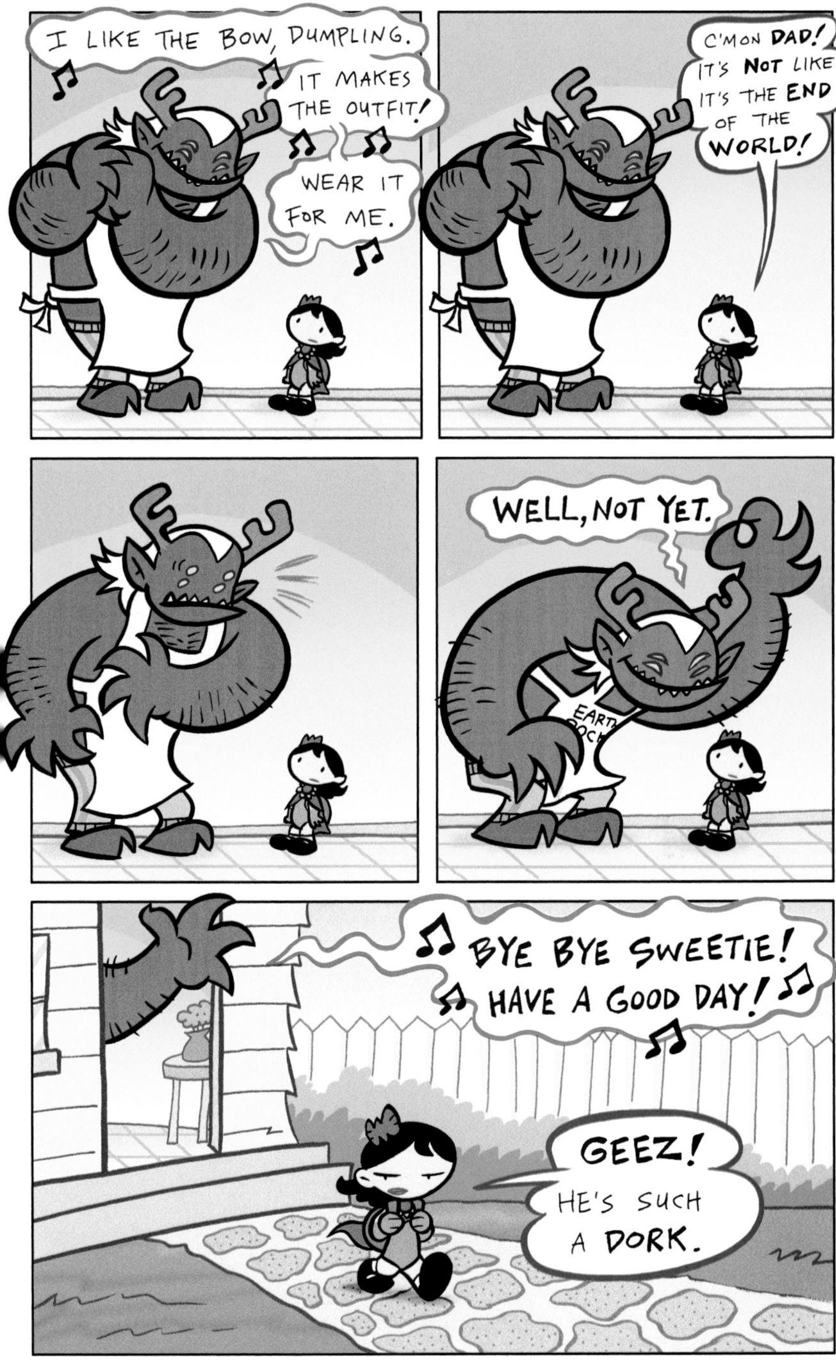
I LIKE THE BOW, DUMPLING.
IT MAKES THE OUTFIT!
WEAR IT FOR ME.
C'MON DAD! IT'S NOT LIKE IT'S THE END OF THE WORLD!
WELL, NOT YET.
BYE BYE SWEETIE! HAVE A GOOD DAY!
GEEZ! HE'S SUCH A DORK.

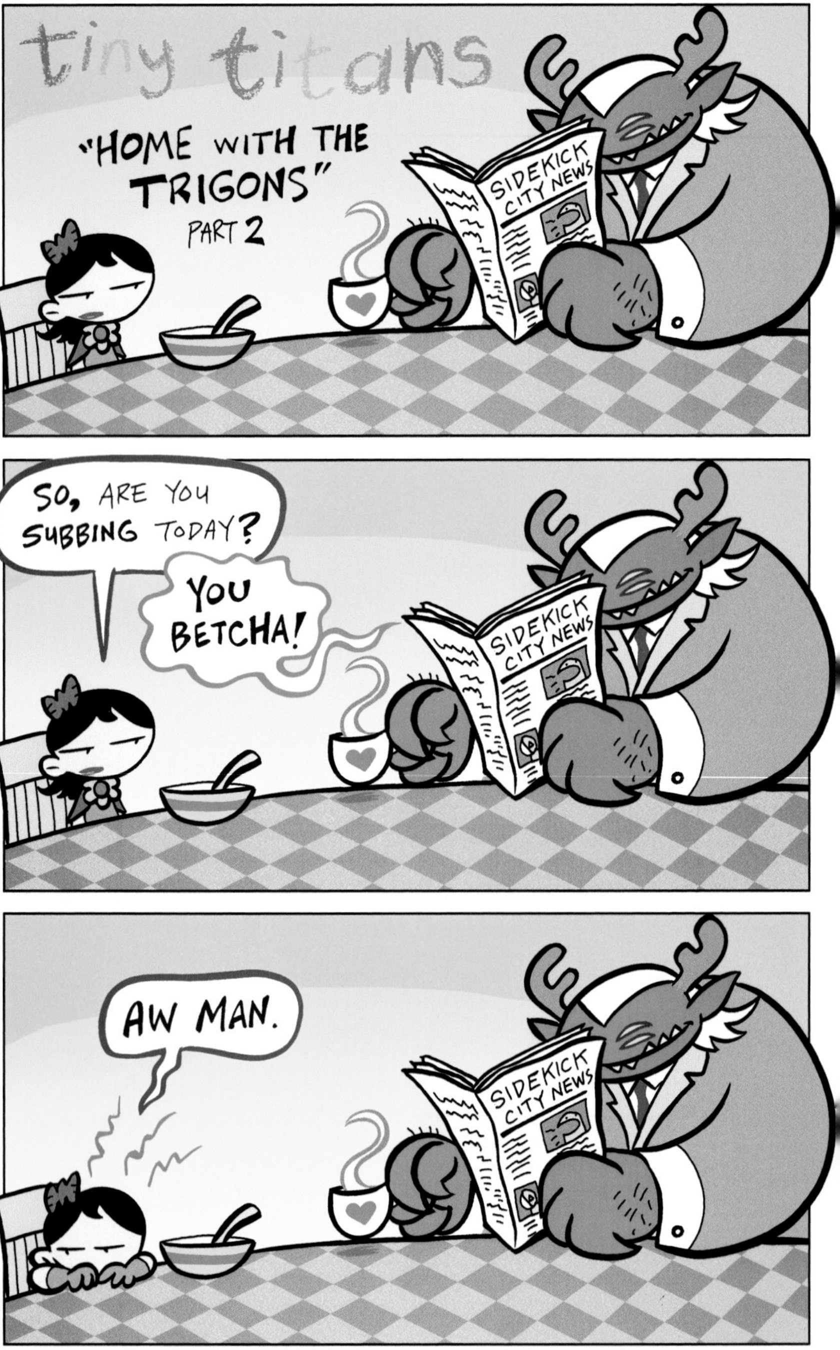
tiny titans
"HOME WITH THE TRIGONS"
PART 2
SIDEKICK CITY NEWS
SO, ARE YOU SUBBING TODAY?
YOU BETCHA!
SIDEKICK CITY NEWS
AW MAN.
SIDEKICK CITY NEWS

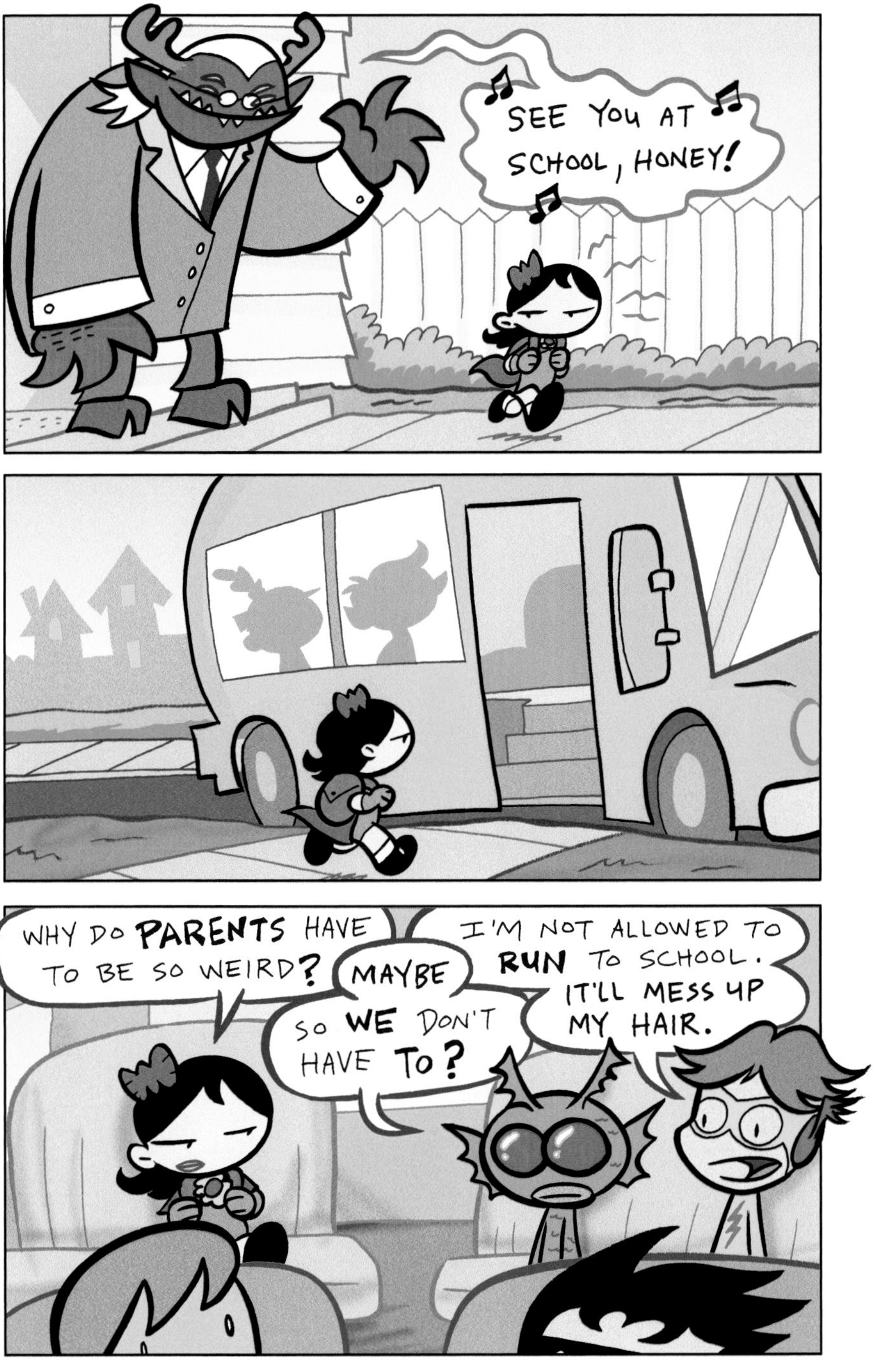
SEE YOU AT SCHOOL, HONEY!
WHY DO PARENTS HAVE TO BE SO WEIRD?
MAYBE SO WE DON'T HAVE TO?
I'M NOT ALLOWED TO RUN TO SCHOOL. IT'LL MESS UP MY HAIR.

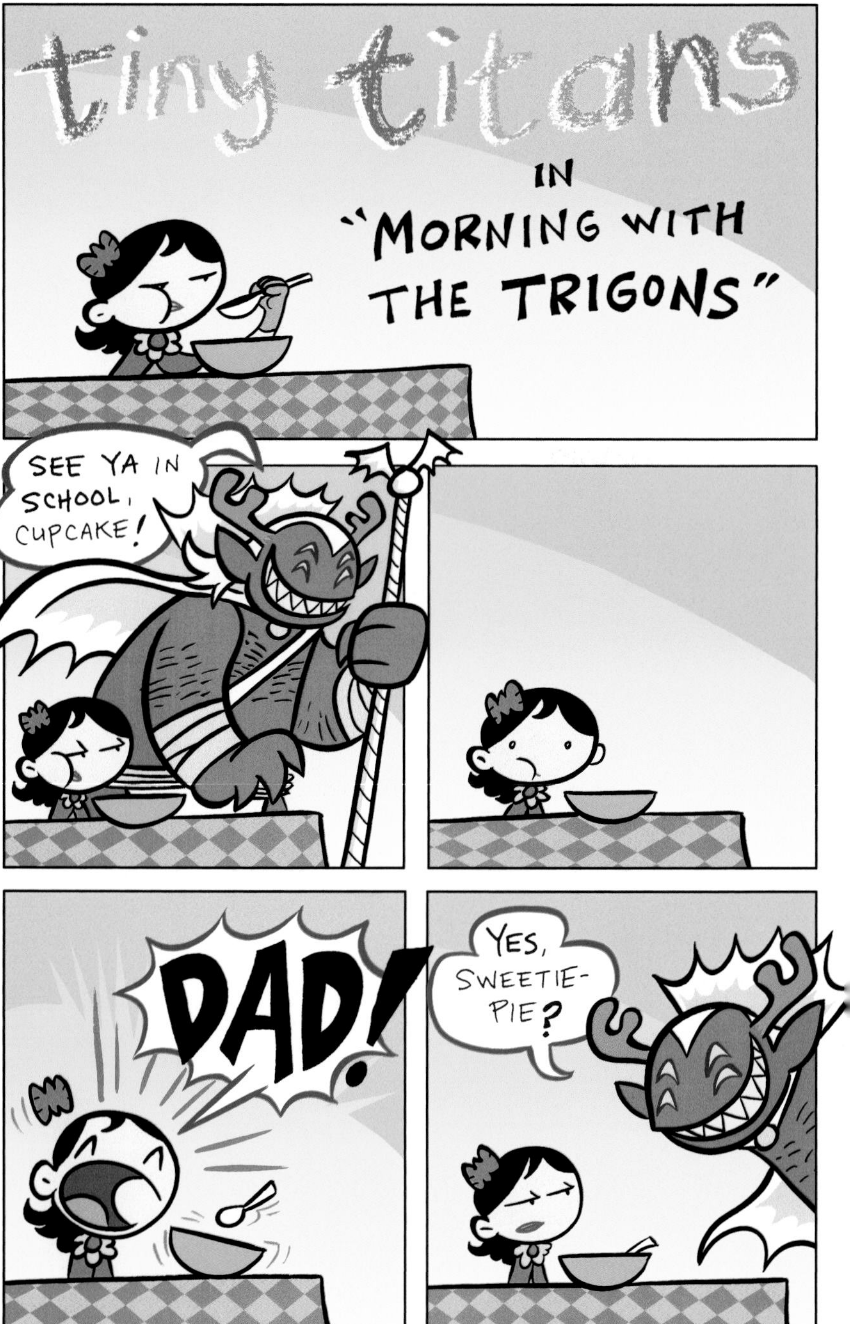
tiny titans
IN
"MORNING WITH THE TRIGONS"
SEE YA IN SCHOOL, CUPCAKE!
DAD!
YES, SWEETIE-PIE?

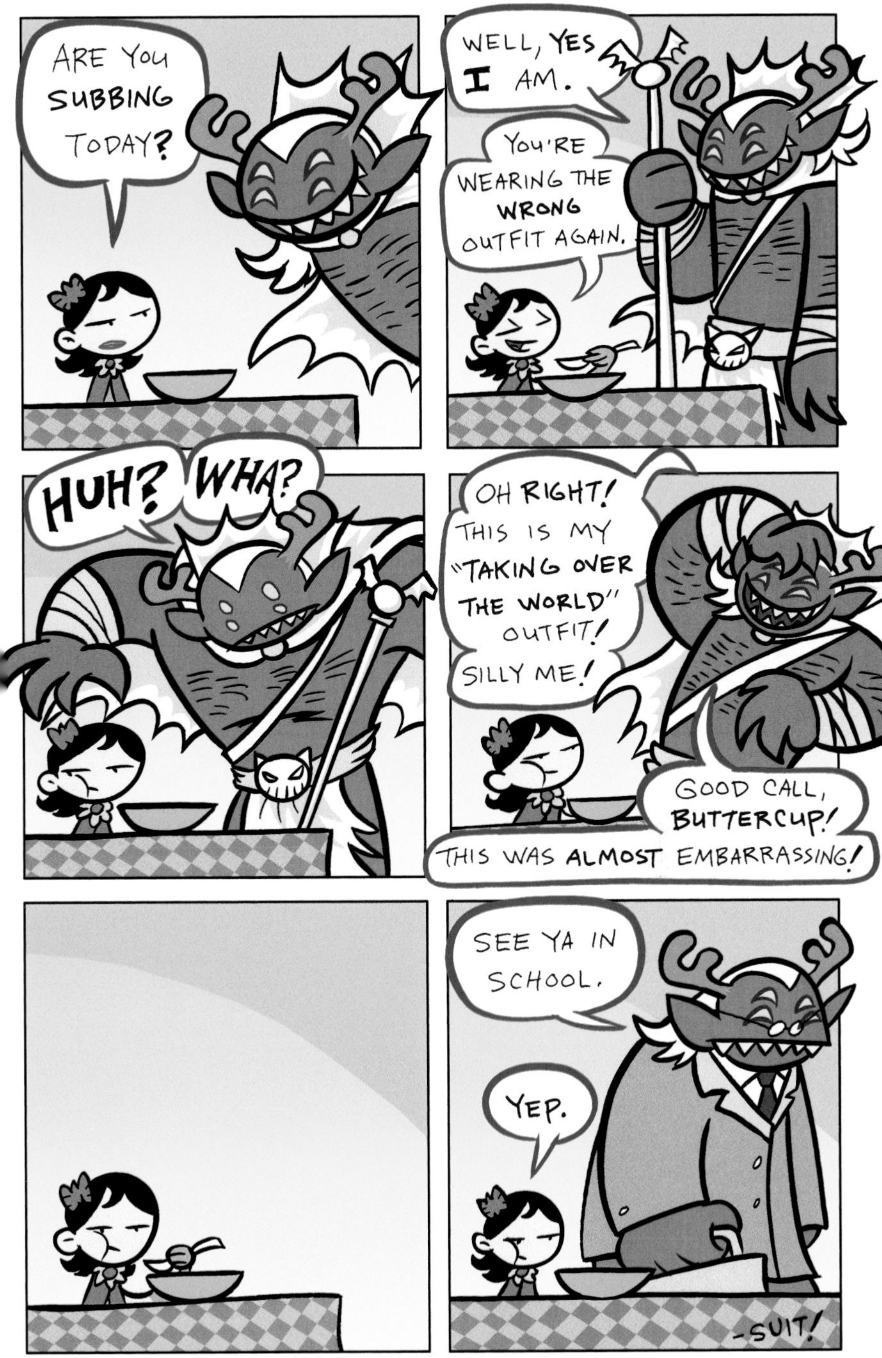
ARE YOU SUBBING TODAY?
WELL, YES I AM.
YOU'RE WEARING THE WRONG OUTFIT AGAIN.
HUH? WHA?
OH RIGHT! THIS IS MY "TAKING OVER THE WORLD" OUTFIT! SILLY ME!
GOOD CALL, BUTTERCUP!
THIS WAS ALMOST EMBARRASSING!
SEE YA IN SCHOOL.
YEP.
-SUIT!

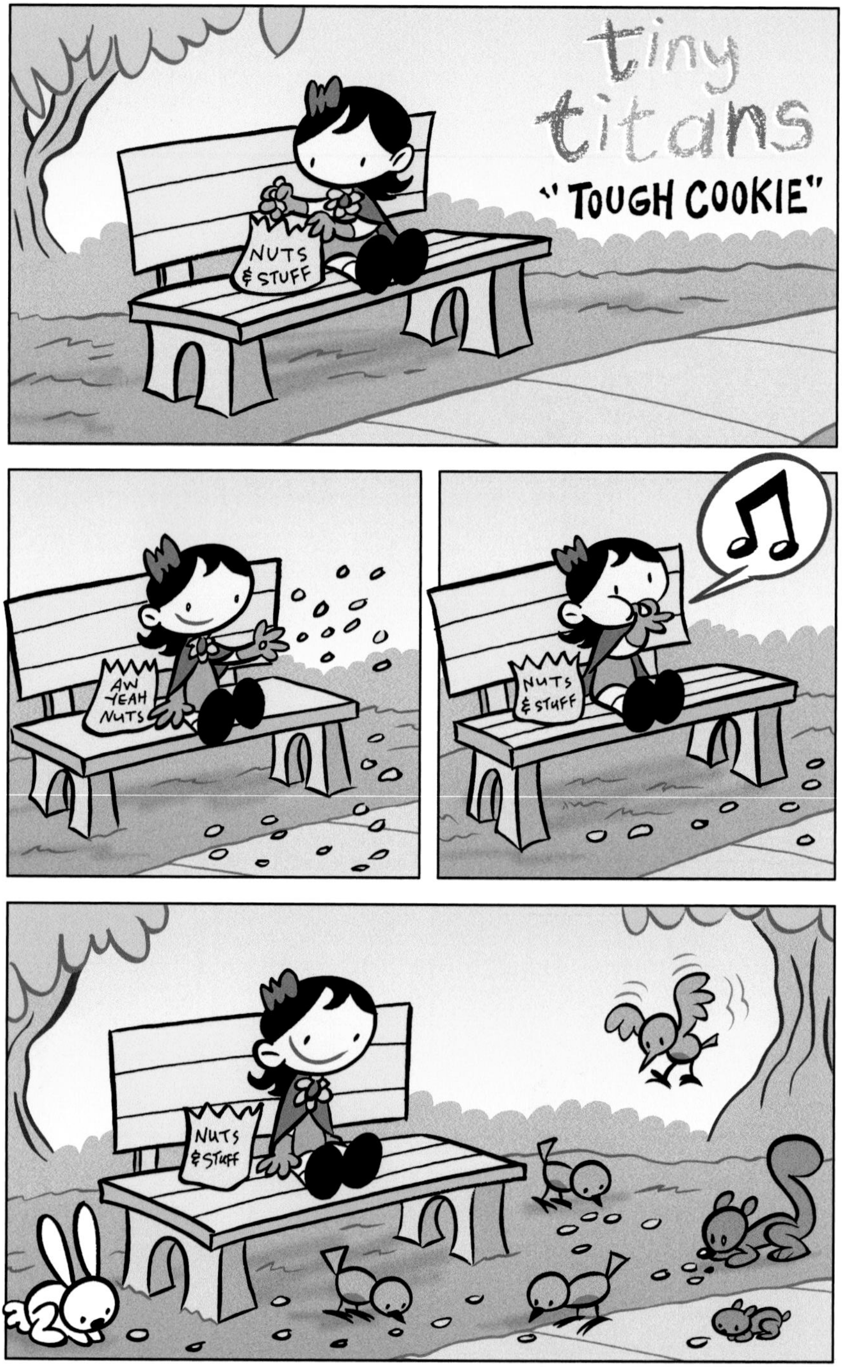
tiny titans
"TOUGH COOKIE"
NUTS & STUFF
AW YEAH NUTS
NUTS & STUFF
NUTS & STUFF

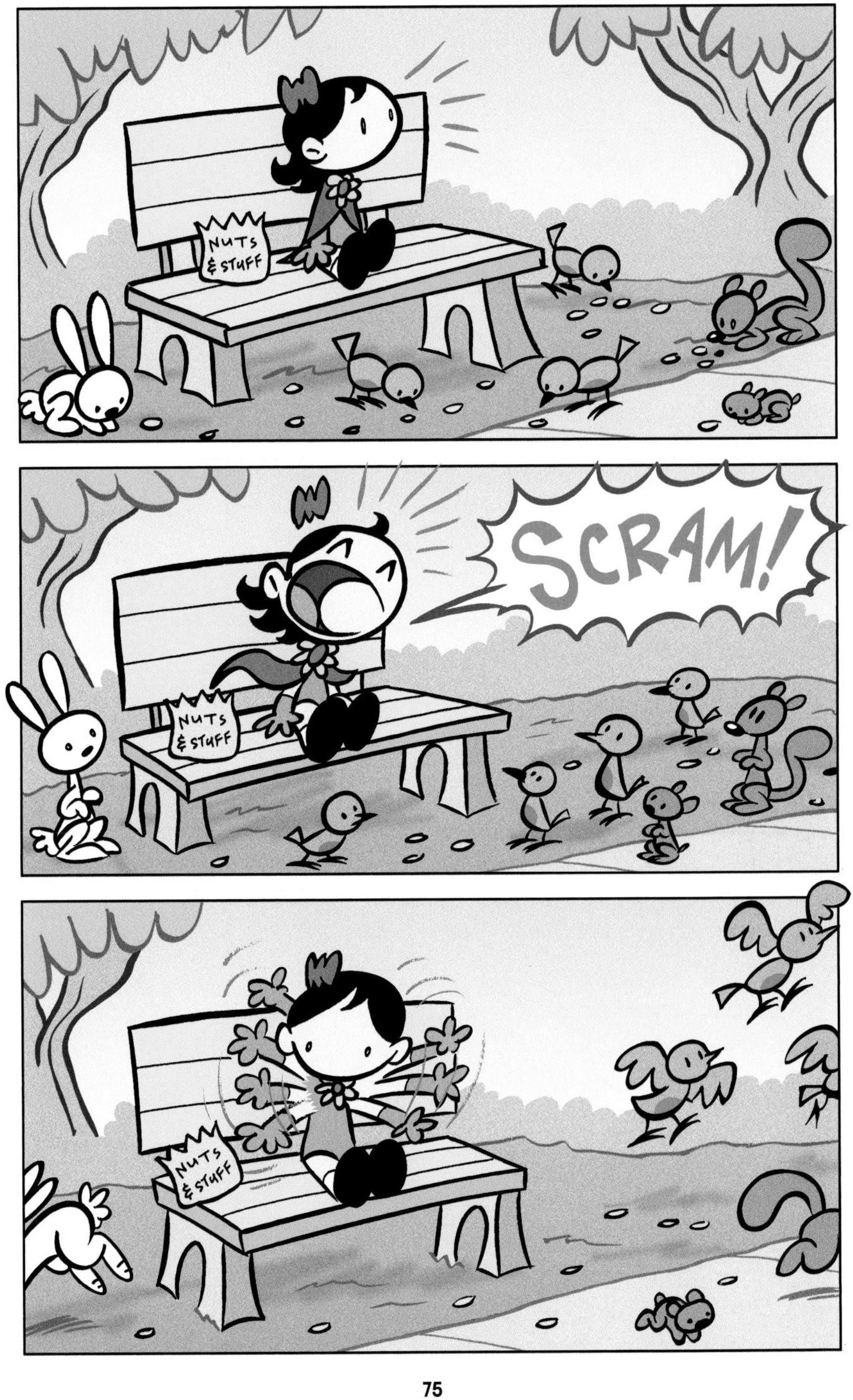
NUTS & STUFF
NUTS & STUFF
SCRAM!
NUTS & STUFF

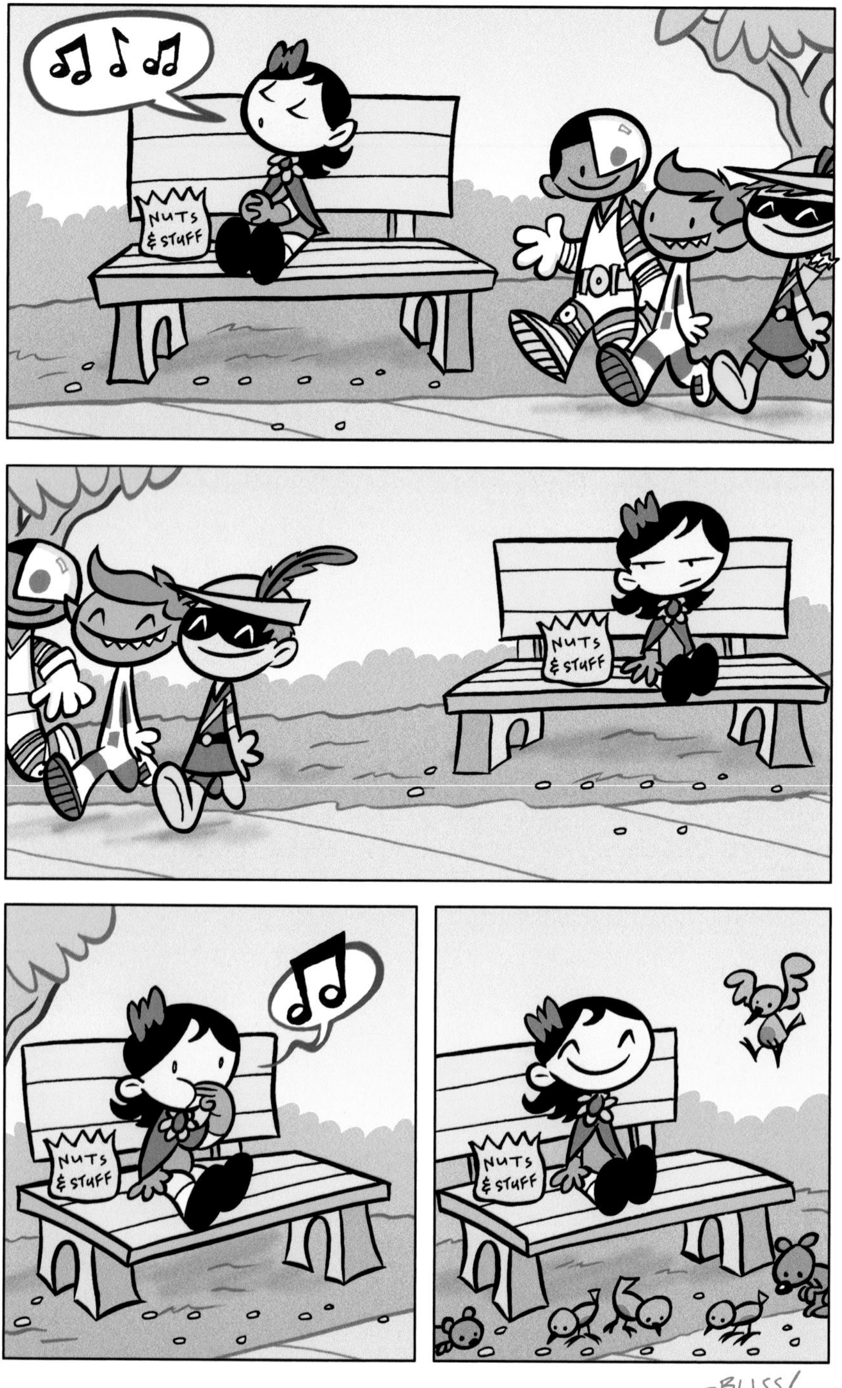
NUTS & STUFF
NUTS & STUFF
NUTS & STUFF
NUTS & STUFF
-BLISS!

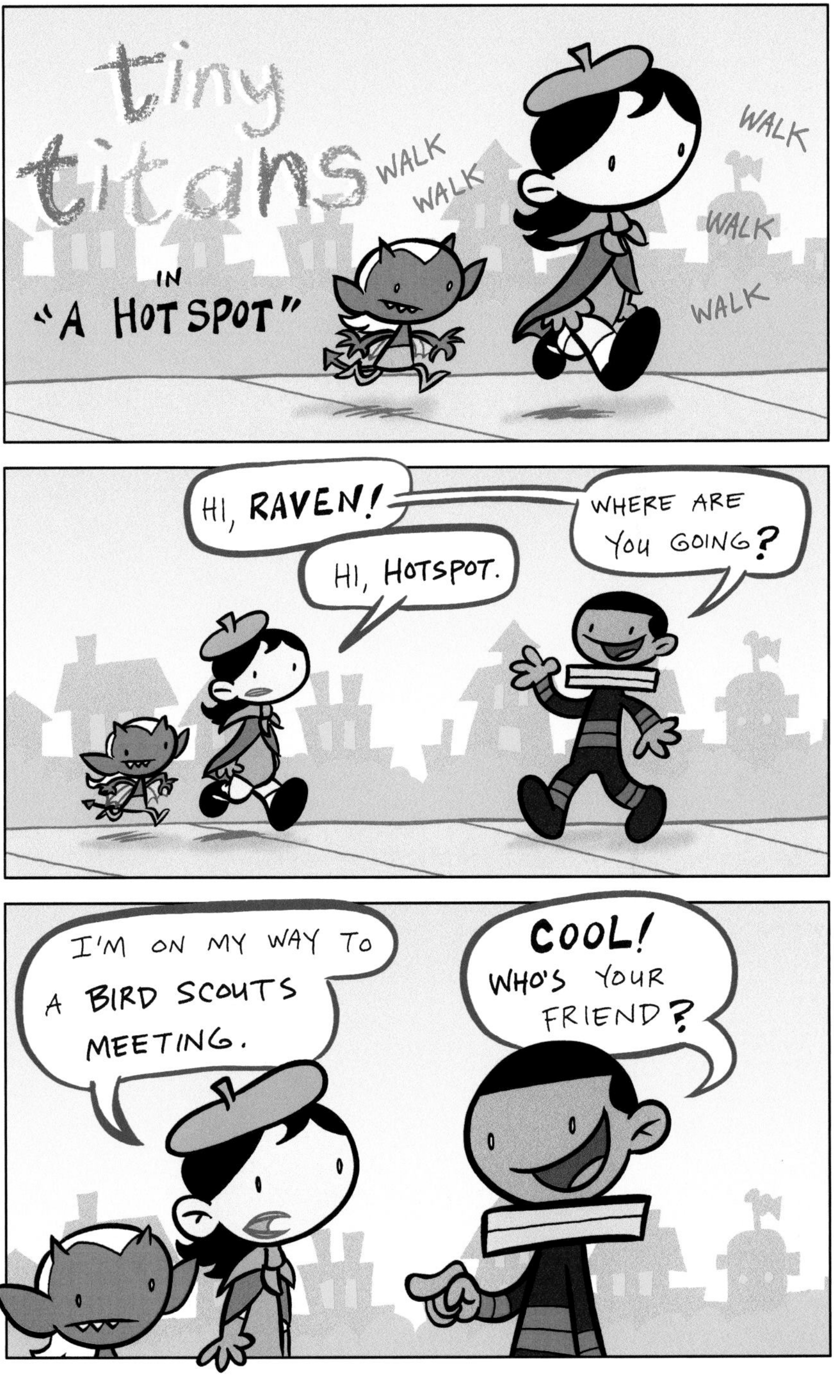
tiny titans
IN "A HOT SPOT"
WALK WALK
WALK
WALK
WALK
HI, RAVEN!
WHERE ARE YOU GOING?
HI, HOTSPOT.
I'M ON MY WAY TO A BIRD SCOUTS MEETING.
COOL! WHO'S YOUR FRIEND?

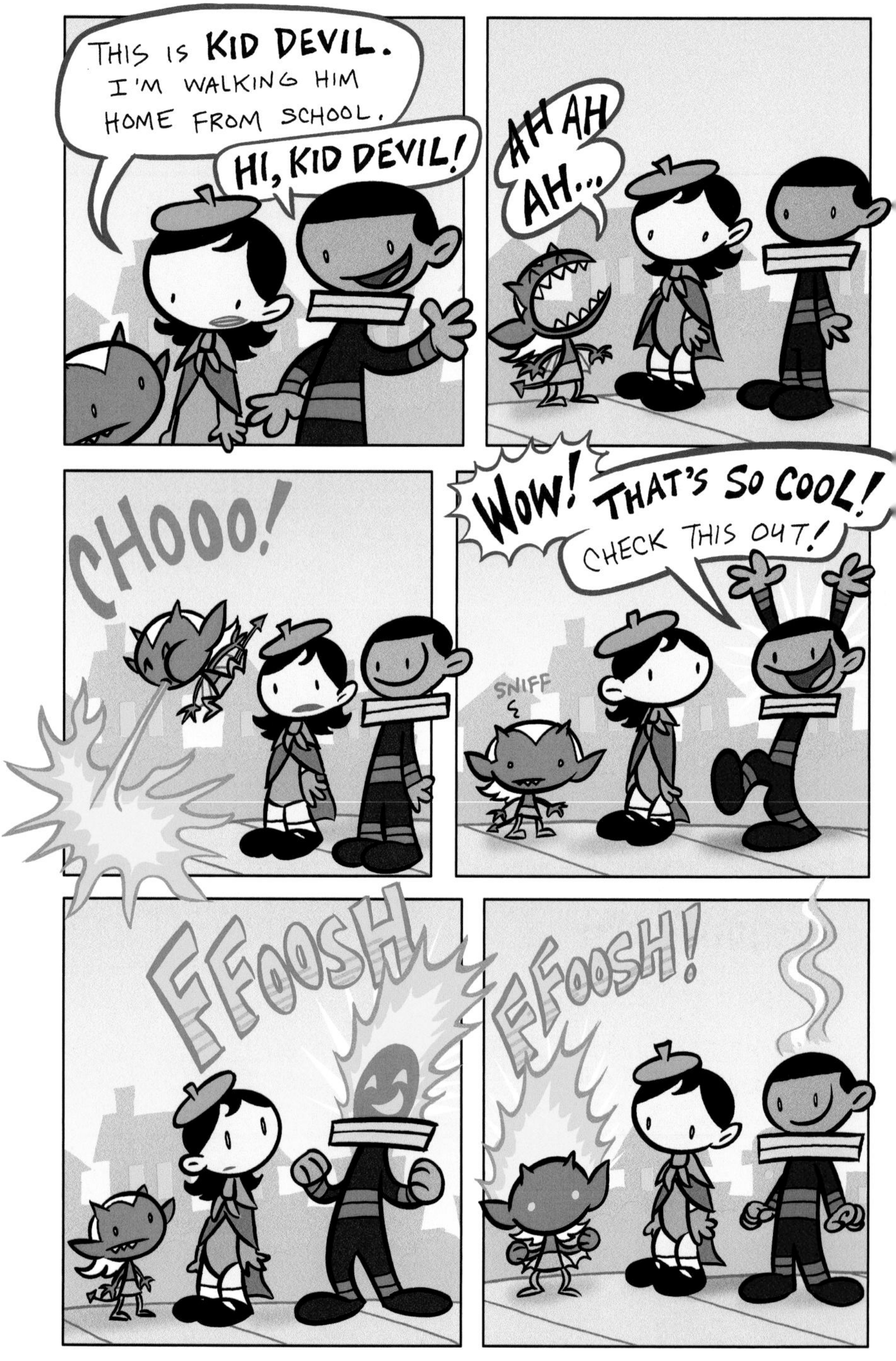
THIS IS KID DEVIL. I'M WALKING HIM HOME FROM SCHOOL.
HI, KID DEVIL!
AH AH AH...
CHOOO!
WOW!
THAT'S SO COOL! CHECK THIS OUT!
SNIFF
FFOOSH
FFOOSH!

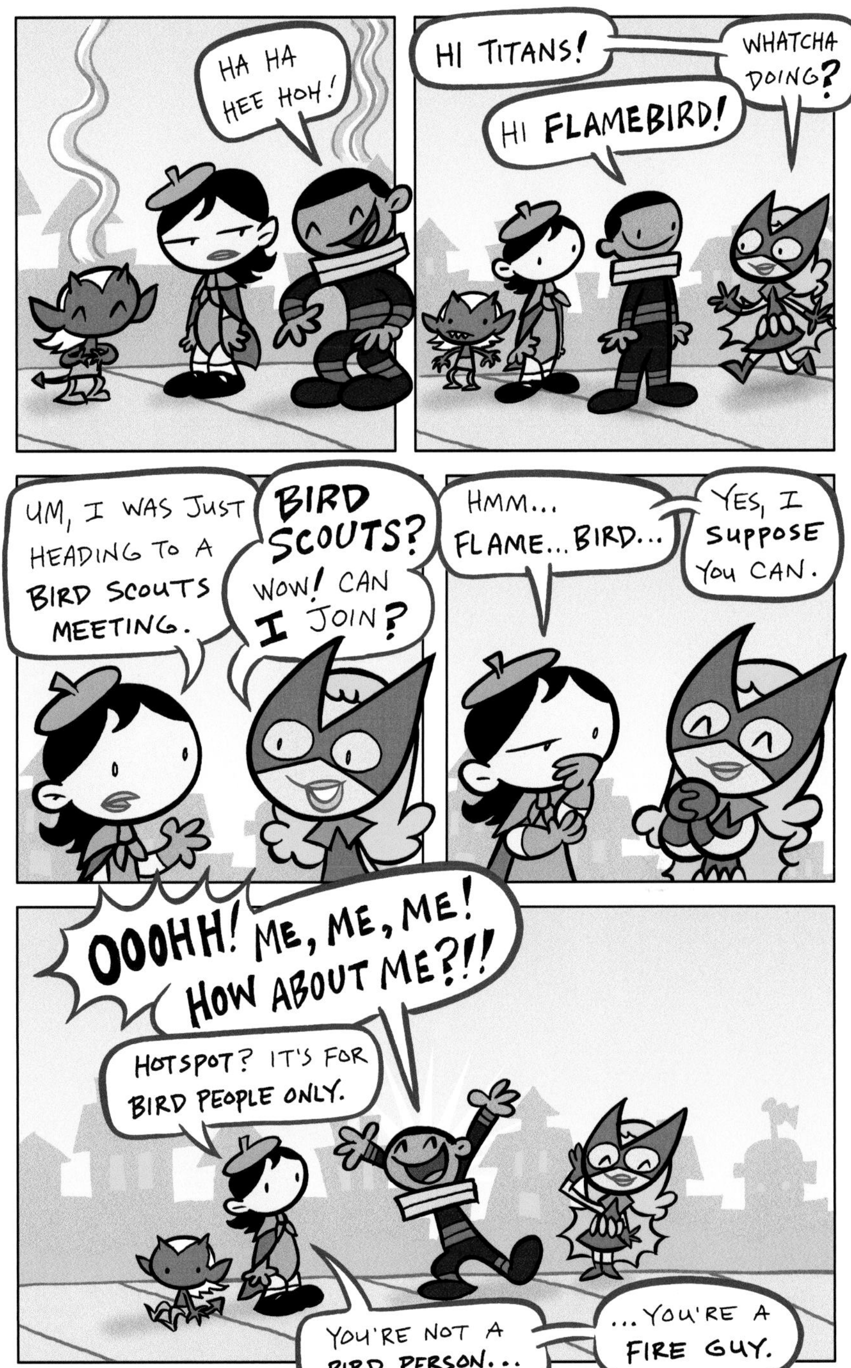
HA HA HEE HOH!
HI TITANS!
WHATCHA DOING?
HI FLAMEBIRD!
UM, I WAS JUST HEADING TO A BIRD SCOUTS MEETING.
BIRD SCOUTS? WOW! CAN I JOIN?
HMM... FLAME... BIRD...
YES, I SUPPOSE YOU CAN.
OOOHH! ME, ME, ME! HOW ABOUT ME?!!
HOTSPOT? IT'S FOR BIRD PEOPLE ONLY.
YOU'RE NOT A BIRD PERSON...
...YOU'RE A FIRE GUY.

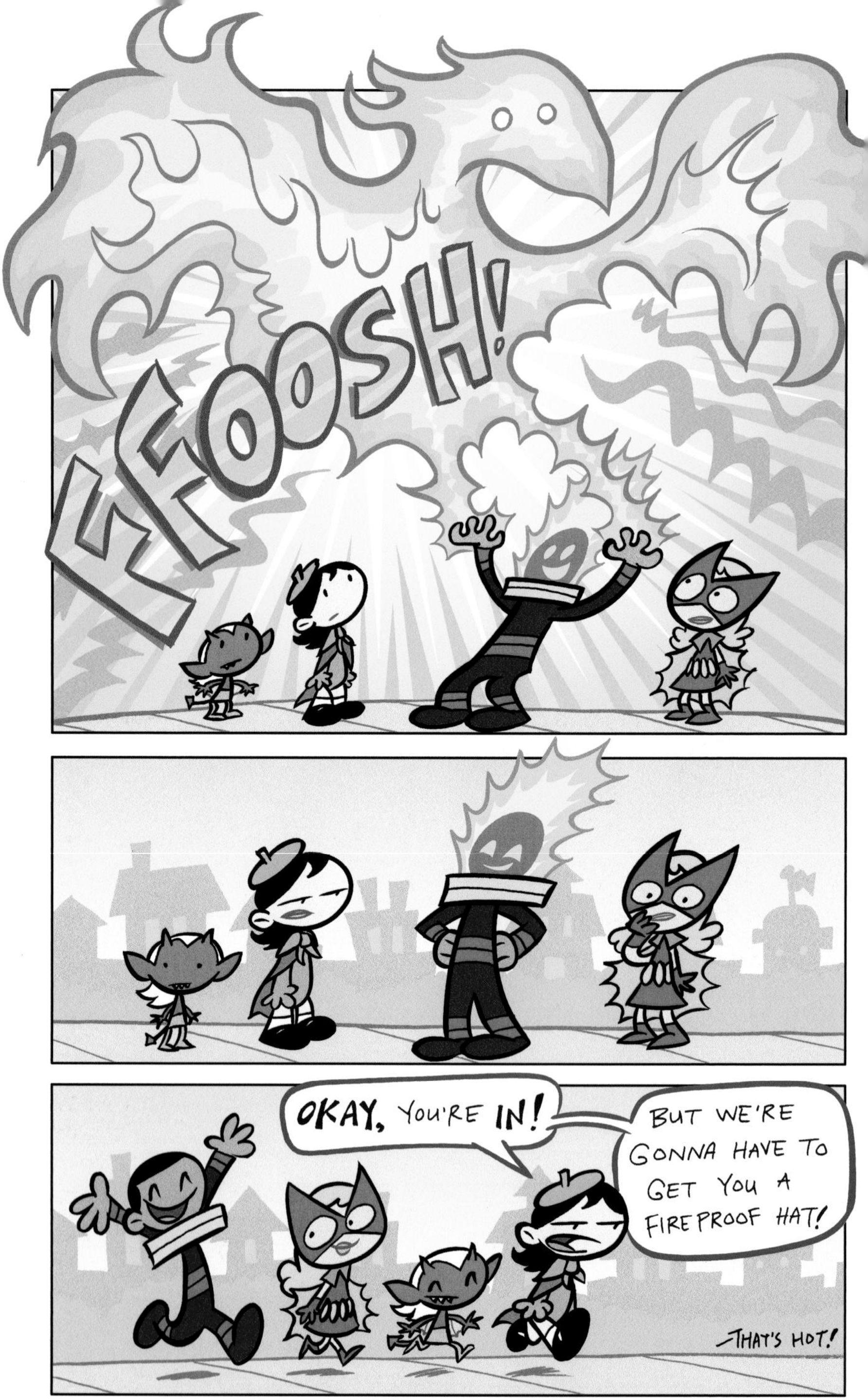
FFOOSH!
OKAY, YOU'RE IN!
BUT WE'RE GONNA HAVE TO GET YOU A FIREPROOF HAT!
—THAT'S HOT!

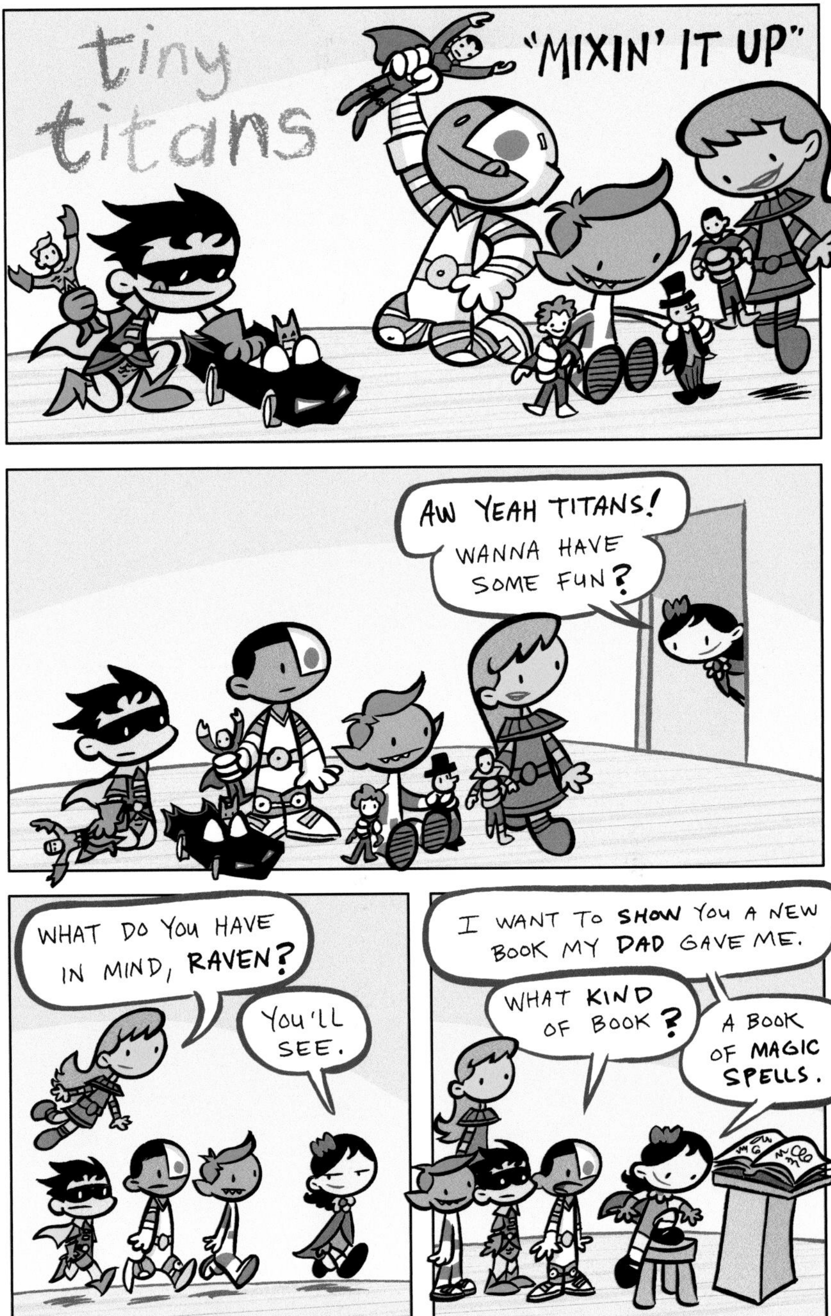
tiny titans
"MIXIN' IT UP"
AW YEAH TITANS! WANNA HAVE SOME FUN?
WHAT DO YOU HAVE IN MIND, RAVEN?
YOU'LL SEE.
I WANT TO SHOW YOU A NEW BOOK MY DAD GAVE ME.
WHAT KIND OF BOOK?
A BOOK OF MAGIC SPELLS.

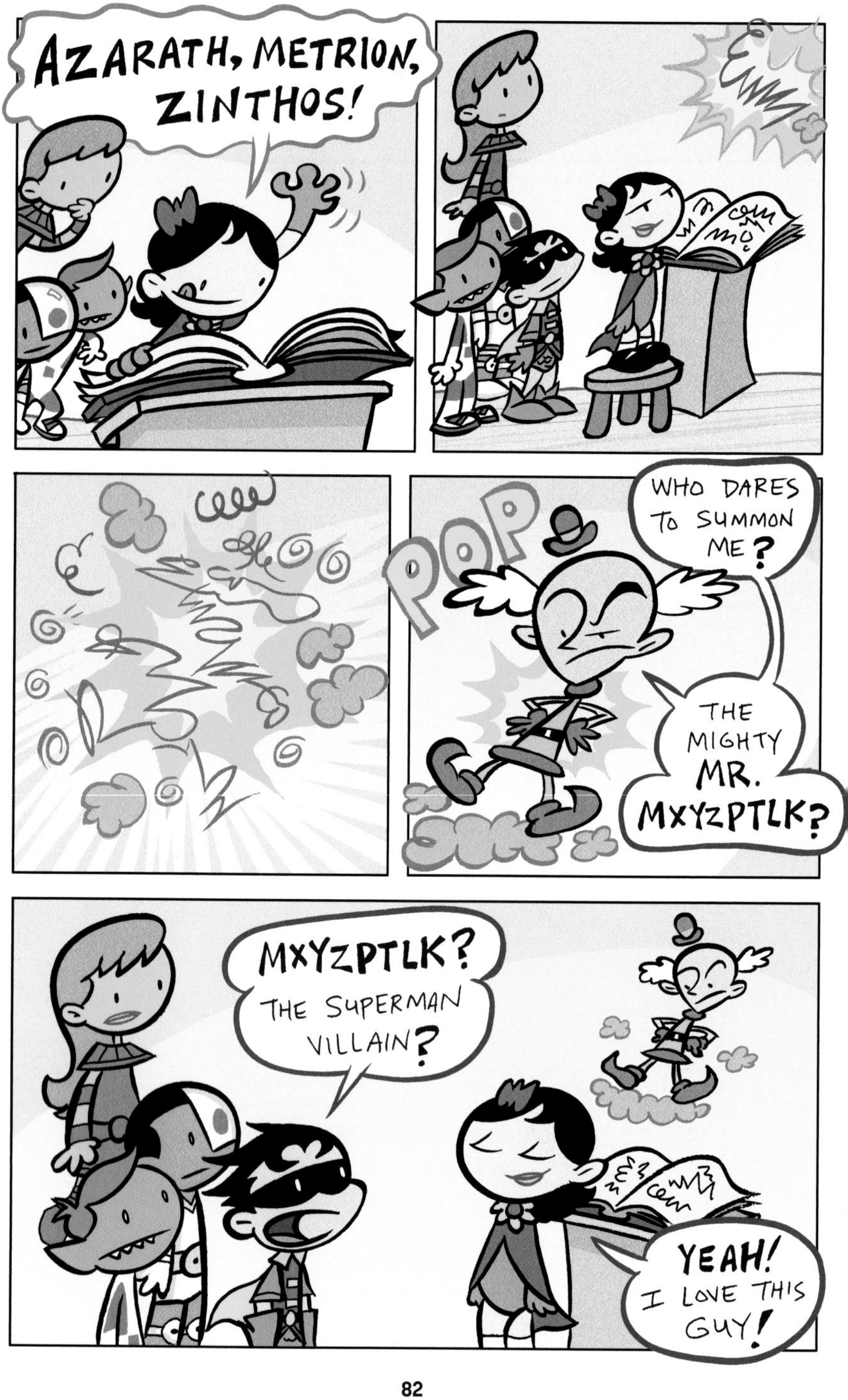
AZARATH, METRION, ZINTHOS!
POP
WHO DARES TO SUMMON ME?
THE MIGHTY MR. MXYZPTLK?
MXYZPTLK? THE SUPERMAN VILLAIN?
YEAH! I LOVE THIS GUY!

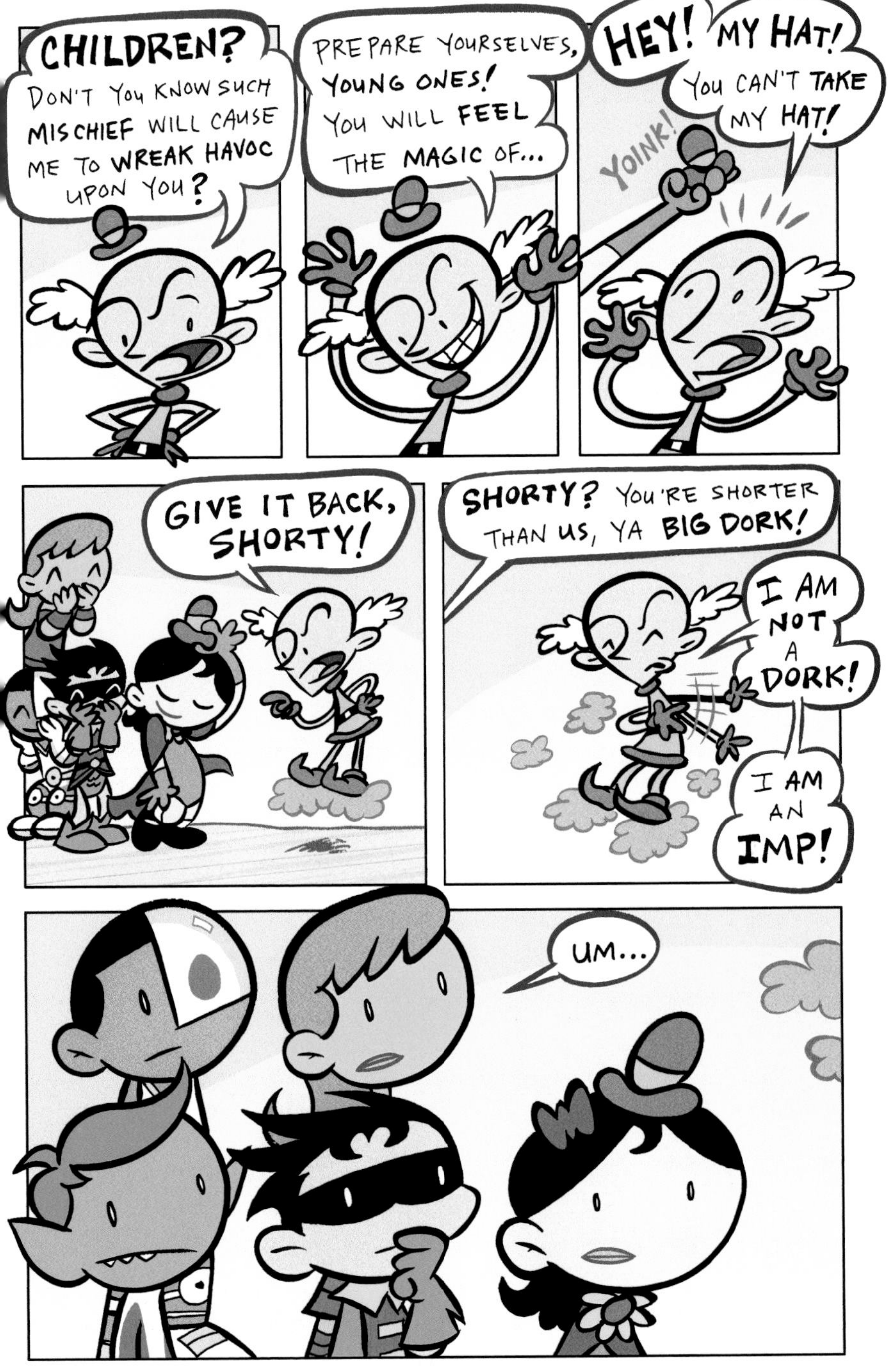
CHILDREN? DON'T YOU KNOW SUCH MISCHIEF WILL CAUSE ME TO WREAK HAVOC UPON YOU?
PREPARE YOURSELVES, YOUNG ONES! YOU WILL FEEL THE MAGIC OF...
YOINK!
HEY! MY HAT! YOU CAN'T TAKE MY HAT!
GIVE IT BACK, SHORTY!
SHORTY? YOU'RE SHORTER THAN US, YA BIG DORK!
I AM NOT A DORK!
I AM AN IMP!
UM...

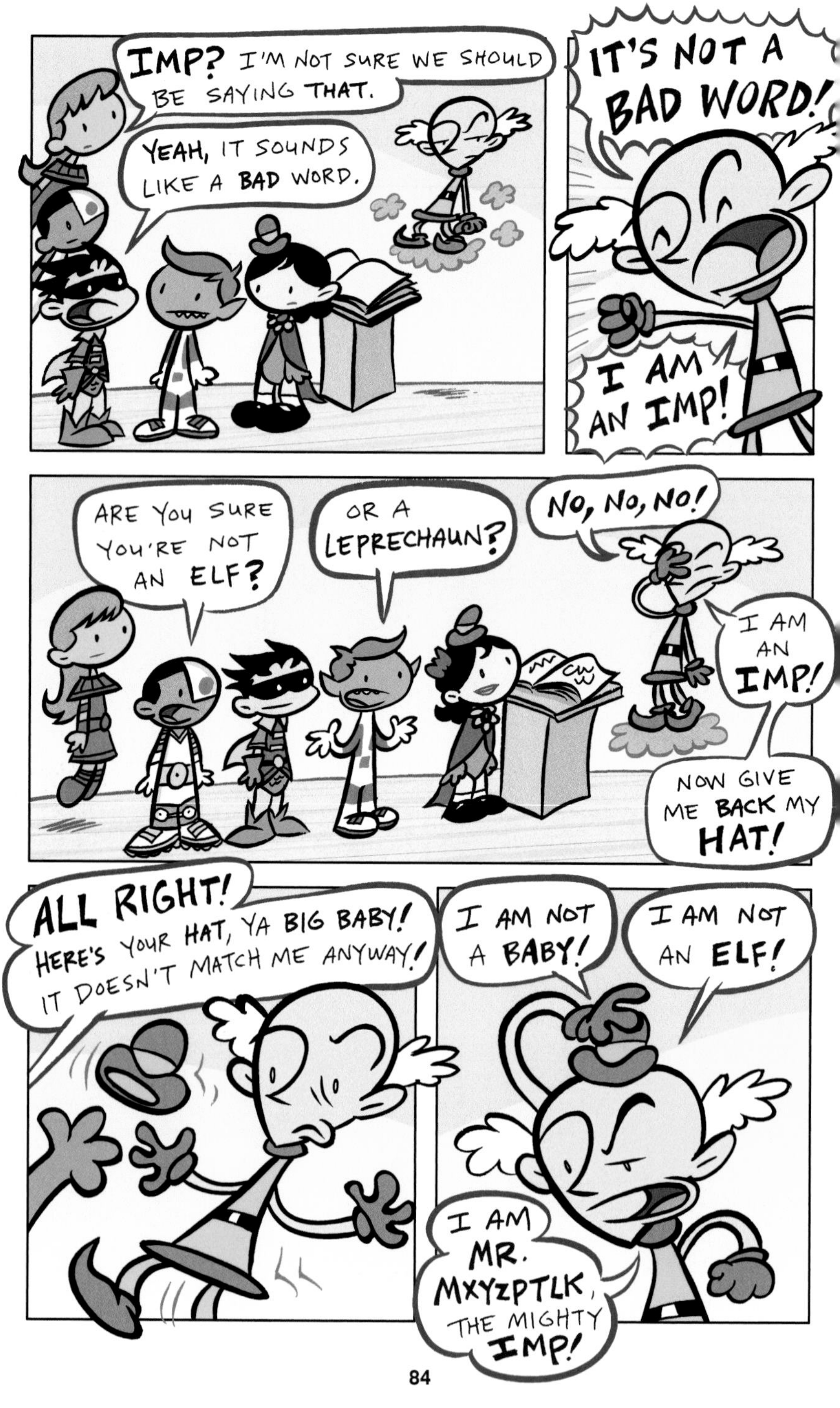
IMP? I'M NOT SURE WE SHOULD BE SAYING THAT.
YEAH, IT SOUNDS LIKE A BAD WORD.
IT'S NOT A BAD WORD!
I AM AN IMP!
ARE YOU SURE YOU'RE NOT AN ELF?
OR A LEPRECHAUN?
NO, NO, NO!
I AM AN IMP!
NOW GIVE ME BACK MY HAT!
ALL RIGHT! HERE'S YOUR HAT, YA BIG BABY! IT DOESN'T MATCH ME ANYWAY!
I AM NOT A BABY!
I AM NOT AN ELF!
I AM MR. MXYZPTLK, THE MIGHTY IMP!

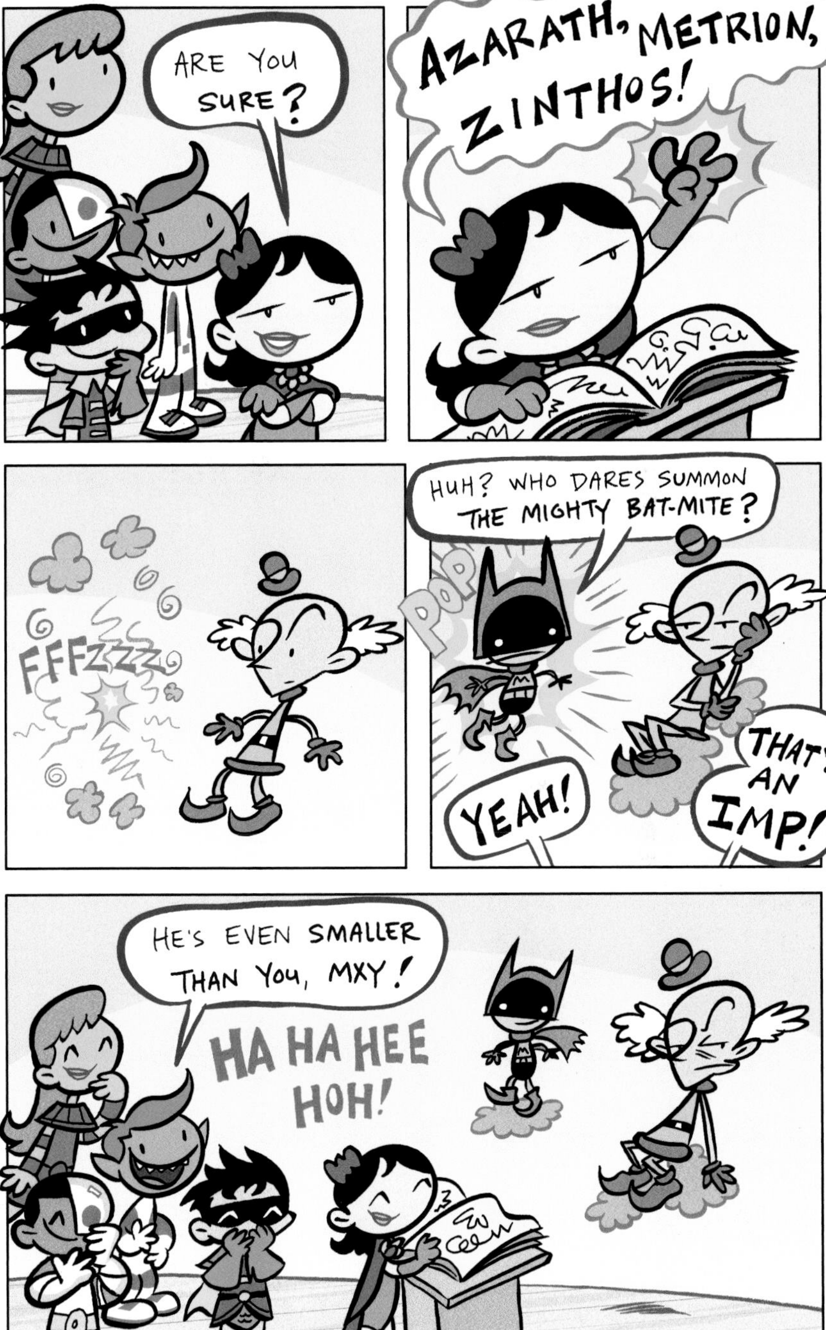
ARE YOU SURE?
AZARATH, METRION, ZINTHOS!
FFFZZZZ
HUH? WHO DARES SUMMON THE MIGHTY BAT-MITE?
POP
YEAH!
THAT'S AN IMP!
HE'S EVEN SMALLER THAN YOU, MXY!
HA HA HEE HOH!

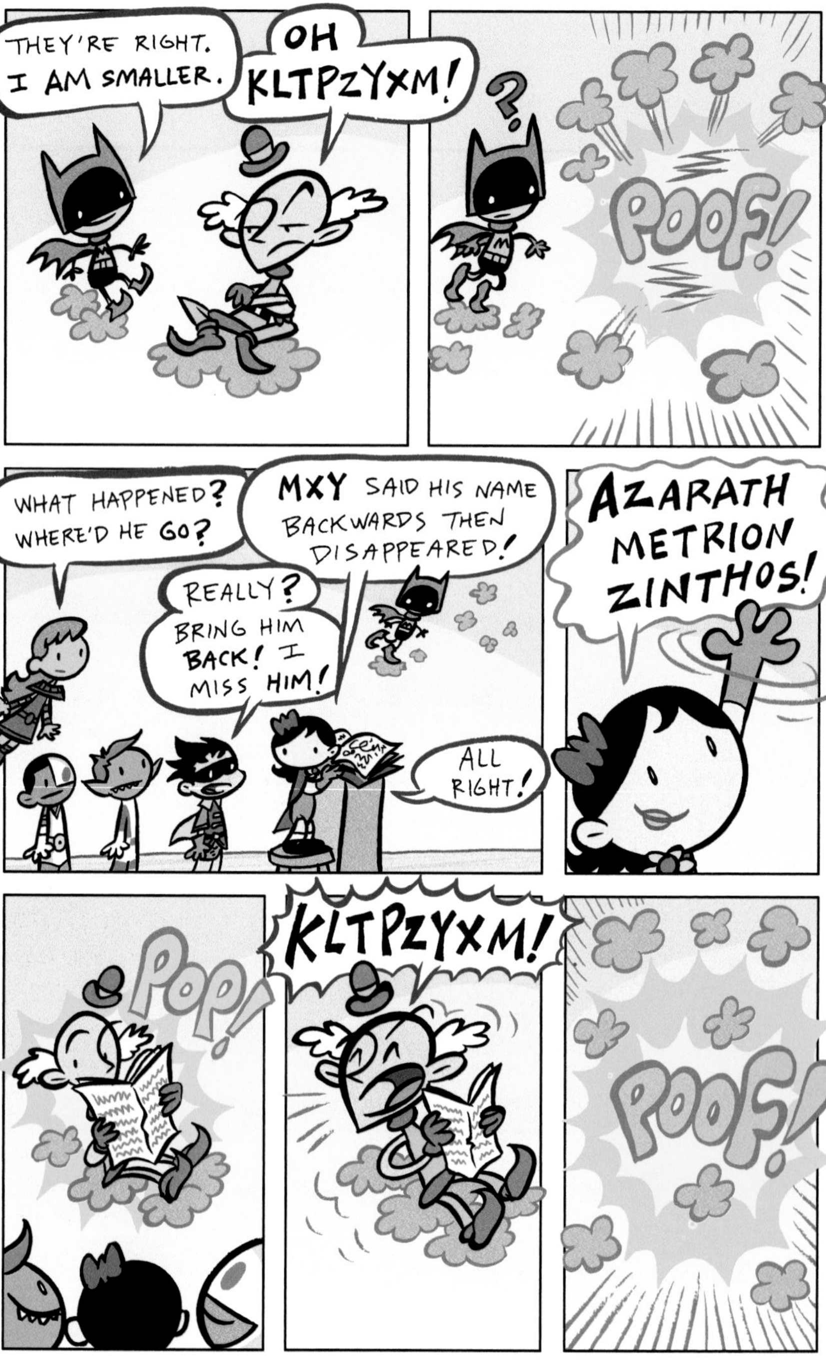
THEY'RE RIGHT. I AM SMALLER.
OH KLTPZYXM!
?
POOF!
WHAT HAPPENED? WHERE'D HE GO?
MXY SAID HIS NAME BACKWARDS THEN DISAPPEARED!
REALLY? BRING HIM BACK! I MISS HIM!
ALL RIGHT!
AZARATH METRION ZINTHOS!
POP!
KLTPZYXM!
POOF!

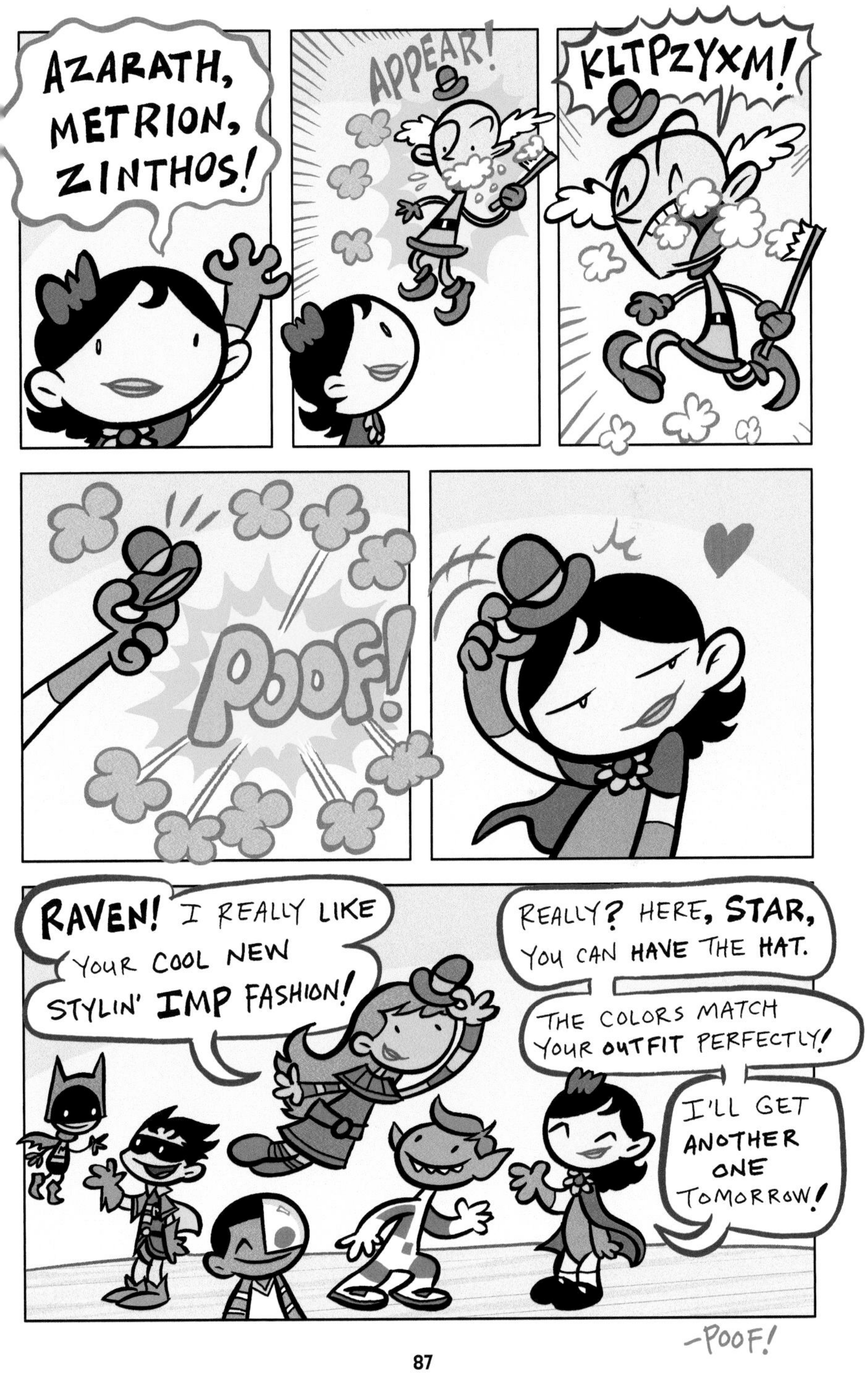
AZARATH, METRION, ZINTHOS!
APPEAR!
KLTPZYXM!
POOF!
RAVEN! I REALLY LIKE YOUR COOL NEW STYLIN' IMP FASHION!
REALLY? HERE, STAR, YOU CAN HAVE THE HAT.
THE COLORS MATCH YOUR OUTFIT PERFECTLY!
I'LL GET ANOTHER ONE TOMORROW!
-POOF!

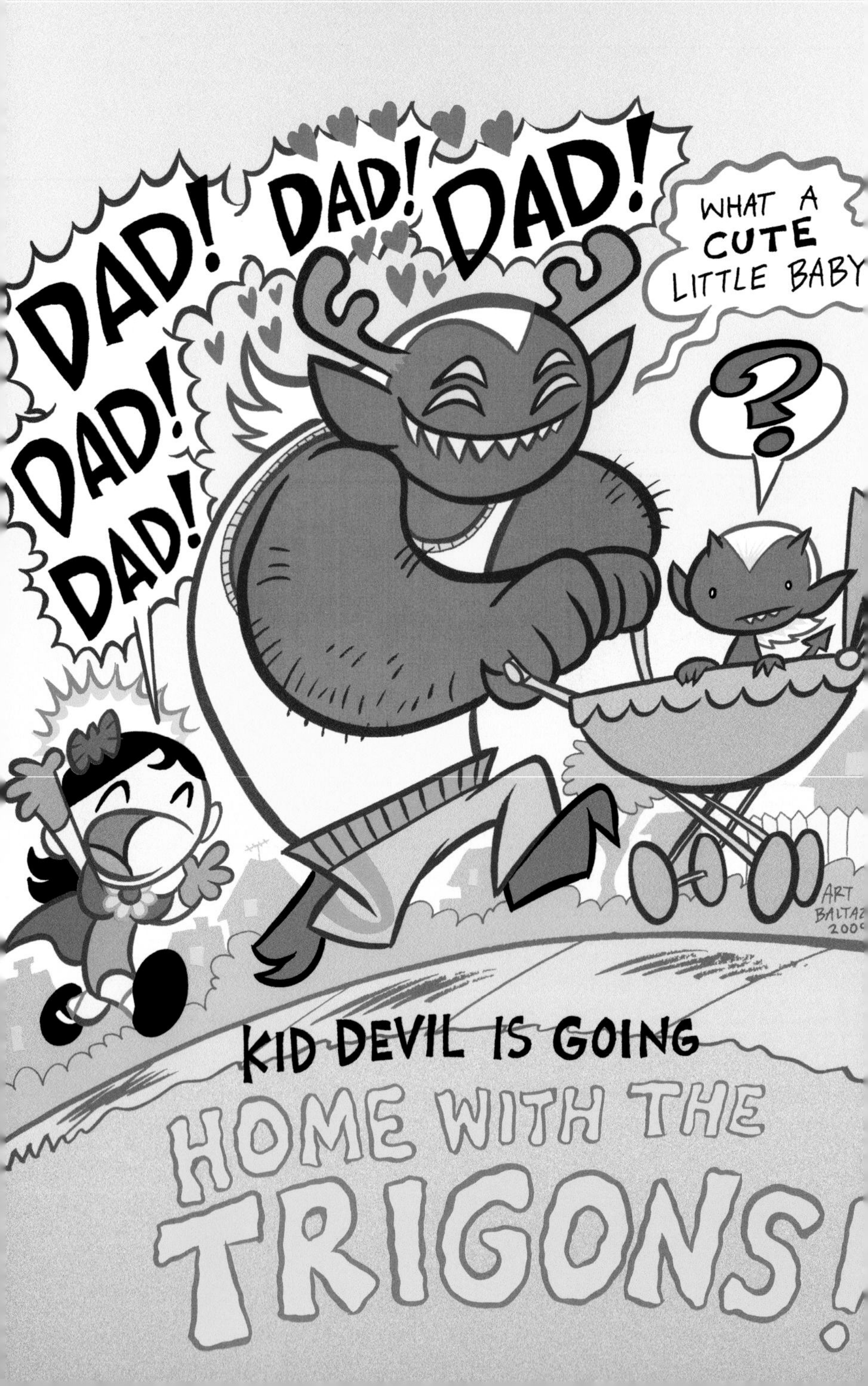
DAD! DAD! DAD!
DAD! DAD! DAD!
WHAT A CUTE LITTLE BABY
?
ART BALTAZ 200
KID DEVIL IS GOING HOME WITH THE TRIGONS!

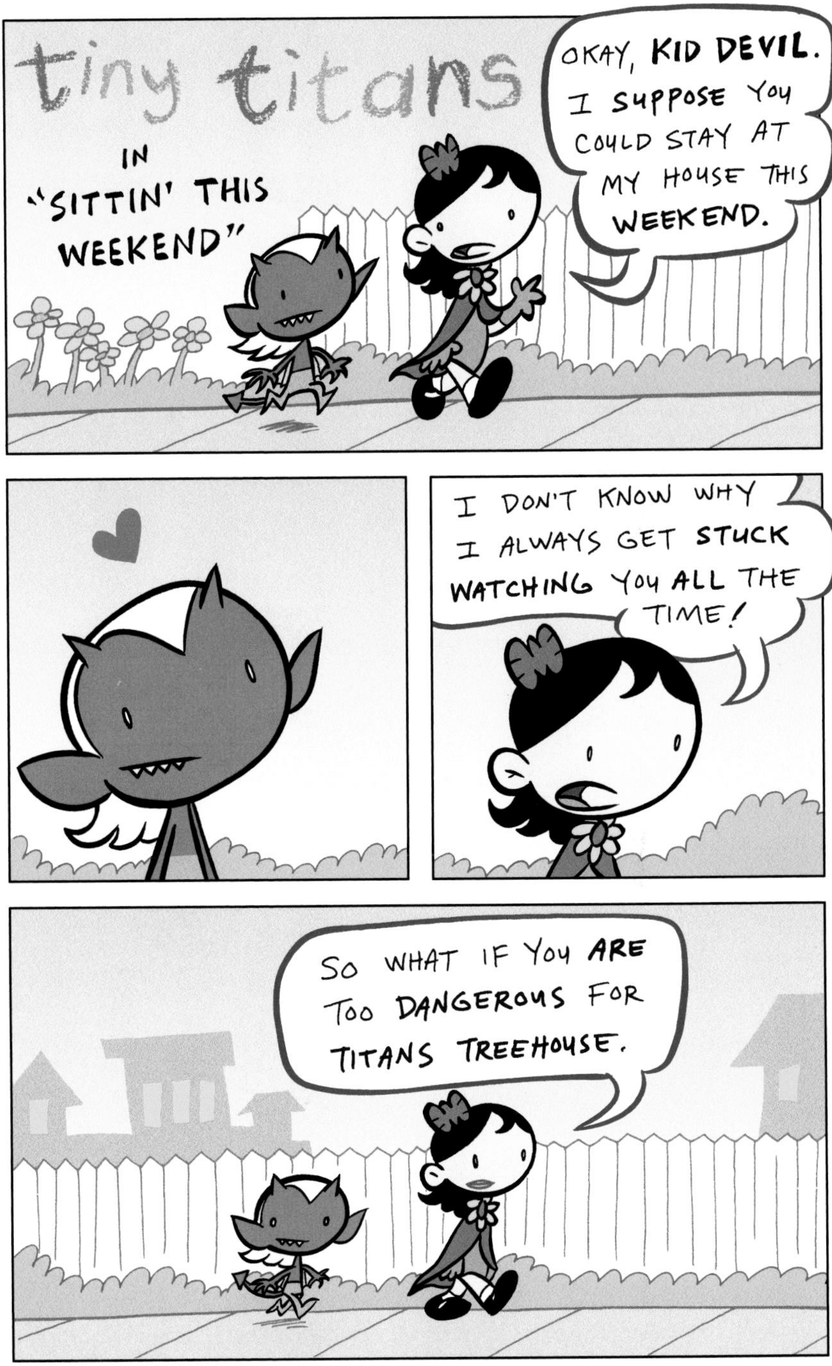
tiny titans
IN "SITTIN' THIS WEEKEND"
OKAY, KID DEVIL. I SUPPOSE YOU COULD STAY AT MY HOUSE THIS WEEKEND.
I DON'T KNOW WHY I ALWAYS GET STUCK WATCHING YOU ALL THE TIME!
SO WHAT IF YOU ARE TOO DANGEROUS FOR TITANS TREEHOUSE.

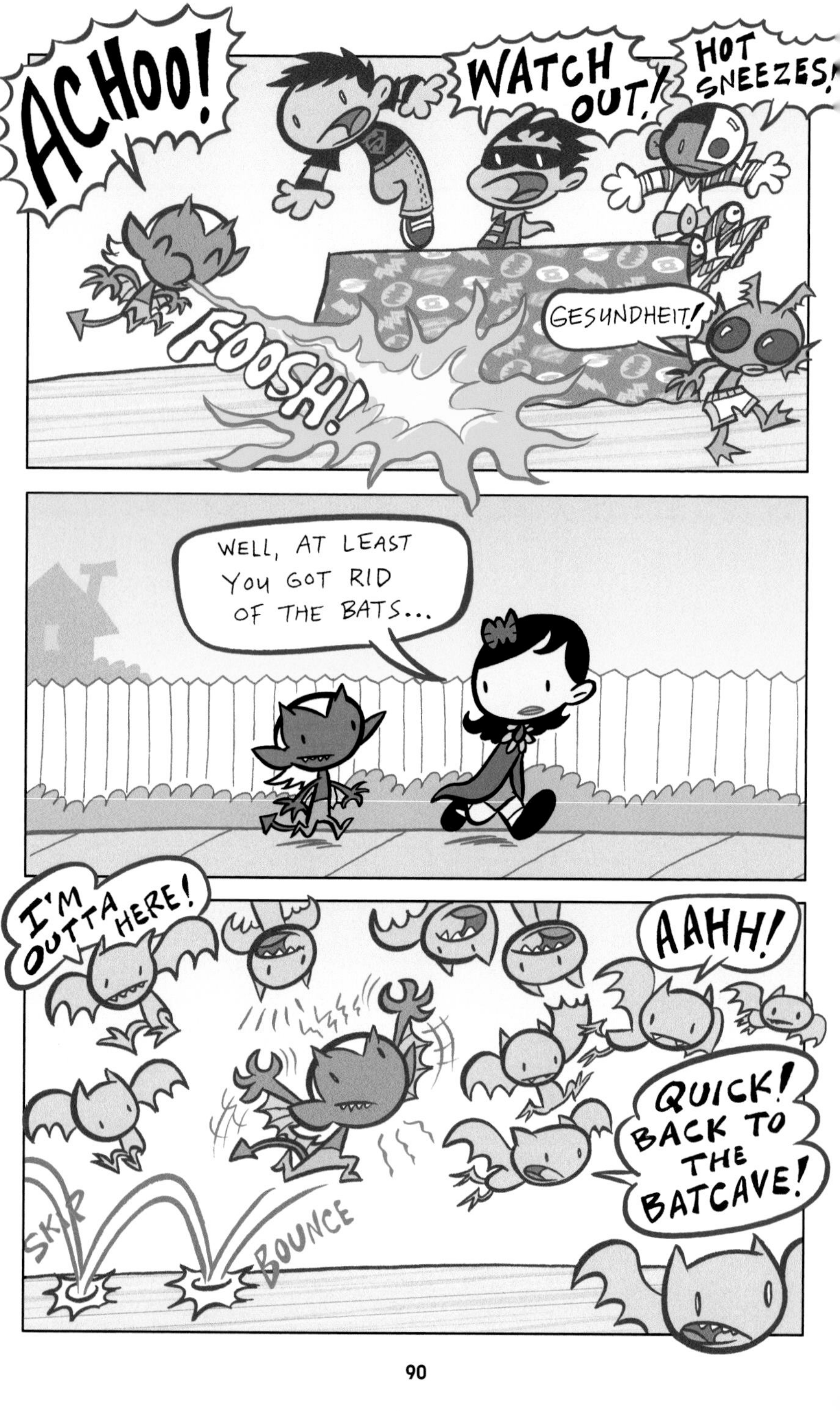
ACHOO!
WATCH OUT!
HOT SNEEZES!
FOOSH!
GESUNDHEIT!
WELL, AT LEAST YOU GOT RID OF THE BATS...
I'M OUTTA HERE!
AAHH!
QUICK! BACK TO THE BATCAVE!
SKIP
BOUNCE

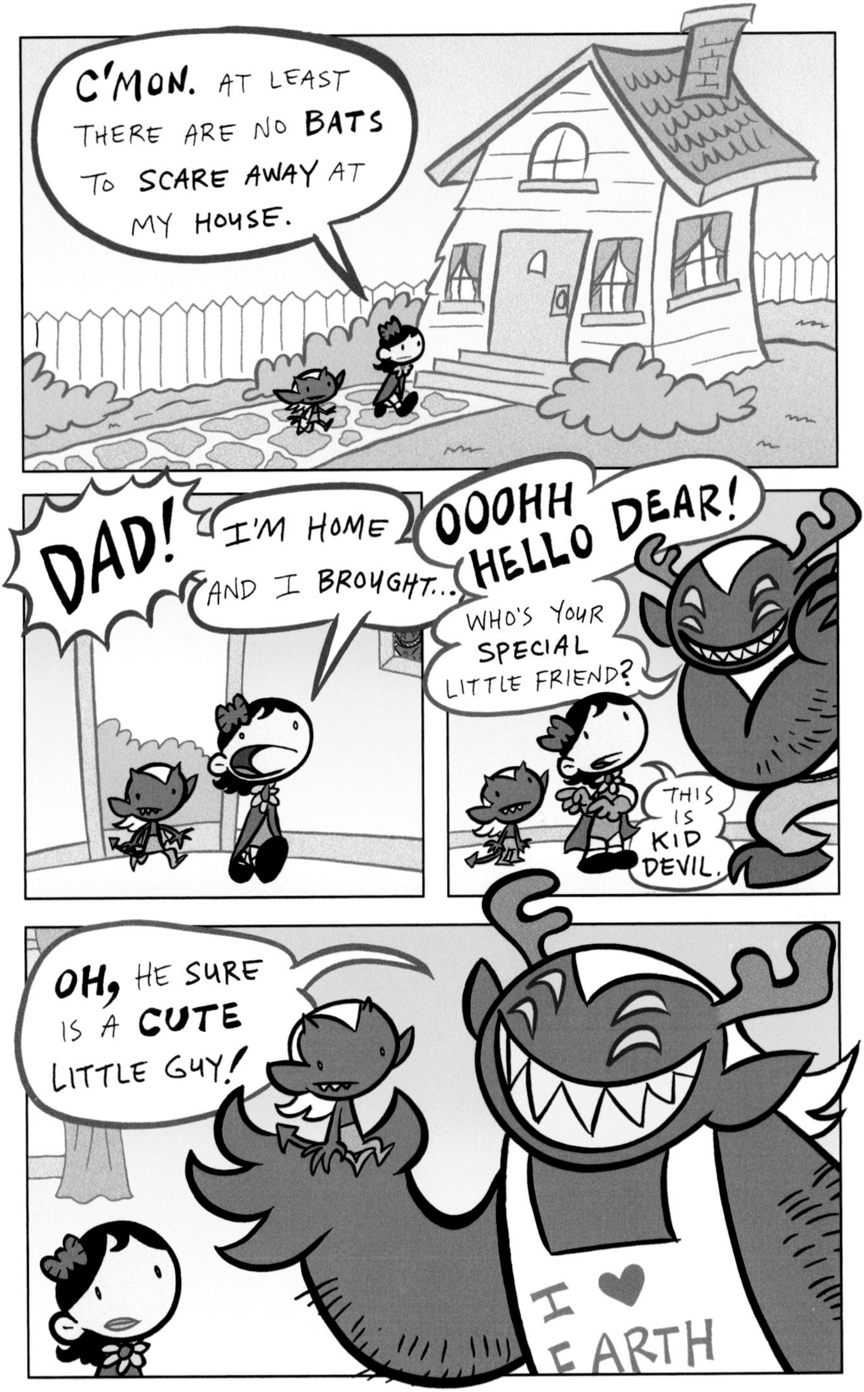
C'MON. AT LEAST THERE ARE NO BATS TO SCARE AWAY AT MY HOUSE.
DAD!
I'M HOME AND I BROUGHT...
OOOHH HELLO DEAR!
WHO'S YOUR SPECIAL LITTLE FRIEND?
THIS IS KID DEVIL.
OH, HE SURE IS A CUTE LITTLE GUY!
I ♥ EARTH

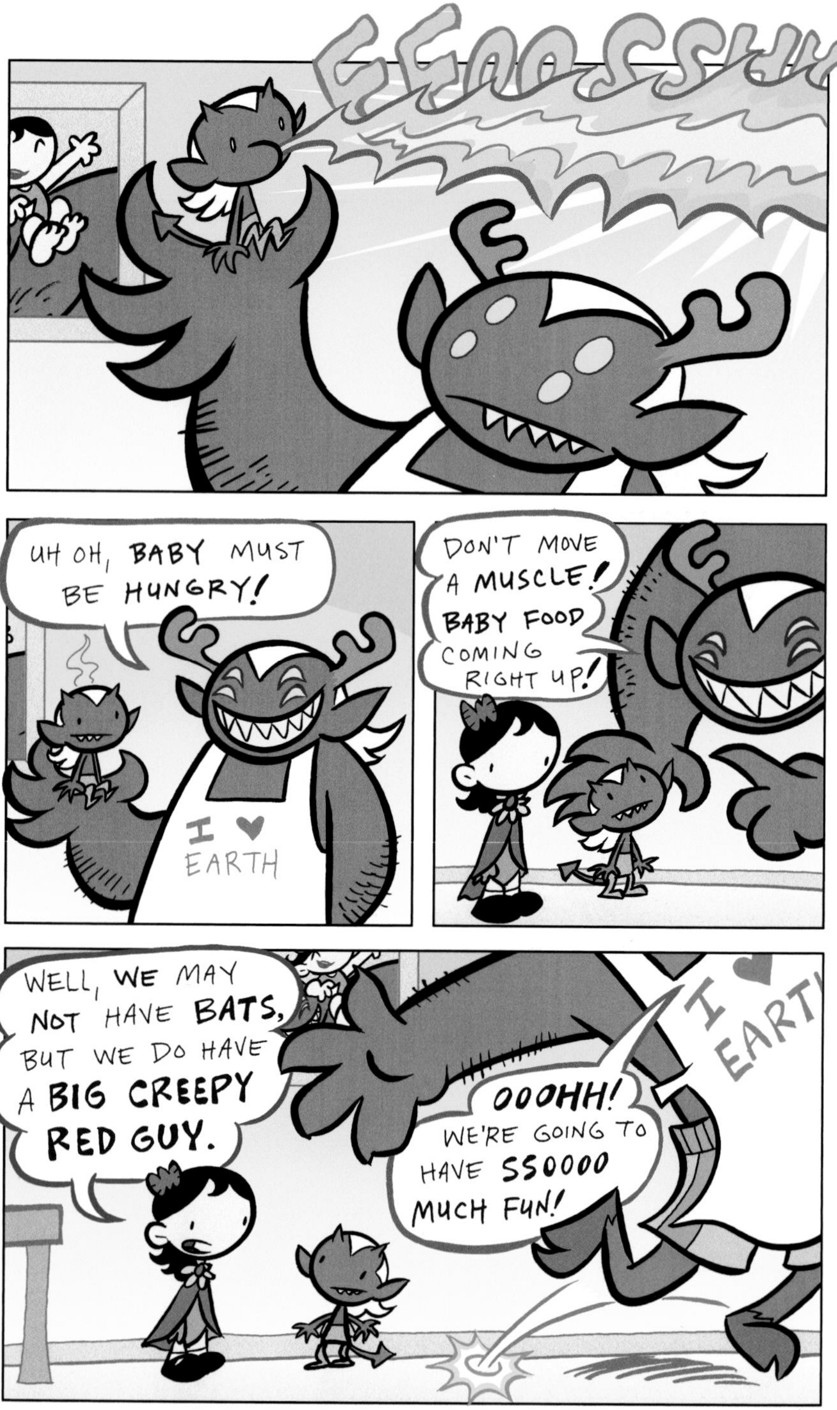
HHSSOOAAGG
UH OH, BABY MUST BE HUNGRY!
DON'T MOVE A MUSCLE! BABY FOOD COMING RIGHT UP!
I ♥ EARTH
WELL, WE MAY NOT HAVE BATS, BUT WE DO HAVE A BIG CREEPY RED GUY.
OOOHH! WE'RE GOING TO HAVE SSOOOO MUCH FUN!

—VISITATION

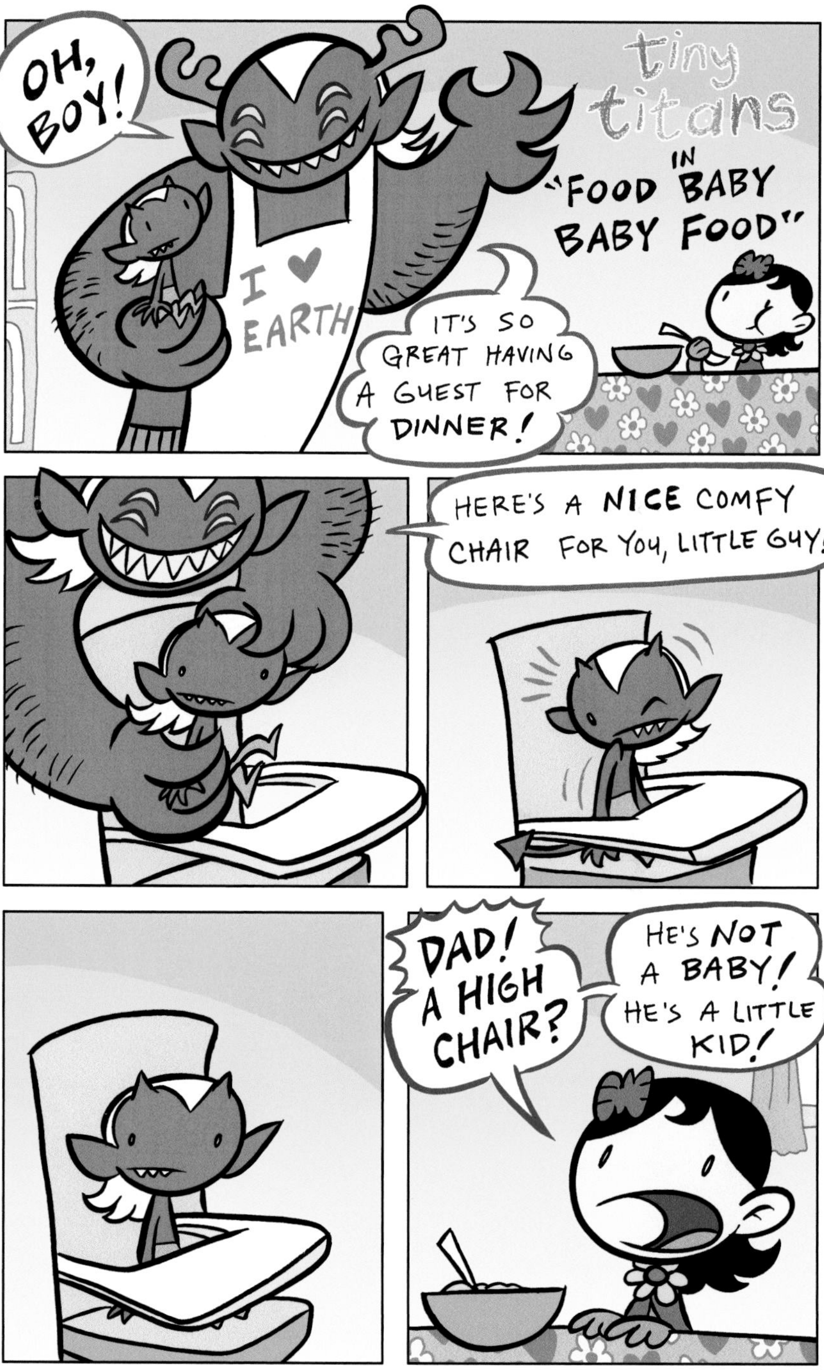
OH, BOY!
tiny titans
IN
"FOOD BABY
BABY FOOD"
I ♥ EARTH
IT'S SO GREAT HAVING A GUEST FOR DINNER!
HERE'S A NICE COMFY CHAIR FOR YOU, LITTLE GUY!
DAD! A HIGH CHAIR?
HE'S NOT A BABY! HE'S A LITTLE KID!

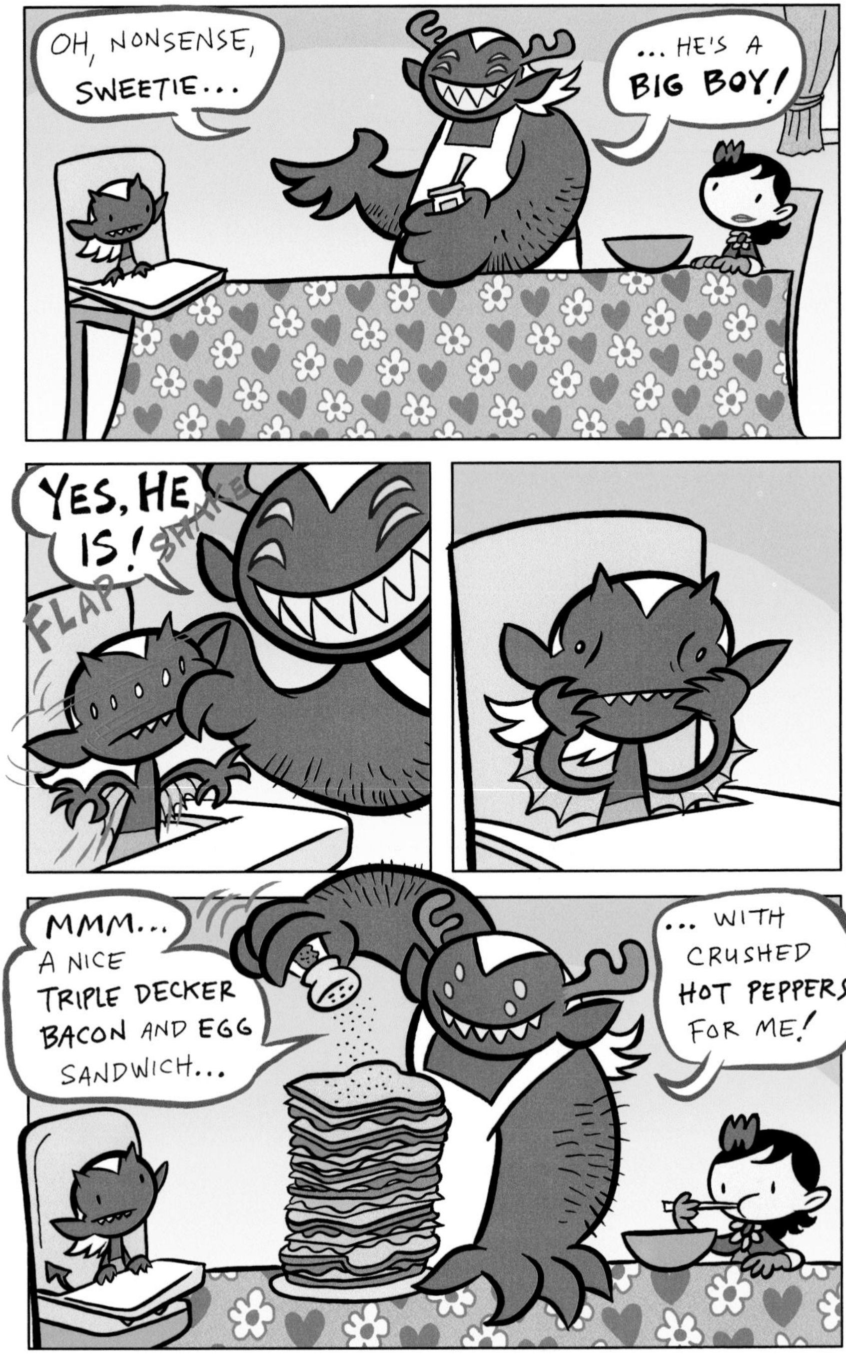
OH, NONSENSE, SWEETIE...
... HE'S A BIG BOY!
YES, HE IS!
SHAKE
FLAP
MMM... A NICE TRIPLE DECKER BACON AND EGG SANDWICH...
... WITH CRUSHED HOT PEPPERS FOR ME!

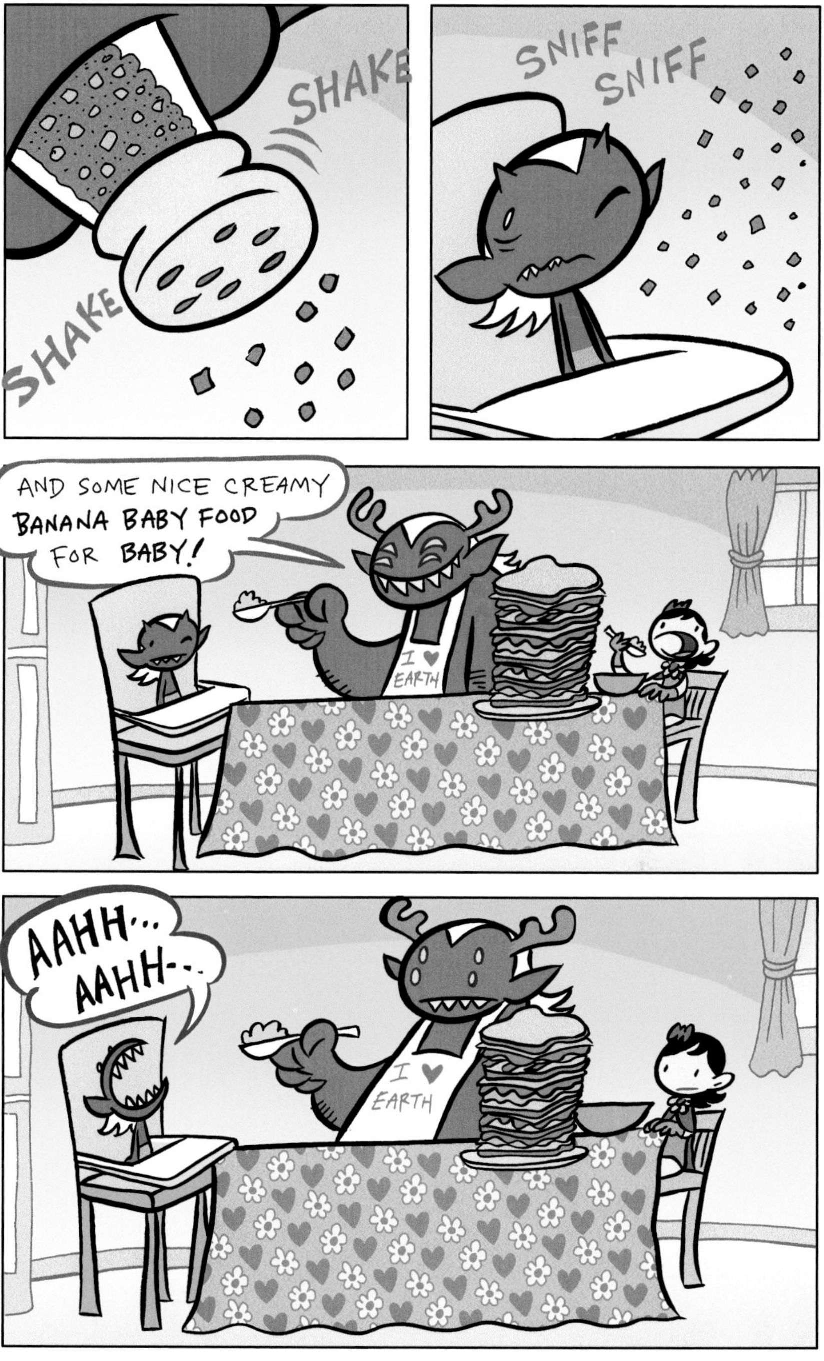
SHAKE
SHAKE
SNIFF
SNIFF
AND SOME NICE CREAMY BANANA BABY FOOD FOR BABY!
I ♥ EARTH
AAHH... AAHH---
I ♥ EARTH

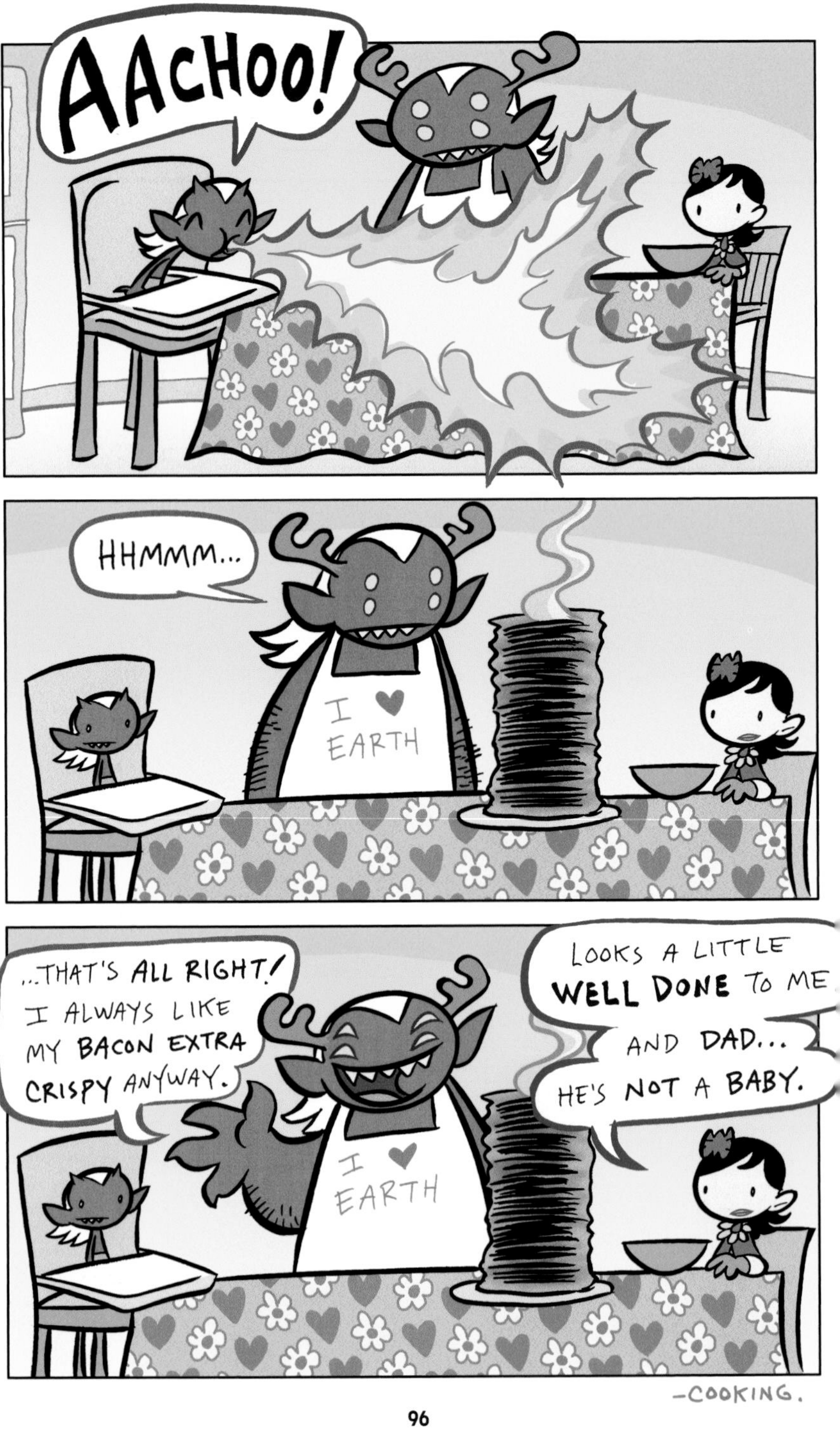
AACHOO!
HHMMM...
I ♥ EARTH
...THAT'S ALL RIGHT! I ALWAYS LIKE MY BACON EXTRA CRISPY ANYWAY.
LOOKS A LITTLE WELL DONE TO ME.
AND DAD... HE'S NOT A BABY.
I ♥ EARTH
-COOKING.

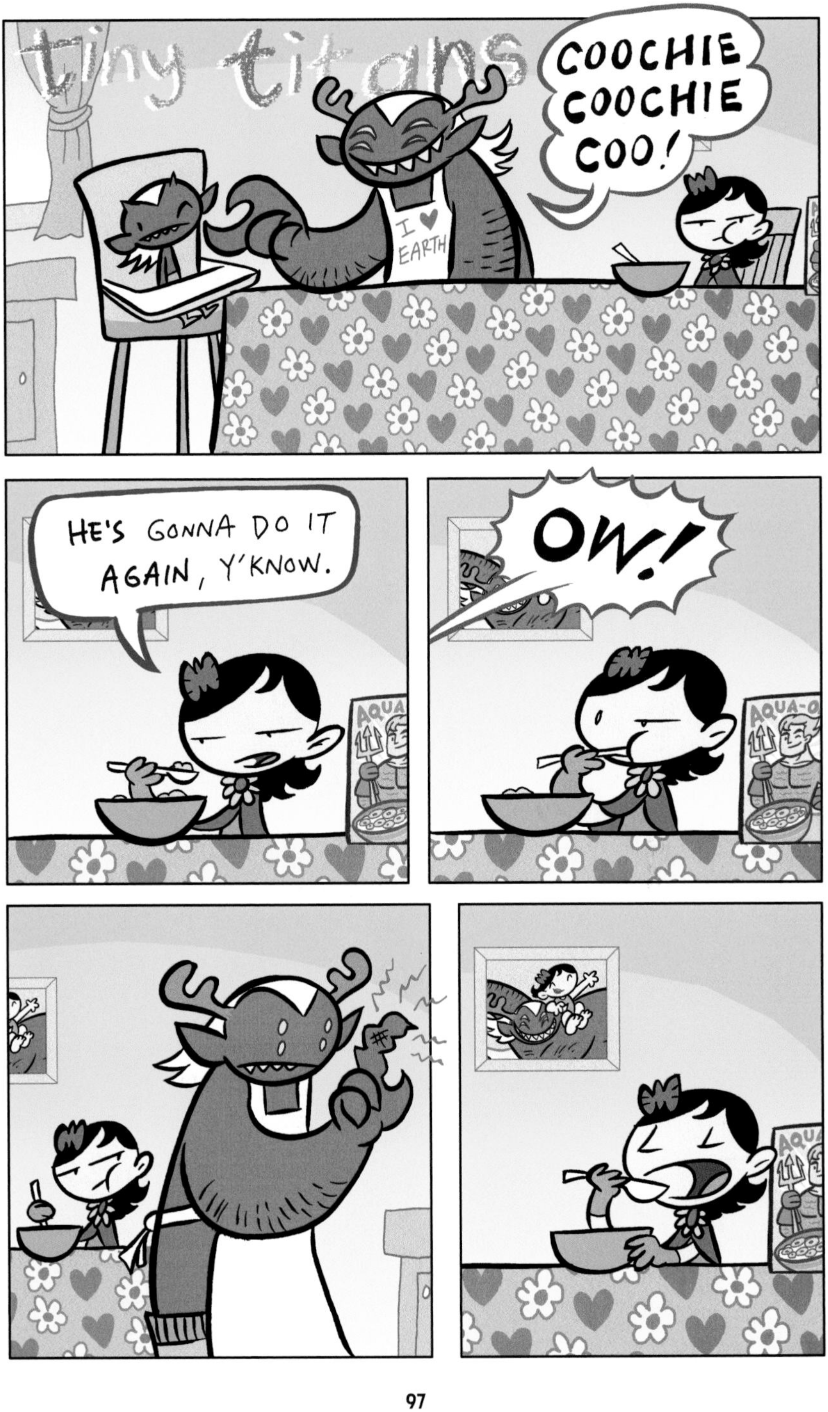
tiny titans
COOCHIE COOCHIE COO!
I ♥ EARTH
HE'S GONNA DO IT AGAIN, Y'KNOW.
OW!
AQUA-O

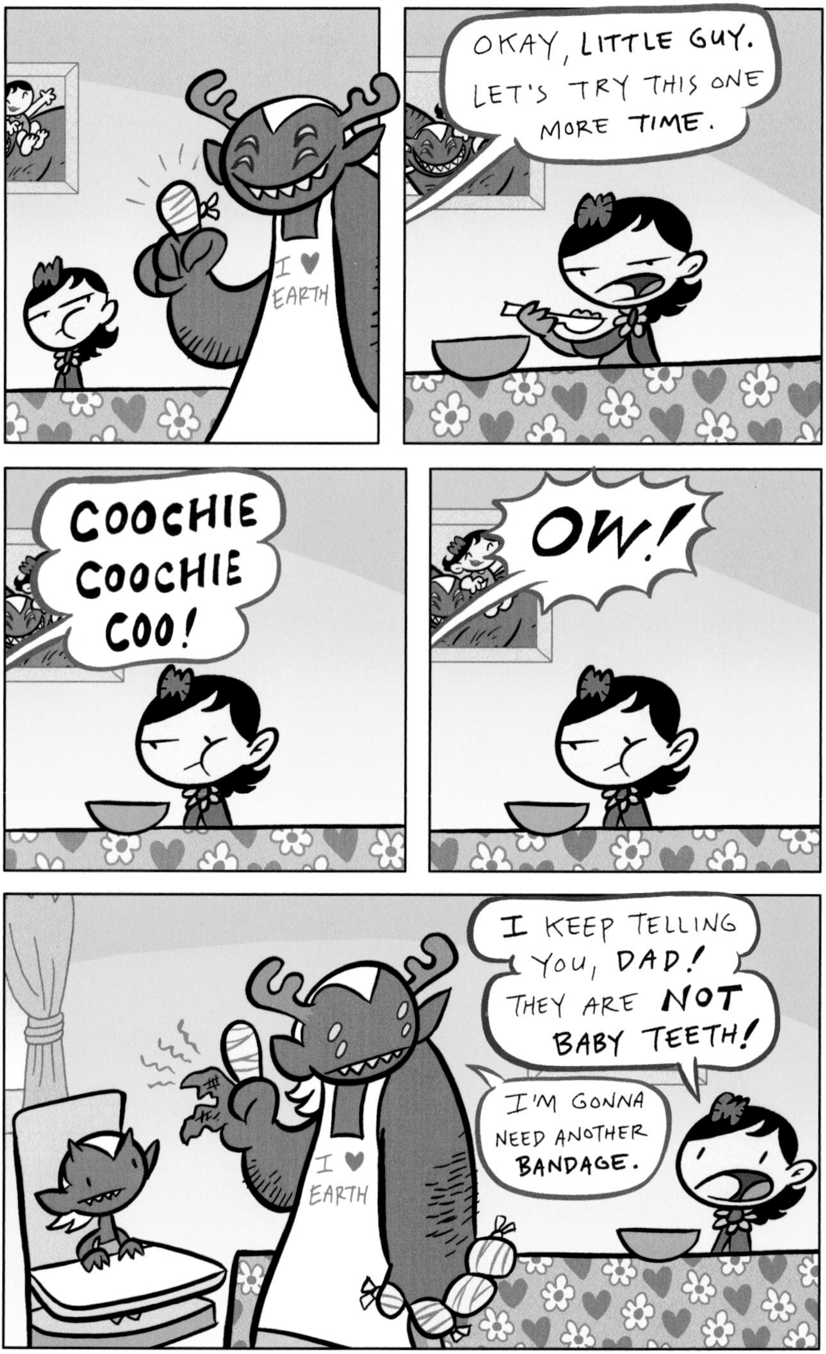

I ♥ EARTH
OKAY, LITTLE GUY. LET'S TRY THIS ONE MORE TIME.
COOCHIE COOCHIE COO!
OW!
I KEEP TELLING YOU, DAD! THEY ARE NOT BABY TEETH!
I'M GONNA NEED ANOTHER BANDAGE.
I ♥ EARTH

—BITE.

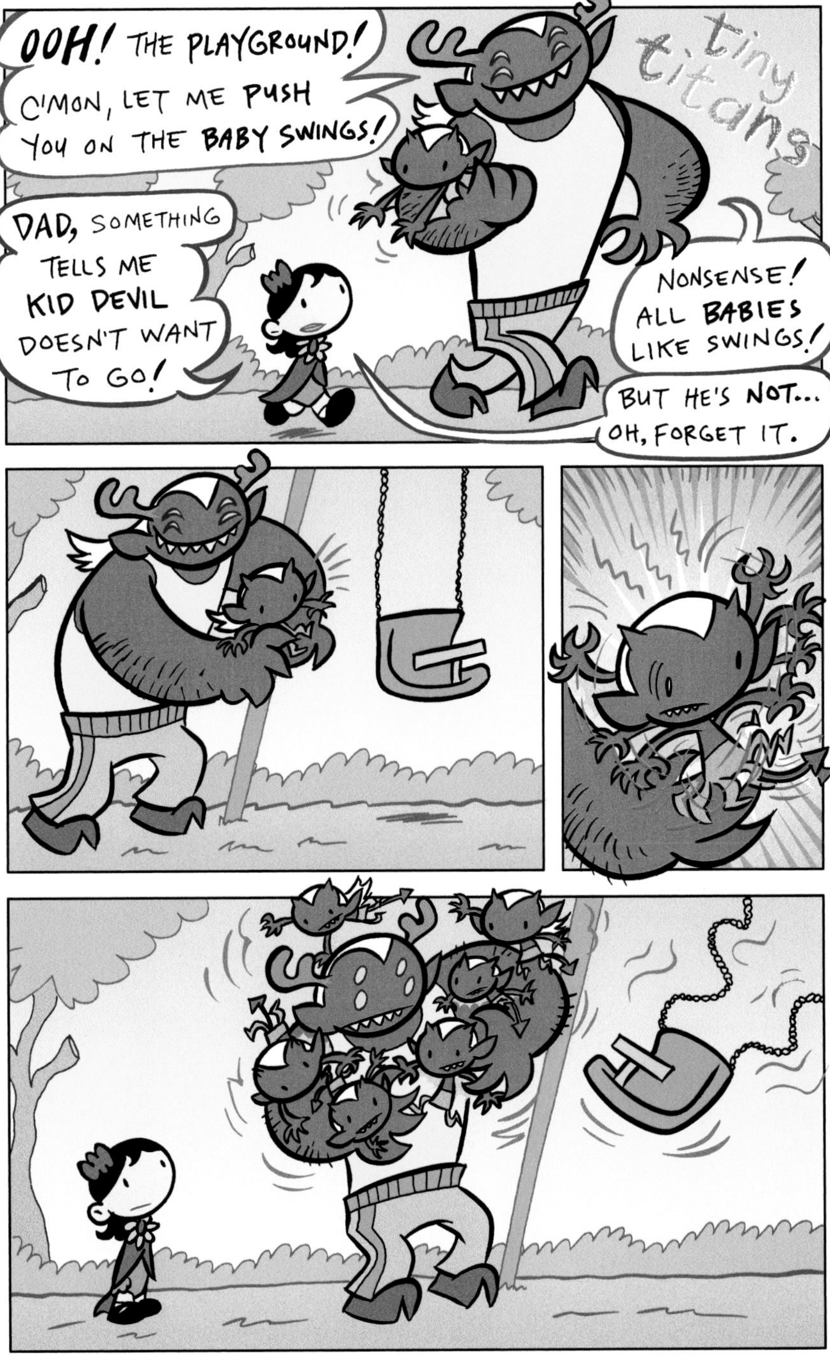
OOH! THE PLAYGROUND!
C'MON, LET ME PUSH YOU ON THE BABY SWINGS!
tiny titans
DAD, SOMETHING TELLS ME KID DEVIL DOESN'T WANT TO GO!
NONSENSE! ALL BABIES LIKE SWINGS!
BUT HE'S NOT... OH, FORGET IT.

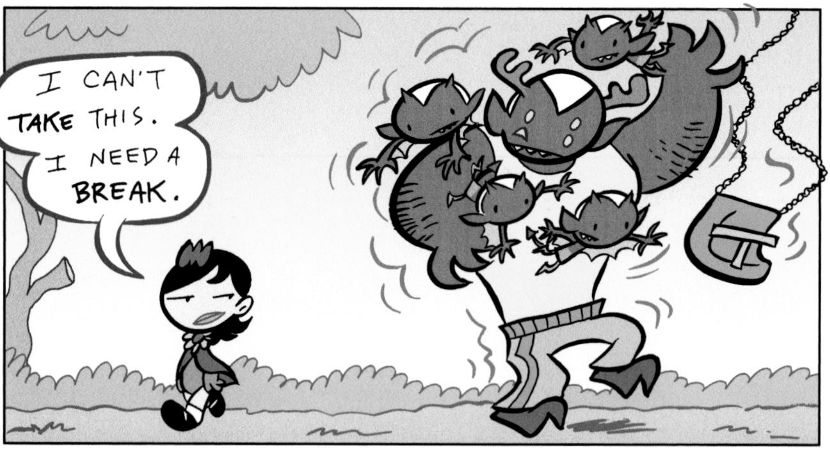
I CAN'T TAKE THIS. I NEED A BREAK.

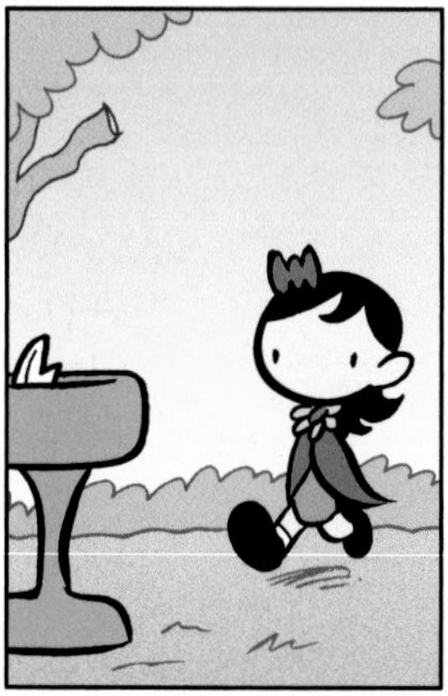

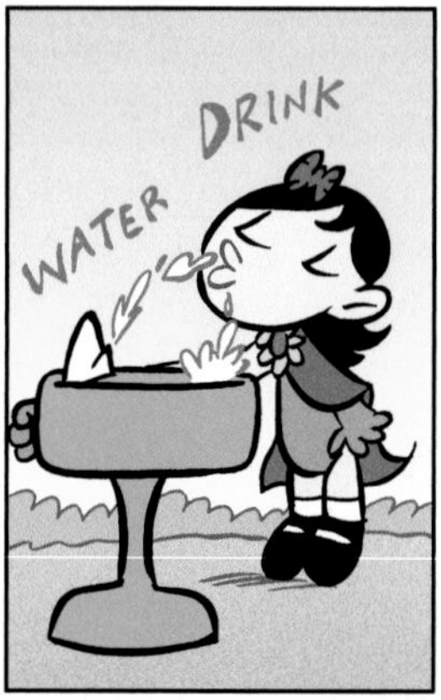
DRINK
WATER

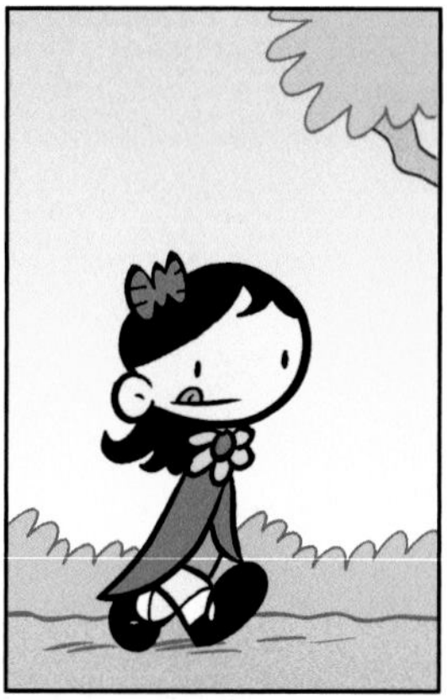

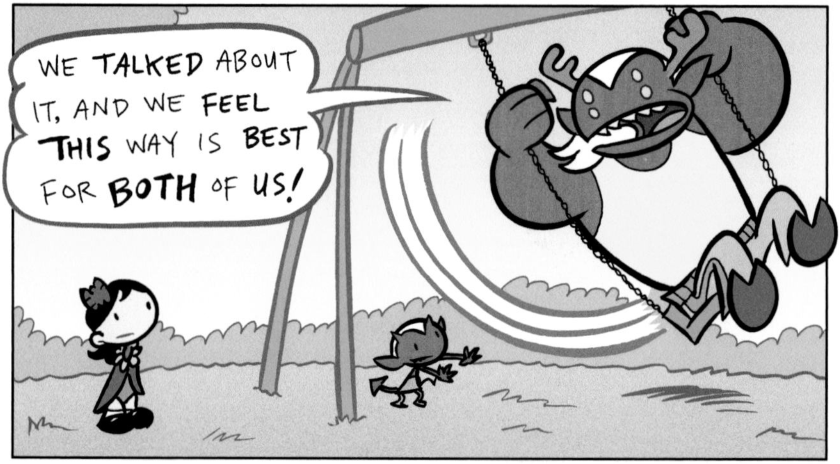
WE TALKED ABOUT IT, AND WE FEEL THIS WAY IS BEST FOR BOTH OF US!

—SHARE IT!

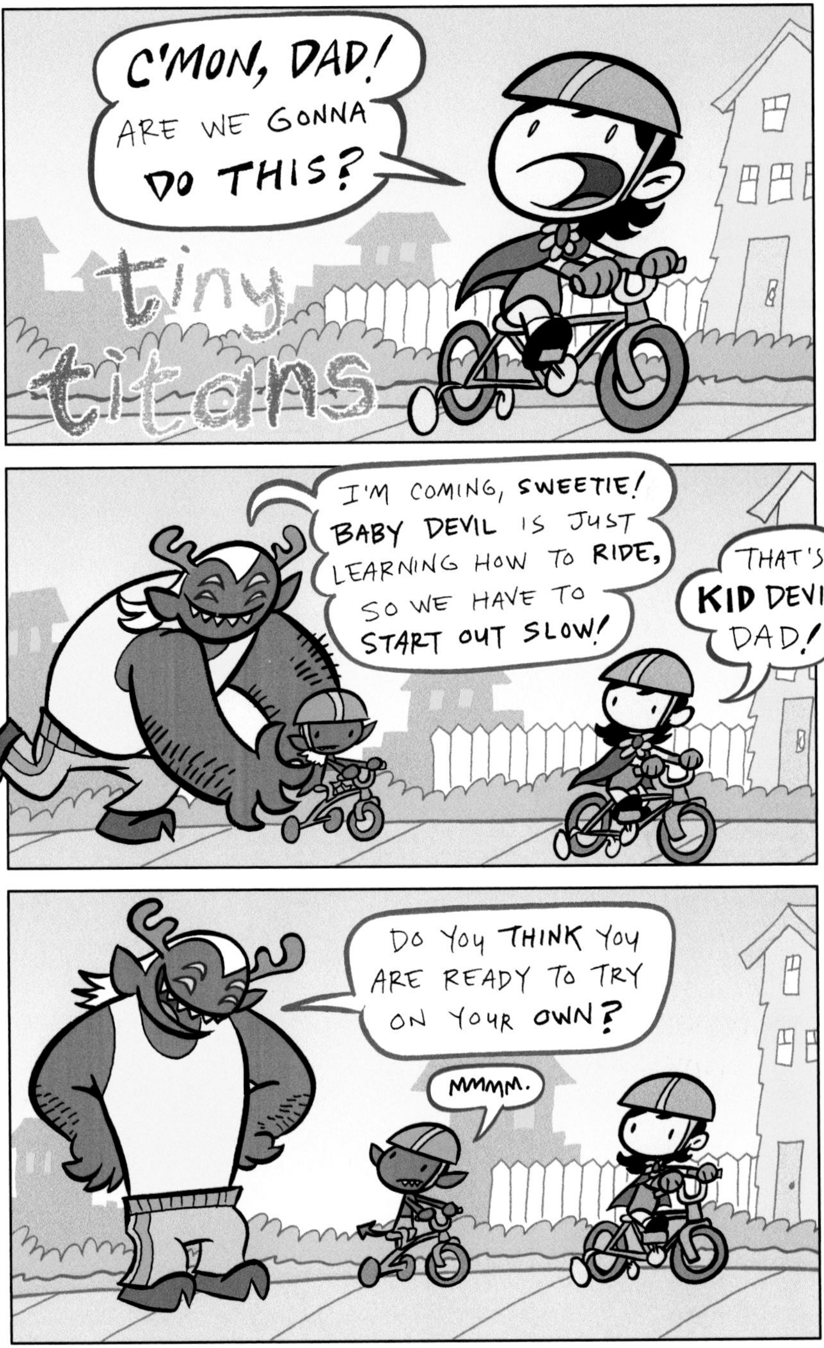

C'MON, DAD! ARE WE GONNA DO THIS?
tiny titans
I'M COMING, SWEETIE! BABY DEVIL IS JUST LEARNING HOW TO RIDE, SO WE HAVE TO START OUT SLOW!
THAT'S KID DEVIL, DAD!
DO YOU THINK YOU ARE READY TO TRY ON YOUR OWN?
MMMM.

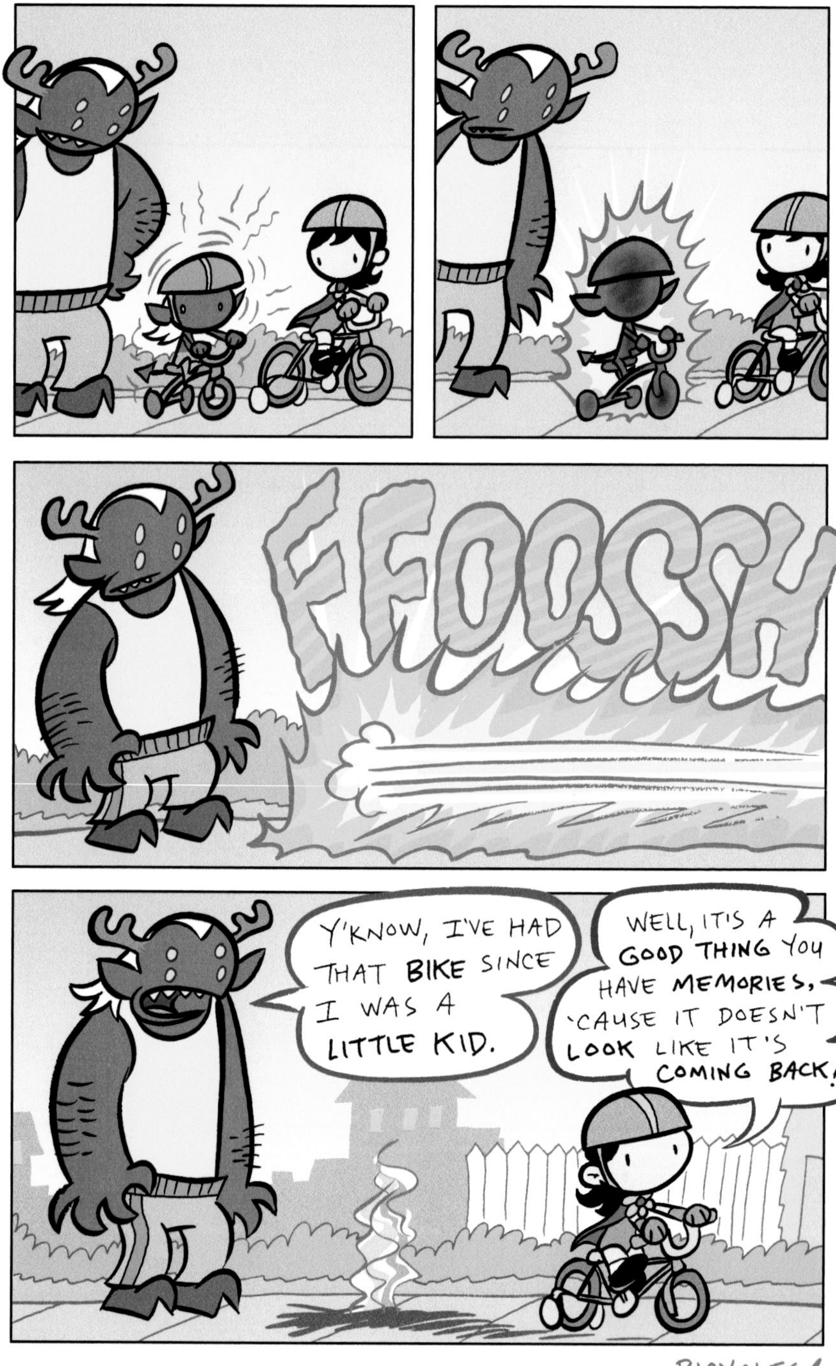
FFOOSCH
Y'KNOW, I'VE HAD THAT BIKE SINCE I WAS A LITTLE KID.
WELL, IT'S A GOOD THING YOU HAVE MEMORIES, 'CAUSE IT DOESN'T LOOK LIKE IT'S COMING BACK!
-BICYCLES!

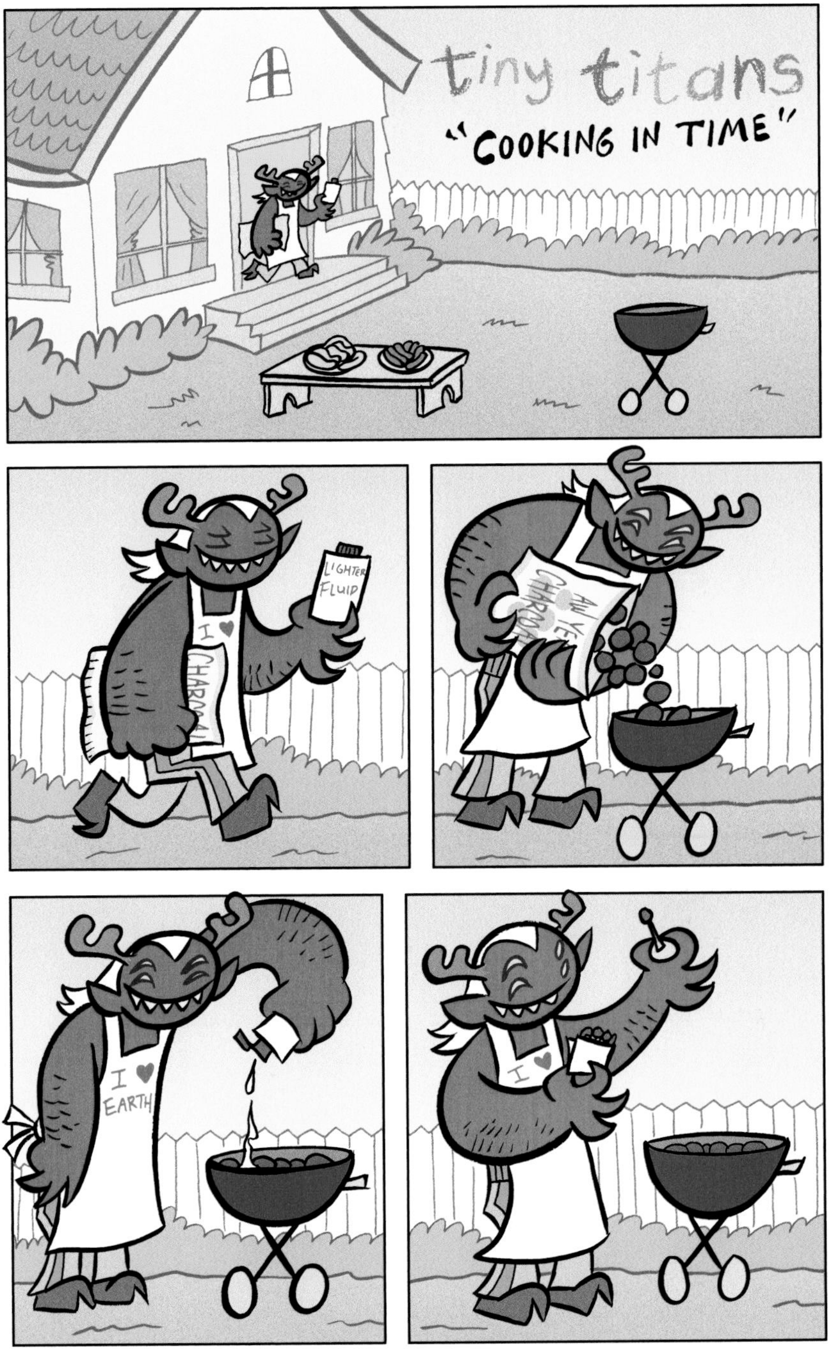
tiny titans
"COOKING IN TIME"
LIGHTER FLUID
I ♥
CHARCOAL
AW YEAH CHARCOA
I ♥ EARTH

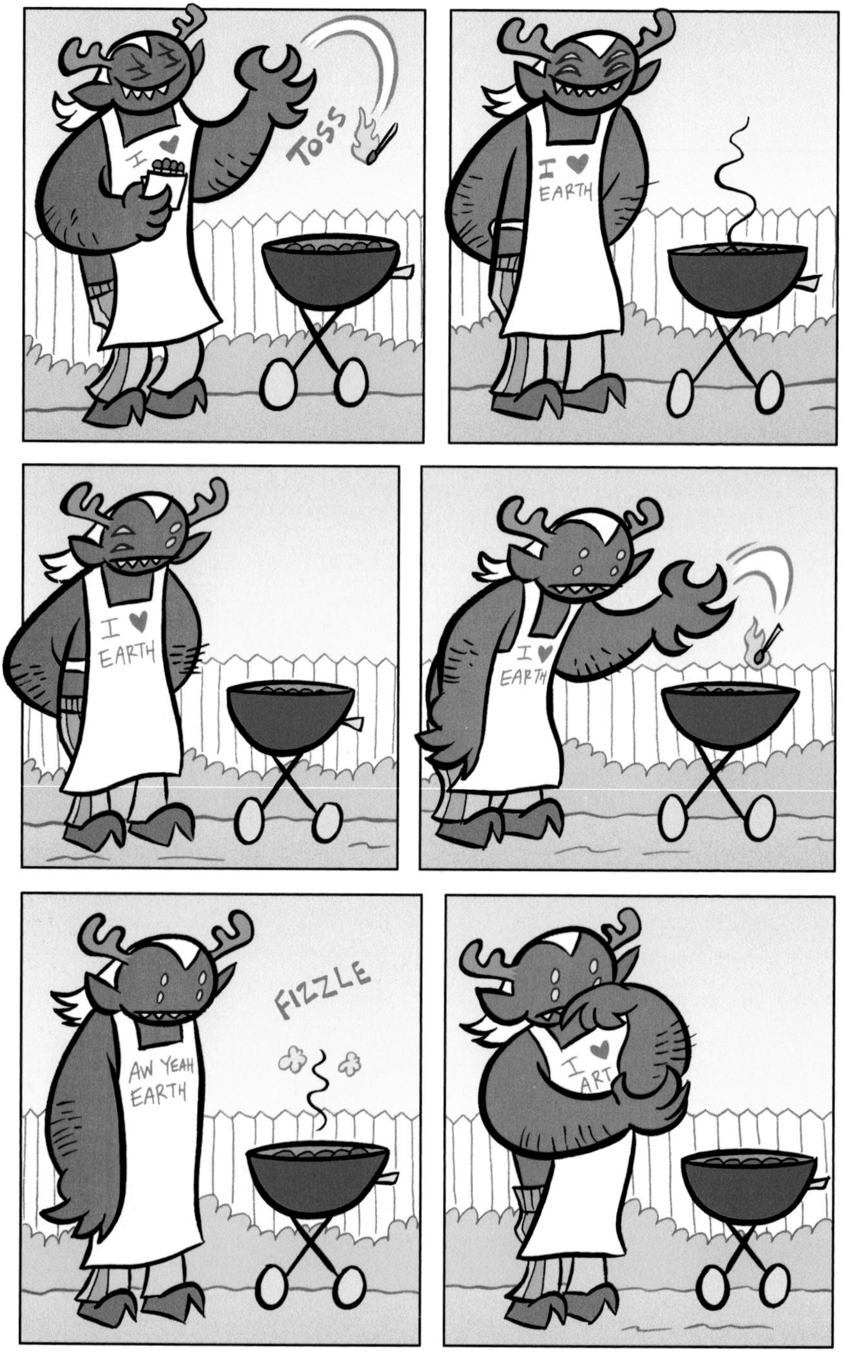
TOSS
I ♥
I ♥ EARTH
I ♥ EARTH
I ♥ EARTH
FIZZLE
AW YEAH EARTH
I ♥ ART

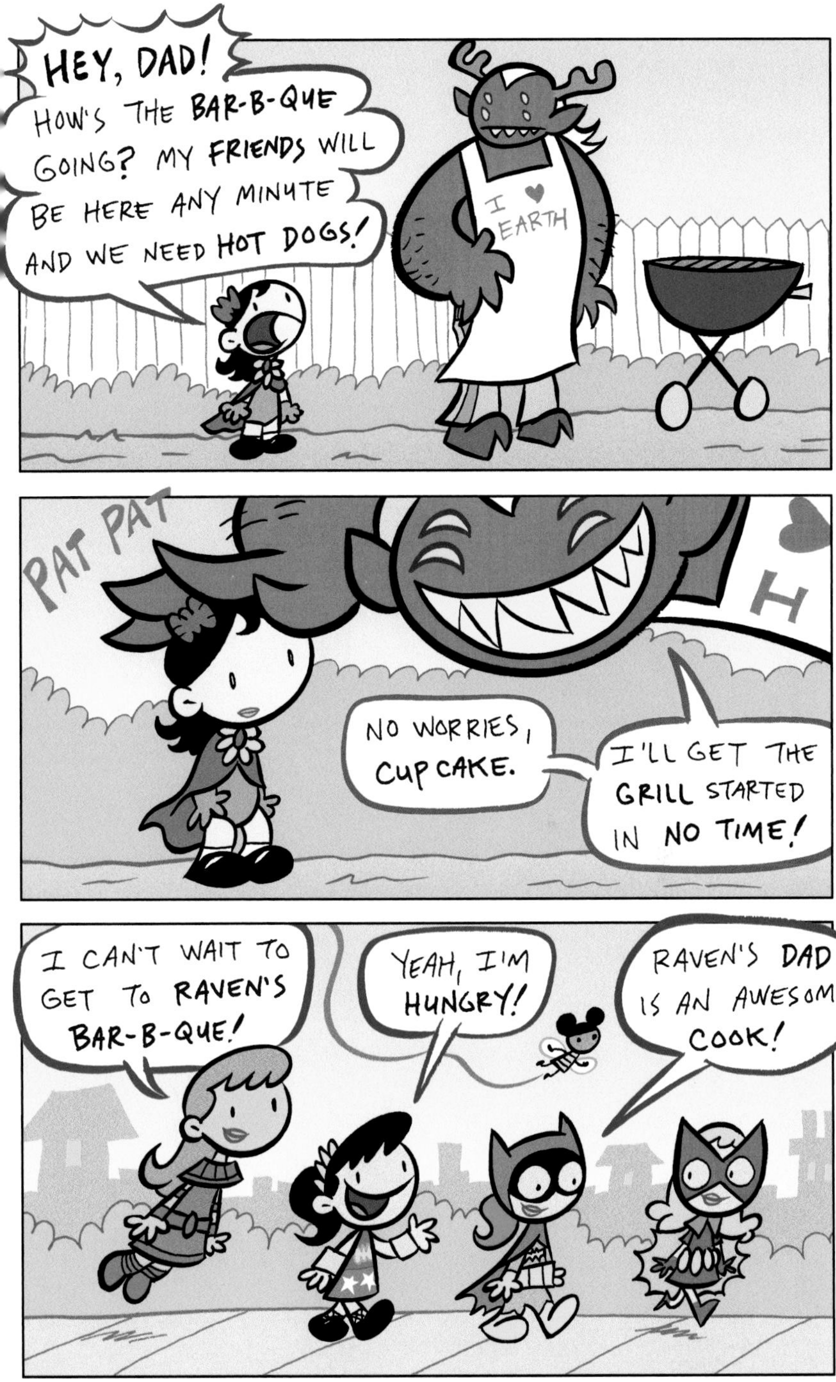
HEY, DAD!
HOW'S THE BAR-B-QUE GOING? MY FRIENDS WILL BE HERE ANY MINUTE AND WE NEED HOT DOGS!
I ♥ EARTH
PAT PAT
NO WORRIES, CUPCAKE.
I'LL GET THE GRILL STARTED IN NO TIME!
I CAN'T WAIT TO GET TO RAVEN'S BAR-B-QUE!
YEAH, I'M HUNGRY!
RAVEN'S DAD IS AN AWESOME COOK!

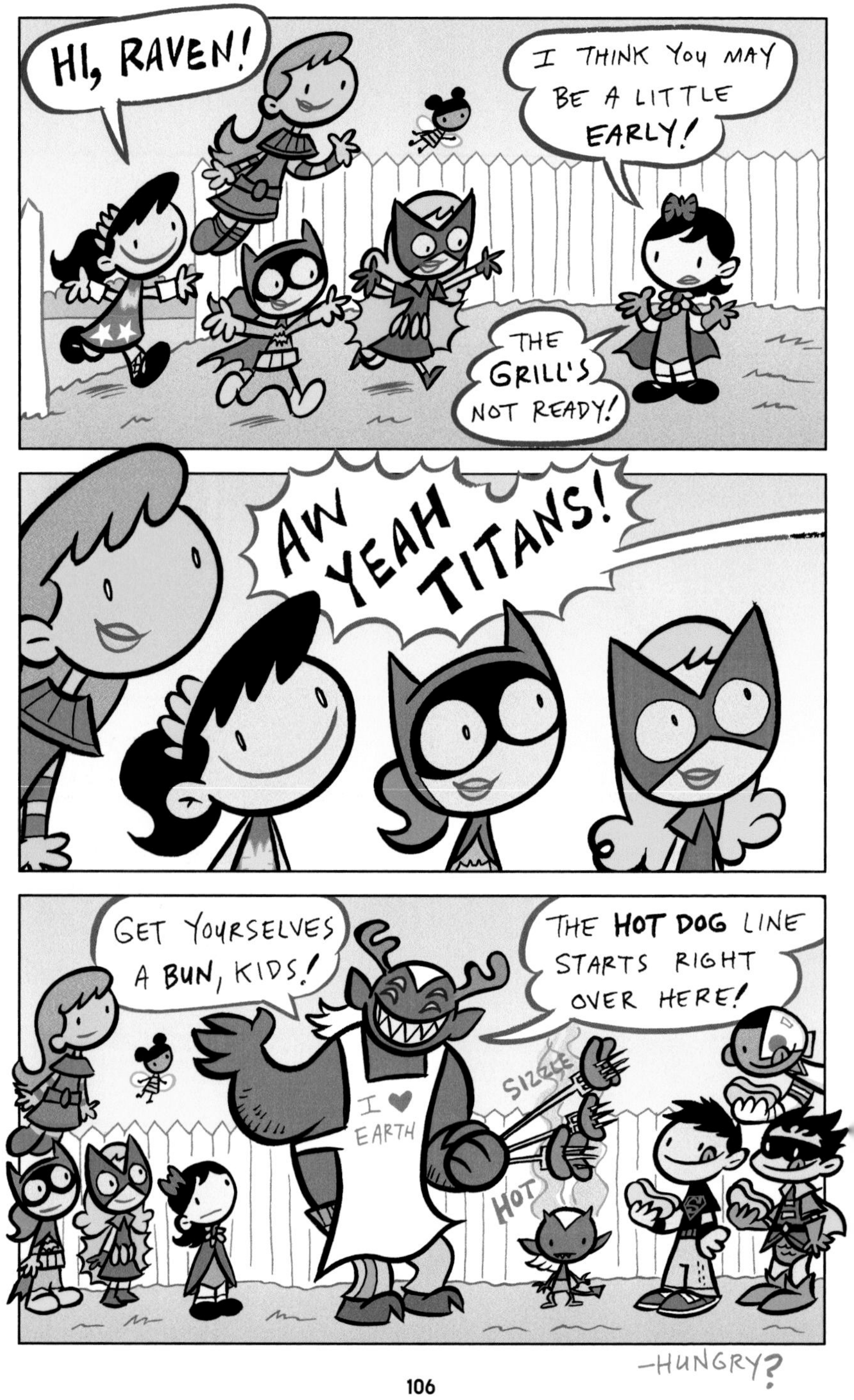
HI, RAVEN!
I THINK YOU MAY BE A LITTLE EARLY!
THE GRILL'S NOT READY!
AW YEAH TITANS!
GET YOURSELVES A BUN, KIDS!
THE HOT DOG LINE STARTS RIGHT OVER HERE!
SIZZLE
HOT
I ♥ EARTH

–HUNGRY?

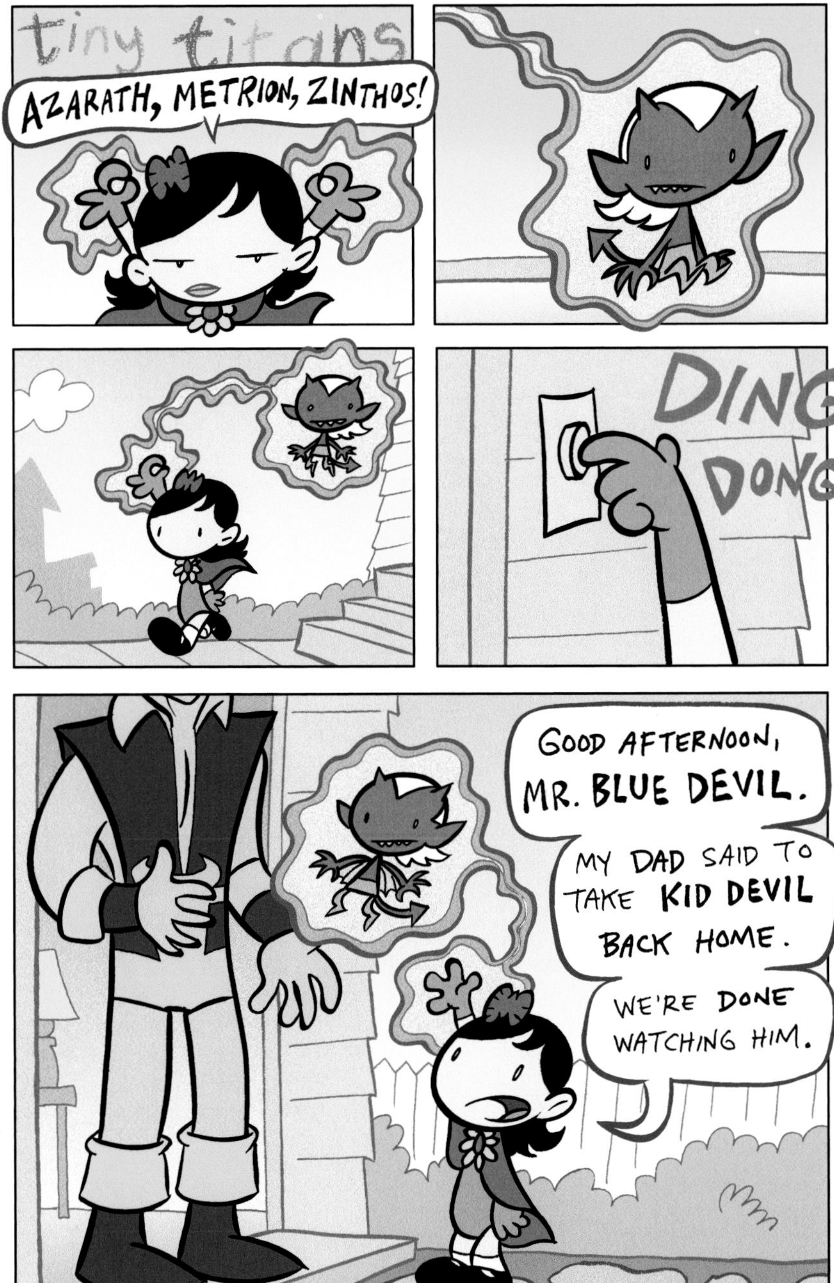
tiny titans
AZARATH, METRION, ZINTHOS!
DING DONG
GOOD AFTERNOON, MR. BLUE DEVIL.
MY DAD SAID TO TAKE KID DEVIL BACK HOME.
WE'RE DONE WATCHING HIM.

—TAKIN' IT HOME!

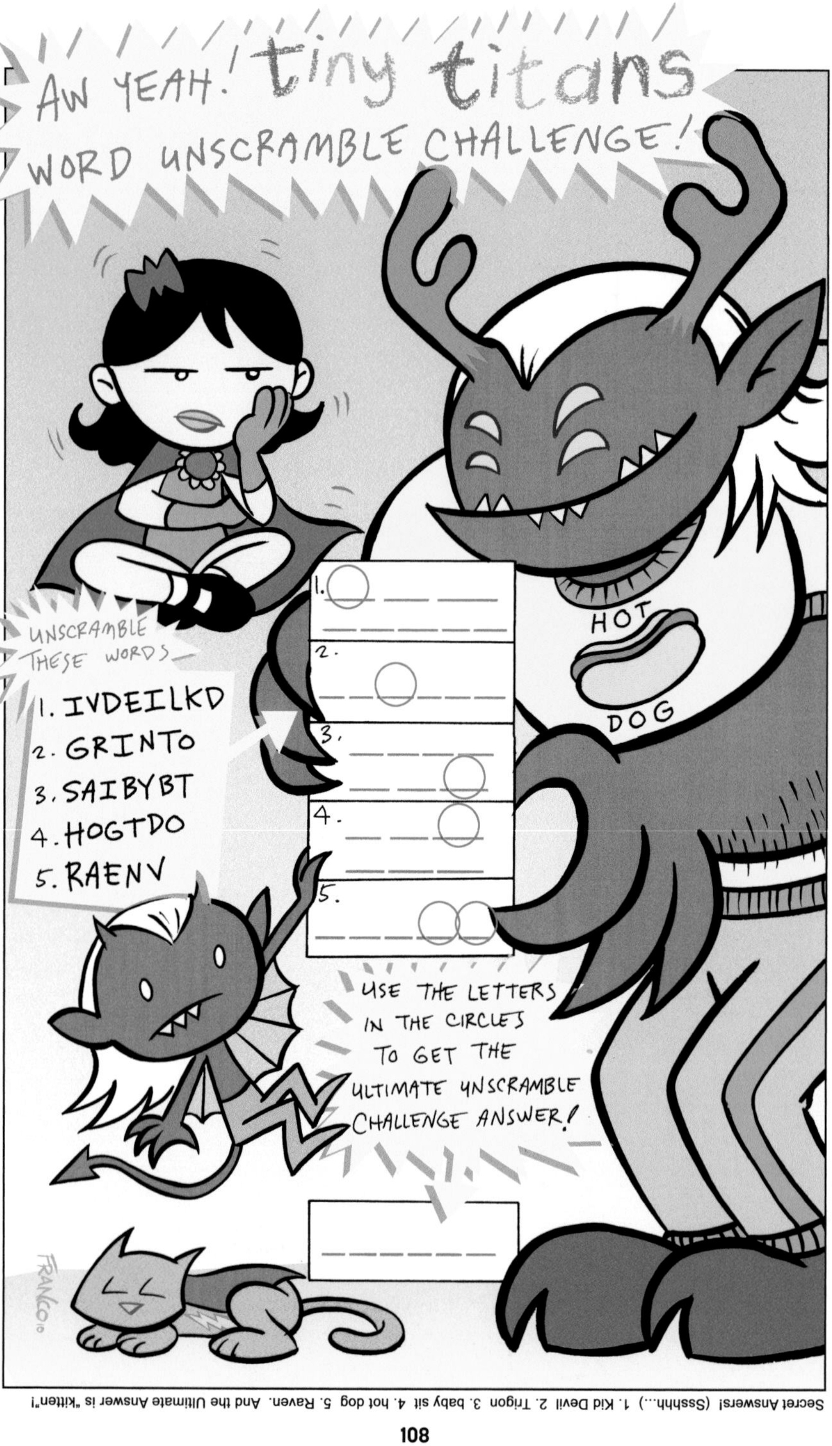
AW YEAH! tiny titans
WORD UNSCRAMBLE CHALLENGE!
UNSCRAMBLE THESE WORDS
1. IVDEILKD
2. GRINTO
3. SAIBYBT
4. HOGTDO
5. RAENV
1.
2.
3.
4.
5.
HOT DOG
USE THE LETTERS IN THE CIRCLES TO GET THE ULTIMATE UNSCRAMBLE CHALLENGE ANSWER!
FRANCO10

Secret Answers! (Ssshhh...) 1. Kid Devil 2. Trigon 3. baby sit 4. hot dog 5. Raven. And the Ultimate Answer is "kitten"!

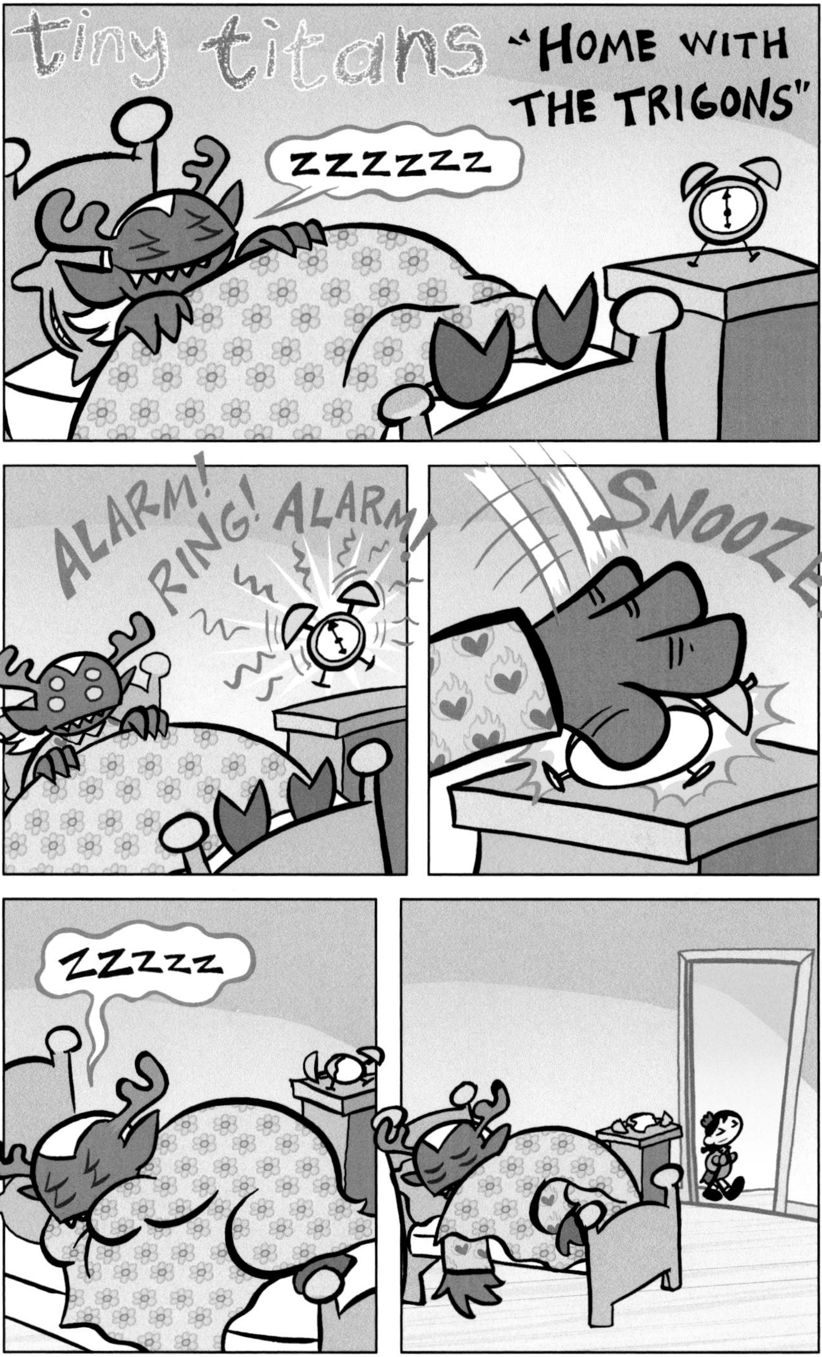
tiny titans
"HOME WITH THE TRIGONS"
ZZZZZZ
ALARM! RING! ALARM!
SNOOZE!
ZZZZZ

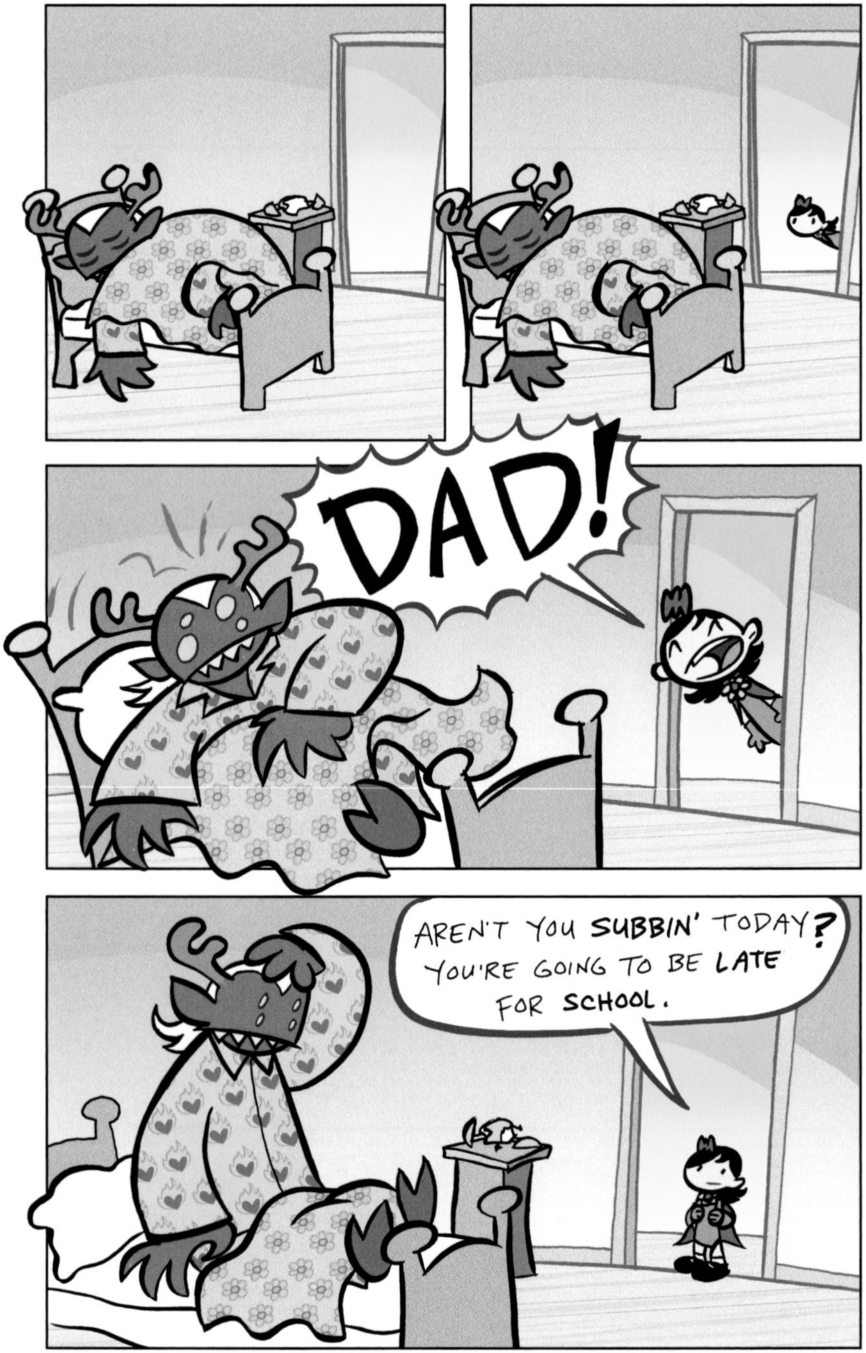
DAD!
AREN'T YOU SUBBIN' TODAY? YOU'RE GOING TO BE LATE FOR SCHOOL.

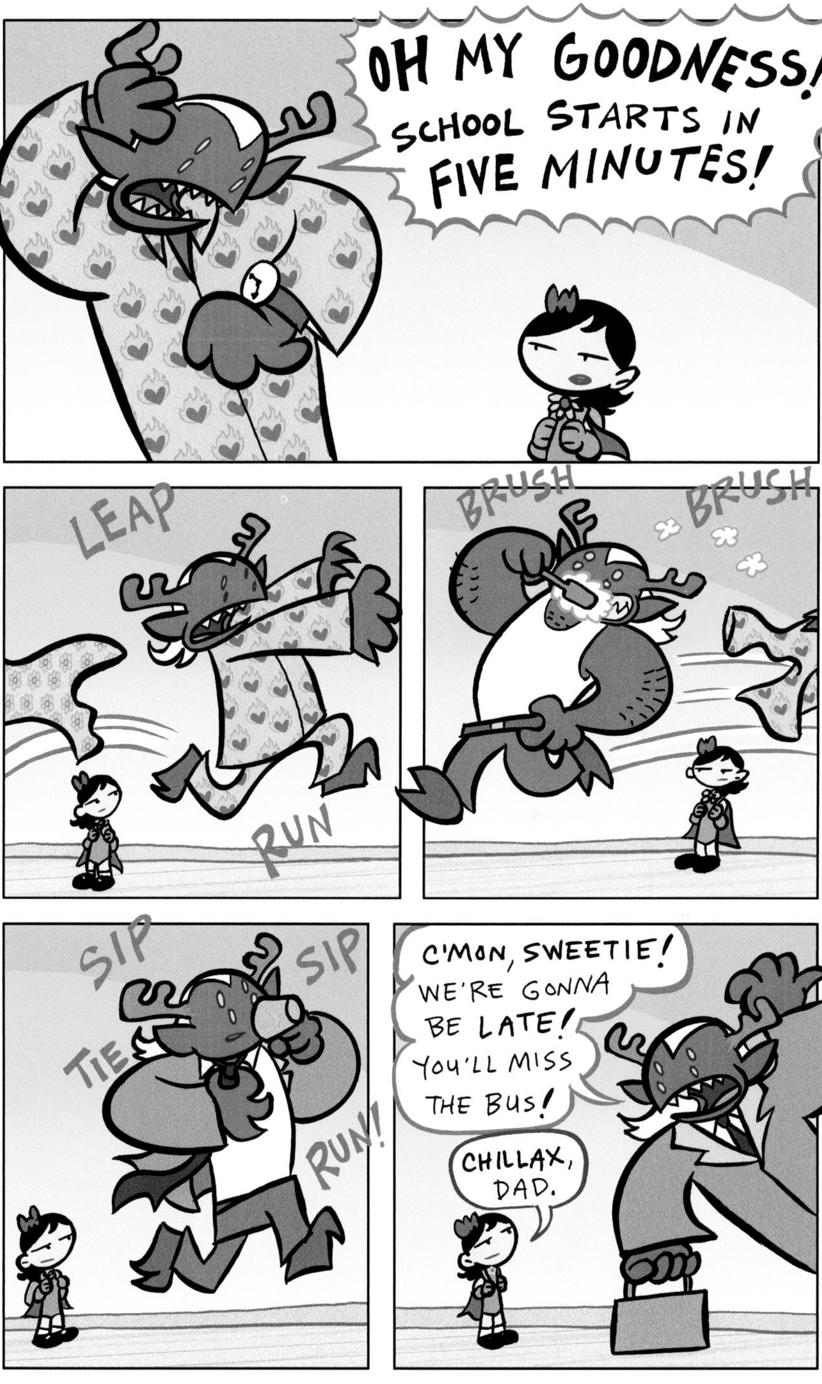

OH MY GOODNESS! SCHOOL STARTS IN FIVE MINUTES!
LEAP
RUN
BRUSH
BRUSH
SIP
SIP
TIE
RUN!
C'MON, SWEETIE! WE'RE GONNA BE LATE! YOU'LL MISS THE BUS!
CHILLAX, DAD.

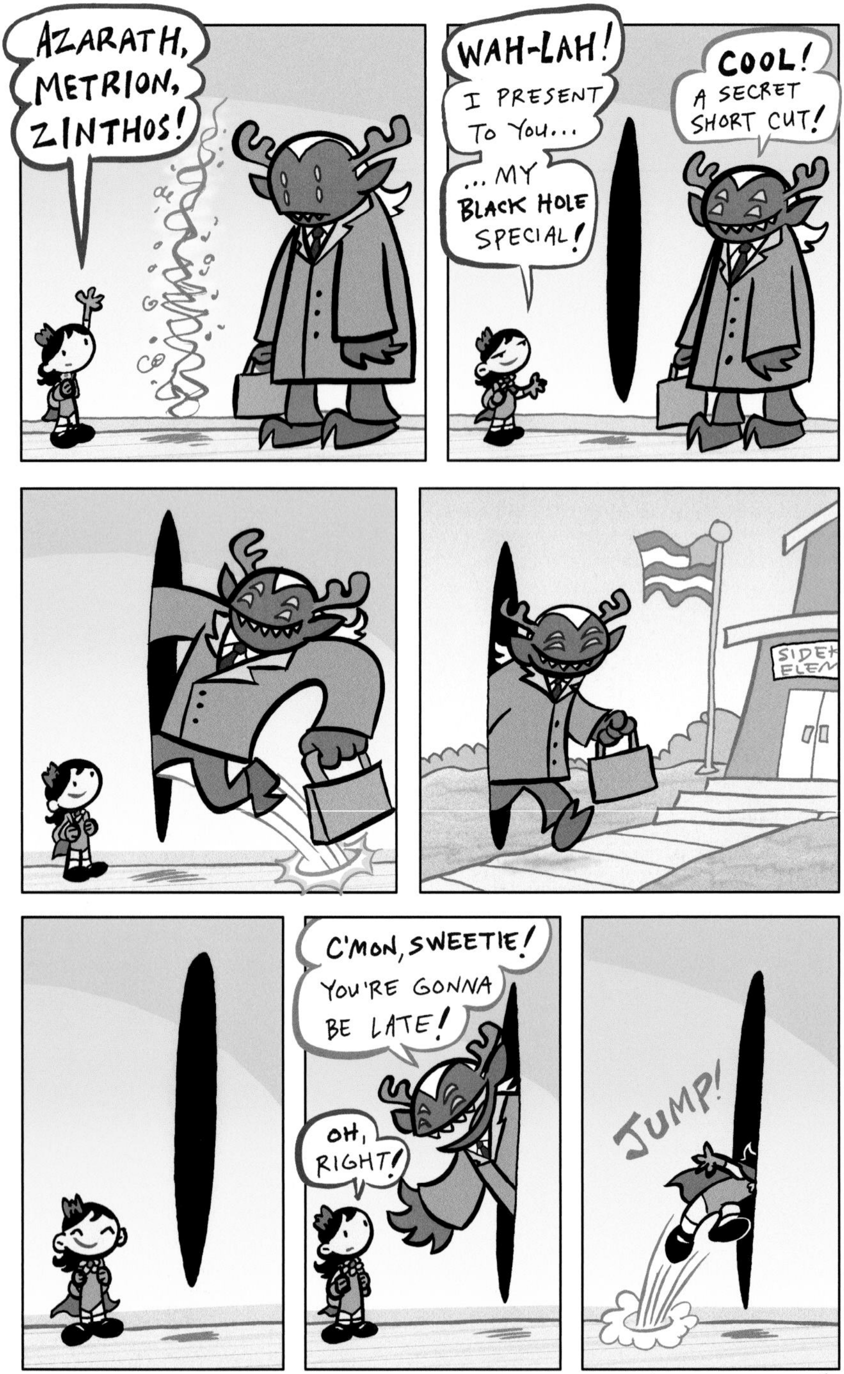
AZARATH, METRION, ZINTHOS!
WAH-LAH!
I PRESENT TO YOU...
... MY BLACK HOLE SPECIAL!
COOL! A SECRET SHORT CUT!
C'MON, SWEETIE! YOU'RE GONNA BE LATE!
OH, RIGHT!
JUMP!

-AW YEAH TELEPORT!

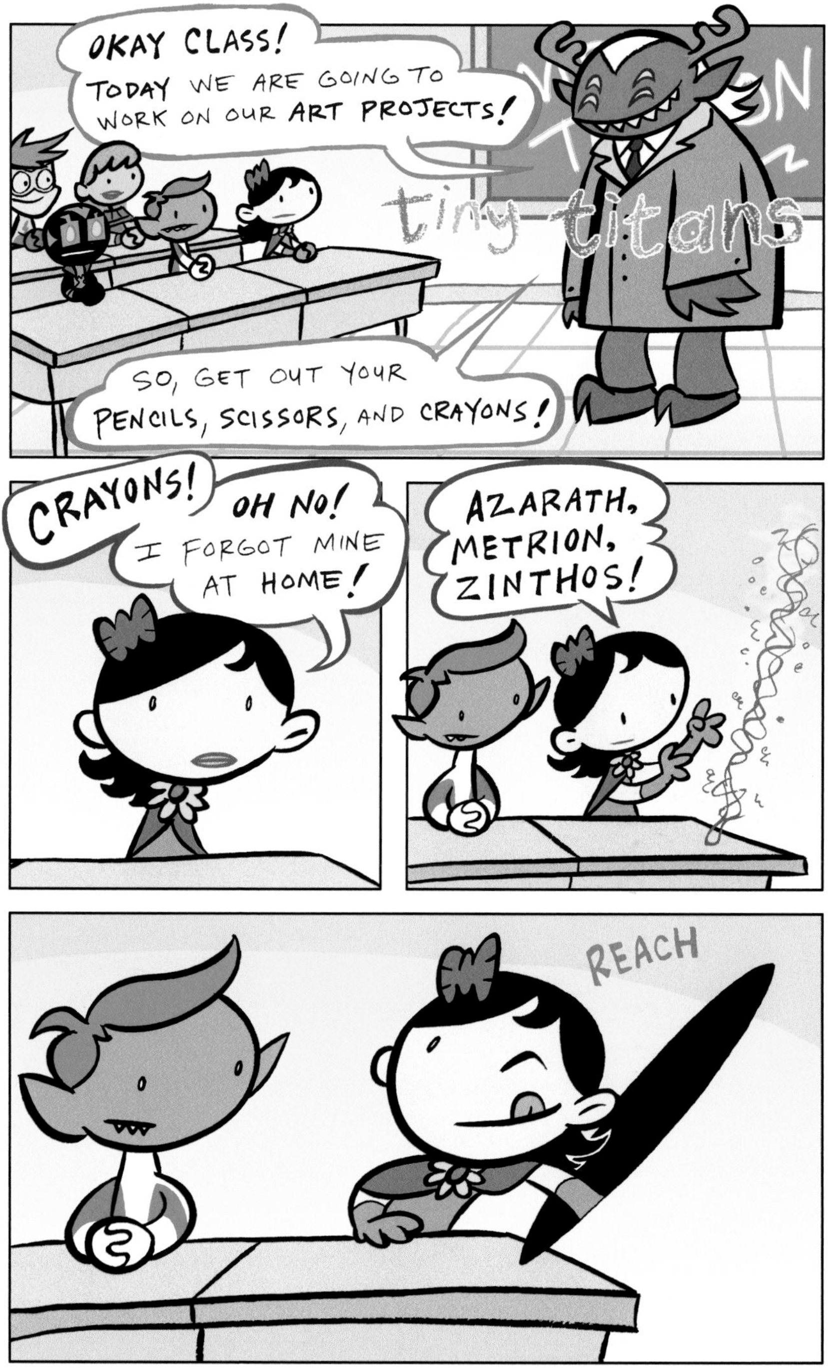
OKAY CLASS!
TODAY WE ARE GOING TO WORK ON OUR ART PROJECTS!
tiny titans
SO, GET OUT YOUR PENCILS, SCISSORS, AND CRAYONS!
CRAYONS!
OH NO! I FORGOT MINE AT HOME!
AZARATH, METRION, ZINTHOS!
REACH

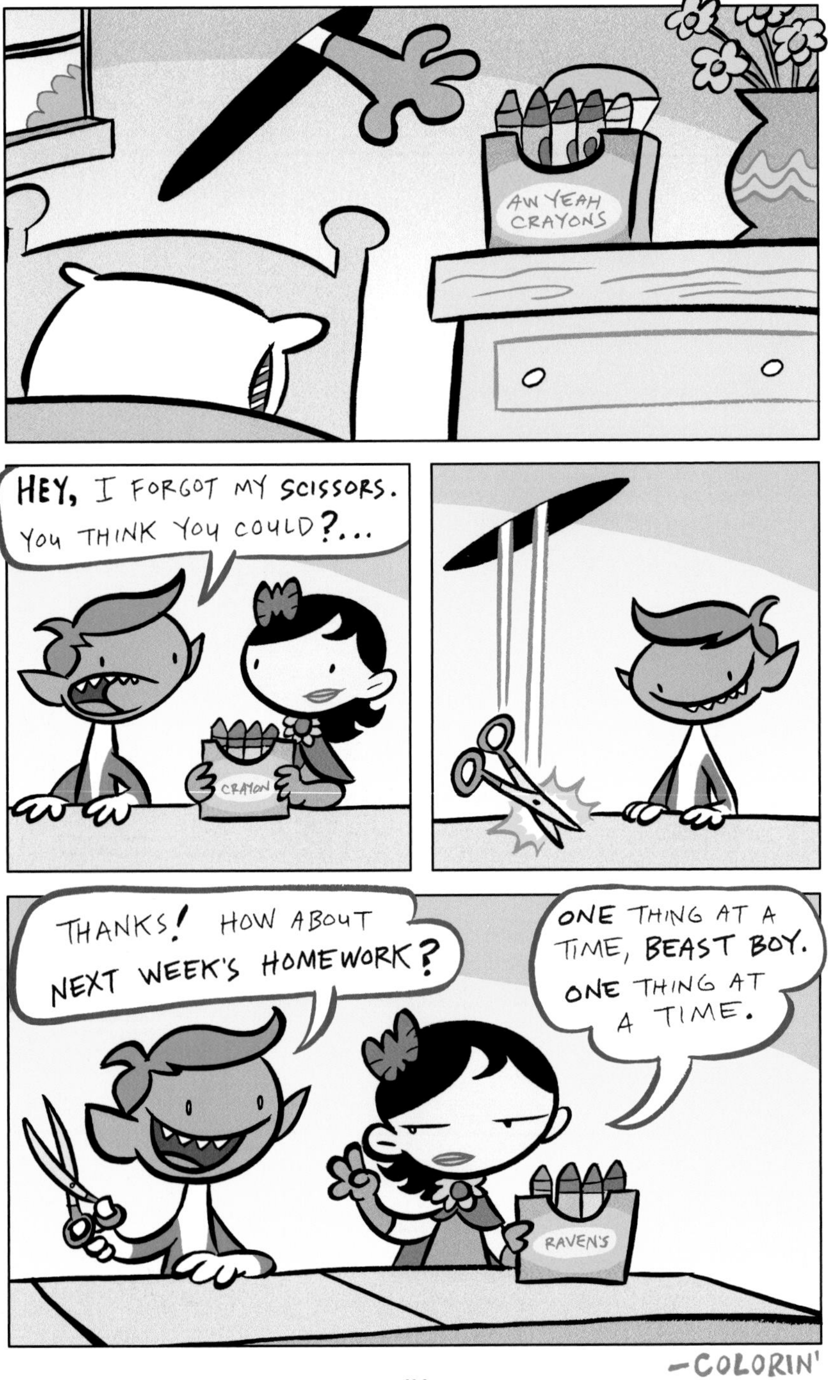
AW YEAH CRAYONS
HEY, I FORGOT MY SCISSORS. YOU THINK YOU COULD?...
CRAYON
THANKS! HOW ABOUT NEXT WEEK'S HOMEWORK?
ONE THING AT A TIME, BEAST BOY. ONE THING AT A TIME.
RAVEN'S

—COLORIN'

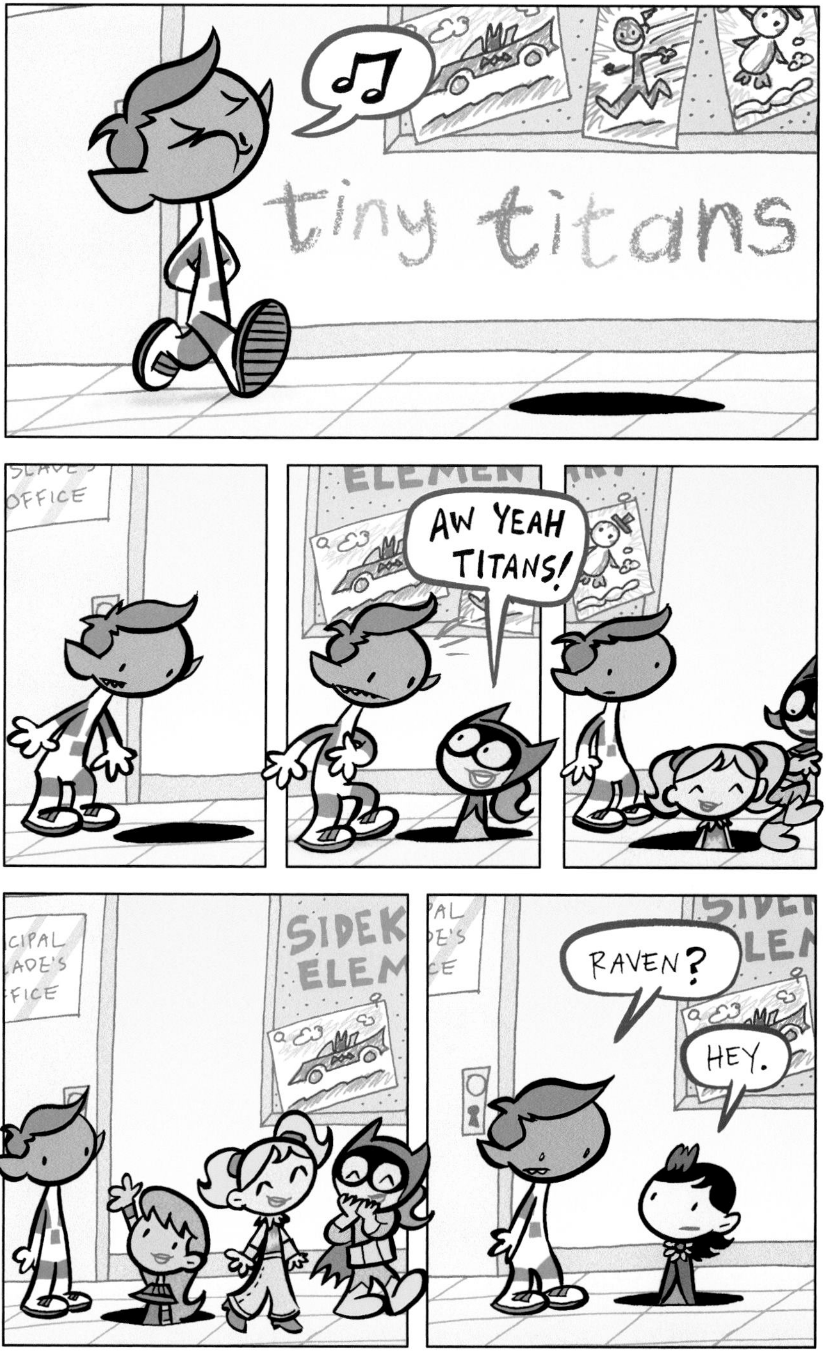
tiny titans
OFFICE
ELEMEN
AW YEAH TITANS!
CIPAL
ADE'S
FFICE
SIDEK
ELEM
PAL
DE'S
CE
RAVEN?
HEY.

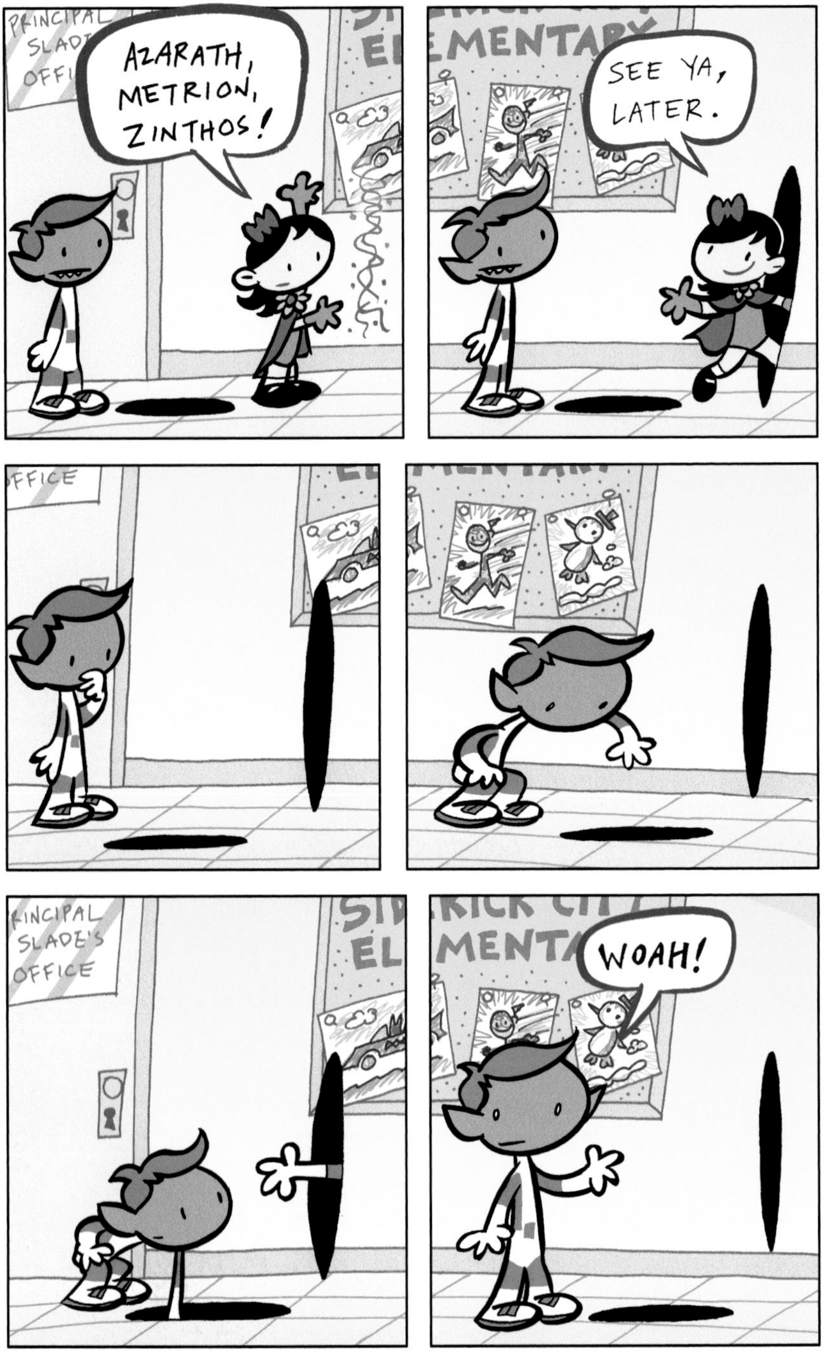
AZARATH, METRION, ZINTHOS!
SEE YA, LATER.
WOAH!

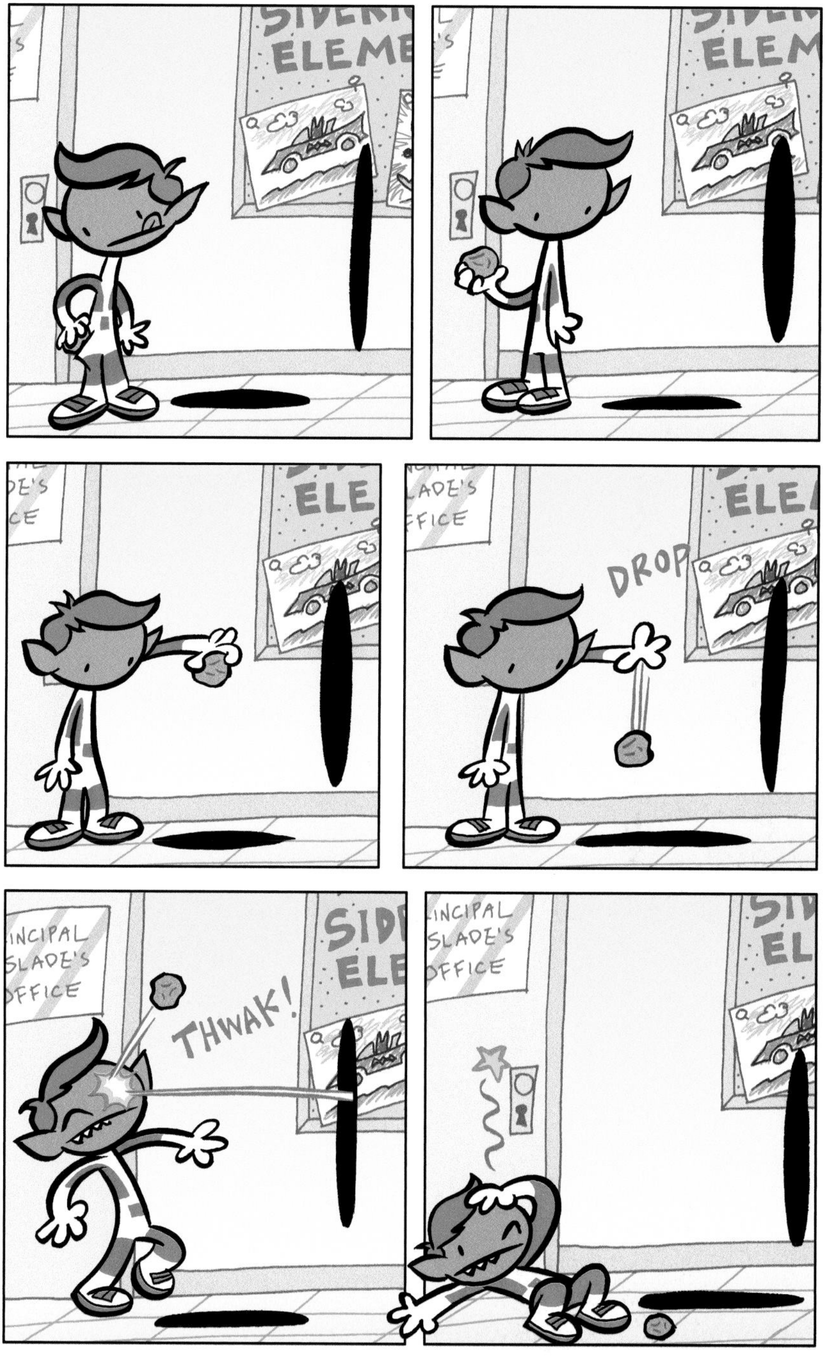
DROP
THWAK!

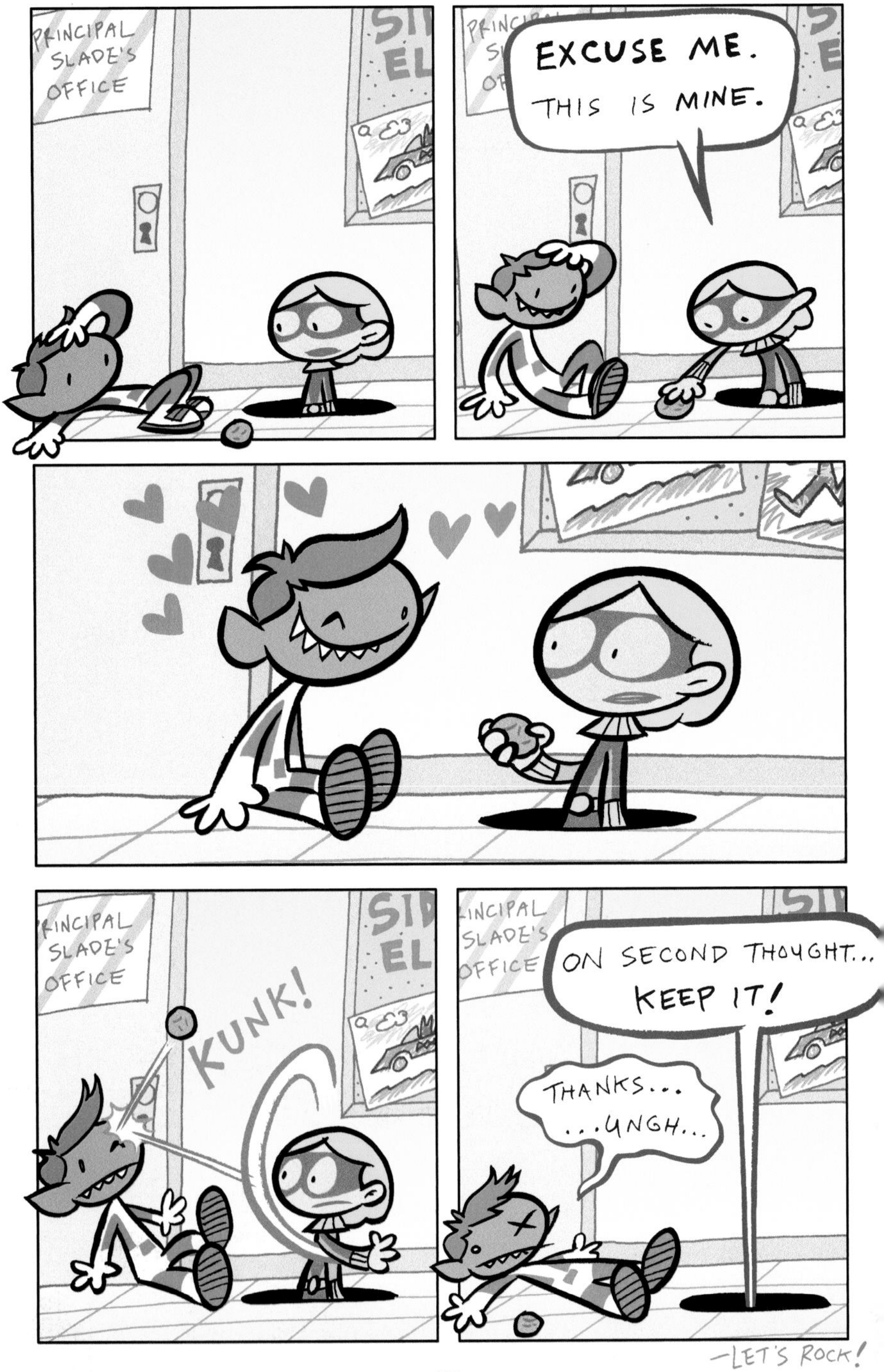
PRINCIPAL SLADE'S OFFICE
EXCUSE ME.
THIS IS MINE.
KUNK!
ON SECOND THOUGHT... KEEP IT!
THANKS...
...UNGH...
-LET'S ROCK!

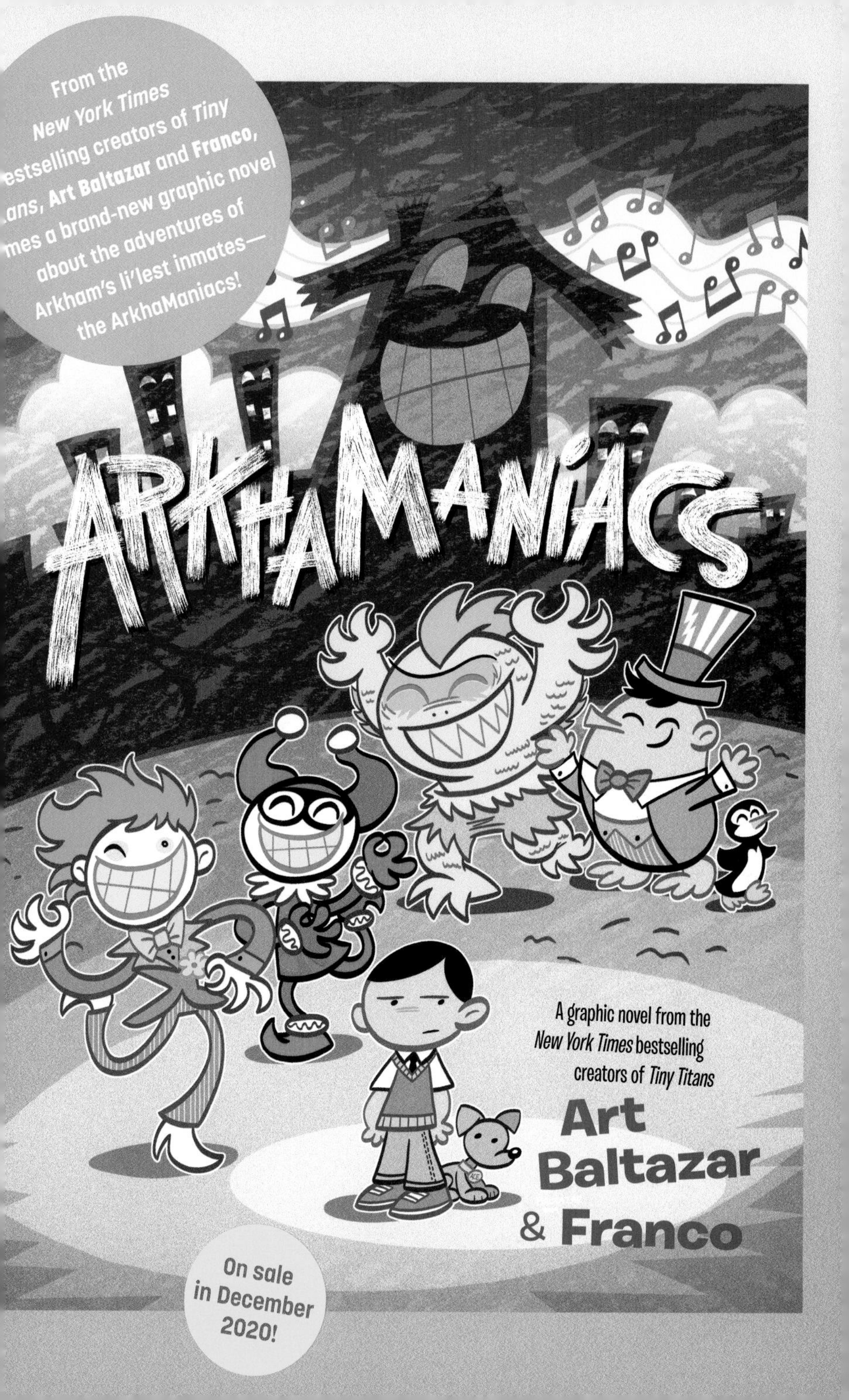
From the
New York Times
estselling creators of Tiny
ans, Art Baltazar and Franco,
mes a brand-new graphic novel
about the adventures of
Arkham's li'lest inmates—
the ArkhaManiacs!
ARKHAMANIACS
A graphic novel from the
New York Times bestselling
creators of Tiny Titans
Art
Baltazar
& Franco
On sale
in December
2020!

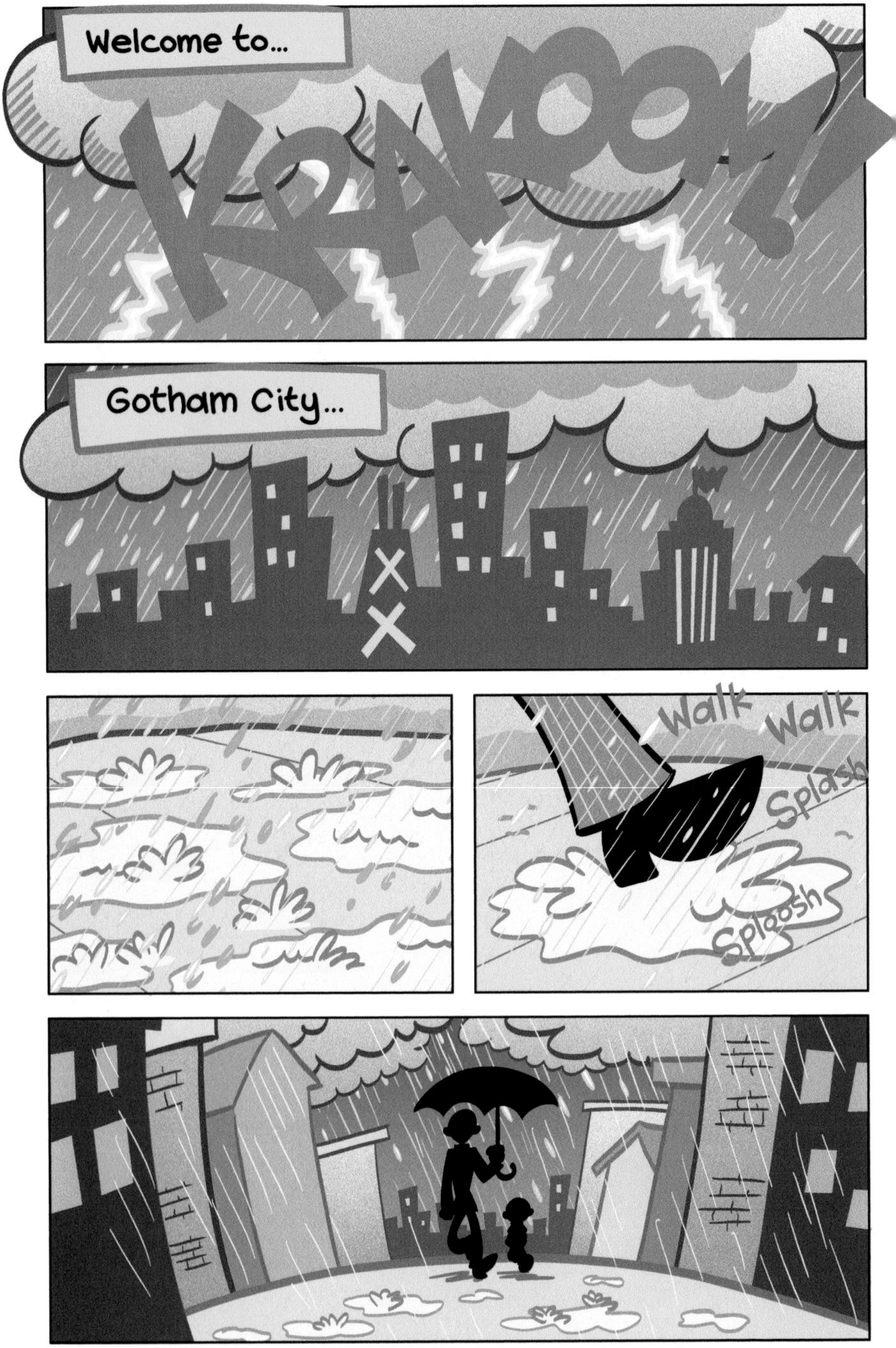
Welcome to...
KRAKOOM!
Gotham City...
Walk
Walk
Splash
Sploosh

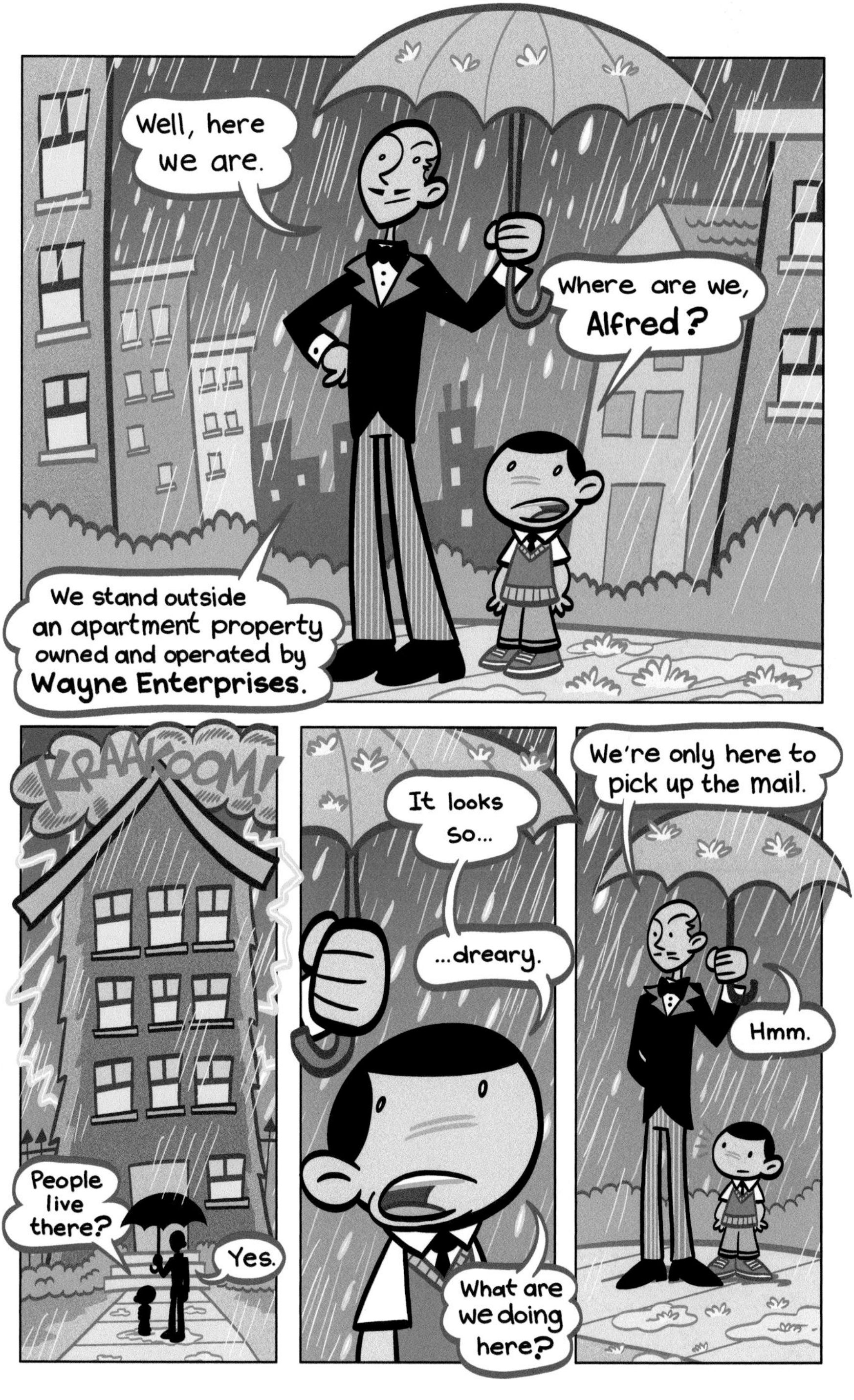

Well, here we are.
Where are we, Alfred?
We stand outside an apartment property owned and operated by Wayne Enterprises.
KRAAKOOM!
People live there?
Yes.
It looks so...
...dreary.
What are we doing here?
We're only here to pick up the mail.
Hmm.

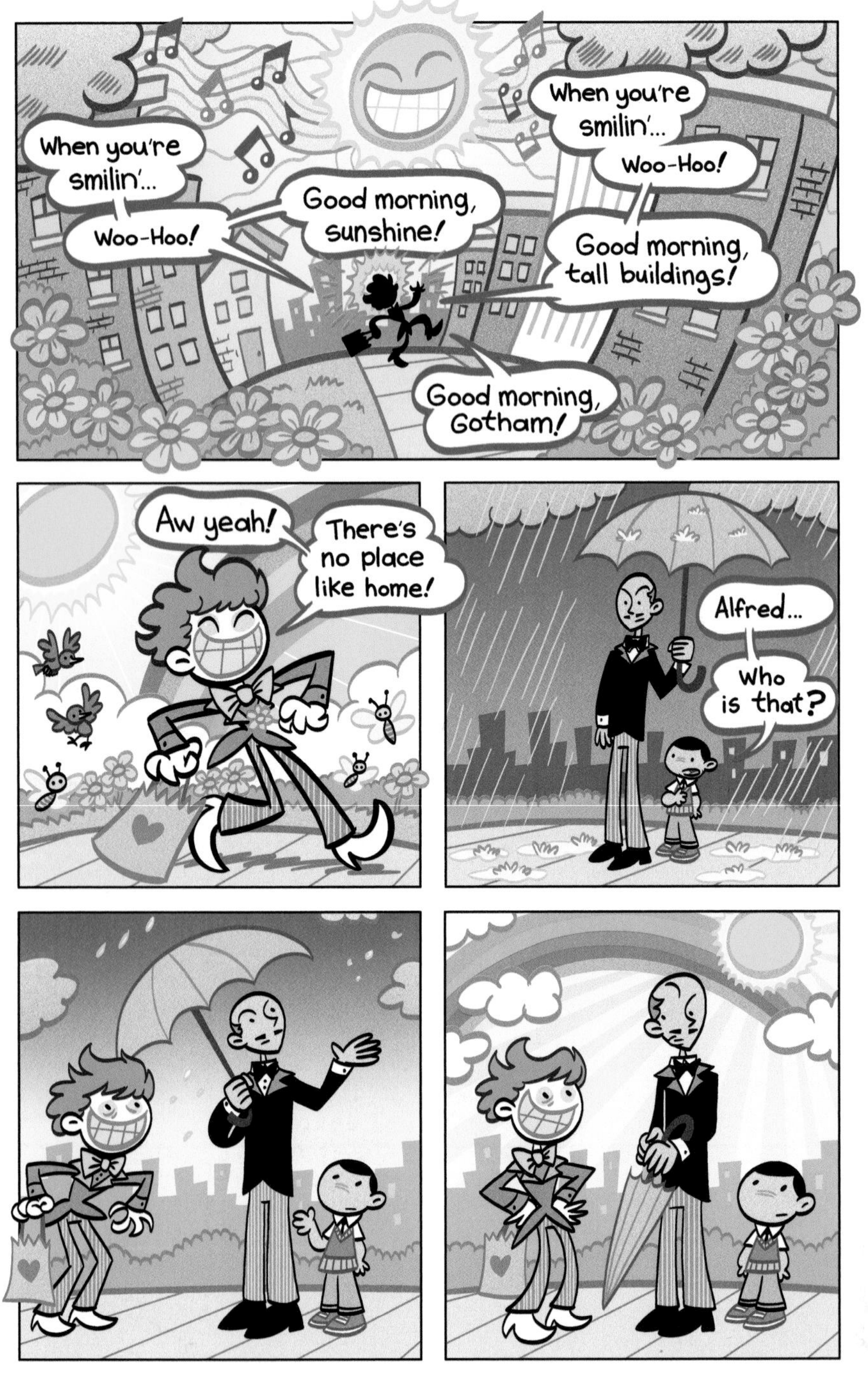
When you're smilin'...
Woo-Hoo!
Good morning, sunshine!
When you're smilin'...
Woo-Hoo!
Good morning, tall buildings!
Good morning, Gotham!
Aw yeah!
There's no place like home!
Alfred...
Who is that?

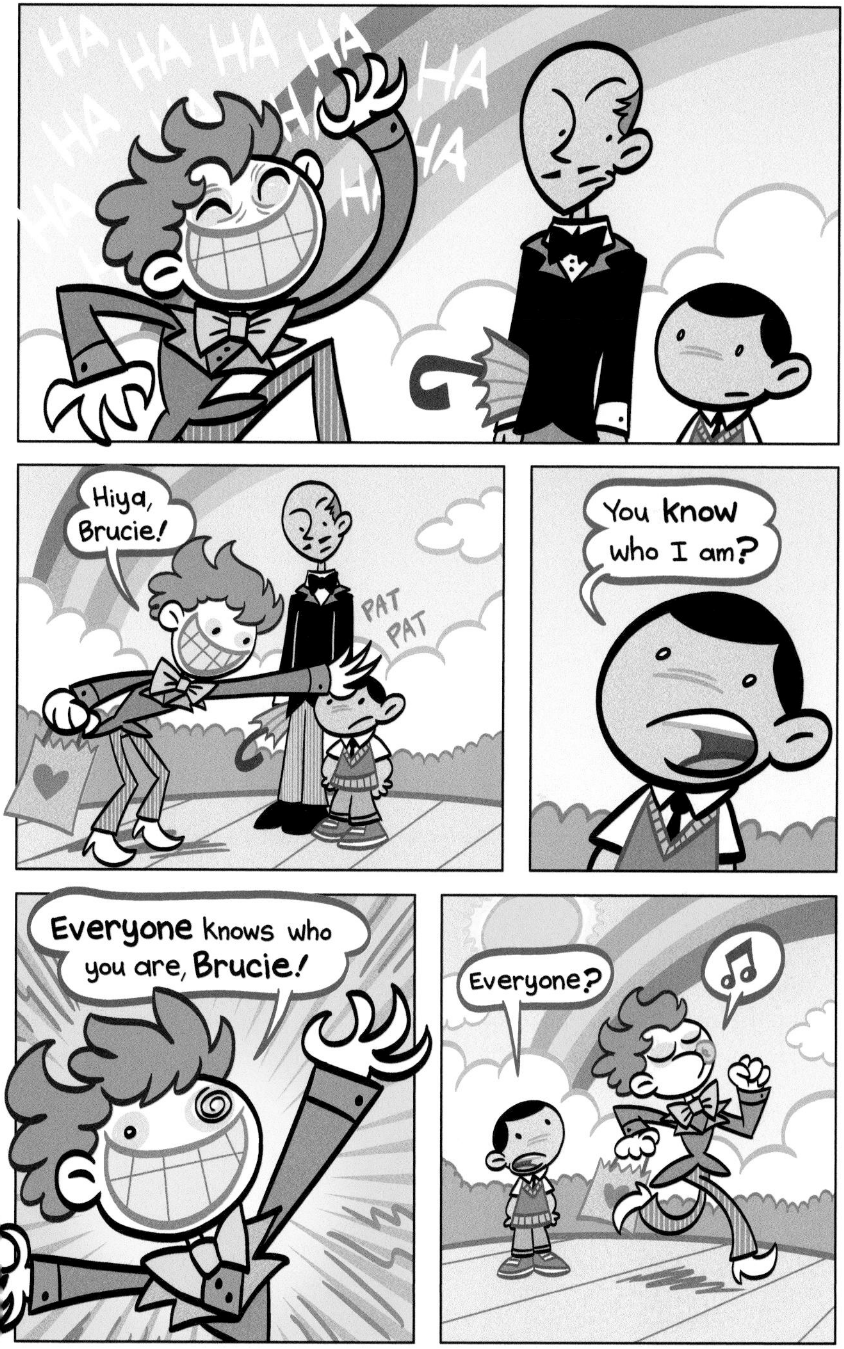
HA HA HA HA HA HA HA HA HA HA
Hiya, Brucie!
PAT PAT
You know who I am?
Everyone knows who you are, Brucie!
Everyone?

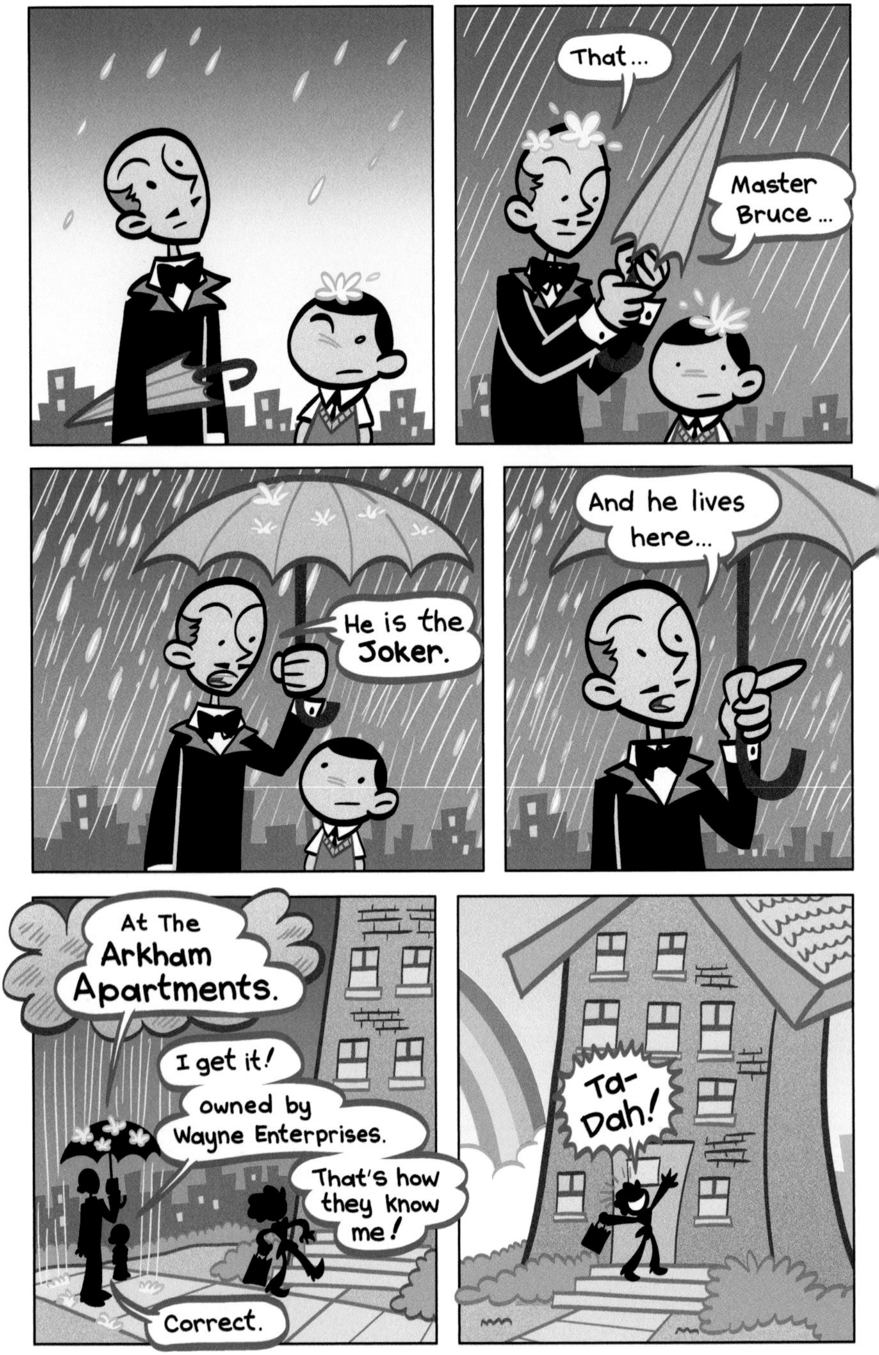
That...
Master Bruce ...
He is the Joker.
And he lives here...
At The Arkham Apartments.
I get it!
owned by Wayne Enterprises.
That's how they know me!
Correct.
Ta-Dah!

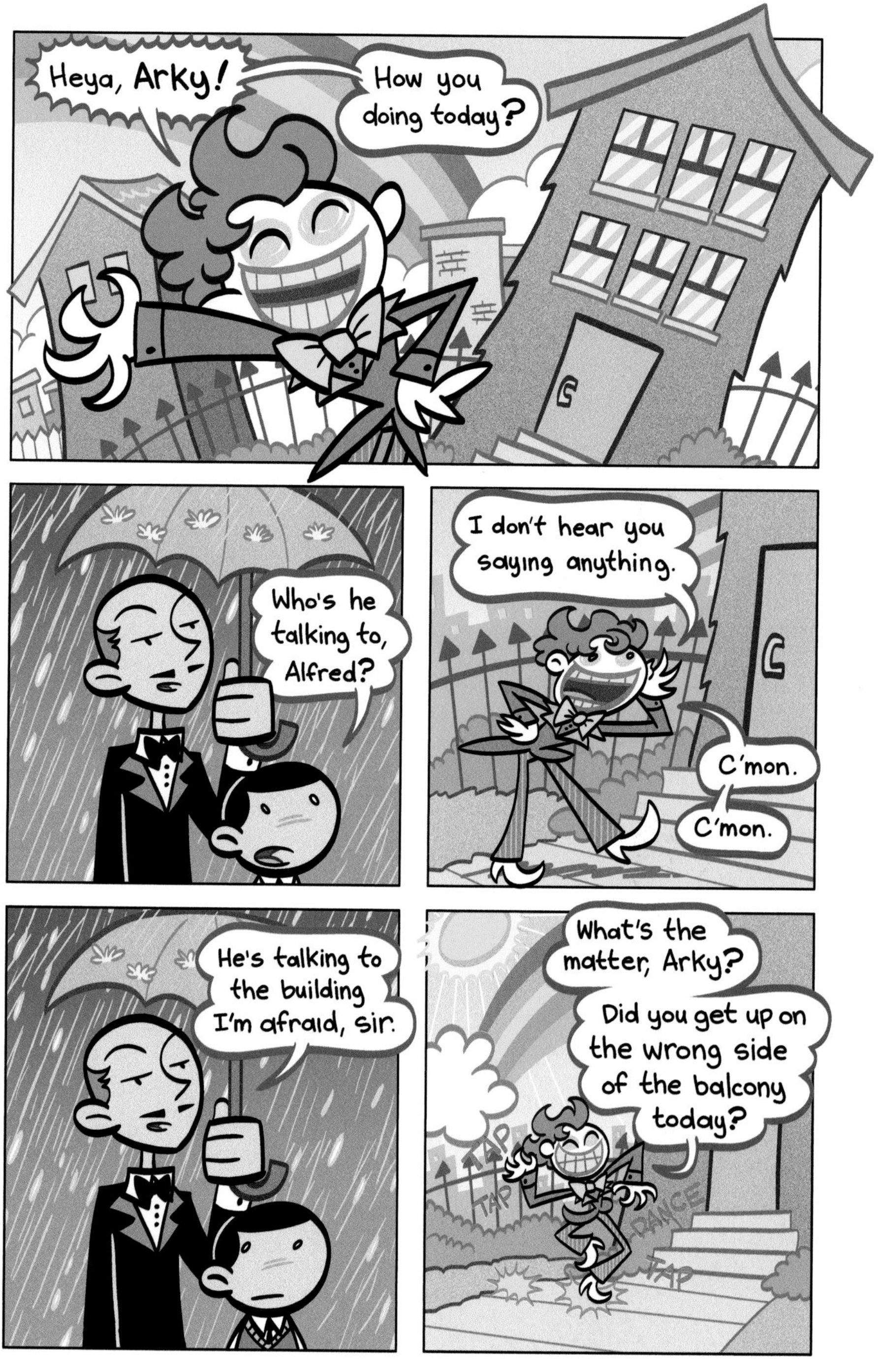
Heya, Arky!
How you doing today?
Who's he talking to, Alfred?
I don't hear you saying anything.
C'mon.
C'mon.
He's talking to the building I'm afraid, sir.
What's the matter, Arky?
Did you get up on the wrong side of the balcony today?
TAP
TAP
DANCE
TAP

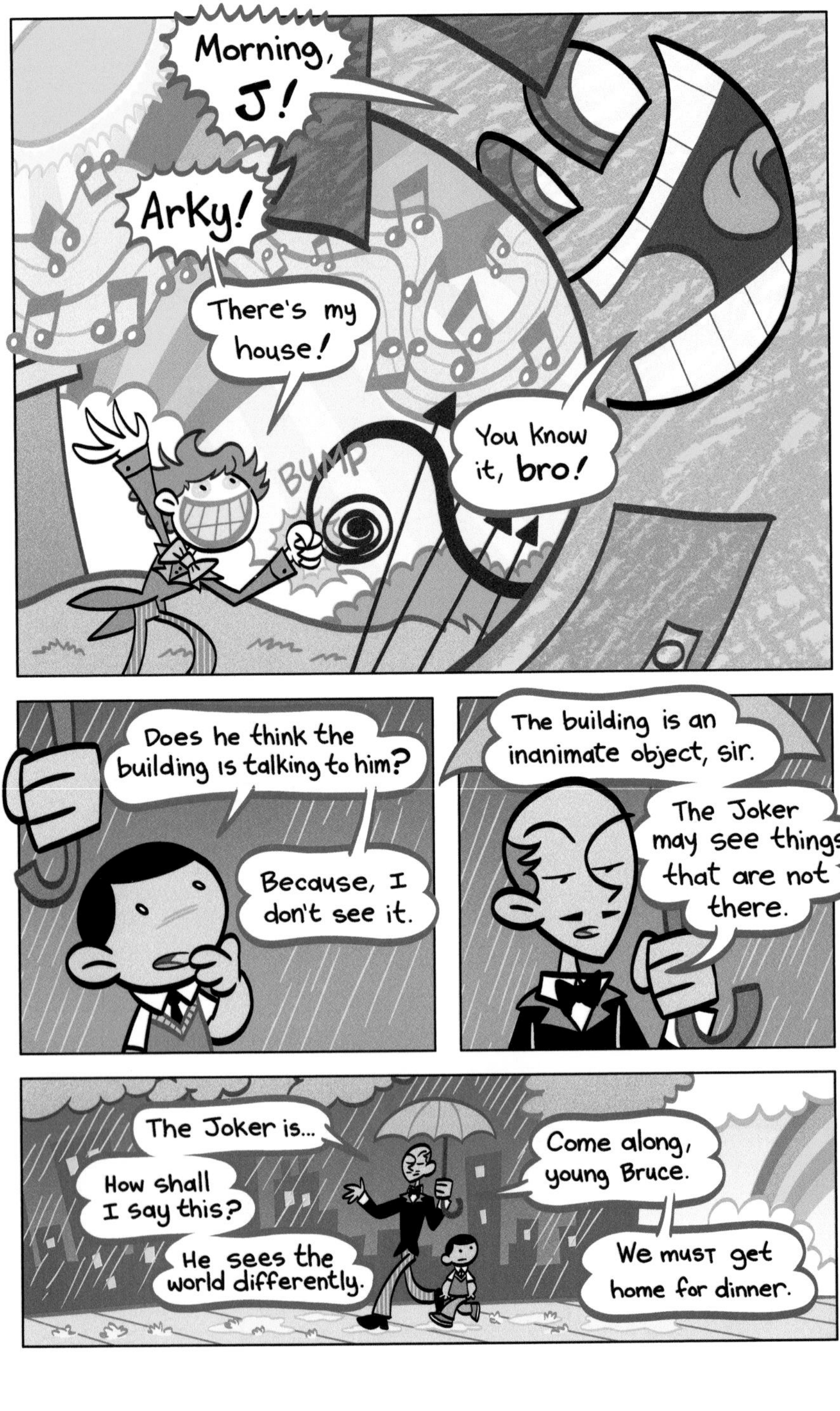
Morning, J!
Arky!
There's my house!
BUMP
You know it, bro!
Does he think the building is talking to him?
Because, I don't see it.
The building is an inanimate object, sir.
The Joker may see things that are not there.
The Joker is...
How shall I say this?
He sees the world differently.
Come along, young Bruce.
We must get home for dinner.

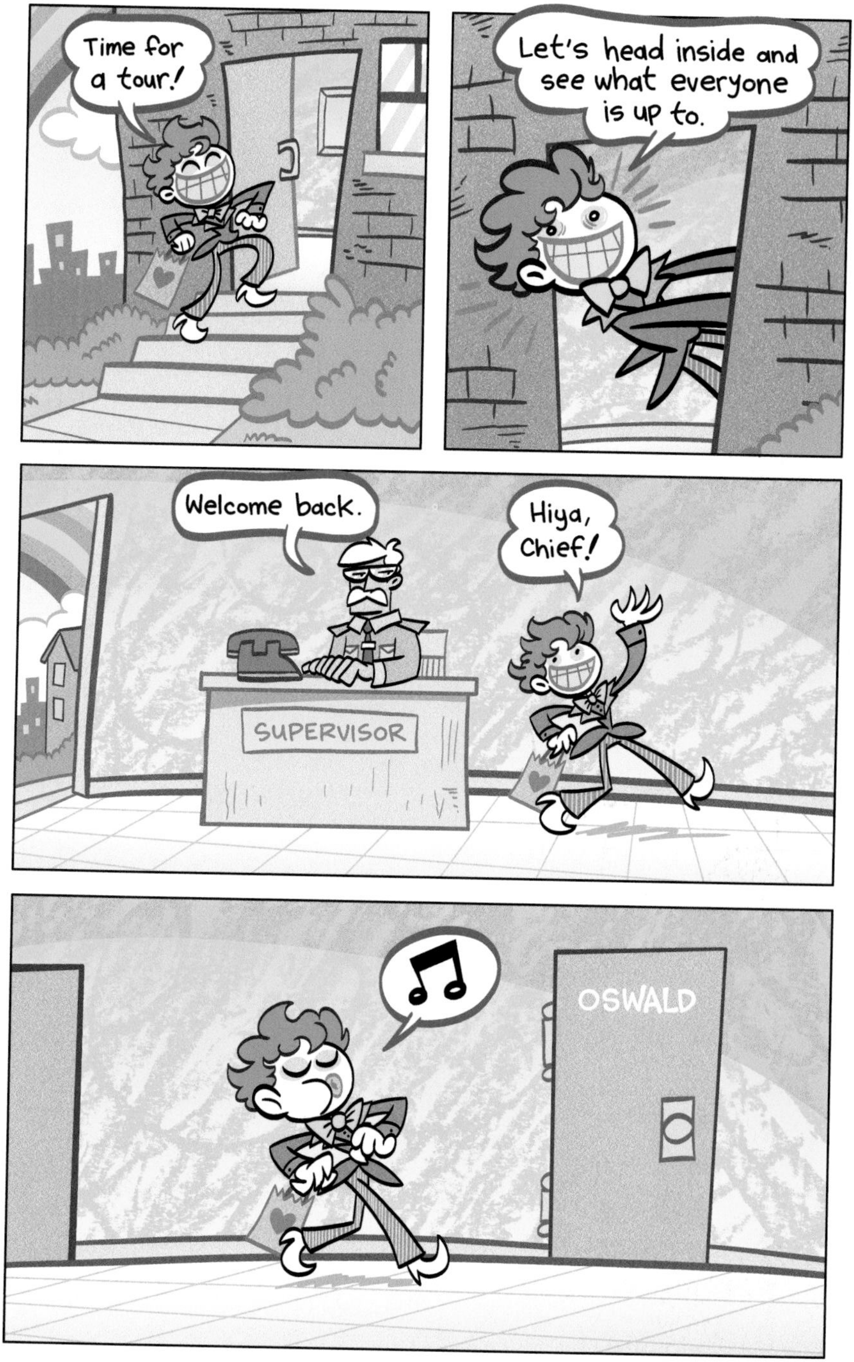
Time for a tour!
Let's head inside and see what everyone is up to.
Welcome back.
Hiya, Chief!
SUPERVISOR
OSWALD

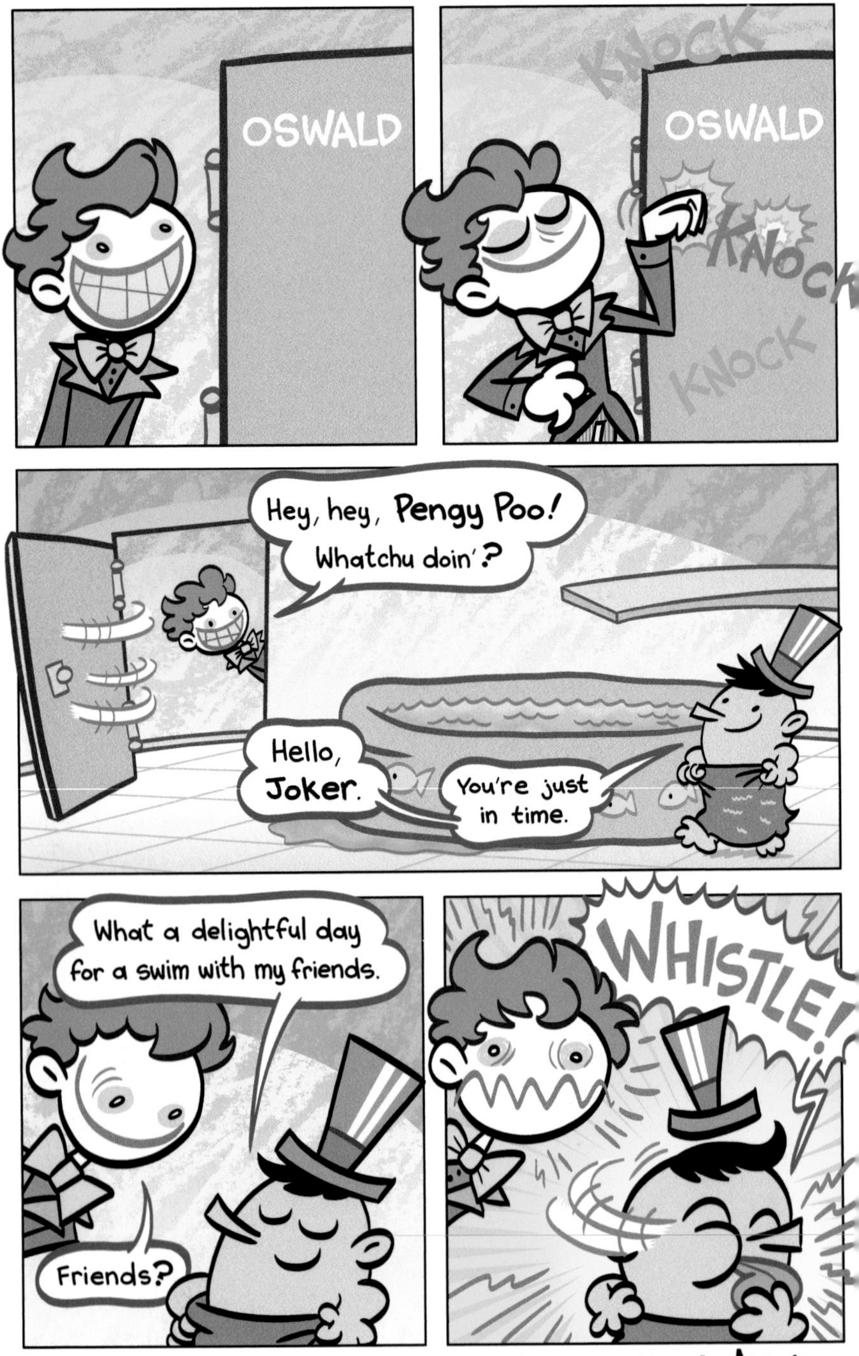
OSWALD
KNOCK
OSWALD
KNOCK
KNOCK
Hey, hey, Pengy Poo!
Whatchu doin'?
Hello, Joker.
You're just in time.
What a delightful day for a swim with my friends.
Friends?
WHISTLE!

To be continued in ARKHAMANIACS